Wherever the Stars Call

S. Jean

ALSO BY S. JEAN

Hymn of Memory
The Devil in the Woods
Forevermore
Born of Scourge

WHEREVER THE STARS CALL

S. JEAN

Wherever the Stars Call
Copyright © 2024 by S. Jean
Star*Cadets

Print (paperback) 979-8-987785959
Ebook 979-8-987785942

First Edition, 2024, Detroit, MI
Cover art & interior design by S. Jean

CONTENT WARNINGS
violence, death, blood, blood drinking, gore, invasive medical procedures, themes of abandonment

To Miranda,
because where there is a weird idea like vampires in space,
you're always down to read it.

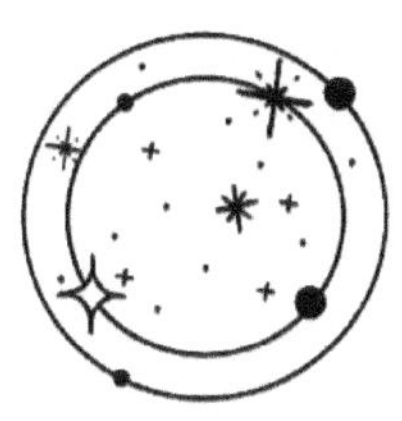

SESSION 1

THROUGH THE NIGHT

01
LAUREL

LAUREL NEVER THOUGHT SHE'D HAVE AN opinion on ceiling ducts either way, but she now knew she hated them. They were filled with cobwebs and dust and she desperately wanted to sneeze, but she couldn't. Not only would that make a racket, but then she'd leave evidence behind. Granted, she already *was* by just being here, but she didn't need to make tracking her any easier by leaving snot behind.

And, it was dark. She hated the dark. If not for the clip-on augment over her glasses, Laurel wouldn't have been able to see at all. It was some kind of augmented reality filament—she didn't know any details other than that—which heightened the brightness and outlined shapes. It was enough so she wasn't hitting every twist and turn the blasted air ducts had. All courtesy of Juniper, her friend waiting for her outside.

According to the blueprints Laurel had studied all night, the space cruiser dealership office where they kept all the keyfobs for their ships was below. All she had to do now was dislodge the ceiling tile and wiggle her way in. Easy.

With nimble fingers, she slid the tile aside and peeked downward. Her glasses didn't point out anything in her path—straight shot down just like Juniper said it'd be. Holding her breath, Laurel twisted and slid her legs out first. Once they were free, she carefully hung from her fingertips to brace herself for the drop.

Then she slipped.

An undignified yelp escaped as she thumped to the floor, ass first. Heart in her throat, she threw herself under the nearest cover and curled up, listening intently for anything that might have heard her. Nothing. She flopped against the floor, exasperated, and peered upward. She was under the dealership's main desk.

She pressed the activation button of the commlink nestled around her ear. It chirped softly and connected to its pair. "I'm in, Junie," she whispered.

The link picked up her voice vibrations and correctly amplified them to the recipient. If she'd been Juniper, all she'd have had to do was subvocalize the words and the cybernetics would do the work. Alas, Laurel had no such augments and had to risk being overheard.

Juniper snickered, their voice always soft. "Obviously," they said and Laurel rolled her eyes. "I watched you drop from the ceiling on my feed. Not exactly graceful."

"Shut up," Laurel said. "My hands get sweaty when I'm nervous!"

"Thankfully, there's no alerts. We're golden."

"How's the outside looking?"

"Street's dead. Chatter on the airway pretty dull."

Juniper was outside near the roof's vent opening. The initial plan had been for them to come in as well, but after looking at it in person, Juniper quickly deduced they would *not* fit. Shoulders too broad. Sure, the rest of them was built like a beanpole, all lanky limbs, but if they got stuck, the whole thing would have gone up in smoke. However, Laurel was small. Easy to squeeze into ridiculous ducts made to augment the acoustics in a dealership.

Like, really. What dealership *cared* about acoustics? Laurel supposed she couldn't complain; it was the easiest way in undetected.

"Phase two." Laurel crawled out from under the desk and peered over the top. The filament in the clip-on flickered before casting an outline around anything solid past the plexiglass surrounding the desk. She nodded to herself. Nothing alive but her.

Afterhours made the entire place creepy, putting it at odds with what it was during the day. What was now dark, near silent, and empty had then been full of people and alive with chatter. Lunar Star Cruiser Dealership was, after all, the best personal starship dealer on this side of the Solar System (at least, according to their ads) and as such, buyers flocked to it whenever it was open.

Their cruisers weren't much compared to the size and power of the Federation-grade starships, but they allowed a couple riders to travel to the nearest space transit system and beyond. With rudimentary life support, a sturdy chassis to protect from space debris, and cushiony seats, only the rich could really afford to own one. Everyone else either used public shuttles or transit cabs to travel from colony to colony.

Laurel and Juniper were definitely *not* rich and public transport was a little *too* public; so, it came down to stealing one.

Information flickered across the clip-on and

disappeared too quickly for Laurel to read. Not for her anyway; the information went right to Juniper's cybernetics as they kept watch.

"No life signs at all," Juniper said. "Got an hour until the security feed reboots. Find our mark and don't forget to grab the fob."

Couldn't hotwire cruisers anymore—the Federation had regulated that kind of build out of existence. Laurel sighed and turned, halfway standing from her crouch. Keyfobs hung on the pegboard behind her, but unfortunately, there were a lot. No identifiers on them either.

Laurel threw them all into her shoulder bag; she'd find the right one when she located their cruiser.

All things considered, the heist was going great. Juniper needed less time than they'd anticipated creating the security feed loop and Laurel was already inside with fobs in her bag. Any security watching the feeds would see what they were meant to see: nothing but the cruisers on display. Lunar Star Cruiser Dealership boasted its security—with their cruisers and *your* information—but to someone like Juniper who was so inundated with cybernetics? Piece of cake. They'd spent four years alone on an orbiting lunar satellite and assuaged their boredom by breaking into all sorts of security systems. A pompous dealership was nothing.

The only thing neither of them could account for was the sole maintenance bot the facility owned. It was just for cleaning—every place had them—but many establishments outfitted cameras to their bots for backup security. Maintenance AIs had closed networks, so Juniper couldn't remotely hack it.

Funny. More security in a little cleaning robot than the entire joint.

Emergency lights in the far back switched on as Laurel headed out onto the showroom floor. Juniper's doing, but it still made Laurel flinch and duck. The red glow from them cast across everything to help Laurel see, but not by much. What helped the most was the skylight above. Scant light from the Lunar Colony around them gave the place a grayish glow, helping Laurel see just a little better. Still wasn't much to work with, honestly. Cruisers aplenty were lined up nearby, though not the one they'd agreed on.

To reorient herself, Laurel looked toward the front glass doors now sealed with rolling metal shutters. If she'd been by herself, those would have worried her, but Juniper had a way to spoof authorization to trick the whole place into thinking it was opening; the shutters would rise on their own, the glass doors would slide open and give Laurel clearance to leave as though she was taking the cruiser out for a test drive.

She'd already done just that earlier this week when she'd come to case the place. She'd managed to look professional enough and the dealer had been happy to let her test drive so he could describe everything their cruisers offered. Baby steered like a dream and was comfy to boot. The dealer was less than enthused, however, when Laurel admitted she needed her daddy's permission to spend that much cash and she'd walked away with finance options and forms to fill out instead if her father was going to pay for it.

Not that he ever would, but also not the point.

Juniper had spent the next few nights afterward coding an injection to wipe all the Federation registration in the cruiser and give it a whole sparkling new set of personal identification numbers so no one could trace it back to the dealership. It would even wipe all the pre-installed Federation spyware and leave only the basic operating systems. All Laurel had to do was what she did best: steal and get away with it.

It wasn't always like this—living in the shadows, dodging the feds, and stealing anything not nailed down—but it sure beat the Federation boarding school Laurel had been sold to. All they churned out were broken husks of workers or 'public safety' enforcers who didn't have a single empathetic bone in their bodies. Laurel had run the moment she found a safe place to go... but not before filching her way up and down the dormitories while everyone was in class.

Running away also meant the feds couldn't scramble her brain like they did to anyone who didn't conform to the system. One way or another, they'd make you fit their mold, even if it meant erasing *you* altogether. She just had to get the hell off the Moon before they found her. Earth wasn't an option; off-limits per fed regulation to preserve what was left (Laurel doubted it; they were just hoarding it all for wealthy investors). Mars and Venus were too close to the hub of the Federation, but past Jupiter, the fed's reach faltered. Easier to hide. All to worry about out there was vampires and space pirates, but if she and Juniper stuck to populated stations, they'd be fine.

They just had to steal their new ride. Laurel knew the basics of how to fly, and besides, AIs did most of the work nowadays. With a cruiser of their own, she and Juniper would start fresh on some far-flung station where no one would tell them what to do or how worthless they were. No family to sell them off when they outlived their usefulness. No expectations—nothing but themselves.

She just had to find the damned cruiser. It was another few silent moments, squinting and slinking, before her foot caught something solid and she thumped forward, landing hard on her knees.

Well, she'd found the small runway that cruisers were paraded down before they flew out of the joint. Always a show. Celebrate someone leaving with their very own cruiser and someone else might be tempted to follow suit.

Laurel turned and on a small podium at the very end was a cruiser. *Their* cruiser, the clip-on noted. Couldn't tell in the dark, but the ship had a sleek crimson chassis that glittered. Like all cruisers of its make and model, it had small wings jutting out from the sides and tailfins along the back, making it rather cute. The front had the typical twin headlights and a moon-shaped hood ornament front and center. Nice, but it'd have to come off to keep it nondescript. There were the standard hover augments along the bottom of the chassis—good for rare ground travel—but the real beauty was the engine and life support system, perfect for shorter interstellar travel. It seated two comfortably (and a third if they squeezed in behind the front seats) and the seats were upholstered with plush black cushions. To protect drivers, the ship deployed a state-of-the-art crystalline top that sealed in all life support and was incredibly difficult to break. Perfect.

All cruisers ready for test drives had their AIs pre-installed, which was the big reason Laurel had chosen this one. AIs handled all the monitoring of the omni-directional radar and alert channels as well as flying during long haul flights through empty space. It was dangerous and exhausting to fly a cruiser without one, but they didn't have the hours necessary to build and install an AI of their own. So, stealing this one it was.

Laurel tried fob after fob, but the top remained

stubbornly locked. She'd tried them at least twice before panic set in. Then a third time and still, no reaction. Laurel's hands went clammy.

"Junie, we've got a problem."

"Ah, fuck," Juniper replied. "I bet that dealer took the test cruiser fob with him."

Laurel slapped her forehead. "These are all blank, aren't they?" Juniper swore on the other end—it hadn't occurred to them either. The dealership must have programmed the fobs after purchase.

Still, Laurel could work with that. She shook out her hands. "I... I bet I can rewrite a blank one." She bent down for the discarded fobs and took out her kit of screwdrivers from her jacket. "J-Just a setback."

"Take a deep breath," Juniper said and Laurel did. No panicking under the pressure. She'd done it enough in school. "We've got time. I believe in you."

Whenever school was too much, Laurel had found solace in talking the night away with Juniper over the underground net. They were Laurel's only actual friend. If Juniper believed in her, then she could do anything.

She slowly exhaled and steadied her hands.

The school's dormitories had a similar keyfob system for their locks. The inner workings were practically identical. Laurel snorted, more panic easing out. The feds controlled the manufacture of all locks, making sure they could get into anywhere they wanted. Thankfully, that worked against them some-times. Like now. Laurel just had to key a blank fob to the cruiser's frequency she'd heard when she tested the cruiser, and not get shocked.

"Ow." Laurel flinched as a spark danced across her fingers. She dropped the fob and went for another one. This time, she worked slower. She had time. She held the memory of the sound the dealer's fob had made a few days ago in her mind as she adjusted the frequency to match.

Then something hit her foot.

She clapped a hand over her mouth to smother her shout. Spinning on her heel, she looked behind her, and her stomach plummeted. She'd been so in the zone, she hadn't noticed the cleaner robot coming.

Disk shaped and black, the motor inside purred softly as it vacuumed around her. It bumped her again, trying to get under her foot and failing.

"What?" Juniper asked. "Is that…"

"The robot found me," Laurel hissed.

Information flashed across Laurel's glasses with the diagnostics of the cleaner. Juniper exhaled. "It doesn't have a camera. I can't tell anything about its tracking software, but it's probably rudimentary given the age of the bot."

"Thank the stars." Laurel gave the robot a pat. It beeped at her. "Thank you for your vigilance, my dear bot." She bent over the fob again. "How's about you and me get out of here when I'm done? Come soaring into the stars with us?"

The sweeper didn't answer. It couldn't; it wasn't that kind of robot. All the AI knew was cleaning and it wasn't capable of rational thought like more advanced androids. Still, it bopped her foot again and settled beside it like it was going to sleep.

Laurel grinned at it. "Junie, we have a new recruit."

Juniper snorted. "You adopted it, didn't you?"

"Already thinking of names." Laurel tweaked the fob a little more. Talking was helping to squash her nerves. "Maybe you can attach a laser to it. Come on. It'd be funny!"

"Yeah, yeah. When you get out, I'll check it for

tracking software so you can keep it."

The sweeper revved back up and bopped her foot again like if it'd waited long enough, she would have moved. Laurel nudged it back and shook her head. "I know you're in a hurry, but I almost got this."

"Are you talking to it?"

"It keeps bopping my foot!" Laurel giggled as the sweeper did it again, almost indignantly. "What else am I supposed to do?"

"It's not a puppy!"

"Well, then it won't piss on our stuff then, will it?"

The fob sang with the frequency in her memory and she lifted her screwdriver. This had to be it. She snapped the fob shut and hit the button. The cruiser's door chimed and the locks hissed, releasing the top so it folded back. Bingo. Just as she opened her mouth to cheer, every single cruiser in the dealership chirped and hissed open.

Well! Not her intent, but no harm done. She'd leave them open as evidence she'd pulled one over on the dealership.

As if in response to her hubris, sirens blared across the building. She crouched and shoved her hands against her ears. *Or maybe not*, Laurel thought and gritted her teeth.

Juniper grunted in pain across the commlink. "What happened?"

"All of them just opened!" Laurel snagged the sweeper and hopped into the cruiser. The bot's engine revved as she put it down behind the front seats and it immediately began cleaning whatever dust was behind her. She repositioned herself and grabbed the controls. "It's fine, just open the gates! Starting this baby up!"

"Oh fuck—oh fuck, no it's not! The security feed

rebooted. They're gonna have your face. You need to get out!"

"Then open the gate!"

Bright fluorescent lights snapped on. Laurel ducked low and ripped the clip-on off before it blinded her. Still left lingering bright spots, however, and she had to blink them back. When the front shutters creaked, however, she jerked upright, her eyes widening. That was too fast, even for Juniper.

Five dark shapes stood in front of the row of spotlights shining inside. Enforcers. These weren't the usual daytime pigs, though; they were clad in all black, with full-face visors, and had their blasters already drawn. There was no way they could have responded to the alarm that fast; they'd been waiting right under Juniper's nose.

"You there!" the one in the center shouted, her voice crackling with the static that came with cybernetic vocal augmentation. "Put your hands up! Now!"

Laurel did as asked, palms facing outward. "Juniper," she hissed through gritted teeth. "Slim sold us out!"

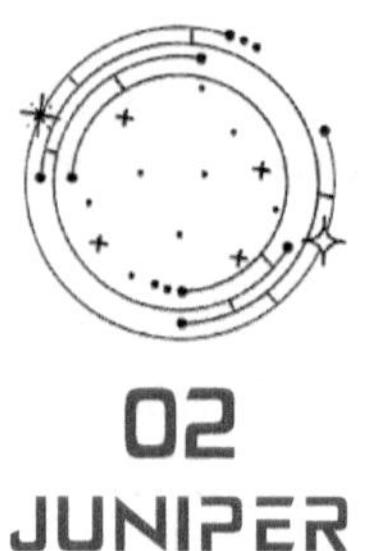

02
JUNIPER

"SHIT!" JUNIPER SHOVED THEMSELF AWAY from the roof's edge before anyone saw them. The circus down below hadn't been there when Laurel wriggled into the vent, so they must have come while Juniper was concentrating. The person calling the shots knew to stay quiet too. Definitely not the usual pigs.

Slim hadn't sold them out—not willingly, at least. He was a good friend of Juniper's, but he was also a Federation-sanctioned android. All the feds needed was probable cause to legally tap into his network feed and find evidence of Juniper asking him about the dealership's security systems. Slim probably wasn't even aware they'd looked.

Besides, it had been up to Juniper to make sure. They'd had to cover Laurel's tracks as she'd palmed stuff from the Lunar boardwalk for Slim to fence at the docks. Then had to plan the heist and make sure it was airtight. Between those two, their usual sleep deprivation, and then the endless inane chatter across the public networks they listened to out of paranoia, everything had become *noise*. If anyone was one hundred percent to blame, it was Juniper themself. Juniper should have done better, but they fucked it up.

"Shit, shit, shit!" Juniper paced, raking their hands through their hair.

Not the time for a pity party. Laurel needed their help. They steeled themself with a deep breath of stale colony air and peeked over the edge of the roof again.

Night enforcers. Clad in all black without the usual identification numbers plastered all over their uniforms. They were usually called in for violent crimes like hostage situations or something—not for lifting a cruiser. Laurel wouldn't hurt a marshmallow, so they were hoping to get someone else.

Shit. They were expecting *Juniper*.

Jumping in boldly wouldn't work. Juniper would get shot before their combat systems kicked in. Thankfully, after a cursory scan, Juniper found that these enforcers used the same network as the day beat. Juniper had their wireless augment connect to it and let their mind sink in. Their body became a dis-associated presence, fuzzy and out of reach with the network between it and Juniper. Always disconcerting at first, but Juniper was well-versed with the feeling by now.

The enforcers only had enough cybernetics to enhance their senses, but there was too much crosstalk between it all for Juniper to misdirect it effectively. What they needed to do was *disrupt* it.

Juniper's mind flitted from system to system until their vision flickered and distorted with images from the enforcers' optics. *Perfect.* The network optics al-lowed the enforcers to see out of each other's eyes, as well as sending the video directly to HQ.

And it was hilariously easy to simply shut off.

They sent in a root level shutdown command, leaving the enforcers with heads full of white noise as Juniper withdrew to their own body. The enforcers stiffened, likely trying to pretend they hadn't been compromised to save face, but the network chatter gave it away with demands at HQ to fix it.

Juniper turned their focus to the dealership's rear door locks so Laurel could escape. The code injection Juniper had prepared to turn the clocks was useless, but they could *still* do this. Just needed more time.

"You are under arrest!" the chief enforcer's voice echoed and Juniper gritted their teeth, trying to block it out. "You have the right to remain silent—"

Juniper squeezed their eyes shut, concentrating. Of course, the chief enforcer was on a secure network from the rest. As they dove back in to do *something* to it, their bio-monitor sent an alarm through their head. *WARNING: heart rate critical.* Fuck, Juniper *knew* that; it was pounding like a fucking bird trapped in their chest. What they needed was a plan.

"Junie!" Laurel's voice cut through all the noise and Juniper snapped their eyes open. "I'm taking off!"

"Hey! Put your hands back where I can see them!"

"Wait, Laurel—"

"Find cover!"

Realization hit Juniper like a splash of cold water. They swore, cutting off all external connections, and heard it. The cruiser engine revving. The shouts below. Juniper threw themself behind the only cover they saw—the vent opening—and ducked low.

Laurel's new cruiser smashed through the skylight glass, shattering it into a million glittering pieces, and Laurel screamed over the comms with a war cry. Laser stun shots pelted the underside of the cruiser, but nothing breached the hull. Juniper found themself laughing, watching Laurel create a perfect arc in the sky among the shattered glass. It haloed her like starlight.

"Stop screaming!" Juniper shouted.

Laurel finished her arc and jostled the cruiser down beside the roof. The top slid open to reveal Laurel within, her two-tone hair of blonde on top and rust red on bottom a mess, her light brown skin glittering with sweat underneath the darkened Lunar Colony lights, and she was giving Juniper the shy little grin she always deployed when she did something mischievous. It made her wide brown eyes twinkle.

Shots pinged off the cruiser, wiping the smile right off her face, and Juniper dove inside. Reunion over. Laurel's description was all over the airwaves, enforcer cruisers were en route, and the ground crew was ordered to keep them in sight. Fat chance of that. Juniper focused on the enforcers' optics again and shut them down a second time while Laurel threw the cruiser into drive and punched it.

Laurel expertly weaved them in and out of the typical nighttime lunar traffic. There wasn't much, thankfully, but the enforcer backup wasn't far behind. Juniper caught their lights in the rearview mirror, lighting up the dark like blinking stars. No matter how many weaves and turns Laurel made, the enforcers were persistent, following each move too closely.

That shouldn't have been possible. Unless...

Juniper looked over the cruiser's console; there were the typical readouts for speed, altitude, and the like, while the bulk of the screen was dedicated to the guidance system. It read *LunarNav v. 5.03.3645.*

"Shit!" they shouted. "Laurie—this still has fed spyware!" Laurel winced and Juniper shook her shoulder. "You didn't slot in the drive!"

"I was kinda busy!" Laurel yanked the wheel to the side, turning the cruiser sideways and squeezing them between two office buildings. The enforcer ships made the turn just as effortlessly. Laurel swore as she righted their ship on the other side.

"Without it, we can't lose them! They'll have the ship's signature!" Juniper searched through Laurel's jacket for the drive and yanked it out of an interior pocket. Juniper jerked to look out the window; they were following one of the higher lanes dedicated for cruiser travel, so not super close to the surface. Their cortex computer finished the calculations. Safe to cut the engine. Hopefully.

Juniper shoved their drive into the console's data slot and braced themself. "We're dropping in five seconds."

Laurel shot Juniper a wide-eyed look. "*What*?!"

"It needs to restart the entire system!"

The systems powered down and the ship dropped. Laurel screamed and despite themself, Juniper did too. After a terrifying few seconds of freefall, the system reengaged with a whir of the engines, and the console's screen flickered back to life as the crucial systems reloaded. It now displayed *JuniNav v. 1.0.0*, a sure sign that their program had worked and wiped the cruiser clean of fed spyware.

Laurel slammed her feet on the thrusters and pulled the wheel back. They narrowly dodged some poor sap on a night drive, swerved between two food carts making midnight rounds, and stabilized before they hit the lunar floor. One of the enforcers following them didn't pull up in time and skidded across the ground, smashing sideways into the pedestrian walk-way barrier. Another one hit its partner with a screech of metal-on-metal, and furious shouts erupted across the network.

And of course, more enforcers were on their way, but they'd be locked onto the cruiser's old ID number. Once Laurel and Juniper lost their pursuers, they'd be home free.

Juniper patted Laurel's arm, a laugh bubbling out of their throat despite how hard their heart hammered in their chest. Their bio-monitor warned them against strenuous activity, but it felt good to be alive like this. Laurel grinned at them even though her knuckles against the wheel were white.

"You're out of your mind," she laughed.

"So are you!" Juniper winked before diving back into the network around them, the physical world receding into distant, fuzzy noise.

Enforcers were still too close for comfort. There had to be something else Juniper could do to lose them... Juniper mentally rifled through their potential plans before remembering the virus they'd been working on back at the satellite. It spoofed the ID of whatever vehicle Juniper set it to and, when pinged, sent out randomized navigation data. They'd only made it to cause chaos for fun, but now it might just save them.

They let the virus slip free and bloom through the unprotected network of the traffic cams. Once the enforcers caught their cruiser's ID on the cams (and they would), the virus would latch onto their network and infect everything with after images of their cruiser, designed to throw them off the chase.

It was almost too easy.

"All right." Juniper pulled back to themself, surprised to find their voice breathless. Unsurprisingly, their vision had turned blurry. Auras glowed around everything, indicating an oncoming cybernetics-induced migraine, and they squeezed their eyes shut again. *So* not the time for one. They had to keep it together. "Get ready to drop again."

"*Again?!*" Laurel whined as she swiped away an incoming call from one of the enforcers.

"Last time. Pinky promise."

Laurel dragged in a tense breath. Juniper slid their hand over her arm, squeezing it. She nodded, bracing herself, and switched the ignition off.

No screams this time as they plummeted, just silent prayers they didn't hit anything. Juniper counted to five before they switched it all back on. As the engine revved, picking them back up, Juniper pointed out the perfect hiding place. Expertly, Laurel guided them into the tight squeeze between two towering office complexes. They jerked to a stop right beneath the pedestrian walkway, effectively hidden in the shadow. Laurel killed the lights.

The enforcers hot on their tail zoomed on—not even noticing the sudden drop—and chased the ghost in their viewfinders. They'd go until they figured out they were getting randomized coordinates and all they saw was an afterimage left behind by the virus. By the time they doubled back, Juniper and Laurel would be long gone.

Juniper slumped against the seat, trying to calm their screaming bio-monitor. *Heartrate too high, adrenaline at dangerous levels, danger, danger, danger!* The headache always following after the auras rolled in and crashed into them like a tidal wave. Something trickled out of their nose and they tasted the blood running over their lips before they could stop it. Typical.

"Ah, shit." Juniper tried to stem the blood flow with their sleeve.

"Here." Laurel handed them a tissue from her jacket. She'd started carrying them for just such an occasion, and while Juniper hated to admit they needed the help, they appreciated the gesture.

Juniper dipped their head forward and pressed the tissue to their nose. It'd stop soon—it always did—but Juniper was all too aware of the way Laurel watched them. She was worried. She always was after they used their cybernetics so extensively. Hard not to be given how wrecked they were after a job like this. But it wasn't like Juniper had a choice.

Their cybernetic augmentation was as much a part of their body as their meat organs. Couldn't turn them off. Couldn't stop the chatter as its various systems assessed the world around them. All they could do was drown it out.

It sucked. Even androids weren't this neurotic. When Juniper had finally admitted to Slim how they constantly felt, believing he'd understand, he'd been concerned; as it turned out, androids could adjust how sensitive their augments were. Juniper couldn't. They were on high alert all the time.

The only way to stop it that Juniper had found for themself—even if only for a little bit—was to over-whelm the system with something euphoric, which was usually sex.

Obviously, not something Juniper could turn to all the time.

"It's too quiet," Juniper said finally. "Need out of my head. You loaded the drive with some tunes, right? Let's hear them."

Laurel smiled and worked her fingers across the console's digital keyboard. When the song loaded, she cranked the speakers. Out came the shouting of some punk band and though Juniper tried not to—it *was* music of a sort, after all—they made a face.

"Hey!" Laurel nudged them, bouncing in her seat with a little dance. "Come on! You told me to load it up with tunes and that's what I did!"

"I was hoping for a classic. Like from Earth or something." Juniper pulled the tissue away and felt their nose with the back of their hand. No blood. The auras had faded. The slightest twinge of the headache remained, but normal enough. "*Ode to Joy*—I told you to put that on there, right? That's victory music."

"You *always* play it." Laurel switched the tracks, rolling her eyes. While it was definitely a more punk rendition, Juniper relaxed into the familiar beat.

Laurel reversed the cruiser, carefully easing them out of their hiding place. "You'd like the Smashing Coffins if you actually listened to them."

"It's just hard to take them seriously when half their songs are about smashing their own coffins." Juniper peeked around Laurel's head, letting their cortex computer scan for danger. Nothing. They gave Laurel a nod and she guided them back onto the floating freeway like they were normal night drivers. "They're *vampires*, they don't die. The metaphor's a little on the nose."

"Pfft." Laurel's voice devolved into a laugh. "It's not meant to be deep. Just enjoy the absurdity."

About as absurd as someone like Laurel—a literal goody two-shoes if not for her penchant for stealing— liking a real-life vampire band. Fangs and everything. Federation didn't like vampires, and if it was up to them, would have eradicated them all by now. But vampires thrived in the deeper reaches of space where the sun couldn't reach no matter how often the Federation tried to cull them. Instead of wasting resources, the feds had made an uneasy truce. If vampires stayed past the inner asteroid belt (although the farther, the better) and didn't feed on diplomats or something, they'd be mostly left alone. That included letting some make noisy punk bands. Even if they never held concerts on this side of the belt, their music traveled vast across the intrasolar net and made them into a hit.

Laurel's lips shifted into a mischievous grin. "Wanna see them live?"

Juniper raised their eyebrows. "Seriously?"

Laurel typed their destination into the console and the AI chirped its affirmation. With any luck, they'd be at the Lunar Landing Station in no time.

"I'm sure between our talents, we can spring some tickets," Laurel said, nodding.

Maybe it wouldn't be so bad. Beyond the stunts Juniper did to chase the euphoria following a hookup, they were decidedly a homebody. They'd been too scared to leave their satellite, so any lived experience was based on what they could find on digital recordings and archival footage. Sometimes they'd use their wireless augment for VR, but it wasn't a match for reality.

"All right, sure. First adventure past Jupiter." They smiled and giggled when Laurel pumped her fist in the air. "No way! Was this your plan all along?"

"I knew you'd come around!" Laurel said. "I bet you'll like them in person. Main singer's your thing." She tapped her chin thoughtfully. "Tall, muscular, and he has long hair! Not to mention, rumors say—"

"Oh, stop!" Juniper laughed, covering their face. Even with their bio-monitor adjusting their autonomous systems, they were still plagued with the ability to blush. Heat flushed through them and only intensified when Laurel hummed and brought up a photo on her palm tablet—likely the steamiest image of the singer available on the public net.

It must have been from one of those pinup digital calendars fans paid to download. Handsome. Devilishly handsome. Flawless skin. His long black hair cascaded down one shoulder. He was giving the camera the bed-roomiest eyes he had alongside a smirk showcasing very vampiric fangs. He lounged naked on a chaise from some bygone era with a blanket covering anything indecent, but Juniper saw enough. At least, their cortex computer did; it gave them an approximation of all what was missing, using rumors from fan sites to fill in the details. Juniper had to cover their face again. Nope. Nope. Did *not* need that kind of information right now, no matter how eagerly their cortex computer encouraged them to chase that line of thought in pursuit of good brain chemicals.

"Okay, okay, you're not wrong," they said and Laurel took the image away. "I'll go for the eye candy and you go for the inane coffin smashing."

"Yes!"

There was a beep behind them and then the softest purr of a motor. Juniper turned, searching in the dark, and found the sweeper bot Laurel had swiped.

"You actually nabbed it!" As they picked it up, the motor went dormant and Juniper let their cybernetics do a scan of it. Maybe a generation old. No tracking software beyond a wireless network useless this far from the dealership.

"Think they'll miss it?" Juniper asked.

"I bet they'll just buy a new one." Laurel patted it gently on the motion sensor and smiled proudly.

"Needs a name." Juniper placed it back down and

it revved up to continue cleaning.

"Got one already!" Laurel was bouncing in her seat again and Juniper waited expectantly. "Sprig!"

Juniper laughed until Laurel shoved them. "No! No—it's good! Just..." They snorted back another outburst. "We gotta start theme naming everything now! We should have found a green cruiser. What are we gonna name a red one?"

"We'll call it Maple!"

The *Maple*'s AI chimed. "Half an hour until destination," it said as it directed them downward into a lane exiting the city proper. They'd left the throng of tall buildings and establishments behind and it was flat and empty until the station in the distance.

The cheerful mood quieted upon seeing it.

Ships came and went at all hours of the day and even now, a few were taking off while others were coming in for a landing. The building itself was an austere white, sticking out of the Moon's surface with towering docks. Each one had blinking lights so no one accidentally hit it. Reminded Juniper of the stars.

Laurel's smile faded and she grew apprehensive.

Juniper patted her shoulder before she said what she was thinking. "Don't be mad at Slim," they said. "He'd never sell us out on purpose."

"You *would* think that."

Juniper shoved Laurel's shoulder. "He's not the kind of guy that'd sleep with you and then sell you out. We're friends. Feds probably just tapped into his network traffic and he didn't even know."

"If they know he helped us, won't they be waiting?"

A possibility, but Juniper swallowed the spike of paranoia and shook their head.

"I told Slim to alert me if there was anything out of the ordinary." Juniper opened their mental inbox with a thought. Nothing. Last one was from a week ago after one of their hookups. "We should have enough time to get our stuff from him before the feds realize anything. Would it make you feel better if I messaged him when I can link to his network? Just to make sure?"

Laurel fell silent, thinking. Juniper understood her hesitation; although bubbly and friendly, she didn't trust easily. Boarding school hadn't exactly been the place to build strong bonds. Juniper was all she had.

Eventually, she exhaled and nodded. "It would." She peered out the front window and a chuckle escaped her throat. "I still can't believe we're actually doing this, you know? Flinging ourselves past Jupiter. I just... I don't want to mess it up."

"Yeah." Juniper watched the empty lunar landscape whiz by outside. Sure, their stomach was suddenly dropping, thinking about what it *really* meant to leave, but this was what they'd wanted. They forced a smile at their reflection.

They really were almost there.

03
LAUREL

SEEING JUNIPER GIVE SLIM THE TIGHTEST hug they had in them made everything real to Laurel. On a normal day, Juniper kept physical touch to a minimum because their cybernetics would overwhelm them trying to scan the other person. But today? None of that mattered. They were really leaving and this was probably the last chance Juniper had to hug Slim at all.

Laurel tried to give them privacy, even if she was only a step away sitting in the cruiser still.

Slim oversaw a number of small docks inside the Lunar Landing Station. He'd always kept one open for Juniper's satellite shuttle and provided maintenance when needed. Slim and Juniper became acquaintances out of necessity and friends sometime later, although Laurel wasn't sure exactly when. All she knew about Slim was he was a regular dock android that made Juniper happy. It was because of him they had supplies in their satellite and no one knew it was there.

Well, it definitely wasn't there anymore. Before the heist, Juniper had programmed it to crash into the dark side of the moon to bury the knowledge they'd ever lived there at all. With any luck, the feds wouldn't notice until they were long gone.

Although, Laurel wasn't sure why that mattered. Anything important was packed away; the only thing they'd leave behind was skin flakes or whatever and she was pretty sure the Federation already had their bio-signatures on file. It really wouldn't matter if the feds realized they were ever there to begin with.

In any case, it was just another thing to cement they were really leaving. With their temporary home gone, they had no other choice.

Instead of staring at Juniper and Slim, Laurel looked elsewhere. The dock was small, only big enough for a single occupant, so not much to really look at beyond the chute their cruiser waited in and the launching terminal Slim had already initialized.

The station chatter around them was too soft to listen to as well, walls thick enough to stop most of it from leaking through. Every time another ship flew off, Laurel was drawn to staring at the glass doors at the end of the chute, at least. Sometimes, she could catch the colors ship fuel left behind.

To further distract herself, she mentally went over what was going to happen once they left the chute. Just to further make it feel real. Doable.

Anyone wanting to leave the inner system had to use the Mars Transit gate. There weren't any around Earth or the Moon, because when gates broke, it was always catastrophic. Pieces would end up falling to Earth and the feds didn't want to put it in danger.

Slim had already given them the command key to his own seldom used transit dock on Mars, which would get them past the asteroid belt for free. After that, the plan was to never come back.

So it was no wonder Juniper held Slim so tightly. He'd been their sole lifeline for years. Their sole friend—sometimes something more. Watching the two of them dropped a stone in Laurel's stomach. Juniper would never see Slim again. Laurel had no one she'd left behind and she and Slim never bonded, so she couldn't wrap her head around what Juniper must have been feeling.

Juniper and Slim finally parted after a soft kiss. As he went over quick docking procedures with Juniper, Laurel studied him. Like most male bio-androids, Slim stood tall and muscular, the very picture of an ideal man according to fed standards. He was a generation behind other bio-androids, however, since he didn't want to upgrade his body and lose what was essentially himself. As it was, he had flawless skin, bright yellow eyes with white limbal rings—the telltale sign of an android—long black hair braided down his back, and a small jack near the base of his skull. Juniper had one the same and it let people like Juniper and androids alike link into digital interfaces or one another.

"I am truly sorry the feds tapped my network feed," Slim said, pulling Laurel out of her thoughts. "I didn't realize it until Juniper messaged me."

"I know." Laurel nodded. He'd already apologized when Juniper contacted him on the ride over. "No harm done."

She didn't mean to sound so dismissive and internally groaned. Somehow, she was bad at interacting with everyone except for Juniper.

Still, Slim smiled, hopefully understanding her. His eyes glimmered and he blinked it away.

"Diagnostics are all done. I've registered the *Maple's* new ID across the transit system's inner network, so no one will know it was ever anything else." He helped Juniper back into the ship. "Just get to the Mars Transit Gate and the Solar System is yours."

Juniper gently ran their fingers through his hair before they let go. Slim reciprocated, long fingers drawn slowly through the faded blue of Juniper's short hair. Probably for the last time.

"I don't know where we'd be without you," they said. "Thank you so much."

The stone somehow grew heavier in Laurel's stomach despite the soft smile Slim turned on Juniper. He probably wanted to go with them, but fed androids hardly had a shot at saying 'screw you' to the rest of the cosmos and flying off. The fed tech inside of Slim was too deep; with it, he'd be found immediately, but trying to extract it might erase the Slim they knew.

Slim stepped away from Juniper, letting them buckle themself in. "You two are trouble," Slim said, winking, and Laurel couldn't help but smile at him this time. "Give them hell out there, all right?"

Slim patted the side of the cruiser and the top engaged, sealing them in. With one more lingering look, he waved and started the launch procedures from his terminal.

Juniper hastily wiped their cheeks, breathing in deep. A countdown displayed on the screen. Laurel didn't know what to say; goodbyes weren't her thing, especially not with someone like Slim, but she squeezed Juniper's hand, hoping it was a comfort.

The *Maple*'s AI engaged life support as the station lifted them into the launch chute. Juniper returned the hand squeeze just as their ship shot out of the station. Fast enough to escape the gravitational pull of both the Moon and the Earth. If they had lingering second guesses, it'd be too late now.

Once the cruiser stabilized, Laurel eased on the thrusters and directed them into the usual space cruiser lane and let the AI handle the driving from there.

Juniper distantly watched the Moon quickly grow smaller behind them. It was too quiet. Laurel had to say *something*. Get her friend out of their head or their regret would boil over.

"Will you miss the place?" she asked and bit down. *Real smooth there, Laurel.*

"Yeah." Juniper tore their gaze away and sniffled. "Years scared to leave and then you had the gall to show up." They nudged Laurel with their elbow, smiling sadly. "I wouldn't change it for the world though, you troublemaker."

"Me neither," Laurel said, nudging them back.

Their meeting on the local underground net had been a complete accident, but Laurel was glad it had happened. She'd found the directions of how to connect to the net in the boarding school's bathroom and to her surprise, the school's uplink hadn't been blacklisted like most Federation-adjacent organizations. Night after night afterward, she trawled the net looking for meaning in her life.

After months spent reading zines, underground articles, and conspiracy theories, she'd grown bored and hopped from chat to chat to find *someone* to connect to. She'd happened across a message board advertising itself as a place to make 'personal connections' and came across Juniper's profile picture. A long face of soft curves, shaggy blue hair tousled to one side, and narrow cybernetic-yellow eyes that seemed to look right through the screen. Laurel remembered the little smile on Juniper's lips, slightly open and most of all, shy and unsure. They'd looked *kind* and sounded friendly, so Laurel shot them a message.

At first, Juniper had been standoffish, but kept replying to Laurel out of politeness, and once they'd found they shared a love of old science fiction novels, Juniper became much friendlier. Soon enough, they were talking late into the night via voice chat. They'd shoot the shit, trade stories back and forth, and even managed to marathon movies together. Before long, Juniper was the one leaving Laurel messages to wake up to and Laurel always left a channel open for Juniper so they could talk to her anytime she was in her room.

It was much later that Juniper had admitted to Laurel what 'personal connections' had actually meant. A message board for sex hookups. Laurel, of course, had been (and still was) scandalized. It explained Juniper's initial confusion (Juniper had very specific tastes, and Laurel was *not* it, but she'd somehow missed the note on their profile page) and why Juniper got Laurel off the site ASAP.

Embarrassing story aside, Laurel was glad she'd found Juniper.

It was only a year later when Juniper revealed where they lived and offered Laurel a getaway. Laurel hadn't thought twice; she'd packed her things, hitched a ride to Slim's dock, and the rest was history.

They'd spent the year learning to live with each other. A stark change for Juniper since they'd been alone for so long, and though sometimes Laurel had felt like she was in the way, Juniper had been always quick to assure her she wasn't. By the time they were comfortable with one another, they'd begun planning their escape from the ironclad reach of the Federation.

And now, they were doing it. Still didn't feel real.

The AI chimed and announced they were close to other cruisers in the space lane, and Laurel peered through the crystalline windshield. They'd caught up to the late-night traffic. No use trying to skip the queue; it'd get them noticed, and if Laurel wasn't careful, she risked crashing into another ship. Better to let the AI do what it did best.

"How long do you think it'll take?" Juniper's voice was weak, the earlier energy and enthusiasm all but lost. The crash after the high.

Laurel frowned. "Going at not-suspicious speeds, accounting for a pee break halfway there... maybe six hours?" She tapped the console and brought up the ETA and the corresponding map. "Can probably sleep the whole way." She smiled sadly as Juniper nodded, distracted. "Is the buzz really bad now?"

Juniper sighed through their nose and opened their eyes. The golden yellow was so bright, they glowed. "I look that distracted, huh?" They scrunched their shoulders together. "I'm sorry."

When Juniper overtaxed their cybernetic systems, their bio-monitor forced them into what Juniper called an equilibrium state to level everything out. Juniper described it as feeling mentally far away, while all physical sensations were reduced to a buzz. It went hand-in-hand with the secret use of the cybernetics feds never told anyone about: the weapon part. What good was a weapon if it experienced the highs and lows of emotion? This would level emotions out if the bio-monitor deemed it necessary.

Laurel had seen it happen many times when Juniper returned from a quick hookup. They'd start on top of the world with manic energy only to crash as their bio-monitor dragged them back down. Anything exciting or strenuous caused it and Juniper hated it. Except they couldn't do anything but endure right now. Laurel honestly hadn't expected it to happen from the thrill of stealing a cruiser and then leaving, but the excitement must have been too much.

Twisting around in her seat, Laurel reached for the nearest bag in search of the one thing that helped Juniper avoid the oncoming malaise.

"We remembered your sleep gummies." Laurel fished the plastic container free. Juniper had decorated it with stickers of sleeping animals, glow in the dark stars, and a big warning symbol dead center. "Sleep will do you some good, right?"

Juniper took it. "Yeah." They winced. "I'm sorry. I really wanted to watch movies with you."

When Laurel downloaded the music, she'd also set aside space for the fluffiest set of kid movies she could find so they could watch them and get their minds off being sad about leaving.

"Sleep's better," Laurel said. "We can watch a movie anytime. No biggie."

"Yeah..." Juniper stared at the gummies. They were star-shaped and multicolor. Laurel had thought they were candy at first, but Juniper had set her straight immediately. Under *no* circumstances was she to ever take them.

Juniper picked out two and plopped them into their mouth. "Down the hatch."

It wouldn't take long. Laurel took the container back and glanced inside. Just one gummy left; Juniper hadn't been able to find a supplier before they left. As Juniper reclined their seat, eyes growing distant, Laurel returned the container to Juniper's bag and pulled a blanket free. Slim had sent it one day, saying it had reminded him of Juniper. Glow-in-the-dark stars decorated it in old Earth constellations. Laurel spread it across their laps and Juniper curled up beneath it.

"Good night," Juniper whispered, closing their eyes.

"Sleep well," Laurel replied.

And Juniper was out. Laurel released the sigh she'd been holding in and thumped back into her seat. How fast the gummies worked always weirded her out. She did not like them; they were a black-market drug and Juniper used questionable ways to obtain them. With their enormous sedative effect, they would *definitely* kill a normal person.

Juniper, however, was not normal.

Cybernetics and nanomachines had been outfitted throughout their entire body at the tender age of eight courtesy of the Prodigy Program. It was run by the best minds in the Federation with a mission to aid and augment the human experience (with a hidden side of human-shaped weapon to boot). It'd done nothing but make Juniper's life hell and they'd escaped the moment they could.

Unfortunately, with their cybernetics heightening their senses, Juniper couldn't sleep well, especially after a high. Sometimes they managed it, but when under stress or anything similar, Juniper simply couldn't. According to them, the cybernetics were too loud, monitoring everything around them, but because the nanomachines kept the body repaired, the lack of any meaningful sleep didn't kill Juniper like it did most people. It just made their mental state deteriorate.

Gummies let Juniper sleep and they were only safe because their cybernetics kept them breathing and the nanomachines detoxed them before the gummies could do any real damage. Once sufficiently detoxed, their bio-monitor would wake them when it judged them to have had enough sleep.

Although sometimes, it never felt like enough.

The cybernetic implants also made it so the feds would never see Juniper as a person—just an expensive experiment on the run. One of their many plans past Jupiter was to find a way to help Juniper deal with their cybernetics so they could be halfway normal. Give them control over their own body.

Although even on the move, it felt like a faraway dream still.

Once Laurel had watched Juniper long enough—the way the lights in the console made their pale skin even paler somehow—and counted enough breaths that most of the anxiety seeped out of her, she freed her palm tablet. Its glare was bright in the dark, making her eyes water, but it soon readjusted to the available light around them and dimmed. She loaded her tasking program and clicked on the plan she'd written before.

Pack everything we'd miss. Check.

Get information from Slim. Check.

Get the Cruiser.

Laurel ticked the box with her finger. Her tablet gave her a chime of a job well done, and she smiled at the absurdity of being encouraged to cause mischief.

Pack everything inside and say goodbye to Slim. She checked it off too.

Head to the Mars Transit Gate. They were on their way, so she ticked the box.

Find out how to turn off Juniper's cybernetics. Unchecked.

Be free to go wherever the stars call. Unchecked.

A little half-assed, sure, but Laurel literally didn't know where to begin on the last two. She hoped they'd find options at the Jupiter Transit Gate. A station that big was bound to have a lead. She darkened her tablet and slid it back into her jacket.

Six hours ETA.

"Hey, uh, Maple?" Laurel said.

"Yes?" the AI replied.

"I'm sleeping too." Laurel popped her seat back to lay down. "Wake us up when we're in view?"

"Affirmative," the AI said. "Sleep well."

As the console lights dimmed, Laurel rested her head on Juniper's shoulder and breathed them in. They always smelled like the juniper trees the boarding school grew on the terraformed campus. A little on the nose, but Juniper never minded. It was their chosen name, after all. Apparently named after whoever helped Juniper run away from the Federation scientists. That person was long gone—Juniper hadn't offered many more details than that—but the name itself honored what they'd done for Juniper. It was sweet.

Laurel closed her eyes, listening to the soft whisper of Juniper's breathing, of Sprig cleaning behind them, and let it pull her under for a deep sleep.

It lasted until the cruiser jerked and the AI blared the debris alarm. Laurel's eyes shot right back open.

Breathing? Check. Warm? Check. First two dangers taken care of. Laurel jerked her seat upright, and her jaw dropped.

Space junk absolutely *littered* the area in front of them. Not errant space trash, though, but like there had been a collision. Laurel peered past the junk, looking for its origin, and froze when she found it. Yep. Exactly that. Two ships. One was made of mismatched ship parts—usually indicative of space pirates—and it had rammed itself into the larger ship, a Class Theta Federation starship. Those resembled barges and were typically used to perform dangerous experiments in the dead of space.

Usually not near Earth. And what space pirate would ram a Federation ship? Especially here in the space lane?

Laurel blinked, looking around them, and her jaw dropped open.

This wasn't the space lane.

Laurel stomped on the brakes as the AI attempted to dodge another oncoming piece. The cruiser stalled from the two contradictory commands and a chunk of debris banged into the side before rolling over the cruiser's top.

"Stop! Stop!" Laurel ordered. "Where the hell did you take us?!"

"There was a Federation blockade in our preapproved lane," the AI said. "You were both unconscious, so I weighed the pros and cons of whether I should elect for a detour. The pros won out." It paused, like it waited for a response, but Laurel was too stunned to give it one. "If I took us through the blockade as originally planned, Juniper's datacrypt would have alerted the Federation."

Laurel swore under her breath. The datacrypt implanted in Juniper's head had come with the cybernetics and was only accessible upon death—hence the name. It housed Federation secrets, but was just a way for the feds to control a cybernetic person's autonomy. Under law, the travel of a person holding confidential information by any means was severely restricted and anyone sheltering such a person who'd fled those boundaries faced serious charges. It effectively made Juniper federal property and easily trackable if they weren't careful.

They almost weren't.

"There's a distress call," the AI pointed out.

"Nothing I can do with that." Laurel turned the wheel, but the ship didn't respond. Not even when she pressed on the thrusters. The ship continued its slow crawl toward the broken mess. "M-Maple?" Laurel squeaked. "What's going on?"

"Oh. That ship has tethered us to pull us aboard."

The AI said it so matter-of-factly, like it was choosing what coffee to prepare. Laurel's jaw dropped again. "What?! Since when!?"

"Since I stopped dodging debris. I am alerting you now. I cannot undo it. The ship's AI is overpowering my controls. Do you wish to hail them?"

"Hell no! I want out!"

"I cannot do that at present."

Laurel ripped the blanket off Juniper. They didn't stir. "Juniper! Wake up!" She jiggled her friend's shoulder. Still nothing.

"You both slept soundly," the AI continued, oblivious to Laurel's rising panic. "Vitals within the correct parameters. It has done you both some good."

"Shut up!" Laurel took Juniper's shoulders with both hands and shook harder. The AI didn't respond and Laurel resolved to apologize to it later. "Juniper!" she shouted. "You wake up right now!"

Something jolted through Juniper and they sucked in a deep breath, like all their systems turned on at once. They jerked away from Laurel, completely awake in an instant, and glanced past her. Their face fell.

"Where the hell are we?!"

"Detour," Laurel said. "Maple said there was a fed blockade and if we'd gone through it, it would have detected the datacrypt in your head." Juniper pressed their hand to their temple, scrunching their face. "That broken fed ship has a tether on us and is pulling us in. I can't get out of it."

Juniper froze, like it was all too much at once, and gazed at the towering wreck of the ship they were creeping toward. After a moment, they swore and tried keying in a few commands into the ship, but nothing worked. They bent over to pry the front console panel off and slotted a cable from within into their head-jack. Their body went rigid, eyes glowing, and after a moment, they gritted their teeth.

"It's got us too good." They jerked the cable out. "Seriously, Maple? You didn't notice any of this shit en route?"

"Negative," the AI said. "I do not perceive as you do. I relied on reports of the area."

"Wait." Juniper narrowed their eyes. "There's a distress call, but it's not on any of the official channels?" They shared a look with Laurel and she shook her head. She was as baffled as Juniper. "Something's not right."

"I agree," the AI said. "My hypothesis is the ship has been waiting for anyone to come by. Ships usually stick to known pathways to avoid incidents such as this."

Just not *their* ship. Laurel bit back her groan.

The Class Theta approached, its size dwarfing them completely, as the tether pulled them toward one of the hull doors near the bottom. If Laurel remembered right, that was where the hangar would be. Knowing one thing going on made her heart slow down a little bit. Until the metal doors slid aside and revealed a dark maw. Heart went right back to hammering in her chest. She squeezed in a breath and counted to ten before she exhaled.

"What's the plan?" she asked.

Juniper chewed on their lip. "When we get in, the

tether has to let go. Once it does, we burn fuel and peel out before the hangar doors shut again. Okay?"

Easy enough. Laurel adjusted her feet against the thruster pedals and held tight to the wheel. The darkness swallowed them, leaving only their dim console lights as guidance. There were emergency lights farther inside, sparking on and off, but that didn't do much for Laurel's rising panic. They were settled neatly inside past the airlocks. Laurel swept her gaze across the hangar to take it in. Escape pods sat askew, a broken cruiser was nearby, and really not much else was around but debris shaken loose by the impact. No one waited for them like she expected.

"Disengaged," the AI said.

"Now!" Juniper shouted.

Laurel threw them in reverse and slammed both feet on the pedals. The ship peeled backwards, but it wasn't fast enough; the *Maple* hit the closed hangar doors and spun from impact. Laurel pushed hard on the brakes, biting back a scream, and they jerked to a sudden stop before they collided into anything else.

"Shit!" Juniper snapped.

"Now what?" Laurel asked.

Juniper considered the hangar, their eyes darting from the mess, the lights, and then finally to the small, upright console against the stairway leading up to the deck above them.

"Bet those are hangar controls," they said.

Laurel's heart leapt into her throat as Juniper attempted to disengage the top. "You want to leave the ship?" she squeaked.

"With how damaged everything is, I don't trust sifting through the network wirelessly." Juniper gave her a worried look.

The AI pinged and a screen opened on their

console, showing a rudimentary diagram of the ship. "The vitals are within livable parameters," the AI added, "and the ship has locked off areas too compromised to traverse."

Not helpful. Laurel did *not* want to leave their ship. Her silent plea fell on deaf ears as Juniper disengaged the top. The air smelled of the steel of a typical hangar, but more prevalent was the stench of an electrical fire, making her nostrils burn. Juniper didn't let that deter them any and hopped out. Laurel resigned herself to being a willing participant. She grabbed the stunner from her bag and checked it; not enough to do any real damage, just numb a limb or two, but better than nothing.

Juniper hurried over to the console near the stairway and Laurel kept up right behind them. As Juniper fiddled with the machinery, Laurel watched the hangar for any signs of... well, anything other than them. After a tense moment of listening to the groan of the ship, flinching at shadows made from flickering lights, and holding the stunner so tightly, her hands hurt, Juniper finally smacked the console with their palm. The screen remained dark.

"It's locked down and I don't trust jacking into it," they said. "If I can find the main console, we can get this unlocked and leave." They gazed upward toward the entrance to the deck above and tightened their jaw.

"No way," Laurel breathed, feeling her entire body rattle from nerves alone. "We don't know *who* pulled us in or *why*."

"We'll be worse off if the feds arrive." Juniper gently touched her arm. "Stay with the ship—I can go alone."

That was a more awful plan. Laurel swallowed hard and shook her head. "Friends don't let friends go alone. I'm coming with." Even if she really wanted to stay with the ship.

She wasn't sure if Juniper was relieved or not, but they nodded all the same and took the stunner. Better in their steadier hands. "We'll be fine," they said, testing it, but Laurel heard how their voice shook. They glanced over Laurel's head and nodded at their ship. "Maple: you see anyone other than us? Lock up."

"Affirmative," Maple said. "Please, be careful."

Laurel steeled herself with a deep breath and followed Juniper up into the derelict ship.

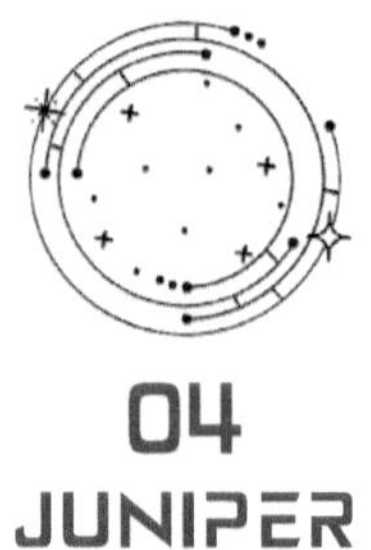

04
JUNIPER

HONESTLY, IT WAS A MIRACLE LIFE SUPPORT still worked and the ship's AI was intact enough to lock off the breached areas. The hallways past the hangar were draped in an encroaching darkness only penetrated when the ceiling lights lit up momentarily. The floor was littered with torn cables, wall panels, and debris too destroyed to know what it had been.

What unnerved Juniper, however, was the complete absence of the crew.

They'd never admit to it because they had to keep it together for Laurel; if they were ready to bolt, then she was one misstep from a full-blown panic attack. Making everything worse, however, was all of Juniper's cybernetic augments were sluggish from the gummies. Their eyes wanted to close back into the bliss of sleep. Their entire body felt so detached from themself, like it was all a dream. Juniper finally bit down hard on their lip and the pain kickstarted their cybernetics back into focus. No sleeping. No dreaming. Had to protect Laurel.

They'd find a working console with an uplink into

the main computer, get the hangar locks open, and leave. Nothing more. Whatever sorry fate had befallen the ship was of no concern to them.

"W-What—" Laurel's halting voice made Juniper jump and they glanced back. Her normally dark skin was ashen beneath the sparking lights and her eyes were wide like saucers, glancing this way and that. "What do you think happened?"

Even if Juniper did not want to know, noise would help. Something other than the rise and fall of their breathing and the soft groan of the ship.

"Maybe pirates?" Juniper peeked around the corner. More darkness and panels ripped off the wall. "There's evidence someone's been through here."

"Pirates are never on this side of the belt, though." Laurel stuck so close, Juniper's bio-monitor was picking up her pulse. Too fast.

"The feds must have been stowing expensive research," Juniper said. "Pirates probably figured it was a chance worth taking to sell on a black market."

"What do you think it was?"

"I wish I knew."

They made it past the flickering hall and up a short flight of stairs into a level with more lights. Not that it helped much. There was a door to the right just off the stairs and then the path continued forward. Juniper tried the door and it got stuck halfway open. Good enough. Juniper shoved it the rest of the way and slipped in. Their optics hardly had the place scanned before they pieced together *what* was inside.

Blood. Lots of it.

"Shit!" They spun around and shoved Laurel out. Laurel covered her mouth, eyes even wider, and they held up a hand at her. "Stay there." She nodded. "Let me check it for a console. Don't peek inside, okay?"

Another fervent nod. Laurel was always the more squeamish of their duo. Couldn't let her see *this*.

Juniper pulled the collar of their shirt over their nose and plunged in. Their optics finished the scan of the room and yep, not pretty. Dead body slumped against the wall to the left. Not wearing fed threads—maybe they were one of the pirates—but it didn't matter. Dead was dead. A huge gouge had been taken out of the neck, leaving blood leaking all over the place. Nothing useful there.

What piqued their interest was the raised section of the floor in the middle. A podium of sorts. It shimmered with fine dust. Juniper held their breath and let their bio-scanner catch up. Dust... no, not dust, but crystalline shards too fine to be called such were left behind from thawed cryogenic ice. Their bio-scanner insisted against inhaling.

Juniper frowned. Cryogenic ice was used to transport organic material through long hauls in space. Since humans died when encased in it, it was usually used for food—and vampires. The feds famously made examples of unruly ones by trapping them in ice and jettisoning them into the sun. Juniper shuddered thinking about it.

With more of the room in focus, their cortex computer reeled off a plausible scenario of what went down. Feds had been transporting an iced vampire. Logical. Pirates breached and boarded the ship. Evidence all over the place attested to that. Then some sorry sap—the body slack against the wall—decided against better judgment to de-ice the probably starving vamp.

That left out the why. Cryogenic ice was basically indestructible; it was why the feds used it against vampires. There was no reason to de-ice what was clearly a violent vampire.

"Junie?" Laurel squeaked from the hallway.

"Yeah?" Juniper swiped the scenario away. Too many holes.

"What's in there?"

"Dead body." Juniper ignored the mess as their scanners pinged a terminal in the back of the room. Probably used to monitor the cryogenic ice, but maybe it had a stable uplink. "Gimme a sec—there's a terminal in here." They edged their way over, dodging the blood, and jacked into it. Fuzzy feeling going in as usual, but the terminal didn't respond. Dead.

They sighed. "Useless."

"Junie..." It came out as a whisper this time and Juniper practically flew out of the room, pushing themself in front of Laurel. She was watching a camera up in the corner. "That camera moved."

Juniper fired up their wireless augment and searched for its network. Everything was a mess of gibberish and alarms, but they found the security feed buried in there. No way to tell if anyone was watching it, but they powered it down all the same before getting the hell off the network. They couldn't risk staying linked for long, lest something—a security protocol or an electric short—scrambled their brain.

"Let's go," Juniper said and hesitated seeing just how scared Laurel was. They swallowed and urged her closer. "Just look at me if you get too scared."

When Laurel nodded, Juniper led the way. They drew themself tight and kept their clammy hands holding the stunner in front of them. Couldn't let Laurel see how scared they were. Had to keep it together for her. Thankfully, Laurel dutifully followed right behind them, keeping her eyes downcast.

Given the way the lights struggled to stay lit,

Juniper didn't trust the lifts, so up more stairs they went. Around the first bend was another bloody corpse. Laurel immediately hid her face against Juniper's back and clung to their shoulders. Juniper gave the body the briefest glance before moving on; a husk with its blood drained. The blood was mostly on the wall and floor. More bodies littered the way up to the bridge's deck, pirates and fed suits alike. All dead.

Juniper vastly preferred not knowing where the crew was.

At the top and down another flickering hallway were the frosted glass doors of the bridge. Intact, but that wasn't a surprise; bridges were always made so they could be sealed off in case of emergency. The doors stuttered aside upon approach, the mechanism within groaning, allowing Juniper and Laurel through, but before they went in farther, Juniper put out their arm to stop Laurel. Had to wait for their sluggish optics to assess the room.

There had been a fight inside. The front window had a shallow crack where a skull must have borne the brunt of the damage. Not to mention the blood all over from what must have been the dark shapes of dead bodies. Ignoring them, the terminals inside were either fuzzed with static or off completely. The only one that had escaped the carnage was the pilot's console closest to the door. Good; that was the one they needed.

Juniper's pulse buzzed suddenly and their reflexes grew fluid as their bio-monitor pumped adrenaline through them. *Why?* Panic surged as they swung their gaze over the bridge again. No one else was here—why was their bio-monitor going so hard? They were missing something. Juniper held their breath and glanced from the dead terminals to the pilot's console, and then to the body slowly rising from its crouch.

The body. Moving. *Alive.*

Vision became sharp and clear. Time seemed to slow and their optics highlighted potential weak points in red, but then auras oscillated around everything, washing it all out. Pain shot through their head, speeding time back up, and all Juniper managed to do was push Laurel out of the way and pull the stunner up.

The body reached them in seconds and squeezed a crushing grip on Juniper's shoulders. They lifted off the ground, but all Juniper processed was Laurel screaming their name.

Fuck. This was it. Their grand plan had gotten them both killed.

Nothing happened. The hands let go. Juniper's fight response fizzled and they crumpled to their knees. The body took a step back, eyes wide.

"Shit," he swore, scowling, and Juniper caught the glint of sharp fangs. "You're kids." His voice was a husky tenor and would have been soothing if he hadn't just tried to kill them. He turned away, raking two hands through his vibrant red hair. "Shit! Shit!"

"Shit your fucking self!" Juniper snapped, undaunted as he spun back around to glare at them. Laurel pulled on Juniper's arm, trying to stop them, but Juniper's mouth continued on sheer panic alone. "What did you fucking *think* we were?!"

The man pinched the bridge of his nose. "Some fucking tiny-ass maintenance crew. Give me a break; everything's been a bit hazy." He turned and dragged a body off a console beside the pilot's chair. Given the fancy coat it wore, it had probably been the captain. Neck torn open like all the others.

"*You* pulled us in," Laurel breathed.

"I did." He dropped the body beside the keyboard and pressed the captain's limp hand to the console. The ship's AI greeted him in a warbling voice and he dropped the body to type. "Needed a way off this damn ship and then you were there."

Realization shuddered through Juniper and they forced themself back to their feet, cybernetics straining to give their legs strength. Laurel came up too and hid behind them. "You're the vampire they had on ice," Juniper whispered. "Aren't you?"

The man turned, smiling wide, and there they were in full view: long and absurdly sharp canine fangs. "Cedar Woods, vampire space pirate at your service." He grimaced and turned back around. "Well, I *would* be if I had my fucking ship."

"You killed everyone here," Laurel whispered.

Cedar shrugged. "Technically, the pirates did most of that. I just cleaned up."

"You don't even care," Juniper said.

Cedar slammed both hands on the terminal and faced them. "Why the fuck should I care? Feds kept me on ice for three fucking years, starving me!" He spread an arm toward the rest of the bridge where many more dead bodies lay below the window. "I'm gonna take what I'm fucking owed!"

Everyone went silent. He continued glaring, like he was daring them to judge him again, but Juniper understood. More than they probably should have. He was right; he had no reason to care about anyone on the ship. The feds certainly didn't care about him and the pirates wouldn't have either. He turned and faced the terminal again. The AI affirmed the hangar console unlocking and Juniper stilled.

"And..." Cedar faced them, smirking. "I'm owed a ship."

"Fuck you!" Juniper snapped, pushing Laurel toward the door. Cedar didn't advance, but Juniper's bio-monitor revved them up for a fight anyway, making everything go sharp and bright. "Take the pirate ship!"

"You saw that thing—it ain't running again."

"Like that's our fault?!" Laurel shouted and Cedar rolled his eyes, advancing another step. She squeaked and Juniper's bio-scanner pinged her racing heartbeat. "Take an escape pod! That's *our* ship!"

"Those have tracking." Cedar spread his arms mockingly. "What, you think you can stop me by blocking the doorway?"

Laurel tensed and Juniper scowled at Cedar. He gave them a smug look—he already knew the answer. Low blow. Even if Juniper wasn't malnourished and had kept their cybernetics up-to-date, vampires were in a league of their own. Fighting wasn't an option, but then what *was*?

"You're going to strand two kids?" Juniper said, frantic. Cedar's smile twitched. "You must care a little bit if you haven't killed us already."

Cedar shrugged and lifted a bag off the floor. Juniper hadn't noticed it before; it was so dark, it'd blended in. It was made of material too thick for scanning to get through. Cedar pulled the strap across his chest and stepped forward.

"Can and will. Feds will show up— probably soon—and save your sorry asses. Nice meeting you, but I'm getting the fuck out of dodge before that happens."

He made another step toward them, this one purposeful. Laurel flinched, trying to yank Juniper back, but they held their ground.

"Why do you have the distress call going if you

don't want the feds?" Laurel asked. Juniper stopped from nodding encouragingly at Laurel; she could keep him talking while Juniper planned their escape.

"As soon as those fuckers rammed the ship, it started on its own." Cedar waved his hand at them. "Move. I don't want to hurt you."

"Just strand us here!" Juniper argued, undaunted as Cedar glared at them. "No—*you* fuck off! I can't get caught any more than you can!"

Cedar raised his eyebrows and scoffed. "What are two kids doing to get on a fed shitlist?" He stopped suddenly, making eye contact with Juniper, and his surprise turned genuine. "Fuck. You're a cyber."

Juniper bristled. "Don't call me that."

"It's what the feds will," Cedar said. "I bet you got a datacrypt too, right? Larceny charge and all that to anyone caught housing you." He glanced away and gritted his teeth. "Shit..."

It almost sounded like that alone made them worth not stranding there on the ship.

The distress call ceased suddenly, leaving everything silent, and Cedar turned to look out the window. Long beams of lights slid into the bridge. Juniper's stomach sank all the way to their feet seeing what was on the other side of the window.

A Class Alpha Federation starship.

The internal intercom crackled to life. "Class Theta, *Globus*, do you read? This is Class Alpha, *Soliloquy* of the Galactic Federation. We have arrived to assist. Prepare to be boarded and meet us in an orderly fashion on deck four."

05
LAUREL

"I REPEAT..."

This was bad. Not even a day on the run and they'd already gotten caught. Beyond caught. There was no way to escape a ship that big. Laurel felt sick, all the blood, death, panic finally getting to her, and she bent low to force herself to take deep breaths to not vomit. Juniper came down with her, smoothing her hair back.

If she hadn't gone to sleep, she could have avoided this. She squeezed her eyes shut, breathed in, and counted to ten. Calm breaths, even as panic wound around her lungs. Calm breaths. One more. A few more.

There was a crunch and she flinched, pressing into Juniper. The fed's broadcast cut short. Cedar had plunged his hand into the ship's pilot console, destroying it. He yanked his fist out, pulling wires with it, and was undaunted as sparks licked his skin.

Then there was another crash down below, jostling the bridge. Must have been the mechanism used to force open ships if they were otherwise compromised. The distinct sound of metal being ripped open screeched through the ship, making the whole thing shudder. The feds were breaching the hull.

"What do we do?" Laurel whispered, throat tight.

Cedar sighed through gritted teeth. "I don't fucking know."

The question wasn't even intended for him, but Laurel bit back from snapping at him as he stalked to the other side of the bridge and then back, pacing.

"We're leaving." Juniper helped Laurel up and dropped their voice. "Let him distract the feds."

Callous, but Laurel wasn't about to object. It was his fault they were in this mess. Juniper moved them quickly, but they only made it just past the bridge doors before a light shined on them. Laurel shielded her eyes, blinking fast, and when she could see, she caught the gleam of blasters and the uniformed feds behind them. She shot her hands up.

"Don't shoot!" she shouted.

"Down on your knees!" the enforcer in the center ordered. Laurel counted three of them. All decked out in black with visors across their eyes like the ones back on the Lunar Colony, but there was a different air about them. A tenseness to their stance. Finger on the trigger. She doubted those were calibrated to stun.

"This wasn't us!" Laurel tried. "Please—we—"

The other enforcers behind the middle one raised their blasters. Laurel swallowed her words.

"I said: on your knees!" the first one repeated. "Hands behind your head! I will not ask again!"

Laurel and Juniper dropped to their knees and Laurel threw a glance back into the bridge. Cedar was gone. Asshole.

The head enforcer—he had to be since he was

calling the shots—stepped closer, mouth in a hard scowl. Text scrolled across his visor, too quick to read. He put the end of his rifle on the underside of Juniper's chin, forcing them to look up. More flashes of text.

"Where's the cargo?" he asked.

Laurel raised her eyebrows. "Cargo? W-We found none. There is a vampire—"

"Doesn't matter," the enforcer interrupted. One of the ones in the back put a hand to his ear, listening to his comms. "Gonna die all the same once we light this baby up like fireworks." Another enforcer went into one of the flanking rooms, leaving them with two. "Again: where is the cargo?"

It never did any good to talk to pigs. Only had ears for what they wanted to hear. Laurel maintained her silence, biting down on her lip, but her body trembled, betraying how scared she was. Not Juniper, though; they'd practically turned into a statue.

It wasn't lost on the head enforcer. He glared back, face twisting, and as soon as the second enforcer with him headed into another room, his visor lit up.

It'd made a match.

"Oh." He suddenly laughed. "Look at that. Cyber on the run." He leaned forward, a sick grin on his lips, and gripped Juniper's hair to tip their head to the side.

Juniper lunged faster than Laurel could register it. One second, they were there, and then the next, one hand had pushed the rifle toward the wall and the other slammed upward into the enforcer's jaw. He staggered backward, grunting, visor knocked askew, but before Juniper could follow up, the enforcer punched Juniper hard in the stomach.

Laurel flinched and Juniper slumped back to the ground, gasping for air. The other two returned, but relaxed seeing it was under control and returned to their search.

"Fucking punk." The enforcer kicked Juniper.

"Stop it," Laurel pleaded. "We haven't done—" She stopped when the rifle leveled with her face.

"Shut the fuck up," he snapped. "You're both a whole lotta nothing, you know that? I don't fucking care what you did or didn't do. What?!" He snapped the last bit into his comms and grimaced. "No. I don't see the fucking cargo. I found some mice. One's a cyber."

One of the other two enforcers returned. They all looked too similar for Laurel to tell the difference. "Come on. The other team will deal with these two. We need the cargo or we don't get paid. Cyber don't matter. Probably broken."

"Tie them up then," the first enforcer said. "If the other team don't want them, then they can blow up with the ship."

Juniper's eyes shot back open, but before they could react, the first enforcer's boot smashed into their side. Laurel squeaked, attempting to reach out until the rifle was back in her face. She glared at him, wanting to scream.

Then a shadow loomed behind her.

The enforcer didn't have time to scream. Not the way Cedar's hand caught his throat, crushing it between his fingers. Blood spurted out, coating the hallway red, and Cedar yanked the man off his feet. The second enforcer screamed an order, lifting his rifle, and Laurel dove on top of Juniper. Laser shots pelted the hallway, missing them outright, and made scorch marks where they'd hit. The shots continued up into the ceiling, smashing the lights to bits. The first enforcer now lay on the ground, eyes wide open and dead, while the second was failing to deal with Cedar. The vampire had pushed the rifle upward, letting it shoot all it wanted, and sunk his teeth deep into the enforcer's neck.

Right, Laurel realized distantly as the man went slack. *He's a vampire.*

Juniper jerked Laurel back to the floor, covering her this time, and the world seemed to restart. Another battle cry echoed across the hall. Shots hit something solid, but when Laurel peeked out from beneath Juniper, it was definitely not Cedar. Just the poor body he held, now drained of blood. Cedar had the rifle in his other hand. Juniper suddenly pushed Laurel's face into their chest, squeezing her tighter, and there was one last shot.

The body thudded to the floor.

Vampires weren't just punk bands with good publicity. They were exactly what Cedar was. An unstoppable force.

"The fuck you two waiting for?!"

Laurel refused to look at what was sprawled on the floor and focused wholly on Cedar. She regretted it. Blood drenched his chin and stained his shirt red. Fingers were absolutely coated in gore. His pupils had dilated, making his eyes almost entirely black.

"Run!" Cedar roared, throwing an arm out toward the dark. "They're gonna send fucking backup. You two want to sit here and gawk!?"

Panic and fear made Laurel tremble so hard, her legs wouldn't cooperate. Juniper tried to haul her upward, but they were shaking too much too, and they both ended up back on the floor.

Cedar released a low growl and reached over, making Laurel flinch, but he'd only taken her other arm. Between him and Juniper helping her to her feet, she found her strength again.

Once she was set, Cedar barreled his way down the hall and Laurel and Juniper hurried to keep up, leaving the mess of blood and bodies behind.

Better the devil they knew, if only for five minutes.

Another trio of enforcers blocked the way down. Didn't stand a chance against an angry vampire once he launched himself; he landed on the first, probably killing them outright, and made quick work of the other two.

Vampires were incredibly hard to kill. Laurel remembered reading about it once. Sure, the sun could do one in very quickly as could completely obliterating the body, but with adequate blood in their system, most wounds healed in seconds, like the ones healing across Cedar's hands now.

Humans couldn't take down vampires on their own, not without serious firepower, and the school's self-defense class always stressed the 'do not engage' bit. It also stressed not to run away, either. They were something like predators, after all, and would chase.

Basically, if you ever met an angry vampire, you were screwed. At least he was on their side. For now.

They made it back to the hangar, and thankfully, it was still free of the feds. The *Maple* was right where they'd left it. Juniper overtook Cedar as he stopped in front of the hangar control terminal. It was lit up, unlocked, and awaiting a command, and as he clacked at the keyboard, Juniper tossed Laurel into their cruiser and threw themself into the driver's seat.

"Disengaging the locks," the ship's busted AI chirped, the voice echoing across the hangar. "Opening the hangar doors upon your command."

Juniper was flipping through the *Maple*'s menus

faster than Laurel ever could, force-starting all the necessary systems. There was a shout above them and Juniper threw themself over Laurel. Blaster shots dinged the cruiser—outside and in—and unlike at the dealership, these left marks.

Cedar threw himself behind the front seats and jerked forward to input a command. The top snapped shut, protecting them from another hail of laser fire.

"Hangar locks are disabled!" Cedar shouted. "Tell your AI to open the damn doors!"

"Please, Maple!" Laurel shouted. "We're in!"

"Affirmative," the *Maple* said and a warning signal blared from the hangar's computer terminal.

No depressurization. No prep. The hangar doors slid open and so did the air locks. The vacuum of space tore out anything not nailed down, including one unsteady enforcer. He went flying and Laurel forced herself not to watch him go while Juniper flew the *Maple* backwards in the poor sap's wake.

They turned the cruiser around with the spin of the wheel and slammed on the thrusters. As soon as they sped out into space, a hail from the Class Alpha immediately lit up the console. Laurel swiped it away and then another and another until she was distracted by Cedar flopping back against the seats behind them.

"Close your eyes," he said.

Laurel jerked to look at him, explicitly not closing her eyes. He held a small black fob in his hand. "What are you—"

Her words died to a scream as the derelict ship exploded. Their tiny ship spun outward from the force and Juniper struggled to right it until Laurel reached over to grip the wheel. Together, they stopped the cruiser from rolling with the space debris and stabilized it.

White explosions almost as bright as the stars themselves lit up across the derelict ship first. The half of the pirate ship inside it was blown off, left to drift away from the force, but the rescue ship wasn't so lucky; the blasts continued up the breaching mechanism and knocked the arms holding the ships together clean off, leaving behind gaping holes in the hull. Two ships with one stone.

The incoming hails ceased and all was silent.

"You blew it up," Laurel breathed.

"That'll keep them occupied." Cedar grinned, his teeth still stained and his breath reeking of blood. "Didn't think the blast would knock back to their ship. Pirates were loaded."

Juniper spun to face Cedar, seething. Their hands were still shaking. "For fuck's sake! You were going to leave us and blow us up?!"

Cedar dropped his grin. "Nuh uh," he said. "That was a last resort. If they got here before my ride did"—he patted their seats and if looks could kill, Laurel was sure Juniper would have murdered Cedar—"I was gonna go up with it. Become stardust and all."

Laurel studied him quietly. He looked so harmless now if she ignored all the blood. Nothing that was the terror he'd been on their escape. It was uncanny. Her eyes drifted downward to the black bag in his lap. She raised her eyebrows.

"That the cargo they wanted?"

Cedar clutched it close, glaring at her. Right back to definitely dangerous. "Probably. What of it?"

Juniper reached back to touch it, but Cedar shoved their hand away. "They were ready to kill us over this!" they shouted. "We deserve to know what it is!"

"None of your business is what you need to

know," Cedar growled, baring his teeth as Juniper tried again.

Not the time for this. Laurel dragged Juniper's arm back before Cedar bit it off. "We have to jet and you're driving, Junie."

"I know a station," Cedar said and leaned forward, undaunted as both Juniper and Laurel lurched to the sides to get away from him. He brought up a map on the center console and zoomed out quite a bit before he pointed to a set of coordinates not super far away, all things considered. "Around here. Feds never go near it. Just burn the fuel to pick up some speed and we'll lose them."

"Ill-advised," the AI chirped. "Burning fuel could leave us stranded. No such station is listed in my internals."

Cedar flipped the console off and fell back. "Calling me a liar?" The AI didn't respond and he blew out a sigh. "I swear, it's there. I'll even pay for the refuel."

Juniper scoffed. "With what fucking cash?" they asked.

"Do you want to be caught?"

Uncertainty laced the air as Laurel and Juniper shared a glance, but Laurel had no better plan. She input the coordinates into the autopilot despite the AI's misgivings. The *Maple* slowly turned on its own and fired up the thrusters to full blast.

Silence lasted until Juniper caught Laurel's eye again. They nodded at her and Laurel nodded back. They needed to Talk. Laurel only wished they'd waited until they got to this invisible station, just to give herself more time to think, but better now. Together, they turned as a unit and faced Cedar. He jerked to attention, hugging the bag tighter.

"Here's how it's gonna go," Juniper said slowly.

"We get there, you refuel us, we leave. Without you. Part ways. All that shit."

Cedar blinked. "Hold up… I need back to my ship."

"We are not a travel service," Juniper said. "I want you off our ship as soon as possible."

"I saved your fucking asses!"

"After trying to strand us!" Juniper shouted right back, looking ready to throw themself over the seat to throttle him. Laurel settled a hand on their arm and they exhaled.

Cedar did look chastised, at least, with eyes downcast and an uneasy frown on his lips. Maybe he felt bad. Laurel tried to think of a different approach—maybe appeal to some paternal instinct that must have kicked in when he decided to save them—and Cedar interrupted her by reaching forward to poke Juniper's head. All regret was wiped clean off his face. Juniper dodged his hand, scowling deeply.

"I know what you want." He smirked like a cat who'd caught a mouse. "What all cybers outside of fed control want. You want that entire system to stop, right? Want it out of your thoughts?"

Juniper didn't answer. It was true, even Laurel knew that, but she kept quiet too.

"I had uh…" Cedar's fingers tapped the bag in his lap. Something like glass resounded from within and he immediately stopped when Laurel glanced at it. "A friend like you, though not of the same caliber of cybernetics. He couldn't escape the feds forever, either. Vampirism shuts the tech down."

Laurel glared at Cedar—that wasn't a viable solution—and Juniper sighed.

"No," they said, sounding hurt. Laurel reached over and squeezed their arm.

Cedar nodded. "I figured, just wanted to provide

the easy option first. I got another." He smiled again, but Juniper didn't look back this time. He focused on Laurel instead. "There's this private facility orbiting Pluto specializing in androids, biotech, and cybernetics. You just won't make it in this dinky ship."

Juniper twisted in their seat again, eyes wide. "No way that place actually exists."

"It does." Cedar leaned forward, excited, and placed himself between Laurel and Juniper. "The Lowell Orbiting Research Facility of Pluto. It's *real*."

The name sounded familiar, but only in passing like she'd heard it at school. Laurel eyed Juniper. They were hardly breathing. "Junie?"

"Does it really exist?" they breathed.

"I did some jobs for the guy a while back," Cedar continued. "I swear: it's real. I've been there. I've seen his shit. It's the real deal."

Juniper flicked a glance at Laurel as Cedar moved back. All she could do was shrug. She had no plan, and if Juniper believed him, it was something. Even if it meant traveling with a vampire, and Laurel wasn't sure how she felt about that right now.

"I'm giving you an out for your problem," Cedar stressed. "People like you don't last long running from the feds. They will catch up and you will lose whoever you are to them. Help me and I can help you."

Laurel slid her hand around Juniper's and squeezed it. They had nothing else.

Juniper thumped back into their seat. "We're thinking on it overnight."

"Sound plan," Cedar said. "There're a few motels at the station. I'll buy." He grinned and Laurel settled back in her seat. After a silent moment, however, he was leaning forward again like a man who was not used to being ignored. The playful smile was back on his lips this time, almost disarming if not for the blood.

Sighing, Laurel cut him off with a wave of her hand and maneuvered it around him to fish out the makeup wipes from her bag. She took one out, intending to hand it over, but after another glance at him, decided to shove the entire package at him.

"Please, wipe your face. Take as many as you need. You're hard to look at right now."

Cedar actually looked embarrassed and quickly wiped his face and hands down. A little better. Not as grisly, especially when he slotted the playful smile back onto his lips. No more blood there either; he must have used a wipe on his teeth too.

"So, help me out here. I'm Cedar Woods. Your names?"

Laurel afforded him a smile. "I'm Laurel Langley. She if you please."

"Oh!" Cedar pointed at himself. "He's good." He turned the same disarming smile on Juniper.

"Juniper," they said. "And they's fine."

Cedar gave them both some thought and a laugh bubbled out of his throat. "Shit, there's theme naming going on here, huh?"

Juniper shoved him back, making him laugh harder. Laurel had to cover her mouth to stifle her own. Either nerves were getting to her or the thought of someone with a plant name pointing it out was too funny.

"Yeah, well." Juniper was laughing now too, gently slapping Laurel to make her stop. "The cruiser's named the *Maple* and you're sitting on Sprig."

Cedar jerked up, hitting his head on the top of the glass, and Sprig whirred out from underneath him, beeping indignantly. He settled back down, shooing it away as it tried to vacuum him up.

"Well, Laurel and Juniper," he tested their names, nodding, "I think this will be the start of something grand. You two just gotta trust me."

Not like they had much choice in the matter.

SESSION 2

VAMPIRES WILL NEVER HURT YOU

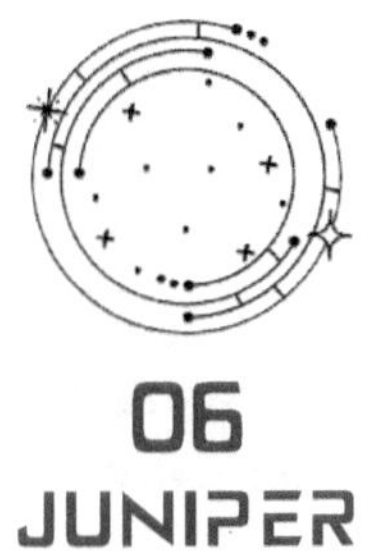

06
JUNIPER

THE REFUELING STATION *WAS* THERE, A dark speck that didn't gleam like stations usually did. Those begged for your business with tantalizing lights, and ships flocked to them like moths to a flame, as the old saying went. Not that Juniper had been in enough nature biomes to see moths, let alone watch them flock to a flame. This one being so dark and unassuming meant only one thing on this side of the belt: vampires.

Cedar handled linking the *Maple* to the station's docking AI. Juniper didn't like handing him control, but it wasn't like they knew how to get in. Usual attempts were ignored. After typing in certain commands on the console, the station requested a code and he gave it his personal one. While Juniper worried it would be three years too old, the AI welcomed him and directed them toward a dock for smaller ships.

Thankfully, most stations resembled one another, even weird pirate ones like this, so Juniper knew exactly where they had to go. The impenetrable dome up top was the actual station and it rested on what resembled a metal spike. That was where the docks were—larger ones near the bottom, smaller ones closer to the dome. Once the *Maple* was on its way, letting the station's AI guide it, Juniper let go of the wheel and unclenched their hands.

Juniper never would have guessed a place like this existed so close to Earth. They were also offended that in all their sifting through the underground net, this place *never* came up. They wanted to grill their resident vamp on how it ran so far under the radar and still existed, but Juniper kept their mouth clamped shut. No chatter. He was not a friend. Merely an asset.

Honestly, if Juniper had been on their own, they would have already said to hell with it and bought into the Pluto plan. Rumors about Clyde Lowell swirled across the underground net, but what Juniper had been able to piece together was he was a hermit researcher with enough technical prowess, even the Federation sung him praises. If anyone knew how to stop cybernetics without killing the person attached, it'd be him. Since Juniper was not alone, however, and had one squishy human in over her head, they couldn't agree. Laurel deserved way better than being some vampire snack because of Juniper's risk taking.

Speaking of Laurel—she was nodding off in her seat. She kept trying to pretend she wasn't, but she was clearly exhausted. They'd only made time for one stop along the way at a tiny rest station outfitted with basic restrooms and a few food and clothing vending machines (Cedar was able to get himself a new, not blood-stained shirt, which made him way easier to look at). The rest stations scattered across the Solar System were always unmanned and often deserted. Juniper had thought about stranding Cedar there, but they didn't know if they could make it to a known station from there on their own.

Besides, Juniper wouldn't have been able to live with themself if they'd knowingly abandoned someone who did technically save them. And, they *did* tell Cedar they'd think about his offer overnight. They owed him that much.

The docking procedure was smooth as the *Maple* linked with the station's interface. Juniper tried not to fret, but they did anyway. It wasn't a place they knew; wasn't a place they'd scoured for details on the net before setting foot in. Juniper chewed on the inside of their cheek hard enough to give their systems something to focus on that wasn't their panic. They had to keep it together for Laurel's sake.

The *Maple* nestled itself into its dock which was a glorified tunnel with basic ship amenities and an airlock. At the other end was a sliding door leading into the station. When the airlock sealed and they were given permission to disembark, Juniper disengaged the top. Fresh station life support air. Always stale.

Laurel immediately set about refueling with a cred stick Cedar produced from his coat. She even took the liberty of paying a repair bot to look at some of the blaster marks on his dime. Though none of them had breached the hull, they were a sorry sight on their otherwise brand-new cruiser.

While she dealt with that, Juniper decided what they were lugging to the motel. Not ideal to grab everything in case they had to run. There were four bags stuffed full and Sprig slumbered soundly beneath a folded blanket. Juniper decided to take the bag Laurel had shoved most of both their clothes into. Everything else, even Sprig, would be safely locked up inside. When Laurel finished, she and Juniper joined

Cedar at the station door.

"Stick close," Cedar said, taking point. He had his cargo bag over his shoulder and Juniper's cybernetics tried scanning it again. Not helpful—just an approximation of the weight as it rested against Cedar's back. Could have been anything.

"Don't want anyone thinking you're fresh meat," Cedar added.

Because that was exactly what they were. Juniper and Laurel stuck close and the three of them blended in with other travelers disembarking. Not everyone was a vampire, thankfully. Juniper's bio-scanner identified typical human vitals (Cedar's vitals were almost silent in comparison) and gave warnings when someone looked for too long, but Cedar was as much defense as they needed. All he had to do was glare and onlookers backed off.

The lift into the station was a tight ride and Juniper was only glad to be off it and into the station proper, but the place wasn't much to look at. The station resembled all other refueling stations. Cramped, smelled like fuel, crowded with different establishments along the main boardwalk lit up by cheap neon lights, and teeming with people coming and going. Their bio-monitor warned them against the shitty air quality, and when Juniper swiped that away, their cortex computer chimed in with a warning about how many security feeds they were on. Enough to make Juniper want to run back to sleep in the ship.

Whenever they'd left their satellite, they had certain items they'd always take to feel like they had control. A black hood, their cloth face mask, and their signal disrupter they used to temporarily disable the feeds directly on them. It kept them safe, but the disrupter had only been tested against fed hardware—

not anything black market. Still, they dug for it in their pocket and clicked it, hoping it distorted *something*.

The growing panic must have shown on their face because Cedar's pace slowed and he glanced back, worried.

"I'm fine," Juniper lied. "I'd just like to get off the street."

"About that..." Cedar pulled them to the side of the boardwalk and nodded to a building a few doors down.

Motel. Neon lights boasted vacancies and free uplinks. Not that Juniper would trust an uplink in a skeevy station. There was a small office facing the street and then two rows of exterior facing rooms on top of each other. Crowding in the alley nearest them were bright vending machines with the motel's logo of a wide-open eye. Their cortex computer pinged the machines and listed everything for sale inside: pills, lubes, prophylactics, and toys for 'enhancing intimate experiences.' Juniper bit back a groan and made a note to stop Laurel from investigating—she'd go looking for candy and die of embarrassment.

"It looks..." Laurel made a face. "Cozy?"

"That's a word for it," Juniper said.

"It's cheap," Cedar insisted. "The thing is, we have to make them and any eyes watching us believe you're with me and not just... hanging on." He leaned toward them, making a useless hand gesture like it would help them understand. "Do you get me?"

Laurel blinked, absolutely oblivious, and it was another beat before Juniper realized what exactly this place was and why Cedar was being so dodgy. It explained the vending machines.

"For fuck's sake," they said through gritted teeth. "Are you serious?"

"All the cheap places are like this," Cedar said. "I don't want anyone thinking you're free. It'll just be until we get in and then we can go back to distancing. Promise."

It finally dawned on Laurel and she gasped, covering her mouth.

"I'll put my arm around your shoulders—is that okay?" Cedar waited and Laurel nodded. "And your... uh..." He glanced at Juniper and looked about as uncomfortable as Juniper felt. "Is your waist okay?"

"It's fine." Juniper faced Laurel. "You good with this?"

Laurel nodded again. "Yes, I am," she insisted. "It'll sell the story, right?" She breathed in and set her glasses straight. "Ready."

"No funny business from me. Pinch me if you get too uncomfortable. Just hang onto me like you actually like me and this will go smoothly."

It must have been a sight. Two runaways hanging off one very tall vampire, forcing themselves to look absolutely smitten with him. Laurel nailed the sweet and innocent look at least, fluttering her eyelashes with a little smile on her lips. She was almost *too* good. Someone might actually try to save her from the big bad vampire. Juniper hung onto Cedar's other side, trying desperately to look like they enjoyed the situation as much as Laurel. A little hard given their bio-scanner decided this was the best time to try and fully scan Cedar for Juniper's protection.

The clerk at the desk watched their sorry trio saunter up, his eyebrows high in disbelief, and he grew interested as his gaze darted from Juniper to Laurel. Bastard even had the audacity to lick his lips and Juniper had to stop themself from launching over the counter to deck him.

"Need a room for the night," Cedar said, his voice easy and slow. He glanced down at Laurel, jiggling her shoulder. "Doll face, get me my cred stick, will ya?"

Laurel stared blankly at him, dropping the sweet and innocent look to one of sheer panic, and then quickly retrieved his cred stick from the exact pocket he'd put it in. Of course; she'd been watching it like a hawk since he'd taken it back. She'd probably been planning to steal it if they ended up running and now Cedar let her know he *knew* she knew where it was.

So much for that backup plan.

She coyly handed the credstick to the clerk, batting her eyelashes, and the clerk smiled at her. Yep. Fangs. Juniper might have missed them if they hadn't been watching for vamps.

Given the way he glanced Laurel up and down, there was only one thing on his mind. Juniper's cortex computer outlined scenarios where they could get away with decking him.

"Why's a guy like you need two?" The clerk slotted the cred stick into his terminal. It pinged and deducted the cash. "You wanna share? I can hook you up with a good suite."

Cedar leaned in, looming over the clerk so suddenly, the man shrank back in a panic, eyes wide. "No," Cedar growled, keeping his teeth bared. "They are *mine,* and if you ask again or disturb us, I will tear out your throat."

Juniper couldn't stop the laugh in their throat in time. Not with how scared shitless the clerk looked handing Laurel the room fob. They tried muffling it, turning into Cedar's shoulder, but the clerk heard them, his face souring. Cedar glanced down at Juniper, smirking.

"You like that?" Cedar purred and as Juniper

looked up to nod, Cedar pressed his lips to Juniper's cheek.

It was for show—no question—but Juniper should have told Cedar *not* to touch his skin to theirs. With cybernetics so highly tuned and too focused on how close Cedar was, as soon as they touched, their bio-scanner took it as a full invitation to finish its invasive scan. Juniper was bombarded with all the information they didn't want to know about Cedar. His height, his weight, his lack of a healthy heartbeat, his natural hair color for fuck's sake. And then it started listing the measurements of *everything*. Way more than Juniper *ever* wanted to know.

They forced themself not to flinch and let out a little coy laugh, even as heat crept through their entire body. When Laurel had touched them the first time, her bio-scanned information had come easily and calmly. This was a blow to the head.

"Come on." Cedar's voice was distant and Juniper forced themself to follow it to find reality again. He'd bent low, picking Laurel up with one arm, and for her part, she let out a litany of giggles. She probably actually enjoyed being tall for once. The clerk curled his lip into a scowl and glued his eyes to his terminal.

Without any other distractions, Cedar kept them both close as he took them up the stairs. Juniper tried to make their cybernetics focus on the other rooms. Check for vital signs within or what dangers might be lurking, but nope. Right back to Cedar and all the faded tattoos his vampirism hadn't healed.

As soon as they were in their room with the door locked, Juniper pushed themself away and held their head. With the physical scan out of the way, the bio-scanner had begun tracking his emotions. All from a single, simple touch.

Cedar's calm became confusion and confusion became outright concern, then he gasped and set Laurel down. "Oh shit." He reached out to Juniper, but immediately stopped and drew back with his hands up. "I am so sorry. I forgot. I—"

"It's fine," Juniper forced out, relieved when Laurel came up beside them. The one they knew. The cybernetics calmed with her nearby, focusing on her, instead. Not a threat. Friend-shaped. "Sold the story very, very well."

Cedar continued watching them, like he wanted to say more, but then finally nodded toward the opened door beside them. "Take the shower and use up all the hot water."

Laurel paused and considered him. "Really?" She jokingly nudged Juniper and a nervous laugh bubbled out. "Junie definitely will."

Cedar's smile was so genuine and relaxed, some of Juniper's panic ebbed. He waved them off. "Serious. I got some digging to do. Figure out what all I missed in those three years."

As Cedar headed into the dark room, Laurel lingered like she intended to stay with him. Not happening. Juniper dragged her into the bathroom and shut the door.

"Neither of us are staying alone with him for now, okay? Not until we're sure."

Laurel nodded quickly. "Sorry. I was just thinking about how it must have felt. Three long years frozen..." She shuddered and flipped the switch for the bathroom light. The fluorescent bulb above the vanity to the side buzzed on and sheathed the room in orange. She gave Juniper a small smile. "Holding up?"

Juniper listened intently. Cedar's careful footsteps moved away from the door. He must have gone to the room's uplink terminal—most motels had them to pay for extras or to look at what the station had to offer. Their aural augments picked up the electric fuzz it made as it switched on. Just as he'd said, then. Juniper sagged their shoulders, relaxing.

"Yeah." They dropped their bag in front of the vanity. "I call first dibs!"

Laurel laughed, covering her mouth to dampen the sound, and Juniper danced around her attempts to stop them. "You always call first dibs! No fair!"

JUNIPER FELT BAD BECAUSE LAUREL WASN'T wrong; they always did call first dibs. They were glad that Laurel let them have it, however. Especially once the torrent of hot water—almost too hot—overwhelmed their cybernetics, quieting them to a distant murmur, and made everything feel right. After lathering up with the provided two-in-one wash and shampoo and rinsing it all off, Juniper curled into a crouch and focused on the pitter-patter of the water on their skin and the way the heat cocooned them. Refreshing. Real. They almost ascended to the right state of mind where everything was and would always be okay, but then their bio-monitor revved up, detecting Laurel moving on the other side of the curtain.

"I'm okay," Juniper said on reflex.

"I know." Laurel's silhouette turned to the vanity.

Juniper wiped their cheeks, trying to be okay as they fell back to reality. Being okay really wasn't something they ever did. Maybe one day it wouldn't be such an obvious lie.

"Your cybernetics went into overdrive, huh?"

"Yeah." Juniper snickered sadly, trying to find the humor in it. Their augments were supposed to keep them safe, not immediately hone onto a body type they liked and give them all the information it could about it. Something told Juniper it wasn't a feature the feds had in mind.

"It... uh. Well." Juniper laughed again, feeling their face heat up. "I know he's packing."

There was the telltale sound of Laurel smacking her forehead. "I think I could have lived without knowing that," she said. "Why does it tell you that?"

"I think it's finally picked up I like guys," Juniper said. "Don't worry. I'll spare you the lurid details."

Even though Juniper couldn't see Laurel, they could practically hear the eyeroll. She went silent for a moment, clearly fiddling with something by the way her shadow moved, and a small clamshell opened in her hands. Juniper raised their eyebrows.

"When did you find that?" Juniper asked.

"When Cedar was scary," Laurel said. "This case was in full view on the desk. Surprised you didn't see it." Juniper had been a little distracted, but leave it to Laurel to notice something she could easily palm. "There's a keycard in here for waste management. Kinda useless... Oh! There's also some lipstick!" She made a sad sound. "Ugh. So not my color. Why can't I ever find a good neon-yellow lipstick? Here." Her hand came around the curtain, holding it out. "Your color?"

Juniper leaned away from the stream of water to get a good look at it. Midnight blue. "I could try it. We'd need a reason to dress up." Laurel capped it, humming, and Juniper inspected their palms. "All right, I am a certified prune. Your turn."

Laurel helpfully threw them a motel towel once

Juniper turned off the water. The towel was actually clean according to their bio-scanner—a miracle. After a quick pat down, they wrapped it around their waist and slipped out, letting Laurel hop in, her own towel wrapped around herself. The water turned on just as fast, just as hot, and Juniper bent over their bag.

"Hey, Laurie, which do you want?"

"Hm..." Laurel giggled. "Going for your meteors?"

Juniper found their meteor boxer briefs and grinned. "You know it."

"Gimme my spaceship ones then. We'll match!"

There was no stopping the smile spreading across Juniper's face. This was why they loved Laurel. She knew how to make the world simple again, down to matching underwear. It reminded Juniper they were human.

By the time they'd dressed in their standard sleepwear of a tank and leggings with their cardigan wrapped around themself, Laurel was done. Juniper handed her the clothes she usually slept in and, knowing her penchant for modesty, turned away as she got dressed. Once they were both done, they headed out as a team.

Cedar didn't bother making conversation as they came around. He saw them, abandoned his search on the terminal, and headed into the bathroom for his turn. It wasn't long before the shower was back on and Juniper didn't blame him.

Besides, his absence let Juniper snoop.

He hadn't bothered with the lights, but the window was seated exactly where the neon sign shined in. Probably intentional on the clerk's park. A lone lamp was on the nightstand beside the bed. Nothing special there. Laurel sat on the bed's edge and gave the mattress a bounce. Not a bad size, but heat crept through Juniper as their cortex computer tried to calculate if they would fit on it with Cedar. No. They and Laurel could outvote Cedar and take the bed for themselves. He could have the couch against the wall.

Juniper dragged their gaze from the bed and noticed the television screen on the wall across from it. Given the kind of motel this was, Juniper didn't trust that it'd have anything worth watching this late, so they kept it off.

Beyond that, the room was pretty barebones. Not many places to sit since Cedar used their single chair to barricade the door. Couldn't be too careful, Juniper supposed.

Laurel had turned on the lamp for more light and busied herself with digging into the nightstand. She immediately closed the drawer, making a face. Juniper rolled their eyes; what had she expected to find? They were in a vamp hookup motel. Definitely not a Bible.

As she flopped onto the bed, pushing her palms into her eyes to block out what she'd seen, Juniper sat on the other side and glanced at the terminal hooked into the wall on their side.

It was so old, it stuck out like an arcade machine. Nothing like the flat ones feds installed in the Lunar Colony. Probably easier to hack, but Juniper wasn't in the mood to try. It was off, whatever Cedar had been searching for left a mystery. Not that it mattered much. Just three years lost to being frozen.

As Juniper drew their gaze across the room again, they heard ticking. Like a clock. It was so soft, a whisper at most. Juniper focused harder. Laurel tugging the covers out from beneath them made it difficult. They held up their hand and she froze.

There. Juniper looked at the couch. Cedar had left the cargo bag there.

No way. It was *ticking*.

"What?" Laurel whispered, leaning beside Juniper.

"Shh!" Juniper craned their neck and peered at the bathroom door. Closed. Water was still running. "I want to see what the cargo is."

Laurel's eyes grew wide and her gaze darted to it. She shook her head and stood. Girl had no qualms stealing anything not nailed down, but even she had her limits... like snooping into something a vampire definitely didn't want her looking at.

Juniper had no such qualms. "It's big." They brought the bag over and settled it between them both. "I want to know exactly what we'll be dragging across the system if we say yes. We have a right to know." Laurel hesitated and Juniper continued. "Look, we know it's sensitive. The way he's acting? The way the feds were after it? But he didn't take it into the bathroom with him. Maybe the heat would have harmed it. You've got to be at least a *little* curious what we almost died for."

Laurel's eyes fixed on the bag. Got her. There was that twinkle of curiosity. She shook out her arms and nodded. "Okay, okay. Let's see it."

Her heart rate was skyrocketing. Pure nerves. Juniper swiped the information away; their heart was doing the same, but they *had* to know what was in the bag. What was so important that those enforcers would have buried them just to get it?

Juniper undid the latches and pulled the bag down around the glass container inside. It was another second before they processed what they were really seeing and their jaw dropped.

"It's a head," they whispered, hands shaking.

Bio-scanner reported it as dead. No fucking shit. Skin looked gray inside whatever goo the head was submerged in. Hair a wisp of pale blond with scant dye still trapped inside the strands, although it'd been so long, the scan couldn't determine the color. Faint freckles were dusted across the sharp cheeks and nose. Pretty, if not for the dead part. The mouth was slightly parted and as Juniper tried to check the teeth, their cortex computer helpfully told them they were indeed vampire teeth. Juniper turned the container and noticed the jack at the base of the skull.

Interesting. Dead, preserved vampire head with cybernetic augments.

And there was the ticking again. So soft, Juniper hardly heard it, and they turned the container so the head faced them again. It was almost like a shy hello.

The bathroom door opened and Juniper's curiosity gave way to panic. They and Laurel couldn't close the bag fast enough before Cedar was at the foot of the bed. Halfway dressed, shirt over his bare shoulder, hair dripping. He wasn't smiling. This wasn't the man who'd felt bad about making Juniper freak out.

"I've told you," he growled, "that is none of your business."

07
LAUREL

"IT'S A FUCKING HEAD!" JUNIPER SNAPPED.

Laurel was too stunned to say anything. A preserved severed head had not been high on her list of possible cargo. She glanced up at Cedar; he didn't answer Juniper's outburst. He glared at them instead, his lips parted to show his fangs.

Juniper held their ground. "We deserved to know! You want us to carry a severed head across the system. One those enforcers wanted to kill us for!"

And still, Cedar did not reply.

"This is the cyber you knew, wasn't it?" Juniper's voice was breaking. "You fucking cut off the head? For what? The datacrypt?"

"No," Cedar said, his voice growing as small and broken as Juniper's. "No. This wasn't my choice. I didn't cut off his head."

"Then why keep it?" Juniper asked. "Are you gonna sell it? Is that it? What did he even mean to you if you're just going to sell it?"

Laurel finally reached across the bed and touched Juniper's arm. They flinched and looked wildly at her.

"Junie." She shook her head and some of the fight seeped out of them. "I don't think it's like that. Look at his face."

While Juniper had yelled, Cedar's posture had completely shifted; he'd withdrawn in on himself, arms tight across his chest, his glare all but gone. A hurt, worried man stared back. The head wasn't to sell—it meant something to Cedar. Something big. Juniper breathed out, and the silent standoff continued for another moment before Cedar slowly lowered himself onto the couch. Laurel didn't mind; a sitting vampire was less scary than a standing one.

He ran his hands through his hair, wiping it back, and his gaze flitted between Laurel and Juniper. He had no idea where to start.

Laurel had a guess of her own. "You were iced by your old crew, weren't you?" she said and Cedar went still. "I can't think of how except if it was people you trusted."

Cedar looked away, shoulders slumping. "Yeah. It was them."

"They did this to him too, didn't they?"

Another nod. "They did." He slowly exhaled and rested his elbows on his knees. Laurel took her chance and sat on the bed to give her trembling legs a break. Juniper settled next to her, completely unreadable.

"He had a huge bounty on his head," Cedar whispered. "The same as yours, I'm sure. It's just the nature of being a cyber. Although his cybernetics were long since dead—he was a vampire. I guess my crew decided it was worth more than the shit jobs I was pulling in. Drugged us." His mouth twisted into a deep frown. "I woke up and it had already happened. They'd lopped his head off in our hangar. One of the only ways to kill a vampire and it's not like they needed his body. Just the head with the datacrypt." His gaze drifted back to the head.

Laurel glanced at it. Ghastly, even with the serene expression. "What was his name?"

"Aster." Cedar chuckled. "He woulda loved you two on names alone."

"And then your crew iced you?" Juniper asked. "Why not kill you too?"

"They thought I'd be under longer, I guess. Why they didn't kill me first, I'll never know," Cedar said. "Once I woke up, they knew they wouldn't be able to stop me—everyone else was human. Icing was probably a last resort and they knew they couldn't ever thaw me to finish the job because I was *awake*."

Trapped in ice for three years while awake. Laurel forced down a full-body shudder.

"Poor pirate who thawed me had no chance." Cedar pulled at a chain around his neck Laurel hadn't noticed before; it held a copper encrusted pair of leaves. "He probably thought this was actually worth something and wanted it." He let it drop back down and shook his head. "None of those pirates stood a chance. Three years boiling with rage and I was so hungry. And then there was Aster's head in the jar and I guess I saw red realizing it was all real and not some fucked up nightmare." He glanced away again, twisting his fingers together. "I'm glad you didn't come earlier than you had. I'd had time to calm down by then."

Something didn't add up. "For three years, the feds kept you on ice?" Laurel asked. "Kept Aster like this?"

"I can't figure that one out either," Cedar said. "They should have jettisoned me into the sun already and had Aster's datacrypt out. I literally shouldn't be here." He tapped his foot, thinking. "Bureaucratic bullshit, I guess. I'm not going to complain, though. I'm alive."

Juniper let out a slow exhale. "But why keep him like this?" they asked. "Holding onto him won't change what happened." Their voice was distant, like they were imagining themself as the head. Laurel gently rubbed their arm.

"Aster was..." Cedar hesitated and looked at them. "Religious? He had this belief—not like 'big man beyond the cosmos judging us for our sins', but that to really die, we had to rejoin the stars from which we came." He smiled gently. "It didn't feel right burning his head with the datacrypt inside. He *hated* it. I wanted to get it out before I cremated him, just so he'd really be free to rejoin the stars without it. It's the least I could do after how long we were together."

Juniper lifted their eyebrows. "Oh."

"He was your boyfriend," Laurel said.

Cedar snorted and leaned back. "He liked the term paramour."

It all slotted into place. Why Cedar had been so angry. Why he hadn't left it behind. Why he was so protective over it. Not just a link to the life stolen from him, but someone who'd meant the world to him. It was a little sweet, but also incredibly tragic. Vampires lived a long time; to suddenly have the one person you trusted above all else be gone while you could do nothing to stop it must have hurt more than he'd let on.

"I won't hurt either of you," Cedar said. "I was a runaway too once and so was Aster." He smiled again when Juniper visibly relaxed. "Well? I poured out my heart. What about you two?"

Juniper sighed and flopped back into the bed.

"You know what I am. Cybernetics since I was like eight."

Cedar grimaced. "Starting younger and younger. Aster said he got his at ten."

"Yep. They implanted the datacrypt a year later when the initial operation didn't kill me." Juniper slid their hands behind their head, gaze growing distant. "Ran away four years ago when I realized how wrong it all was. Then I was hiding on an abandoned satellite until this runaway found me." They freed a hand and jiggled Laurel's knee. "Your turn."

"My parents sold me to the feds," Laurel said. Once, just admitting it made her tear up, but more and more, she'd come to terms with it. Created a stormy indifference. "I outlived what they wanted me for and the feds gave me to one of their boarding schools to be set straight. Didn't really envision lasting there long, so I ran the moment I could find a place to run to."

She hated talking about *why* her parents sold her. 'Outlived what they wanted her for' was the truncated version and she hoped it'd be enough. The practice itself wasn't unheard of; parents sold difficult or simply unwanted children all the time, and the feds absorbed them into their fold. Many were turned into enforcers like the ones they'd seen, perfect workers, but others simply disappeared. Either dead or sent to work at far flung mining colonies to be made useful. Laurel was sure there was an outcry, but at every criticism, the feds just reminded people the program made good citizens. All those too volatile or disturbed were simply gone.

Laurel probably would have been dealt with.

"I'm sorry," Cedar said. "You two are pretty tragic."

Laurel didn't mean to, but she laughed and Juniper followed suit. Cedar smiled again at them both, but before long, it faded, leaving him vulnerable.

"Look," Juniper whispered as they sat up on their elbows. "I'm sorry for digging, okay?"

Laurel quickly nodded. "We just wanted to know what we were getting into."

"Shoulda just told you both to begin with." Cedar cleared his throat. "I can't promise I can fix everything, but if you can help me get back to my ship, I will do whatever it takes to stop your cybernetics and give you a life outside fed custody." He nodded to them each in turn. "Space pirates are a little unscrupulous—you've already seen me at my worst—but some of us still have hearts."

Juniper watched Cedar sadly. "Your old crew seemed pretty heartless." When all Cedar did was look away, Juniper finished sitting themself up and drummed their fingers on their chin. "Think they kept the ship?"

"Definitely," Cedar said. "Tremaine—the ringleader—was always gunning for it. Asking me all the time if I was ever gonna retire." He snorted and rolled his eyes. "Vampires *don't* retire. We either keep going or finish dying. Didn't know him more than two years, but didn't think he'd screw me and Aster over like that."

The ship had to be still out there, then. Somewhere. Laurel made a face. The Solar System was pretty vast—there was no telling *where* it was.

"And you're serious about the lab?" Juniper asked.

"Yes, I am."

"And he's not with the feds?"

Cedar shook his head. "Clyde would sooner fry them than let them in. When he figures out something worthwhile, he puts his findings publicly on the net. The feds like to claim the research as theirs, but if you cut out all their bullshit and follow the trail, almost all recent android advancements and then some can be traced to Clyde Lowell. He's a researcher. Nothing more." He shifted on the couch. "But I told you I'd give you time to think. Just know there's no real way to stop cybernetics without the dying part. Not without his help."

Juniper sighed. "Fine. Yeesh, I am beat." They flopped back into the bed and spread out their arms as though they were claiming it all for themself.

Cedar waited a moment, amused, before he stood and gently took the head back. He wrapped it in the bag and dropped himself back on the couch, spreading his legs across it. Laurel felt bad; he barely fit as it was. As she opened her mouth to suggest something (although even she wasn't sure what that would have been), Cedar waved his hand dismissively.

"Couch is fine. I've slept on worse."

"Do vampires really sleep?" Laurel asked as Juniper smirked in victory.

"Sometimes. Looking forward to it." He rolled over, turning his back to them, and nestled the head's container against his chest. "Good night."

Laurel doubted it was night according to Federation Universal Time, but in places like this, Laurel didn't think anyone cared. With the lamp off, it was dark enough, and she was tired. She left her glasses on the nightstand, bade Cedar good night, and happily curled herself under the blankets with Juniper. It almost felt normal. Slotted into their usual positions, like they could have been back on their satellite.

"You need a gummy?" Laurel asked.

Juniper shook their head, eyes bright from the

neon light shining in behind Laurel. It was oddly mesmerizing. "I'll be fine." They drew their fingers through Laurel's hair absently. "You sleep, okay? Don't worry about me."

There had been many times Juniper had said the same on the satellite. It meant Juniper had no intention of sleeping. Laurel had never been able to convince them otherwise back then and she didn't bother trying now. Juniper knew their limits. She rested her head against Juniper's chest and closed her eyes, searching for the heartbeat within.

Sleep was a dreamless dark and Laurel awoke to the inane buzz of a news show. She blinked and groped for her glasses. Once she had them on, she wished she hadn't.

The TV displayed a celebrity gossip bit about Lola, practically the most popular idol in the Solar System. She was also the last person Laurel *ever* wanted to hear about. And it wasn't because Laurel disliked her music. It was because Lola was her sister. One who abandoned her just as quickly as her parents had. To all the system, Laurel didn't exist in their family unit. Made it that much easier to get rid of her and Lola never cared.

Good riddance to that.

Juniper sat at the foot of the bed, watching it.

"Nothing better?" Laurel asked, trying not to sound as annoyed as she was, and sat up. It had been an agreement between them that Juniper wouldn't bring her up or even listen to her music, just for Laurel's sake.

"I was hoping they'd go back to general news," Juniper said, turning the volume all the way down. As they set the remote back down, Laurel noticed the bowl in their lap. Then she smelled what it was: apple and cinnamon oatmeal.

The smell made her stomach give the loudest growl it had in it. She couldn't remember the last time she'd eaten anything substantial. "Where'd you get that?"

Juniper grinned, revealing another bowl on their other side. It was still covered and they nodded toward Cedar. He was still sprawled out on the couch with a sheet covering him, although he now had a shirt on.

"Big guy went foraging for food and then immediately passed back out. Mumbled something about forgetting we had to eat." Juniper gave her the covered bowl and Laurel crawled closer.

As she peeled the top back, she breathed in deep. Maple syrup and apple. It smelled absolutely divine. On the satellite, they'd lived off crappy fake food with the occasional treat. It'd given them all the required nutrients, but didn't really do much for bulk. It was the reason Juniper was so scrawny. This, though? Real food. She gulped down the biggest spoonful she could handle, thoroughly enjoying the warmth as it spread through her body on the way down.

"Well?" she asked after she had a few more mouthfuls and dropped her voice into a whisper. "What do you think?"

Juniper crossed their legs. "To be honest, once we got past the belt, I had no plan."

"I didn't either."

"But we might have a lead now and someone to latch onto until he shakes us off."

Laurel snorted. "You make us sound like leeches."

"Are you okay with it?" Juniper faced her, suddenly serious. "Yeah, sure, your favorite band is some punk vampires punching coffins, but a space pirate vampire with no public image to worry about is a lot different."

Laurel glanced at Cedar. He slept still with Aster's head up to his chest like a teddy bear. Completely non-threatening. She shook her head. "You think he'd hurt us? After last night?"

"No, but it's a possibility," they said. "And vamps go for non-nanomachine-ridden blood first." They fidgeted and Laurel frowned. "I looked it up. Had to know."

She could have done without knowing that. "You remember what I said before, right?" she asked and set her bowl down. "Before we left? I'll go with you until the ends of the stars. I meant it. Nothing good is waiting for me and this guy seems like the only chance we're gonna get. I'd rather strike out with him than on our own."

"I thought so too." Juniper smiled, and after a moment, they pinched Laurel's side, making her giggle. "You're such a marshmallow, you know that?" They deftly dodged Laurel's counterattack and rolled to the other side of the bed to stand. "Guess we're this vamp's crew now. Go get dressed." Laurel noticed Juniper had already donned their usual black-everything getup. "I'll wake him up and let him know the good news."

There was one last bite in her bowl and Laurel took the time to savor it before she got up to gather the clothes Juniper had laid out for her. Sweater, leggings, fuzzy socks, and her boots. Some pirate outfit, but Laurel didn't have much that screamed pirate.

As Juniper made a game of poking at Cedar until he brushed their hand away only to do it all over again, Laurel ducked into the bathroom.

She smiled at herself in the mirror. Yes. This was

her life now. Space Pirate Laurel. She liked the sound of it, although she wished her name sounded a little fiercer. Oh well, no one would suspect *her* at least. She dressed, humming to herself, and as she finished tying up her boots, the lights went off.

Odd. Given the voices rising across the motel, everyone must have lost power at the same time. She exited the bathroom and immediately ran into Cedar. He quickly handed her off to Juniper and continued his trajectory for the door. It was practically pitch-black, Juniper's eyes a faint glow matching the emergency light outside. It made everything more eerie as she and Juniper stayed quiet to listen.

Not that listening told her anything. As Laurel opened her mouth to ask what was going on, the television buzzed back on. None of the lights did. It wasn't even the news this time, but instead an image of a dark figure sitting in the center of a bright room.

Juniper gasped, their eyes growing wide. "Oh, no, not him! He can't be here!"

08

JUNIPER

BLINDING LIGHT ENVELOPED THE ROOM behind the Answer. Somehow, being draped in light made him look more sinister. Juniper didn't know *what* he was—human, android, something else—but his job was a bounty hunter. He was always dressed in his uniform of a black leather duster, a black vest paired with a pinstripe shirt, leather pants, and gleaming steel boots. An antique android faceplate and cranium encased his head like a helmet, its screen changing as he spoke. Right now, it oscillated with CRT lines like it was looking for a signal, something from a bygone era to spook people.

"Who is that?" Laurel edged into Juniper. "Can he see us?"

The Answer tilted his head as if in response. Laurel flinched to hide behind Juniper. All he'd done was rest his cheek on a gloved hand. Juniper tensed anyway.

"No," Juniper said and ignored their bio-monitor warning them of their rising heart rate. "He's probably broadcasting it all over the place. Listen to how quiet it's gotten." They swallowed, praying they were right. "People call him the Answer. He's a bounty hunter." A shadow loomed behind them and Juniper spun to face it, panic spiking. Just Cedar pulling on his coat.

"He's bad news," Cedar said.

A massive understatement.

"Remain calm," the Answer said, his voice always easy and smooth, and it resonated as a haunting echo across the silence. His faceplate shifted into a pixelated smiley face. Always in black and white. Most of the time done mockingly. "I am only after one individual today." He languidly held up the finger of his other hand. "I will spare the lot of you if you heed my commands. Of course, I won't say *who* I am after. You'll simply steal this individual right from under me." He rested his cheek against his hand again. "All I ask is that you remain calm, remain where you are, and don't resist me. I repeat..."

Juniper sucked in a breath; it was a loop. Not a live broadcast. They watched the pixels on the screen shift, restarting the short video. He was already searching. Noise grew across the station, individuals yelling and panicking to leave; no one was taking his words to heart.

"Who is he after?" Laurel asked. "The vampires?"

"No," Cedar answered and he secured the bag with Aster's head across his chest. He'd already closed their bag and held it out. "For some reason, he doesn't go after vamps unless we *really* fuck up."

Laurel took the bag and shot Cedar a look. "What you did to that ship isn't fucking up?"

Cedar sighed. "It's too soon after. He's gotta be after someone else. His methods are ruthless—especially if the feds aren't watching. We want to leave."

"He's after me," Juniper said quietly and Laurel whipped around to face them. "Has been for years. He was watching the satellite, waiting, and I-I thought if I made it burn up—made it crash—he'd believe I was on it and died." They turned away, shaking with frustration. "He must have seen me on the feeds somewhere."

The racket outside was rising and Cedar headed to the window to peek out. Juniper didn't blame anyone any; everyone here probably had *some* bounty on their head. There was no way for them to know who the Answer was really after. Likely his intention. People get sloppy when they panic. Maybe he was hoping the same of Juniper.

"What *is* he?" Laurel asked.

"No one knows," Juniper said. "He's the fed's answer to their problems, hence his name. Officially, though? Even they pretend he doesn't exist."

The motel shuddered as something deep below powered off. Juniper's cybernetics pinged a restart in the central station mainframe. Not good. Emergency sirens turned on one by one outside and soon the station was filled with the blaring noise.

The station's AI's voice rang out louder than the sirens. "Life support switched to auxiliary power. Remain calm and orderly."

Cedar shot a wild look at them, only lit up by the looping video on the wall. "More of his MO. He's trying to smoke you out."

"Are we safe here?" Laurel asked.

"No," Juniper said. "This is deliberate. He's probably betting on us either waiting for this to pass or trying to escape on the cruiser."

Cedar was already shaking his head. "He probably has your bio-signature then. Even if we fall into the crowd, he'll find you." He swore, scrunching his face.

"There's gotta be a way to our ship without being seen."

"Oh!" Laurel dug into her bag. She pulled out the clamshell case she'd swiped before and popped it open. She brandished the keycard. "I got this. Probably a maintenance worker's, right?"

Cedar whistled, impressed. "Where'd you get this?"

Laurel shrugged, smile tugging at her lips, and the tension eased off Juniper. Having a magpie as a partner always had a way of coming in handy.

Cedar took the card to the terminal at the back of the room and swiped it. Auxiliary power always kept terminals like this up and running alongside life support so the station's crew could still access their basic systems. A profile appeared, featuring a woman Juniper didn't recognize. The screen displayed a list of what areas she had access to and Cedar was nodding.

"Maintenance walkway." Cedar tapped the screen. "It'll get us to the docks unseen."

Juniper liked the idea, but there was a missing key component. "He likely knows what our ship looks like. If he sees us leave, he'll follow us. We're not gonna outrun him."

Laurel's eyes went wide and she squeezed in beside Cedar. "Not if we make some mayhem!" She pointed to the woman's main job. Waste management. "She can control the garbage and recycling locks with her card. What if we evacuate all the trash? It'll jettison it into space, giving us cover. And if we do *everything*, it'll scramble the feeds." Her grin widened. "With that and everyone else trying to take off at the same time, I bet we'll be able to fly by unnoticed and get out before he realizes we're gone."

No matter what the boarding school might have

told her, no matter how her parents made her feel, Laurel was a genius. No one could convince Juniper otherwise.

"Good idea," Cedar said before Juniper could. "Come on. Let's get moving before he starts busting down doors."

THE MAINTENANCE WALKWAY WAS BEHIND A gated entrance their keycard got them through, and it was a tight, snaking path that seemingly wound between every single building. Perfect getaway, but Juniper felt too closed-in once inside. Walls of pipes and wires, warning signs plastered everywhere, and emergency lights with attached speakers for the blaring siren. Every time there was a respite from the crammed hallway, they found a gaggle of workers at a terminal trying to get the power back online. Not likely; whatever cybernetic augments the Answer used were supposedly ironclad. If he wanted your systems, they were his, no question about it.

For any workers who happened to see them passing, one look from Cedar and they pretended the three of them didn't exist. Helpful.

Laurel took the lead, following the directions pasted near the warning signs, and they found their way to the main waste terminal tucked down a smaller hallway. She swiped the keycard along the reader, but all it showed her was the station's logo against a black background.

"This isn't working." She swiped again, but the screen simply reloaded.

Juniper squeezed in beside her and swore; it wasn't responding because it expected a different kind of login alongside the card. "It's a cybernetic interface. Needs a jack."

Head-jacks with a processing augment were more widespread than Juniper's all-encompassing cybernetics and a lot less invasive. It'd started as fed technology, but covert stations like this must have required it of their employees because it meant added security. Although imagining getting it implanted by some back-alley doctor made Juniper's entire body shudder.

They felt around the terminal and found the aux cord along the bottom of the keyboard. They grimaced and cleaned the end with their sleeve. "Give me a minute, okay?"

Juniper had no idea what awaited them when they slid the cord into the back of their head. Every system was different; with Slim it had been a pleasurable warmth racing through their limbs. The *Maple* was friendly in a professional manner. Juniper shuddered as an icy, staticky feeling washed over their body. Should have figured; terminals were always stone cold.

"Greetings," the AI said and Juniper opened their eyes to a dark room. It was only a moment before a slew of glowing options flickered to life. Too many to sift through. "Please speak a command."

"Eject trash," Juniper said.

"Unknown command."

Oh, for fuck's sake. There was no reason it wasn't the simplest set of words. Juniper scowled. "Spew trash?"

"Unknown command."

"Reverse trash intake," Juniper tried and when the AI didn't immediately dismiss it, added, "in ten minutes."

"Affirmative. Please swipe your keycard when you disengage to begin the countdown," the AI responded.

Juniper disconnected, blinking, and came back to reality. The screen displayed their command and they had Laurel swipe the keycard again. Ten minutes and counting. Juniper ushered Cedar close. "Pull out the whole reader so they can't override it." They yanked the aux cord free too so no one else could use it either.

Vampire strength had the reader off in seconds. Not the cleanest job, but it got it was done. As he dropped the remains on the ground, a light shined on them. Cedar immediately placed himself between the light and Juniper and Laurel, baring his teeth.

The maintenance worker peeking in shot up her hands. She was young, barely older than them. Everyone was silent, like they waited for the other to speak. Cedar clenched his hands.

"You should leave," he said.

The worker glanced at them, the terminal, and then back at them. She thought for another moment and then turned. "Nothing down here!" she called.

Before she returned to her coworkers, Cedar jerked forward and yanked her back with a hand over her mouth.

"Wait!" Juniper squeaked. "What are you doing?"

"Where are the docks from here?" Cedar asked in a low whisper.

The worker froze, eyes wide. Cedar gently removed his hand and, thank goodness, she didn't scream. "Two lefts, straight for two forks, then hang a right. There's a map there for how to get to the individual docks and ladders to bypass the lifts."

Cedar let her go and she didn't linger this time. She all but ran out and called to her fellow workers that she was coming.

Laurel shared a wide-eyed look with Juniper; she'd covered her mouth, likely expecting exactly what Juniper had been. At least Cedar hadn't hurt the poor girl, but part of Juniper wondered if it was because they were there. Cedar didn't comment and led them forward.

The directions took them more accurately to the lift's maintenance stop and indeed had a tiered holographic image of all the docks currently in use. All of them were lit up in red, like the individual docks were locked.

Cedar found theirs, and with the station on auxiliary power, they took to the ladders on either side of the main lift. By the time they got to their dock's doors, Juniper's arms were heavy with exhaustion and, given the look on Laurel's face, so were hers.

It was then the garbage chutes beeped in unison and opened.

Trash spewed everywhere inside, causing shouts of alarm from the docks around them, and Juniper and Laurel had to duck behind Cedar to dodge the first wave. Juniper shot their gaze to the window. Trash was ejecting out there too. Mayhem like Laurel wanted.

All that was left to do then was get out.

Their ship was still safely nestled in its dock, all refueled. Juniper let out a sigh of relief; the Answer hadn't found it, which meant he didn't know as much as they feared. Laurel settled into the pilot's seat this time, Juniper back to their usual copilot spot, and Cedar hunkered down behind them.

"Greetings!" their AI chirped. "Currently, all of the dock doors have been locked down. The station's AI tells me it's sabotage."

Laurel engaged the top to protect them from the

flying trash. "Are you serious?"

"I got it." Juniper quickly jacked into their cruiser's systems and used the *Maple's* uplink to get into the station's lock system. It wasn't complicated, but the station itself was wrestling control from the Answer. He was letting it have it back in waves, clearly using it to keep track of who was leaving... except now it was at a standstill with all the trash.

Juniper couldn't stop the Answer, but they could do one better. They connected to the unguarded master controls and gave it a command to power down all the locks. Someone might lose a cruiser or two when the airlocks opened, but it'd give individual ships the ability to just leave. With any luck, the pirates would escape en masse and Laurel could fly out with the crowd.

With the commands in place, Juniper pulled back to themself, and as soon as their vision stabilized, they saw the dock doors sliding open. "Let's go!"

Laurel pressed her foot against the thrusters and flew out into the wave of trash and all the other ships taking their chance to flee. Home free and Juniper let themself smile.

Until the world melted white around them.

They blinked, but the whiteness didn't go away. A hand pressed against their shoulder from behind, making them flinch, but Juniper refused to turn. This wasn't real. A headspace forcing Juniper to network with it. The hand was just a digital ghost. All this from touching the station's systems. Juniper should have known the Answer had been waiting for them.

"Juniper." His voice was always the same, dripping with honey and lies. "It's no use running."

Juniper forced a laugh, knowing they were quite possibly the only one who had ever laughed in the

Answer's figurative face and lived. "Yeah?" They grinned, hoping the Answer could feel it on his end. "Haven't caught me yet."

His fingers squeezed and if Juniper didn't know better, they would have sworn there'd be a bruise there the next time they looked.

"I gave you time—what you asked for. You're the one reneging on our deal."

"It was never a deal." Juniper swallowed. "And I still want time."

"It appears you have friends now. One particularly soft. Was she always with you?"

Juniper's body chilled. "Leave them out of this."

"That remains to be seen. You're a job and if they get in the way... Well, I can't be held liable for what happens to them, now can I?"

"Eat shit and die."

With a deep breath, Juniper forced a shutdown of all their external connections. It threw them out of the headspace, but it was jarring; being pulled in so fast and getting out so fast felt like a snapped rubber band. The warmth of Laurel's hand on their arm helped them bridge themself back and their bio-monitor helped the rest of the way by reporting their heart rate. Too high. It recommended a few calming breaths.

Juniper opened their eyes. Blessed darkness. Laurel watched them, worried, and the ship's screens reflected off her glasses. Past her, they saw the *Maple* had escaped the trash. They were now traveling in the shadow of a large vessel. Juniper wondered if Laurel had thought of it or if it was a happy accident.

"Are you all right?" Laurel asked.

Juniper smiled. "Peachy. Sorry. I'm here now."

"Your nose is bleeding." Cedar was leaning forward between their seats.

And there it was. Sticky warmth against their clammy skin. Juniper swore and wiped their nose with a sleeve, noticing the tissue Cedar was holding out too late. They took it anyway and pressed it to their nose.

"T-Too much excitement," they said, trying to brush it off. They were trembling, way more than they usually did after strenuous use.

Because it was more than just overuse. It was the way the Answer reached out to them. Forcing a connection then plunging Juniper into it overtaxed the systems. He knew that, of course. He'd do anything to unnerve Juniper, and this always did it. His presence was always like a black hole even now, sucking Juniper inside until everything was wrong.

"No," Laurel said slowly. Her brows were drawn tight. "Your eyes do this thing when you're not mentally here. I saw it happen with Slim, but it was the Answer, wasn't it?"

Leave it to Laurel to notice the subtle things.

"He talks to you?" Cedar asked, surprised.

"Not often." Juniper tipped their head back. "I told him to eat shit and die." They snickered when Cedar laughed, clapping a hand on the seat, but Laurel didn't. "I swear: I'm fine. He's gone."

"How long has he been after you?" Laurel asked. Cedar's laugh faded and Juniper caught him leaning forward again, probably hoping for the selfsame answer. "He left you alone when you were in the satellite. Why now?"

It was bound to come out. Juniper had just hoped he'd never catch up. It wasn't fair of them; they should have told Laurel the danger she'd be in if she accepted their invitation. But Juniper had craved the friendship as much as Laurel had. It could have ended so, so badly if he'd known.

"He... he never touched me in the satellite because the last time he tried, I threatened to blow it up. I had charges set and everything. It was a waiting game and he figured he could outwait me. Every time I left the satellite, I expected him to find me, but he never did. I was just fast enough to do what I needed and get back before he noticed."

Juniper didn't want to admit it aloud, but they'd gotten a thrill leaving the satellite and knowing the Answer could have been out there waiting for them. Time and time again, however, and he'd never showed his faceplate. Maybe that was why they'd let Laurel into the satellite and never told her. Maybe they'd tricked themself into believing the Answer would never touch them. Except now he was here.

"Would you have blown it up?" Laurel asked.

"Not when you were there." Juniper stared so hard at the lights on the console so they didn't have to look at her directly. "It's why I was so okay when you suggested leaving. With you around, the Answer suddenly had leverage over me and it was only a matter of time."

If he'd known Laurel had been there and discovered Juniper wouldn't hurt her, he could have come up anytime he'd wanted. Slim would have stood no chance. It was a miracle it had never happened, but Juniper had dealt with plenty nightmares where it had. It was another miracle they'd gotten this far before he tracked them down. He must have been on another job and hadn't noticed until they were already gone.

And now, they *were* his job.

"Well," Cedar said and Juniper chanced a glance at him. He'd reached forward and opened a screen on the console. It pinged the area around them, but all that it found was the ship they were tailing. Everyone else had split. "Nothing's tailing us. He might have been blowing smoke for all we know." He swiped it away and rested back, hands behind his head. "For anything more drastic, especially in fed space, he needs permission. By the time he gets it, we'll be past Jupiter and hopefully on my ship."

Juniper sniffled and wiped their nose again. "I hope you have a plan to actually find it."

"Just get to the Mars Transit Gate. I'll get some feelers going."

They certainly hoped so, because otherwise, they had nothing. Staying in one place didn't sound smart, especially with the Answer so close. They glanced at Laurel and found she hadn't stopped watching them.

"Laurie, I promise: I'm okay."

Laurel finally looked away, exhaling slowly. Juniper's bio-scanner measured her apprehension, but that was obvious without its input. Juniper bit their lip. They couldn't fix it now. They just had to lose the Answer.

What they both needed was a distraction. Push the Answer far from their thoughts with something silly. Juniper's gaze landed on Cedar and as they considered him, a question sprung to mind.

"Hey," they said and Cedar raised his eyebrows. "You ever meet the Smashing Coffins?"

Cedar snorted and Laurel looked back at him too. "What? You serious?" He grinned. "You think because I'm a vamp and they're vamps, we talk?"

It sounded silly hearing it aloud and though heat crept up Juniper's neck, they forged on, shrugging. "I'm not hearing a no."

Cedar rolled his eyes. "Okay, *yeah*, I've met them before, but you don't gotta say it like that. They pay me for protection sometimes. Met them when some self-righteous vampire haters were crashing their gigs.

I took care of them."

He noticed the way Laurel stared at him, eyes wide in awe. She vibrated so fast with excitement. Juniper was surprised she hadn't phased through the seat.

"Ah, are you seriously a fan?" Cedar asked and Laurel nodded, beaming at him. "No kidding! You'd get on with the bassist, I think. Real chill gal. She had these optics installed that makes holograms as she plays. You see them in action yet?"

They went back and forth, totally absorbed, and Juniper let them be, glad to throw off Laurel's scrutiny. They eased back in their seat and rested their eyes for some peace of mind of their own.

Except their thoughts went right back to the Answer. Absent-mindedly, Juniper ran their fingers over where his hand had been. They could still *feel* it there—the way his fingers had pressed down. His presence was like a virus; one Juniper wouldn't ever notice until they were already infected.

After a moment, beyond all the talk about the Smashing Coffins and thinking too hard about the Answer, Juniper heard a faint sound from the cargo bag again. It sounded like a worried whisper this time. Wanting to make it all better. Juniper found a little solace in it and kept their eyes closed, listening to it.

09
LAUREL

SLIM'S CONNECTIONS GOT THEM INTO A private dock with minimal fuss once they reached the Mars Transit Station. Even a free refuel, which they sorely needed when they arrived. They'd hung onto the shadow of the pirate ship for as long as they could, hiding, and although Laurel had been worried about leaving it to get them back on course, no one had followed them and the rest of the ride was easy.

The station was a typical shape, but beyond it, the transit ring hung huge and golden, as large as the station itself to accommodate all sorts of ships coming and going. It also had a nice view of Mars with its many terraformed colonies down below, dotting the once copper hue with greens and yellows. Laurel's grandmother had lived down there and Laurel fondly remembered the time before boarding school when she had been able to visit.

Not anymore. Needed clearance to go planet-side, and now, she'd never have it.

To get her mind off the sudden thoughts, Laurel wanted to explore the station—she'd never been on one this large before—but Cedar made them stay put with Aster's head. Typical. It was only after Juniper complained loudly about being hungry did Cedar also part with his cred stick.

Laurel was sure she or Juniper could have helped locate his ship, but he stressed they had to stay here. Too easy to get lost, noticed, or even kidnapped. Especially with the Answer on their trail. Besides, Cedar claimed he knew a guy who knew a gal who knew a fella who might know an android who kept tabs on ships coming and going.

Whatever that meant.

The food Juniper took the liberty of getting delivered was *good*, at least. Steamy noodles with fresh vegetables and diced chicken (Laurel couldn't tell if it was real or synthetic), all liberally seasoned with a delectable ginger sauce. Laurel wanted to tell the cooks how amazing it was, but since she and Juniper promised they'd stay with the cruiser, she instead dictated a review and Juniper put it on the station's net. Way more than five stars. Especially since it came with a full serving of dumplings and egg rolls.

Cedar was certainly taking his time, though. As distracting as the food was, it didn't help Laurel ignore just how long he'd been gone. She thumped her head against the side of the ship where she sat sideways, legs dangling over the console in the center. Juniper was on the back of the cruiser, facing the dock doors leading into the station, and had Aster's head in their lap while they ate.

"Yeah, yeah," Juniper said. "I'm bored too." They reached back with their chopsticks for the platter of egg rolls they'd put on Sprig. The bot vroomed out of their reach, proving what a bad idea it'd been despite Juniper's insistence otherwise. With a huff, Juniper grabbed the plate with both hands instead. "If I'd known Cedar would take *this* long, I would have ducked out with our flirty delivery guy. I can't believe I let him go."

Laurel rolled her eyes. "Oh, come on. You might have been noticed out there."

"Killjoy." Juniper chewed thoughtfully on an egg roll. "Honestly, I'm sure I could have tricked the network. It's not *that* different from the Lunar Colony. The same fed bullshit."

Laurel ate a dumpling to stop from pointing out the obvious. This *wasn't* the Lunar Colony. Risk-taking in a place you'd never been was a bad idea, especially with a bounty hunter looking for them. It made Laurel anxious that Juniper didn't care.

Except they probably cared. This lack of caring was a veneer to hide any and all vulnerability. Laurel was just frustrated Juniper had *never* mentioned the Answer or the danger they'd both been in before. Then again, she would still have agreed to join them in their satellite. It wasn't like she'd had many other choices.

"Hey." Juniper peered over their shoulder, frowning. "What's up?"

"Nothing," Laurel said quickly, brushing it aside. Didn't matter. "Just mad that Cedar's not back yet. Did the sleep gummy help earlier?"

Juniper had taken the last one shortly after they'd left the vamp station when Cedar was sure no one was following them or the pirate ship. For the most part, since they'd awoken, they were back to being normal. Although, now Laurel wondered how much of *that* was a veneer.

"I think so." Juniper stretched over to take Laurel's empty bowl. She handed it off and Juniper slipped off the back to throw them into the recycle receptacle nearby. "Still a little high-strung, but better." They gathered up Aster's head in one arm and the platter of egg rolls in the other before coming back to the copilot's seat. Laurel scrunched her legs closer as Juniper slipped in, placing the plate beside the container of dumplings on the center console.

Their eyes went wide suddenly. "Listen!" They pressed their ear to the head container. "It's clicking again—I swear it this time. Listen!"

Juniper had told Laurel about it as soon as Cedar had left them alone, but the head then had been silent. Still kinda was. Laurel indulged Juniper anyway, and pressed her ear to the top of the container. Besides being cold, she didn't hear anything right away. Just the usual thrum of the station around them. She closed her eyes and concentrated.

Something was faintly there, but she wasn't sure if it was what Juniper heard.

"Are you sure?"

"Come on, Laurie!" Juniper said. "You've way better hearing than me. It's like... cybernetics shifting? I swear, it's doing something."

Not that Laurel knew what to do about it if it really was. She chewed on another dumpling, thinking, but before she came up with a plausible scenario, the dock door swiped aside. She and Juniper ducked into one another, wide-eyed, but it was only Cedar striding inside, confidence to his steps.

"Oh!" His face brightened as he sniffed the air. "That smells good!"

He leaned in on Juniper's side of the cruiser and immediately tried grabbing an egg roll. Juniper jerked the plate out of his reach.

"Hey!" he whined. "Share some. It's my money!"

"Money you got off a dead guy," Juniper muttered and Cedar pouted at them.

Once again, Laurel could easily forget this was the man responsible for what befell the feds and pirates on the Class Theta ship.

Juniper sighed. "Fine, just don't use your fingers. Here." They picked one up with their chopsticks and held it out. He smiled and happily ate the offering while Juniper tried not to laugh. It was a little ridiculous—even Laurel had to bite down on her laughter. Feeding a vampire like he was a pet or something.

"Wait." Laurel adjusted her glasses and studied Cedar. "Vampires need food?"

Cedar swallowed. "Kinda? When we have blood in our system, we're almost normal."

Laurel frowned. "You still have blood in your system from the fed ship?"

"Uh." Cedar cleared his throat. "No. I found a willing donor on the way back." Laurel gave him a look and he held up his hands. "Serious. Totally willing. He was into it. Don't look at me like that! I got a stash on my ship so once we get it back, we're golden. No more back-alley blood-sucking."

"Did you find your ship?" Laurel asked.

Cedar nodded and happily ate another egg roll Juniper held out for him. They were enjoying it, a shy smile across their lips, and Laurel rolled her eyes at how adorably domestic and absurd it was at the same time.

"Yep," he said. "Fucker renamed it though—it's what took me so long." He finished chewing and swallowed. "The *Challenger*. Not sure if naming a ship after one that blew up is good luck, though. Look, I got a plan."

Laurel perked up. "Are they here?"

"No—next transit over at Jupiter." Cedar waved off the next question she'd hardly started to ask. "Let me talk."

She shoved a dumpling in her mouth to stop herself.

"We can't confront them in a station. Rather not start a brawl and get fed attention. I figure we head there, watch them, and when *they* leave, we follow." He pointed at Laurel and Juniper in turn. "You two act like lost joy riders and play up some sob story. They pick you up and I do what I do best. Mayhem."

Laurel frowned. That sounded way too simple.

Juniper crossed their arms, thinking. "They won't notice you on their scans?"

"Usually, no. Vamps don't have enough of a bio-signature unless you specifically look for it."

"And they won't?" Laurel asked.

"He's an asshole. He'll just see two stranded rich kids he can exploit."

"We're not rich," Juniper reminded. "What if he asks us for money up front?"

"You *look* rich." Cedar patted the *Maple*. "Only rich kids get cruisers. And he won't ask for it up front; bad luck out there. We space pirates are superstitious about that shit. Look: we get in, I take out the trash, and bam!" He clapped his hands together. "The ship's ours."

Put so simply, maybe it'd work. Cedar eyed the dumplings next, drumming his fingers. Laurel happily leaned over Juniper to feed him one. Maybe being a space pirate with him wouldn't be so bad. He was really growing on her.

"Well, we ready?" Cedar hopped into the back. "We've got my ship to reclaim."

TRANSITING THROUGH SPACE ALWAYS LEFT Laurel's stomach out of sorts. Food probably hadn't helped, but she was proud she hadn't thrown up when they arrived at the Jupiter Transit Station. She had the first time she'd ever transited, although, to be fair, most in her class had. Transiting bent the rules of space travel and shot ships to their destination at speeds no vessel could match on their own. She had no idea how it worked, but as long as it got her from one place to another in one piece, the details didn't matter.

The Jupiter Transit Station looked exactly the same as the Mars', but while Mars' had been red, this one was a sheen of champagne white with spirals matching the planet it orbited. Juniper wasted no time in slipping into the station's logs to locate Cedar's ship and then they waited. And waited. And *waited*. Laurel was just starting to nod off from boredom when Juniper announced the *Challenger* was on the move. Laurel launched the *Maple* just as the *Challenger* exited and she set them on the larger ship's tail.

Much bigger than their little cruiser, it was a gunmetal black and the front was shaped more like the aircraft carriers Laurel had seen in old war movies. The rest of it was smooth and typical ship fare with large thrusters in the back in pristine condition.

Juniper tapped at the screen on their side. "Have they noticed us taking off?"

"Negative," the *Maple*'s AI said. "They haven't even done a sweep of the area. Their blind spot is near the left thruster."

Laurel eased the *Maple* into the blind spot and

drifted along the *Challenger* like Cedar had shown her when they'd left the vamp station. Pirate hacks for traveling undetected.

"He's being sloppy," Cedar whispered, leaning forward between the seats. "Should've had Lily run a scan right as they left. Little ships linger around stations all the time."

"Lily?" Laurel repeated.

"My ship's AI. She'll be happy when I'm home. Never liked Tremaine much."

Juniper made a face at him. "What if Tremaine messed with her? You've been gone for three years."

"He'd have to catch the cyber cat," Cedar said. "Only Aster could do that and the cat's smart. I'm sure Lily's biding her time. 'Sides, she's the life of the ship. No one would risk ruining the ship entirely by messing with her. Good AIs are hard to build."

"If they didn't even do a scan, will they notice a distress call?" Laurel asked.

"They *should*," Cedar said. "Those are hard to miss. We just need to get far enough away from the station so no one there picks it up." He scratched his chin and sat back. "Just enjoy the ride until they stop. They've got to be going somewhere nearby."

Laurel glanced back at Cedar, curious. "Where'd you get the ship, anyway? I'm assuming you didn't buy it outright."

Cedar snorted. "Hell no. I stole it." He watched it, eyes growing fond. "Was with some other vamps at the time and I really wanted my own ship. My own crew. We were doing some digging and found it in some abandoned secret fed base. Lily could have killed us—she had control over the base's life support—but instead, she told me she wanted to see the stars."

Juniper cocked their head. "Why didn't she leave?

She sounds really advanced."

"The base had locks that needed a human hand." Cedar shrugged. "Vampire hand worked just as well. Seeing as the place was abandoned, she was probably going to end up as scrap metal if the feds ever came back. Guess she was a failed experiment. So, I told her I could help her see the stars, and off we went. Been together since."

The story made Laurel smile. She was feeling more and more at home. Runaways from the feds on a runaway ship. "Is Lily nice?"

"I think she'll like both of ya."

It was another hour before the *Challenger* began slowing and then another half hour to idle altogether. Laurel guided their ship away and Cedar's gaze lingered. "Must be setting up to sleep," he said. "Bet he didn't want to pay for the dock overnight or a motel."

Juniper checked their screen and Laurel looked over as it lit the cockpit. "Still not even seeing us," they said. "Ten minutes and then do the distress call? Suspicious if we start too soon." Juniper smiled at Laurel. "Want to handle the crocodile tears?"

Laurel grinned and set her glasses on her forehead so they didn't fog up. "Got it."

Juniper waved their hand at Cedar. "Hide under something. We've got blankets in the bags, just look like luggage." They jumped with a yelp as Cedar thrust Aster's bag at them.

"Hold onto him again," Cedar said.

The trust was seriously touching. Juniper settled the bag gently in their lap while Cedar rummaged for a blanket. It looked a little ridiculous when he curled up underneath it, though. Definitely wouldn't pass a sight check, but Laurel hoped with how dark it was, no one would notice the lumpy body behind them. She dimmed the lights and waited.

After a few more minutes, Laurel turned on the distress call.

It was a series of beeps in Morse code and broadcasted the SOS on the frequency universally reserved for distress calls. Laurel mouthed the letters to herself in time with the beeps to help herself stay calm. It was an agonizing few more minutes before the console lit up with an incoming hail.

Bingo. Laurel contained her cheer and Juniper flipped it open.

"*Challenger* to Distress Call, do you read me?" The woman's voice came through as a wash of static in the cruiser's speakers. "I repeat, *Challenger* to Distress Call, do you read me?"

Laurel glanced back at Cedar. He'd peeked out of the blanket and tilted his head, confused. Maybe he didn't recognize the voice. Laurel didn't like that; it meant an innocent person might get dragged into Cedar's mayhem.

Time to get acting. Laurel turned on the waterworks.

"Oh my god!" Her voice made Cedar jump as she let tears flood her eyes. "Thank goodness you're there! We're stranded! I thought no one would come by. We've been drifting for hours!"

"Really? No one mentioned seeing a ship out here." The woman clicked something on her end and groaned. "Asshole! You didn't do a fucking scan!" There was chatter too far away to hear and the woman audibly huffed. "We could have run these guys over." Another voice replied to hers and she sighed. "How'd you get this far out? A joyride? There's nothing even cool here."

Juniper made a face and Laurel sniffled. "I didn't

mean to come out this far. We just wanted to enjoy the view of Jupiter," she mumbled like she'd been scolded, "but diagnostics went haywire and I panicked. I can't see where I am and my sweetheart and I thought this would be it! Our fuel is like, all dry. Some joyride."

"Okay, okay—calm down and take a deep breath for me. My name's Clary, what's yours?"

Laurel sniffled. "Laurel."

Juniper slapped her arm too late to take it back and Laurel cringed. Should have come up with fake names. Too late now.

"All right, Laurel," Clary said her name incredibly softly. A good effort if Laurel was actually hysterical. "Captain's telling me we can bring you aboard. Do you think you can make it? Or do I have to corral you? I got a grappler ship I know how to use."

Grapplers were cruiser sized ships with arm appendages the pilot could control, and usually used on space maintenance detail work. Not as cushy as a cruiser. Laurel was supposed to learn how to pilot one, but she'd left school before it happened. She made a mental note to ask Cedar about it later.

"I should have enough fuel to get to you," Laurel said. "Can you link up so I can follow your signal until my screen clears?"

"Wait! I got a better plan." There was clacking on the other end and Laurel hesitated. "You're close enough I can just reel you in."

Laurel shot Juniper a worried look and their ship jolted. "Reel me in?" she squeaked.

"Easier this way. Lily's already made friends with your AI too! I'm kinda impressed with this thing—you guys don't have any fed bullshit in there, do you? Swanky." Clary paused at the silence. "You good?"

"Yes." Laurel swallowed, forgetting the act.

"Yeah!" she said with a little more vigor. "Thank you so much. See you soon?"

"See you soon."

They waited until the ship moved of its own accord toward the *Challenger*. Juniper made sure their side of the hail was muted before glancing back at Cedar. He hadn't peeked out again.

"You know her?" they asked.

"No," Cedar said from beneath the blanket.

Laurel frowned. "What are you going to do with your previous crew?"

Maybe it was too late to be asking, but a stone sunk in Laurel's stomach when Cedar didn't answer. He didn't even try lying.

"I'll hold up my end of our deal," was all he said.

Laurel tried to breathe out the sudden spike of anxiety as they approached the ship. She felt stuck, like a fish on a hook, and flinched as the cruiser landed on the front deck. The *Challenger's* AI turned the cruiser and they faced the hangar doors slowly sliding aside for them. Lights lit up as they were pulled into the lift and, once they were settled, it descended.

The hail channel popped open again. "Okay, you're in," Clary said, her voice clearer. "Lily will put you down, so just stay in the ship until I get there, okay? Lily won't be happy if you get out."

Laurel agreed and disconnected. Cedar snorted from below the blanket. "Oh, she is *so* gonna rob you."

Laurel made a face. "Really?"

"It's what we used to do when we robbed people. Lily's got you hook, line, and sinker."

Juniper shook their head. "What do we have to defend ourselves with?" They opened the compartment below the console. The stunner was somewhere in a bag, probably not even charged now, but Juniper found a laser knife instead.

Not exactly strong, but good in a pinch.

"You have me," Cedar said. "Just let her open the top. I'll handle it."

Laurel whipped to face him. "Don't kill her."

She couldn't believe she'd suggested it. Asking a vampire not to kill someone who wouldn't think twice about killing them. She was glad she couldn't see Cedar's face, especially when he didn't answer. Slowly sinking into her seat, she eased out another breath. Their ship slid into the hangar, out in the open, and the lift closed.

It was dark and cold. Laurel's hands were trembling already.

The lights switched on around them, bright fluorescents embedded into the ceiling. Laurel shielded her eyes until she got used to the brightness. There wasn't much in the small hangar. The grappler was nearby with its arms locked against its honey-yellow chassis. Otherwise, there were storage boxes and some kind of cargo underneath tarps. Along the far end was a metal staircase leading up to a door to the ship proper which whooshed aside after a moment.

A woman came inside—probably Clary. She was dressed comfy in a crop top, shawl, and leggings which were tucked into her boots. She hurried down the stairs, a spring in her step. Her skin was pale underneath the lights and she had long, glossy jet-black hair pulled high in a messy ponytail that swished as she walked. Though she appeared unarmed, Laurel noticed a strap inside the shawl. Definitely a blaster hidden there.

She was smiling at them, waving as she came up. Laurel and Juniper returned the gesture, trying to smile too, although neither of them could match her enthusiasm. There was a small fob in her hand and before Laurel asked about it, Clary injected it into the ship's exterior lock. The entire ship powered down and Laurel couldn't hide her shock as the top peeled back.

"Heya." Clary pulled the blaster out from her shawl and leveled it on them. "So, this ain't a free ride. Tell me what you lost chickadees have for me."

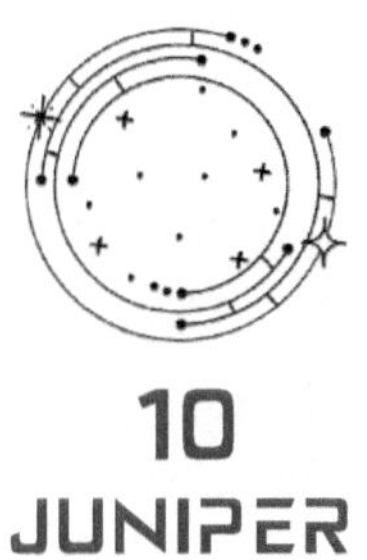

10
JUNIPER

A VERY ANGRY VAMPIRE WAS WHAT THEY HAD.

Juniper barely had time to duck before Cedar sprung upward. The woman's haughty cockiness was gone in a flash as Cedar clattered over the side of the cruiser and landed on top of her, hand over her mouth. The blaster went flying, spinning to a stop a little ways away, and Cedar pinned the woman to the floor.

Juniper stood to see the damage.

Not dead. Not yet. Maybe Cedar had taken Laurel's desperate plea to heart. Clary had her hands up in surrender and Cedar bent closer to bare his teeth at her.

He paused. "I don't know you."

Clary shook her head, eyes growing wider.

Cedar glanced at Juniper and Laurel. "Get her blaster and watch her."

Laurel threw herself out of the cruiser and scooped up the blaster like if she didn't, Cedar might really kill the woman. The blaster was already primed and Laurel turned it on Clary before Juniper disembarked with Aster's bag on their back. They tuned their cybernetics to listen to the ship around them, but heard nothing.

"No one watching your feeds?" they asked, stepping around to Cedar's other side.

"She's probably the lowest grunt." Cedar glared at Clary and she immediately glared back. "You gonna scream if I let you go?" Clary paused a moment, like she was giving it actual thought despite there being only one answer, and shook her head. Juniper wouldn't have believed her, but they hoped she was smarter than that. Cedar slowly took his hand away.

She didn't scream, but she did have the gall to slot a smug smile on her lips. "The door's locked. Can't get in without my code."

Cedar scowled at her, but Juniper had to hand it to the lady; back-talking a vampire wasn't for the faint of heart. She saw leverage and took it. Cedar hauled her up by her shoulders and didn't let her feet rest all the way on the floor. "You two stick close," Cedar said. "We're opening a door."

Well, he hadn't killed her yet, but his voice chilled Juniper. They shared a worried glance with Laurel; she'd gone ashen, but kept her hands steady.

Cedar never broke eye contact with Clary, and, for her part, she maintained it. They reached the unmoving door and Cedar settled the woman down to the side. Just as her expression turned haughty, he punched in a code.

The door opened with no help from her.

Clary's face fell and she yelped as Cedar jerked her into the hallway. Her lips started moving—some silent plea with her only bargaining chip gone, no doubt—and Cedar pushed her into the corner beside the door.

"Stay there," he said and faced Juniper and Laurel coming in behind him. "Stick to her."

A soft pitter-patter echoed from somewhere down the hall, interrupting them, and Cedar turned, smiling. "Lily? That you?"

A black cat with white paws sprung out of an opening along the bottom of the wall and stopped in front of him. There was a white star pattern on its forehead and its tail was the same white. A device resembling a set of headphones was wrapped around its neck, indicating cybernetic augmentations.

After a quick glance, the cat trotted up to Cedar and rubbed against his legs like he was an old friend. Still smiling, Cedar scooped the cat up and let it hop up to his shoulder. He gave it a scratch under the chin.

"Welcome home," came an AI's voice from the collar. "I have missed you, Captain Cedar."

"I've missed you too." Cedar walked down the hall with purpose. "Got some trash to take care of. You good with that?"

"Affirmative."

Clary went still, her eyes bulging wider, as Cedar left through the far set of sliding doors. She flinched like she intended to go after him, but stopped when Juniper and Laurel tightened their ranks around her. She grimaced and straightened her back. About Juniper's height, but with a lot more muscle. After assessing them both, Clary locked onto Laurel and her face softened.

"You're holding that wrong." She reached out. "Let me—"

Juniper swatted Clary's hand away and Laurel glared at her.

"You think I'm stupid?"

Clary put her hands up. "Worth a shot."

The three of them flinched as muffled shouts erupted from beyond the glass doors. Juniper couldn't understand anything, but their cybernetics helpfully pointed out there was a lot of tension.

"So." The woman cleared her throat. "I'm Clary."

"You already told us," Laurel squeaked and swallowed. Her hands were starting to shake. "I'm Laurel. T-This is Juniper."

Juniper gritted their teeth, frustrated. Not the time for re-introductions.

"Did you know who that was?" they asked, trying to make it sound like a threat. Gain control of the situation. Laurel was no good at this, but it wasn't her fault. Juniper should have taken the blaster.

Clary closed her eyes. "Cedar fucking Woods. Once the Red Bandit in the stars and once captain. He's going to kill me."

"He won't," Laurel said.

Juniper gave Laurel another look—there went that bargaining chip. Clary didn't need to know that. Not right away. "He's just taking his ship back," Juniper added. "Do what we say and *maybe* he won't."

Clary eyed them both and Juniper clenched their jaw. It wasn't like they didn't know what taking his ship back entailed. They weren't naïve. No maybes about it. Especially as the shouts continued. Their bio-monitor made their flight reflex kick in.

"You don't want to be here," Clary said. "You're kids. You don't know the stories they told me. He'll eat you."

"Hasn't yet," Laurel said.

"He will. Once the crew's gone, you're next! Why do you think they iced him?"

Laurel glared at Clary. "Is that what they told you?"

Clary bit her lip. "Look, Tremaine's a giant fucking dick. Maybe he's lying. Either way, I owe him a lot of cash. If he dies from this, great! But I don't want to be in debt to another asshole and neither do you two. This life sucks." Her face suddenly lit up, like she thought of an idea. "We can take the grappler—it's better suited for space. I can take you back to the transit station and find your parents and get you out—" She stopped short as Laurel tightened her grip on the blaster.

"No," Laurel snapped. "We won't go back."

"You're sticking with us," Juniper said.

The yelling finally turned into blood curdling screams. Juniper tensed. The screams abruptly stopped. Their bio-scanner reached out, searching for heartbeats, and found only one racing with panic. Three people already dead. Laurel began to tremble, looking like she was going to be sick, and Juniper was too late to notice Clary moving.

She disarmed Laurel with trained efficiency, and though Juniper expected her to turn the blaster on them, she shoved it back into her shawl. Before Juniper could lunge for it, Clary had her arm around Laurel, dragging her closer, and then did the same with a stunned Juniper on her other side. Juniper immediately thrashed, but stopped when they noticed Clary was pushing Laurel behind her.

To protect her. Both of them. Even as her own heart raced with clear panic, Clary was putting herself between them and what she considered the threat.

It came soon enough. The door at the end of the hall swiped open and a light-haired man ran through, gasping for breath. He was a mess; shirt torn, a gouge taken out of his shoulder, and his bright red blood ran down the broken arm hanging at his side. He spotted

Clary, eyes wide, but the distraction cost him his balance. He hit the ground and turned to face the door again, making panicked noises that failed to become words as he attempted to push himself backwards.

Cedar had followed him through.

His pupils were dilated to the point his eyes were simply black. Blood ran down his chin, staining his shirt red. It even dripped from his hands. It was way worse than the fed ship; there, the lights had been sporadic and dim. Here, Juniper saw every single bit of gore. Their stomach twisted.

"I won't eat you, Tremaine," Cedar said, his voice dark.

"You fucking ate *them*!" Tremaine shouted. "Don't you remember what they fucking did for you?"

Cedar swooped down on him so fast, Juniper flinched. Clary pulled them closer, a strong arm across their chest to keep them still and her other arm pushed into Laurel to keep her in the corner.

Cedar yanked Tremaine to his feet, then higher until the man was dangling.

"You mean how they drugged me and Aster?"

"Fuck—Cedar!"

"How they helped you chop off his fucking head?!" Cedar screamed and his voice broke. He swung Tremaine into the wall and held him against it. "You think I care what those fucks did for me in the past? They killed Aster! You fucking killed Aster!"

"God—we-we saw the writing on the wall!" Tremaine cried as he kicked his legs uselessly. "We made it quick! I was doing what was best for them!"

Cedar leaned dangerously close to Tremaine, baring his teeth, and Tremaine whimpered, trying to turn away. "For petty cash! I trusted all of you! Aster *trusted* you!"

Juniper's cortex computer pinged the wall behind Tremaine with a warning. Wait. Juniper went cold. That wasn't a wall. That was an airlock door. The scan finished and gave them just how quickly they'd have to move in the worst-case scenario.

Their heart skipped, finally catching up to what their augments were implying. No. Cedar wouldn't. He *couldn't.*

"Do you know," Cedar said quietly, turning Tremaine back to look at him, "how it feels to have ice collect in your lungs?" He laughed suddenly and Tremaine stilled. "Right, humans don't. You die. Vampires feel every single moment. How it's like a bunch of little knives filling you up."

No. Juniper's cybernetics measured the length from where they stood to the airlock door. Not far enough away. He couldn't seriously be considering it. Not while they were right there. Clary held them tighter, a gasp from her lips.

"Lily!" Cedar shouted without looking away. "Open Airlock Door M-C. Both sets."

"No!" Clary screamed. "Don't you fucking dare!" She shoved her arm across Laurel and grabbed the guard rail near the corner. Laurel latched onto her arm, no order needed, and squeezed her eyes shut. "Please! Don't!"

"Lily!" Tremaine screamed, renewing his futile struggle. "Please! Don't do this!"

"There are others at risk in the corridor," Lily said over the intercom. "Are you sure, Captain Cedar?"

Tremaine froze, his mouth opening uselessly. He must have just realized he'd never had control over the ship. That Lily had been biding her time, waiting for her real captain to return.

Clary redoubled her efforts, pressing Juniper

even closer, and braced herself.

"Yes," Cedar said, taking hold of the guard rail beside the airlock with his free hand. "I'm sure."

A lot happened at once when the airlock hissed open. Tremaine was gone in a panicked blur, no time for a prayer, as the vacuum of space claimed all he was. Cedar held onto the rail, as still as a statue, even as his coat flapped around him. There was an empty kind of solace written across his face. Clary shouted at Lily to shut the doors, her grip ironclad around both Juniper and Laurel, and Laurel was screaming.

The door resealed and the three of them collapsed to the floor, breathless.

"Acceptable outcome," Lily said over the intercom.

Acceptable was a word for it. Juniper placed a hand on their chest, willing their heart to slow down. Their bio-monitor had already released a calming chemical which left a cooling sensation seeping through their body. For once, they were glad for it.

Especially when Cedar faced the three of them with the same empty expression. Clary got her wits about her first, scowling, and shot to her feet.

"You were going to get them killed!"

Cedar tilted his head. "I didn't."

"You're a fucking asshole!"

Cedar chuckled, a sad smile on his lips. "I knew you had them. You're a decent person, right?"

It sounded like a challenge. Clary sucked in a breath, tensing back up. Cedar approached her slowly, as though he didn't want to spook her. Laurel scrambled to get between him and Clary. Girl had heart, but she was no shield. Juniper stood and tugged her to the side; this wasn't their fight to decide. It was between Cedar and Clary.

"I won't hurt you," Cedar said. "You've got a

chance here. You can leave—and don't come back—or stay and be my pilot."

"What?" Clary whispered.

"The way I see it, I just freed you from whatever that asshole was asking you to do," Cedar said. "But I'm betting you got nowhere to go, which is why you stuck it out here as long as you did. All I need is a pilot who knows Lily. No funny business."

Clary went still, hardly breathing. She glanced between Juniper and Laurel, suddenly aware they were watching her too, and after another tense moment, she collapsed against the wall.

"Okay, sure. Pilot," she said. "I've got nowhere to go. You're right. Just... don't do that again."

"I don't think I'll have to." Cedar smiled widely, his expression at odds with the blood all over him. "Lily! New roster! You ready?"

The cat slinked out of a hole in the wall and sat in front of them. Her bright yellow eyes scanned each of them individually.

"Ready," she said.

"Juniper and Laurel!" Cedar introduced, like he was announcing stars coming down a catwalk. Juniper couldn't help but snort.

"What shall I categorize them as?" Lily asked.

"Uh." Cedar blinked. "Trainees?"

"Affirmative."

Juniper fully laughed this time, covering their mouth, and felt better when a laugh also left Laurel's throat. Trainees. Better than fresh meat.

"And... uh." Cedar looked Clary up and down, gesturing at her.

"Clary Sage." She crossed her arms. "She. Still pilot."

This time, Cedar laughed. "For fuck's sake, I'm

collecting plants up in here. Might as well rename the ship the *Gladiolus*."

The cat's ears perked up. "I liked that name much better anyway."

A smile played on Clary's lips, but she turned to hide it. Lily repeated all their names, jobs, even taking care to confirm pronouns, and once she finished, Cedar held his hands out toward Juniper. He'd wiped them off on his poor shirt, but at least they were clean. Juniper happily handed over Aster's head.

Cedar carefully slung the bag over his shoulder. "We all need some rest after all that—but don't you dare go into the bridge."

"Someone has to clean it," Clary said.

"I will. My mess and all... just..." He turned and glanced down the hall. At the bloody handprints Tremaine had left. The trail of splotches of blood from Cedar himself. "I want to see what I left behind. Then you can show them to a room they can sleep in while we hash out some details." He inclined his head toward them. "Got it?"

Clary nodded. "Got it."

"Crew quarters are this way. Ignore Tremaine's blood on everything. It's up the stairs right before the doors to the bridge."

All in all, ignoring what the bridge must have looked like—Cedar blocked it with his body as Clary quickly shuffled them up the correct hall—the ship was nice. Homey. A little cold. A scan showed Juniper that some of the tech was out of date, but well cared for. Juniper glanced at Laurel beside them, trying to gauge her reaction; even after the laughter, she was shaking. Bio-scanner pinged her heart. Still racing. Needed more than nonsense.

Juniper should have been shaken too, but they

were used to locking away their trauma almost immediately. Cybernetics helped, too. They squeezed their arm around Laurel's back, keeping her close, and she fully leaned into them as they walked.

Most of the crew quarters were full of stuff. Clary started to name who owned them, but she caught herself and bit the names back. Those people were dead. Lives never to be reclaimed. Cedar didn't linger. He'd already put aside whatever he'd once felt for them. Clary awkwardly said she'd go through it all, keep what was useful and sell the rest. Cedar nodded and led the way to the farthest room. It was darker down here.

Clary cleared her voice. "I guess this *is* your room. Tremaine never got the door open, so he told me to ignore it. Said there was nothing to clean in there."

"I'm sure it was Lily keeping him out," Cedar whispered.

"Affirmative." Lily came between their legs and stood proudly beside the door. "I knew you would come home one day and wanted to preserve it."

Cedar nodded and the cat's eyes shined. From an unheard command, the door hissed open and Cedar pulled Aster's container free. Still ghastly. Still dead. None of that mayhem had changed a thing. Juniper wasn't sure why they thought it might.

The smell of cedarwood and rosemary escaped into the hall with the room open and Cedar breathed in deep.

"We're home, Aster," he whispered and held Aster close. "Just like I promised."

He sounded like he might break. Three years trapped in ice, knowing the people he'd trusted with his life willingly killed his partner for petty cash. Knowing the love of his life wouldn't really be coming home with him. It was a miracle he hadn't broken down yet. Juniper's throat tightened and they patted his arm.

"We'll leave you to it," they said. "Clary's got us."

Cedar took in a shuddering breath. "Thank you," he said. "I owe you two so much. We'll talk later. I promise."

He stepped inside and the door slid shut behind him. Juniper ordered their systems to ignore the room, begged them to behave for once, but the bio-scanner still reported Cedar's shuddering breaths and his barely concealed sobs. Juniper didn't need it spelled out for them. Cedar deserved his privacy.

Ignore it. Ignore it. Ignore it. Juniper repeated it to themself, drowning out the information the best they could. They were so in their head trying to stop it, they didn't notice Clary trying to nudge them away until Clary physically touched their arm. The bio-scanner switched tactics to the new person to invasively scan, but thankfully, Clary had only touched their sleeve, so it couldn't get a full read on her except for superficial details. Like the fact her pulse quickened.

Juniper followed her and Laurel away from the door and it was only when they'd left the hall, did they realize how fast Clary was trying to move them through. Why her pulse was going so fast.

Juniper planted their feet. "Wait."

"Listen to me." Clary rounded on them and glared at the cat following them. She nudged it with her foot. "Lily, shoo for one second, will you? You like me. I always remembered to feed you, didn't I?"

The cat considered it before it sauntered away to chase after something down the hall.

Once the cat was gone, Clary leveled with Juniper and Laurel. "We can still run." She waved her hand when Juniper opened their mouth to argue. "Stop with your bullshit—we can hide. There are so many places we can go that isn't where a vampire might snap at any moment. No one's in their right mind after being iced for three years. And that is his partner's *head*."

"I'm not leaving," Laurel said. "I can't. *We* can't. He's all we got." She pulled Juniper closer, making a show of a united front. "You can leave if you want. We'll learn how to pilot this thing. We won't even tell him where you went."

It was endearing how much Clary was trying to give them an out. She wanted to protect them, like some misplaced sisterly instinct was kicking in. Juniper wished she would *listen* to them, though. Clary stared at them a moment longer, biting her lip, and eventually retreated with a long sigh. She pulled a charm attached to a necklace out from inside her shirt. She shoved it at Laurel.

"Take this, then," she said. "My moms gave it to me when I left home."

Laurel took it awkwardly, eyebrows high, and let Juniper touch it gently with their fingers. It was a silver hoop with a spike through the center. At the top of the spike was a button that could be pushed in. Juniper jerked their hand away.

"Wait." Their cybernetics confirmed their suspicion. "That's an icing needle."

There was enough cryogenic ice inside the loop to freeze whoever happened to be on the receiving end of the needle. Black market self-defense tool, typically advertised as protection against vampires. Laurel flinched, eyes growing wide.

"One use," Clary said. "It won't accidentally activate—believe me, if it did, I'd already be dead. I have its pair in my room if we ever need to thaw whatever you ice. Keep it. Things go south? Use it. Don't hesitate, because he sure as hell won't."

Laurel stared hard at the needle, like she considered throwing it, but Juniper squeezed her fingers together around it. Better to have it than not.

"We understand," Juniper said. Laurel swallowed, nodding, and slipped the chain over her head. "You leaving, then?"

Clary snorted, blowing her bangs off her forehead. "Fuck no. I'm the pilot, ain't I?" She turned and beckoned them to follow. "There's a spare room down here with no one's shit inside. Stay there until I say the bridge is clean." She smiled sadly at them over her shoulder, halting Juniper's attempt to volunteer their help. "I've cleaned worse messes. Promise."

The room was sparse. Bed was barely big enough for two people and it was dressed in gray sheets. Shelves were embedded into the wall on one side next to the closet. Behind the bed was a circular window peering out into space.

Clary left them be, heading down the hall shouting she'd get their things. Only when the door slid shut did Laurel turn and wrap her arms tightly around Juniper.

Juniper hated they flinched, but when their cybernetics remembered Laurel as *safe*, they fully melted into her touch and wrapped their arms around Laurel just as fiercely. She buried her face into Juniper's chest, trembling harder, and without needing to look, Juniper knew there were silent tears on her cheeks.

"Oh, Laurie." They smoothed her hair back. "It's okay—it's okay. Shh. We're alive. We're safe here. I know we are."

"I-I know." Laurel's arms squeezed Juniper tighter

as she looked up. Tears were fogging her glasses. "I-I just keep thinking this is a bad i-idea, b-but I don't know what else I could have done—and-and—"

Juniper pressed Laurel closer and rested their head against Laurel's. "I know," they whispered. "But it'll be all right. One of us has to say it, right? It can be me." It felt like they were just rambling, but they were glad when Laurel nodded. She released Juniper a fraction, taking a few deep breaths and calming down.

Then she took in a sudden sharp breath and pulled her head up so fast, she nearly smashed her forehead into Juniper's nose. "We forgot Sprig!"

The sudden declaration made Juniper laugh, quietly at first, until Laurel joined in. Together, their laughter was broken and bubbling, but neither of them could stop. Juniper rested their forehead against Laurel's. "I still can't believe you stole that thing."

"It's one of us!" Laurel grinned despite the streaks running down her cheeks.

The grin made Juniper's worries melt. All the pent-up thoughts and fear dissolved into background noise, and they held Laurel tighter. They'd get through whatever life had in store for them so long as Laurel was there beside them. They only hoped they could be the same kind of pillar for Laurel.

"I'm sure we can sneak back down there and scare the shit out of Clary to retrieve it." Juniper returned the grin as Laurel's eyes practically twinkled. "You in?"

"I am *so* in. Let's go."

SESSION 3

THEY DON'T CARE
ABOUT US

11
LAUREL

SOMEHOW—LAUREL DIDN'T KNOW HOW— she slept. After she and Juniper had collected their things and set Sprig loose, Juniper had wrapped her up in a blanket from their bag, the smell reminding Laurel of home, and she'd immediately passed out. Another dreamless dark, but she preferred it that way. No regrets. Nothing enticing her to go back to a yesterday that didn't exist anymore.

She awoke from distant commotion echoing across the ship. Something would clatter, there'd be chatter muffled beyond the walls, then things would fall, and it would start again on another part of the ship. It was distracting enough, it kept her from rolling over to fall back asleep.

Her room was different than it had been last night, too. Instead of the stars beyond her window, lights from sun lamps outside streamed inside. Must have been docked somewhere, then.

With light to see, she peered groggily around her room. It was decked out with some of her items now. Her palm tablet was on the shelf nearby, the time in bright yellow—it was just after morning. Her glasses were propped up beside it. The bag of mostly her things and clothes sat beneath the shelf. All of Juniper's items were absent, but Laurel didn't mind after finding the quickly scrawled note next to her glasses. Juniper had written they were on the other side of the bathroom and signed with a smiley face. Made sense. After a year of forced close proximity on the satellite, Juniper would want their own space. Laurel wanted her own too. Clary must have already cleaned out the other rooms.

Thinking of them—the people that used to be—made Laurel shudder and she immediately scrubbed yesterday from her mind with better thoughts. New day. New her. New ship. Cedar was on their side.

Besides, he'd listened to Laurel. Clary was alive. Laurel hadn't helped doom everyone. Just... most of them.

Laurel rolled over and slapped her cheeks. No dwelling. From what the previous crew had done to Cedar, they deserved it. She breathed out and opened her eyes to her new life. Trainee crew member aboard the *Challenger*. No—the *Gladiolus*. A sword lily. Much more fitting.

Sprig's whirring disrupted Laurel's thoughts. It had left the room in the night through the small cat door, but it must have been time for its return. It came back to the bed and bumped the legs before it chimed a full bin. Laurel sighed. Time to get up, then.

New day. New Laurel.

After emptying Sprig's bin in the recycling chute she found in the hall and setting the robot loose again, she grabbed some clothes—an oversized t-shirt, leggings, and colorful socks—and headed into the bathroom next door. Juniper had already spread both their toiletries across the vanity, making it more their space than anyone else's. Laurel hoped Clary didn't mind; some of what must have been her things had been neatly pushed to the corner of the counter.

She freshened up—brushed her teeth, washed her face, ran a brush through her hair—and smiled at herself in the vanity mirror. She'd make this work. After throwing on new clothes, she quickly fastened her hair back into its usual twin buns and exited into the hall.

The commotion was still ongoing. Something was being upended, someone was frustrated, and then it would start again in another part of the ship. Laurel followed the sounds and paused as she passed the bridge. Its sliding glass doors had been propped open and a chemical smell wafted into the hall. Smelled clean, at least. Like lemons. No bodies to speak of, no blood, and maybe new upholstery. A wonder how fast a pilot and a vampire worked.

Laurel made a detour inside to check it out. The pilot's console was near the doors on a small overlook. A screen was lit up with ongoing maintenance and beside it was a map of the station they'd docked at. Omega Mall Station. She'd heard of it before; it was the biggest mall past Jupiter and had pretty swanky casinos, too. Her parents had gone to the casinos once when she was little, leaving her with her grandmother for a week. She immediately cringed, trying to wipe them from her thoughts, and looked at the rest of the bridge to distract herself.

Flanking the pilot's console were short slopes leading downward into the rest of the bridge. Pretty typical, then. There were terminals set up for drones on one side, a seat for scanning the feeds around the ship on the other, a hologram table for larger maps in front of the main windows, and then finally there was the couch near the table. Someone had hung fairy lights across the bridge, and they cast a pale, orange glow across everything.

Not bad, all in all. Definitely not Federation-grade, but homey.

As she gave in to the temptation to sit in the pilot's chair, just to see how it'd feel, she noticed the cat there. The cat cocked her head and considered Laurel, eyes a vibrant yellow like Juniper's. Right—cybernetic cat.

"Good morning, Miss Laurel," Lily's voice came from the cat's speakers.

"Just Laurel's fine," Laurel said. "And you're Lily, right? The ship's AI?"

"Yes." The cat swished her tail. "The cat and I are one."

Laurel had heard of ships keeping animals as uplinks to their AI. Unlike Juniper, they had rudimentary cybernetics in the form of the cortex computer specifically interfaced with the AI's systems. They were always something small to be able to move through the ship with ease and easy to grab in case of evacuation. Cats were preferred, but many also appreciated the companionship of small dogs and Laurel had even read about a rabbit once.

"Can I pet you?" The question left Laurel's lips before she'd considered if it'd be rude.

"I would enjoy it, yes."

Laurel dutifully pet Lily's head and the cat leaned into her hand. Laurel scratched her under the chin like Cedar had done and the cat let out a satisfied chirrup. Before she got lost petting a cat all day, she pulled back. "Where is everyone? They've been loud."

"I think they reconvened in the den," Lily said. "It's just down the steps to your left as you leave. If needed, I can escort you."

"I'll be okay," Laurel said. "You're watching the bridge."

Lily licked her paw. "Affirmative. Another AI's doing routine maintenance while we're docked and I have to keep an eye on it. Simply a formality. This AI and I have crossed paths before."

"I'll leave you to it then." Laurel gave Lily one more pat, earning another chirp, and exited.

She followed the flight of stairs to her left, the commotion growing louder as she went, and paused at the bottom. The stairs opened up to what definitely reminded Laurel of a den. Near the stairs was an open shelving unit full of physical books of all shapes and sizes, and while she wanted to peruse them, find something new to read, she drew her gaze across the rest of the space first. Two distinct areas. One was the kitchen nook on the far side with a half wall acting as a barrier. It looked pretty basic with typical countertops, cabinets, and appliances. Over the sink was a large, circular window looking out into the station. Golden light spilled inside from sunlamps, making the place even cozier.

On the other side was a carpeted area with a squishy couch facing the large TV screen hanging on the blank wall. Below the TV was a small entertainment stand where someone had spread out game systems, controllers, and movie discs. Maybe there was a party game Laurel could make everyone play so they could get to know each other better.

Juniper sat on the couch and peered over the back while Clary leaned on the half wall, watching with interest as Cedar tore through the kitchen. He repeatedly opened and closed the cupboards, the refrigerator, and even what Laurel pegged as the dishwasher. Each time, he grew a little more frantic, seemingly stuck in a loop of expecting something to have changed since the last time he glanced in.

Laurel plopped down on the couch beside Juniper. "What's going on?"

"There's no blood!" Cedar said, shocked. "At all. No fucking blood!"

Juniper rubbed their forehead like a headache was coming on. "He's been up and down the entire ship for the past hour."

Clary made a face as Cedar opened the fridge again. "Tremaine sold all the blood for cash. No matter how many times you open that thing, it won't magically make the blood reappear."

Cedar raked both hands through his hair, turning in place. He'd dressed in something less disheveled, at least; a clean white shirt with its sleeves rolled up and a well-worn pair of jeans tucked into his boots. "For fuck's sake." He dragged his hands down his face. "I need another stash." He faced Clary so quickly, she tensed like she was ready to bolt. "Where'd you say you docked us?"

"Omega Mall Station," Clary stressed and relaxed a fraction. "They have a blood store. Pricey, though."

"It's a start."

Juniper suddenly straightened with a gleam in their eyes. They must have received a virtual message; Laurel had seen it all the time when they were messaging Slim... Except, it definitely wouldn't be Slim now. Juniper didn't look at Laurel as they stood.

"What's up?" Laurel asked as Juniper tried to leave.

They paused and glanced at everyone, skittish. "Just gotta pick something up."

"Pick what up?" Clary looked over her shoulder at

them, curious. "How'd you even get an order in? Usually, pickups are slammed in the morning. I can go if you want."

Juniper shook their head. "N-No. I'll go." They swallowed and shrugged. "When we docked, I checked their net. Found something I needed. Won't be long."

"With what cash?" Clary asked, but it was too late; Juniper had already left. She rolled her eyes. "You know what, I don't care." She plucked a bag of popcorn from the mess Cedar had piled on the counter.

Laurel left them to their cleaning and headed after Juniper. By the time she'd caught up at their room, Juniper had already dressed. They'd thrown on their black hoodie, a pair of tight jeans, and even had a facemask to obscure their face. Typical escaping-the-satellite outfit. Except this wasn't the satellite. They were just tying up their boots when Laurel peeked inside.

"You want a buddy? We can find something shiny," she offered, grinning.

Juniper winced and set their feet down. "You don't want to come with. Found someone selling the sleep gummies." Juniper stood and fidgeted with their sleeves—rolled up or rolled down—until they decided on rolled up. "Just didn't want to air it out to those two."

"You don't have any money."

Juniper hesitated again and Laurel regretted bringing it up. They never had money for the sleep gummies. The narcotic was incredibly expensive and cash was never how they'd bought them before.

"Right..." She sighed. "Be safe, okay?"

Juniper nodded. "Pinky promise. I'm taking the laser knife. I'll be back soon."

Laurel hated seeing them go. Their very first

adventure at some place they'd both never been, and Laurel couldn't go with. Not that she'd want to go on this particular adventure; the one dealer Laurel had met on the Lunar Colony had been so skeevy, she never wanted to meet another.

But still.

New normal was a lot like the old normal. Bigger than their satellite with a few more bodies added to the mix, but Juniper went out, did something a little risky, and Laurel stayed behind. She hated that it immediately got to her and dragged her hands down her face. Deep down, she had no reason to be out of sorts about it. They were two different people with separate lives; Laurel didn't have to go with Juniper to everything, but Laurel hated being left alone, especially when it was a whole new place.

She shook out her arms and headed back to her room to decorate. Maybe she could finish hers and surprise Juniper with decorating their room too.

Laurel didn't even get any of the things she'd packed pulled out before she gave up. She didn't want to be alone with her thoughts.

Her feet took her back to the den. The mess was still there, but Cedar wasn't. Clary had sprawled out on the couch with the popcorn bag in her lap, watching television. She'd tuned it to one of the many Federation news stations accessible from just about anywhere in space.

She noticed Laurel peeking in and shook the popcorn in her direction. "Breakfast?"

Laurel snorted and came closer. "Popcorn for breakfast?"

Clary shrugged. "After that night? I think I need a little junk." She shoved a handful of popcorn into her mouth and turned back to the television. "Big guy went out for blood sniffing. That's what he called it—not me. Where exactly was Juniper going? Swore you two were joined at the hip after last night."

"Just getting something," Laurel said. "They'll be safe."

Clary eyed her. "Uh. Is Cedar cool with that?"

"What do you mean?"

"He's kinda in charge of you two. I figured he'd throw money at you if you just asked. No need for weird favors from the net." Clary tapped the side of her head. "'Sides, datacrypt and shit?"

Laurel frowned. "Cedar told you about us?"

"Well, yeah?" Clary glanced away. "We had to talk about something as we scrubbed everything top to bottom in record time. Definitely not gonna talk about his past crew. Besides…" She waved a hand in front of her face. "Juniper's got that gold shimmer in their eyes. A little obvious."

Laurel crossed her arms and leaned on the armrest of the couch. "Juniper can take care of themself. They've been doing it long before they met me."

Clary tilted her head. "Feeling left out?"

"Shut up."

"Come on. Eat some popcorn." Clary shook the bag at her again.

Slumping her shoulders, Laurel gave in. Maybe it'd help. At least the sound of chewing would drown out her simmering thoughts. She settled beside Clary and took a handful.

Clary cheered. "Good! And now some trash TV over breakfast!"

Laurel wanted to laugh—it was so absurd—but the cheer immediately dried up when trash news became a breaking story about a press conference with Lola.

Shimmering chestnut brown hair in perfect waves tumbled down her back, the double twin buns atop her head just like Laurel's, and brown skin scrubbed of any imperfection. She wore a glittering red dress beneath a sheer white shawl—one of her better dresses. She'd had it for years. Laurel had helped her pick it out before... Well, before she was sold.

The dress always made Lola the center of attention, especially as crocodile tears glimmered in her eyes. The camera focused on her face as she spoke, leaving her agent unfocused behind her. Lola's face was a mirror of Laurel's own, only older and more mature.

If Laurel wasn't in a bad mood before, she was now, and she scowled.

"Isn't there anything else?" Laurel shoved the handful of popcorn into her mouth. Buttery and warm. Chewing helped block out whatever Lola was saying.

"Morning news is slow today," Clary said. "She's relevant. Bopping tunes, but it's all drama all the time with her, isn't it?"

Curiosity got the better of Laurel. "Why's she relevant now?"

"She's going on hiatus," Clary said. "Family problems or something? Beats me. Reporters are acting like the world's ending or something." She paused and stared at Laurel for a little longer than necessary. She flicked a glance back at the screen, then back at Laurel. "Don't like idols?"

"We've just got a history." Laurel looked away.

Clary watched her for a minute that felt like an hour before she continued. "You've got the same face."

"Shut up."

"I don't like my sisters either, you know." Clary held up her hands in surrender when Laurel glared at her. "Just saying! If you ever want to commiserate, I'm right here."

'Didn't like' was an understatement. Laurel stopped short of shoving Clary off the couch. There was nothing to talk about, anyway. Family problems probably meant one of their parents gambled their money away again and needed to be bailed out. Typical bullshit the news stations would never report because Lola bribed them not to. Like any evidence of her having a little sister sold to the feds. Lola had curated a perfect persona as an idol, and she maintained it at any cost.

Laurel brought her knees to her chest and rested her forehead against them, trying not to think. Clary, thankfully, got the message and switched the station. This one was a roundtable discussion about the ethics of allowing androids to choose their own jobs versus having one assigned to them. Not much better; just a bunch of talking heads spewing fed lies.

"What about you?" Laurel asked, wanting different noise. "What's your story? You already practically know ours."

"It's not really anything as tragic." Clary spread her legs out in front of her. "Grew up in a military family. Joined the Federation Quarters looking to broaden my horizons and scout new places to make colonies. I was a pilot." She inspected a popcorn kernel and threw it back into the bag. "That's what I thought I'd do. It was about as shitty as any other fed job, though. We just look good on paper. New colonists don't conform? Bam, down they go, courtesy of us. There were always more desperate people we could toss into unstable colonies.

"My group got raided by pirates one night and I sold them out just so I didn't die. The pirates were just as bad. Tremaine helped me get away for a price, but then, surprise! He was a shithead too." Clary dipped her head back. "I think he turned out to be the worst. All he wanted was some bitch to look pretty, mother everyone, and somehow do all the dirty work for him. It was complete shit."

Laurel tightened her arms around her legs. "Do you want to go back home?"

"Can't. Feds know I sold them out. Probably watching the place to see if I ever turn up again." Clary inclined her head toward Laurel and reached out to jiggle her knee. "Well, what's really up with you? Your own words. Not Cedar motor-mouthing everything in a single breath as he reupholsters the seats."

Laurel could picture Cedar doing just that and it gave her a momentary smile. She breathed in and tried to set her thoughts straight.

"I was born as replacement parts for my sister because she kept getting sick as a child," she said, immediately knowing how awkward it'd make the conversation. "She and I grew up together and she stopped getting sick. No replacement parts needed. She went on to bigger and better things—an idol everyone loves. My parents didn't want me anymore. I wasn't pretty enough. I couldn't sing. Do anything they thought was worthwhile. So, they sold me to the feds and I was put in one of those boarding schools. I ran before they could scramble my brain."

There was a distinct pause of awkwardness.

"Shit, girl." Clary eased out a breath. "I'm sorry."

"It doesn't matter now." She shifted and watched the screen. It was showing local ads for the mall now. "My family never cared and I made no friends. All I have is Juniper."

It sounded pathetic spoken aloud and all at once, she felt lonely again. She pressed her forehead against her knees to hide her face.

"Hey," Clary said soothingly. Her hand pressed against Laurel's shoulder. "Are you lonely here already? Look, girl—we can—"

"I just thought things would be different," Laurel admitted, a lump lodged in her throat. She didn't want to cry. "For a year I spoke to Juniper every day on the underground net. And then for another year, I lived with them on their satellite. Sure, they left sometimes to do what they had to, but they'd always come back to me. God, I don't even like them like that, but I was so happy every time they came back to me. And then we agreed to escape together and now we're here. And it's the same bullshit."

She breathed in, suddenly like she'd forgotten her lungs needed air, and blinked back tears. "I thought I'd finally find something to do in my life, but I feel lost and we haven't even done anything yet. I don't know how to feel or even what I want."

The words spilled out so fast after being dammed up so well. It'd been everything she'd been holding tight since Juniper sent their satellite into the moon. All her apprehensions and all her doubts. It was her idea to leave, strike out on their own terms, but she'd expected it to feel different. Not more of the same. All she wanted to do was be confident in who she was and not rely on Juniper, and of course, now when Juniper left to do something uniquely Juniper, Laurel floundered.

With the ensuing silence however, Laurel wished she hadn't dumped everything on Clary. She didn't even know why it was so easy. Something about her just screamed 'sister', even if it was so far removed from her actual sister. Rounder eyes, a bridge piercing, and a smaller nose to boot.

Clary stared at her for so long, Laurel thought for sure time had stalled specifically to drag out this awkward moment for as long as possible, just to show Laurel how wrong she was for feeling it at all. She wanted to run back to her room and shut the door.

"You know," Clary finally said, breaking the stalemate, "when those two come back, we should go shopping."

Laurel raised her eyebrows in disbelief. "What?"

"I'm not good with my feelings," Clary admitted. "You're trained to suppress them in fed work. Shopping always cheers me up. There's this tea shop that sounds divine out there, too—or maybe milkshakes? The mall's gotta have something you like." She smiled at Laurel, warm and inviting. "I got some money squirreled away we can blow. We go out, just you and me, and do whatever. Something stupid and fun. Not thinking so hard." She was half-rambling by the end, eyeing Laurel for an excuse to stop.

Laurel found herself smiling at Clary, worries melting away a little bit. "Yeah," she said. "I think I'd like that."

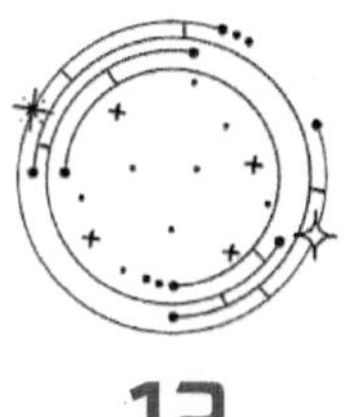

12
JUNIPER

JUNIPER BASKED IN THE POST-HOOKUP BUZZ on the walk back. Everything was weightless, bright, and complete somehow, the usual cybernetic bullshit distant. A perfectly normal person without the constant barrage of information, like their heart rate, possible exit scenarios, or how many people were on the street. Silence and bliss in their own head.

Except the euphoria would wane. Always did somehow. Reality would drag Juniper back with something small and out of place in their newfound bliss. Like the pain in their neck. Asshole had found the most sensitive spot—where their cybernetics fit into their spine at the base of their skull—and bruised the shit out of it.

The pain grounded them enough to notice one of the security cameras scanning them. They dropped their hand into their pocket and fiddled with their signal disrupter. A soft ping confirmed they'd been fuzzed out of the feed.

Juniper rubbed their neck and seethed as pain etched itself further down through their shoulder. At least they'd gotten the sleep gummies they needed. Vamps typically sold them—they were some kind of vampire narcotic—but most left Juniper's neck alone as some unspoken rule. Until this last guy. Asshole had gotten a little too excited with his love bites. Next time, Juniper was putting an ironclad 'no biting' rule up front. No matter how good it felt in the heat of the moment, not worth the risk or the pain they were in now.

Between running from the feds to everything happening with Cedar, they could have used someone way gentler. Like Slim.

The sudden realization of just how much they missed him hit them like a wave, tears immediately prickling their eyes. They furiously blinked them back. They should have tried harder to convince Slim to escape with them and Laurel. Maybe things would have been different.

Except if they'd brought Slim, Laurel would have felt even more left out. Juniper frowned and breathed out a sigh. Barely even out on their own and already nothing was going well on that front. Juniper's response to trauma was to immediately lock it up—cybernetics made it easy to scrub the mental images away—and what Cedar had done to his crew was definitely traumatic.

Laurel, though... She'd still seemed shell-shocked when they'd put her to bed. After scaring Clary and all the giggles thereafter, they'd thought they'd set her right, even cuddling with her until she fell asleep, but given how distant she was before they'd left this morning... Juniper had screwed up somewhere. And they'd only realized it halfway down the mall's boardwalk to meet up with some vampire asshole.

They should have taken Laurel out on the town.

Helped her swipe something pretty and have fun for a change. No one knew either of them this far out; they could have done it without checking over their shoulder all the time. Maybe it wasn't too late to apologize and explain... Except what would they do if it didn't work?

Juniper slumped their shoulders, frustrated. Even after a year with Laurel physically present, Juniper wasn't used to thinking of someone else's needs. It'd be easier if their cybernetics weren't so loud, vying for attention or even just shutting down thoughts so Juniper could focus on staying alive. Their cybernetics didn't care about the feelings or needs of anyone else, so Juniper didn't always notice things like that right away. Although, maybe it was just easier to say that than to own up to their own flaws.

Hopefully that part would be dealt with soon and Juniper could learn how to people better.

For now, however, they were in some space mall full of unknowns, and they refocused on their surroundings. Bliss had come and gone, leaving a residual fuzziness, but not enough to drown out their cybernetics completely, and not enough to expect a crash.

The Omega Mall Station was awash with lights from the sunlamps turned bright for daytime. Not strong enough to burn a vampire (their hookup was proof of that), but warm enough to feel like actual sunlight and not feel like they were orbiting Jupiter.

The boardwalk teemed with people brushing up too close for comfort, and Juniper focused on their end goal: the docks. There, it would be quieter, less security cameras, and maybe they could find an ice pack for their neck. The mall was full of distractions, however, easily capturing Juniper's attention again and again as they walked. The main part of the mall was the gleaming tower in the center they were passing now. Walkways jutted off it at every level to connect it to the smaller mall towers. Images glittered off the sides of the buildings as ads for the shops therein. Juniper made a mental note of a few Laurel would love and continued on.

The next distraction came from the mouth-watering aromas floating out from the restaurants and cafés lining the boardwalk. Juniper's stomach grumbled loudly. Most of the foot traffic was going toward some restaurant or another, given how close it was to lunch, and Juniper paused in front of one to consider how easy it would be to sneak inside and swipe a waiting order. They might not have Laurel's sticky hands, but how hard could it be with cybernetic reflexes?

They were letting their cortex computer configure a few potential scenarios where they could get away with a meal for both themself and Laurel when their bio-scanner flashed an immediate alert. They jerked their attention back to the street, panicked, and found Cedar right next to them.

He looked... normal. For him. Same shirt from this morning with his worn jeans, but he'd hidden most of himself beneath a jacket with the hood pulled up, a flat brimmed cap under that for more shade, and completed the look with sunglasses. Just an average guy who happened to be sensitive to sun lamps walking the boardwalk.

Juniper swatted his arm. "Don't sneak up on me like that."

Cedar gave them a look over the glasses. "I said your name." He poked Juniper's head. "You used to me now that I just blend in?"

"No. Everything's just fuzzy right now." Juniper

peeked at his other hand and pouted. He held a cup from the café one storefront down. Strawberry mocha with vanilla cream drizzled inside. "You could have bought me one."

Cedar snorted and handed it over. Score. Look pitiful enough and anyone will give up their food.

"Too sweet for me anyway." He shoved his hands into his pockets and started walking again. Juniper happily kept up, hunger satiated for now. "It's what all the kids like apparently."

Juniper pulled down their mask for a long sip and shivered as it went down. Perfect blend of strawberry, coffee, and vanilla washing the morning away. Their bio-scanner interrupted their delight by noting a change in Cedar's pallor. Juniper studied him. "Did you get what you needed? Your cheeks are pinker."

"Nah," Cedar said. "Too expensive. Clerk let me have a nibble though." He slowed and nodded to the bench near them. "Sit there. I'm gonna try another drink."

Juniper looked up at the establishment nearby and rolled their eyes. Vampiric Delicacies Café. Bunch of reds, blacks, and purples for the aesthetic. They sat on the nearby bench, crossing their legs, and happily waited with their strawberry mocha. Cedar wasn't inside long and looked chipper as he sat down with a frosty white drink swirled with lots of red.

"Seriously?" Juniper leaned over to look, but Cedar immediately pulled it away before their cybernetics could scan it. "Is that real blood?"

"Raspberries." Cedar sipped and smiled. "Totally fake. Barista was geeked out about seeing my fangs, though. Got a discount." He showed them off, grinning wide.

Juniper laughed and tried to hide it by taking

another drink. Cedar's grin immediately dropped when a security guard floated by on his hovercraft. He slowed, eyeing them both, but eventually continued on.

This side of Cedar was nice—not the vampire space pirate with a penchant for mayhem, but the easy-going guy underneath it all.

"So?" Juniper asked when the silence itched at them. "About your blood predicament?"

Cedar rested his arm on the back of the bench and stretched out his legs. Passersby made it a point to avoid him and the bench entirely. Not a bad idea; kept the eavesdropping down. Juniper mimicked him and stretched their legs too, keeping them crossed at the ankles. Not as much reach as Cedar, but enough.

"I'm not biting anyone on the ship," Cedar whispered. "Never worked that way."

Juniper lifted their eyebrows. "Not even Aster?"

Cedar leveled a look on Juniper over his sunglasses.

"They don't put cybernetics in vampires. Therefore, he wasn't always one, was he?"

Cedar eased out a sigh and dipped his head back. "You're too astute for your own good. But Aster was very different. I'd never do it to anyone else."

Good to know. Juniper noisily sipped on their strawberry mocha, nodding.

"What about you?" Cedar asked, glancing back at them. "Who were you letting bite you? Thought you and Laurel were a thing."

Juniper snapped back against the bench, face flaring, and tried to hide the bruise. Too late. Cedar gingerly moved their hand away to look at it and Juniper stammered. "N-No. Laurel and I aren't a thing like that," they said, focusing on the second comment.

"She's ace. I like guys."

Cedar slowly nodded. "Noted. I'm more concerned about the first question, though."

He hadn't moved away. Juniper felt too warm all of a sudden; their bio-monitor flooded them with notifications about a surge in adrenaline, their heart rate skyrocketing, their blood pressure rising—everything they didn't need to know. Like their cybernetics were making up for lost time. Little glimmers began to appear around everything from the information overload, prompting a migraine, and Juniper swallowed.

"No one important," they said and jerked the vial of gummies out of their pocket. They shoved it at Cedar, pushing him to back off. "I just needed these, okay? I ran out. It's not like we have the cash for it so I just used me. It's fine." It definitely didn't sound fine, not with the edge of panic to their voice. "I've done it before," they added a little too quickly as Cedar opened his mouth. "I'm safe. Promise."

Cedar turned the vial in his hand. "Only 'cause your nanomachines keep you clean," he murmured and narrowed his eyes. "Vampires sell this to other vampires. Usually they're stingy."

"Most vampires are willing to make exceptions. This one was no different."

"Because he wanted to bite you," Cedar said. "Vamps are way more dangerous than humans or androids—Juniper—"

"I—"

"No. Listen to me." Cedar bent forward so that Juniper had no choice but to look at him. "He told you that bruise was an accident, right?" Juniper shrugged and covered it with their hand again. "Vampires never do it by accident. We're incredibly aware of ourselves.

He was trying to break the skin and make it look like an accident. Then he would have drunk enough to leave you delirious. Did you even have a plan if he'd done that? I didn't even know where you'd gone."

"Shut up!" Juniper pushed Cedar away as their entire body thrummed, cybernetics' fight or flight response kicking firmly into flight mode. "You are not my parent. I'm nineteen. I know what I'm doing, okay? I have it handled."

Blurting everything out so fast, it certainly didn't sound like they knew what they were doing. It sounded more childish than anything else. Besides, Cedar was right. Even they knew that. They'd rushed, going with the first asshole to respond since they'd had no idea how long Cedar would keep them docked. Maybe it was a blessing all Juniper had to show for it was a bruise that hurt like hell.

"You're right, I'm not your parent." Cedar looked back at the vial and settled against the bench. "I'm your captain, and I don't want you doing risky bullshit—especially without giving me the heads up you might not come back." As Juniper opened their mouth to argue, he pushed the vial into their hand, stopping them. "Next time you need this stuff? Tell me and I'll get it. I've got experience finding dealers for this. Way better than some washed up vamp hiding in an alley looking for defenseless people like you to take advantage of."

Juniper exhaled through their nose, trying to stay calm. "I am not defenseless."

"He was able to bruise your neck," Cedar stressed. "Anywhere else, I'd believe you. But that is not 'having it handled', do you get me? You never let vampires get that close to your neck unless you trust them."

Juniper scowled, biting back a snappish reply.

They'd done the exact same thing tons of times in the Lunar Colony, and they'd always come out unscathed. Except… Their scowl faded, annoyance washing out of them. The vampires there had been few and far between because they weren't allowed in the inner system. They wouldn't have risked being caught. The vampires out here were different.

Juniper studied the gummies; each one shimmered multicolor beneath the sunlamps, looking so innocuous. Cedar's offer would be easier, even if Juniper hated thinking of having to rely on him for something so basic.

"What do vampires use these for?" they asked, curious.

Cedar shrugged and noisily sucked on his straw. "Puts us in a dormant state. If I lost an arm or something, I'd want to eat one, go dormant, and then have someone watch over me with a steady pack of blood going into me. Quicker limb regrowth that way." He glanced away and slid his glasses back up. "And it's what Tremaine used to drug me and Aster."

Juniper almost dropped the vial. "Oh, no. Shit! I'd never use it on you," they said. "I swear. It's for me. I-I can't sleep usually. This makes it so my cybernetics revert to keeping me alive instead of keeping me awake."

"I know," Cedar said softly. "Aster used them too, before I turned him. Some days, he was too scared to sleep." He smiled gently at Juniper. "I always told him I'd watch him. Calmed him down enough. 'Cept his cybernetics weren't nearly as finely tuned as yours. He had an easier time."

If only Juniper could talk to Aster. Maybe he could have helped Juniper not feel so miserable. Cedar was a start. Sort of. It felt easier talking to him about it than Laurel. Juniper never wanted to dump all their problems on her because she had her own. Cedar was completely acceptable.

Juniper leaned against Cedar's shoulder. Not a bad pillow, especially since their cybernetics had finally sorted him into the 'friend-shaped' category. Leaning on him wouldn't be so bad.

Together, they watched the crowd amble by on whatever errands they were running. Some had large bags in their hands, some were friends without a care in the world, and some were couples enjoying the sights. A few security patrols hovered by overhead, darkening the road momentarily, but no one ever stopped. All normal lives, unaware of the ones outside theirs.

"Is…" Juniper glanced at Cedar after a few moments. "Is vampirism worth it?"

Cedar didn't answer right away. Juniper thought he wouldn't at all—it seemed like such a personal question to ask out of the blue—but eventually, he sighed. "I don't know."

"Did you kill that clerk for the free sample?"

Cedar snorted into his drink and gave Juniper another look. Three in one day; Juniper was on a roll. "No! What the fuck do you think I am? I know how to lay low. Ask nicely, bat my pretty eyelashes, and just be handsome." He made a show of batting his eyelashes and Juniper clamped down a sudden laugh. It was so ridiculous looking.

"Old crew and fed grunts just different?"

"That was personal," Cedar said. "Most vampires get by with a certain amount of blood in their system as a baseline. If we dip below that for too long, we get… violent. Go too high above and you forget where your baseline was. Starving for three years messed me up, but I've got a handle on it after all those feds. Promise." He finished his drink and tossed it toward the trash receptacle nearby. He cringed when it nearly missed. "I'm usually good at that..."

"Do you ever get lonely?"

Cedar eyed Juniper. "Can you stick to one conversation, please?" He laughed. "First you ask one thing and then another. Giving me whiplash over here."

Juniper glanced away. "Sorry. Questions are just kinda popping into my head. Buzzing is going down. Talking helps."

After some thought, Cedar continued. "I think most vampires are lonely to some degree. At first, I wasn't going to turn Aster—he liked life, but he didn't want to go on without me." A warm smile brightened Cedar's face. "He made things less lonely."

"Did either of you ever regret living so long?"

"Vampires can't do regrets. Life's full of them. If we linger too long, they'll undo us." Cedar leaned his arm back on the bench again. "'Sides, if I didn't live this long, I wouldn't have met Aster. He made it all worth it."

But he was gone now. Juniper heard what was left unsaid. They leaned against Cedar again, hoping the presence was a comfort, and Cedar draped his arm across their shoulder. A kind of half hug, but it was nice.

Juniper finished their strawberry mocha and handed the cup to Cedar. He gingerly tossed it after his own cup and this one went in perfectly.

"Well, I'm done bonding," Juniper said. "We should figure out your blood situation."

"Still working on that." Cedar gazed at the towering stores and lights looking down at them. His lips shifted into a sly smile. "Security's pretty lax down here." His sly smile turned into an outright grin. "You think Laurel wants to show me how she'd take whatever's not nailed down?"

Juniper returned the grin. Just the thing to make it up to her. "She'd have a field day if we let her loose."

13
LAUREL

LAUREL WAS ALL OVER THE PLAN. EVERYONE hashed out the details together over dinner with a map Juniper had found on the station's underground net. According to Juniper's digging, no inventories would be taking place tonight, so no one but maintenance bots and overnight security would be present. Both easily circumvented.

The following day, after a night of excited tossing and turning, Laurel and Clary headed out to case the stores under the guise of a shopping spree with Clary's stashed away funds. They didn't buy much, but Laurel did score a store's keycard which Lily could hack into opening all the mall's doors. By the time the sun lamps were darkened for the evening, Laurel was practically bursting with excitement.

Laurel was glad to deck herself out in her usual lifting threads again. Black everything to blend into the dark, of course. Felt like old times, like she was sneaking around the Lunar Colony to find something to palm just for the sake of doing something.

And though Laurel had expected to only go in

with Juniper, Cedar insisted he come with. He stood out, even in dark clothes, but Laurel wouldn't let him cramp her style.

After she finished dressing, she dumped out the rest of her items from her duffel bag and took it to Juniper's room to let them know she was ready. After they'd planned yesterday, Juniper had immediately retired to their room and had been in there ever since. Laurel had been too distracted with hanging out with Clary to notice it until it was too late and then she was too distracted with the shopping spree to check in. She felt a little bad about that, but she could fix it now.

As she knocked, the door swiped aside, and she peeked in.

"You ready?" Laurel immediately frowned, noticing the glaring bruise against Juniper's neck. Had that been there last night?

Juniper quickly threw on a sweater with a cowl, effectively covering it. It was such a deep blue, it must have hurt. Laurel stammered, not sure what to say. Juniper noticed her staring and glanced away, idly rubbing it.

"Is that from getting your gummies?" Laurel finally asked.

"It's fine," Juniper said, their voice stilted. It was very much not fine. "Cedar already dad-ed out on me over it. I was stupid. Got it. Won't happen again." They smiled at Laurel. "Okay?"

So quickly brushed aside. "Sure, but you could have told me," Laurel said. "I could have lifted one of those fancy bruise fading bandages while we were out."

Juniper shrugged. "Hindsight, I guess. Maybe we can snag some tonight."

Laurel couldn't help but feel like there was

suddenly a wall shutting Juniper away from her. Sure, everything was a lot lately, but it felt like one of them had hurt the other and neither wanted to admit it. Except Laurel had no idea what she'd done. She opened her mouth to ask, clear the air, but before she could, Juniper came over and looped their arm with hers.

"Come on." They grinned, normalcy slotting back into place. "You've been dying to do something like this for ages, right? A whole-ass mall?"

Whatever the wall was, maybe it didn't matter. Laurel returned the grin. "You fucking know it!"

"Just no adopting a maintenance bot again."

"Fiiine!" Laurel dragged out the word and Juniper laughed as they headed into the hall as one. "Don't deny it—Sprig has been doing good work!" At least, when the cat wasn't riding it in and out of rooms like it had been earlier.

The two of them headed to the bridge where Clary had the surveillance ready. Cedar was waiting with her and had two more bags over his shoulder.

As they came in, Cedar tossed a bag at Juniper. "We all get a bag. I'll carry whatever's heaviest," he said.

Clary swiveled the holographic map of the mall on her tablet so everyone could see it. The map outlined the entire place with all the stores crammed inside, including the many basements and loading bays. Almost labyrinthine at first glance, but they were going through the maintenance hallway behind everything which was a lot simpler.

"Four stores. Should be in and out, easy." Clary pointed to each of them. Three different levels, but not far from one another. Two stores for clothes, one for food, and then lastly, the blood clinic. Anything to get ready for a trip to Pluto without breaking the bank.

Clary handed Laurel the stolen keycard. "Lily set this up to open all doors and has her little paws in the feeds. They'll loop as soon as you get to the loading bay." She rotated the map around and pointed out the bay where shipment arrived during the early hours. "Take this entrance into the maintenance hallway. There's a lift that will take you to another hallway with the backdoors of all our targets. Fill up the bags then move on." She eyed them. "I want edible food, by the way. Not just sugar shit."

"Yeah, yeah, I know." Cedar snorted. "This is a mall. Ain't hard."

Clary rolled her eyes. "If anything does happen, get out immediately. Don't try and salvage it. Got it?" She waited for them all to nod before a grin passed her lips. "All right then! Get going! Don't fuck this up!"

THE OMEGA MALL STATION WAS DIFFERENT with the sun lamps off. The glass dome showed the stars above, each one twinkling bright, with Jupiter looming along the horizon between buildings. Earth was one thing, but Laurel liked this view better. Down the boardwalk, bars were lit up with neon lights, trance music spilled out of opened doors, and the casinos in the distance were bright pillars, hoping to attract nightcrawlers. Foot traffic had died down considerably; the families, the dates, all the usual day folk gone and replaced with those who stayed to themselves. Security patrols were about the same, but easy to spot from the lights on their hovercrafts.

Most of the nightcrawlers helpfully kept their distance as soon as they spotted Cedar. Wasn't a bad idea adding muscle to the outfit; Juniper's enhanced reflexes paired with Laurel's penchant for going straight for the balls got them out of most trouble, but Cedar could outright throw someone.

The loading bay was empty aside from a few androids working overnight. Thankfully, beyond a cursory glance, the androids never acknowledged them. Either Lily's doing or the androids knew to leave them well enough alone. The keycard got them through the maintenance door and Laurel ticked phase one off in her head.

The cramped hallway within had industrial piping crossing between its buzzing fluorescent lights. It led to a lift that looked like it was out of an old horror movie; rickety with metal grates and gears that probably hadn't seen maintenance in years. Cedar tested it by jumping on it. When it held, Laurel swallowed back her fear of falling and stepped on with Juniper.

"Starting at the top." Juniper hit the button on the outdated controls and it lit up beneath their finger. "And then we work our way down."

The comms Clary linked with them crackled in Laurel's ear as they ascended. "Bingo. Stay out of sight. Be smart."

The first store they hit was the posh lounge clothing store that had turned its nose up at Laurel and Clary earlier. Expensive threads supposedly made from Earth-grown cotton. Laurel mostly picked it as payback for the snide looks she'd been given.

As Cedar stayed in the hall as lookout, Laurel and Juniper went to town. New clothes were desperately needed between them, and undergarments were even more so. There was only so much more Laurel could sew her bras and underwear back together, and

Juniper was in similar straits. Laurel had even gotten Clary's and Cedar's sizes so she could get something for everyone. As Laurel crammed her bag full (she could sort it later), Juniper took a moment to peruse the lacy delicates for themself. Until Cedar grumbled about them both taking so long. Laurel supposed he didn't understand that comfy underclothes were serious business.

The next store was more clothes. This time, shirts, pants, outerwear—anything to make their new life on the *Gladiolus* comfortable. Whatever they grabbed that didn't fit, they could always resell later, and Laurel wasn't picky. She was just glad to have new clothes. When her bag was close to bursting, they moved on.

They were well into the small grocery and variety store when Laurel noticed Juniper acting antsy. The fluorescent lights from the freezer Cedar was raiding illuminated Juniper's pinched expression and the way they were tapping their fingers on their knees.

"What's up?" Laurel asked.

"Sorry," they whispered. "Just some chatter on the feeds. It's encrypted, though." They pursed their lips, narrowing their eyes. "You hearing it, Clary?"

"Yeah," she replied slowly. "I thought it was just noise, but that's definitely chatter." She hummed on the other side and Laurel heard a few decided clacks on the keyboard. "Lily doesn't have the resources to decode it right now, though. I know there was some hullabaloo over at the casino about a half hour ago. Someone tried to empty the creds and got caught. There's been buzz since. Chances are it's related..."

Laurel snorted and Cedar returned to digging through the freezer. "That's too obvious," she said, although deep down she wanted to heist the money from a casino just to say she had. She just wasn't good at counting cards yet. "What did they think would happen?"

"You got me," Clary said. "Not everyone is as good as us. Come on. The chatter's making me nervous."

No argument there. Cedar zipped his duffel bag and then they were on to their last hit: the blood café. It was also the *coldest* hit. Laurel had to burrow deep into her sweater as they took stock of the place.

Blood cafés never had much up front aside from some couches and holographic information stands. This one was especially minimalistic in a chic way, suggesting swanky clientele. Cedar was most definitely not it.

"How'd you manage to get in earlier without getting security called?" Laurel asked.

"Clerk was sweet on me," was all Cedar said with a sly grin.

The blood was kept in a cryo-vault in a small room behind the checkout desk. Taped to the vault's door was a list of dates when the latest pack had come in and when to revitalize them. Laurel wrinkled her nose.

"Revitalize? What does that mean?"

"It's synthetic," Cedar said while Juniper knelt down beside the vault's lock to look at it. "Gotta get shaken up or it starts to coagulate. Remind it that it's supposed to be a little alive." He nodded to an apparatus to the side of the vault. It looked like a drink shaker. "Got one of those in the kitchen for the same thing."

There went Laurel wanting to use it to make milkshakes.

"Is synthetic as good as real blood?"

Cedar shrugged. "No, but it works. Door. Let's focus on the door."

Juniper was already on it. While there was no card slot to abuse their keycard privileges, Juniper had already jacked into the terminal. Their eyes flickered bright, then not, and then bright again between blinks. It was unnerving whenever Juniper was jacked in; they went completely still, like a mannequin. It gave Laurel the creeps.

With nothing to do but wait, Laurel got fidgety. Cedar was no help—all he did was watch Juniper like a hawk, as though staring made their hacking faster. After a peek through the metal gate into the mall to check for security—no one; it was an eerie ghost town—Laurel did what came naturally to her: searched for something to nab.

She headed through the café's 'Employees Only' door, right next to the cryo-vault. Shelves with bro- chures, binders with schedules, and lists of frequent customers and known troublemakers, but nothing interesting to take. No personal belongings at all. Laurel killed a little time looking for Cedar and Aster on the lists, but they weren't there.

Laurel checked the security terminal tucked into the far corner. Still on Lily's loop. Good. She slinked out to the main counter and dug around. Maybe someone left a cred stick behind.

A calculator. A scalpel. Someone's punch card for the Vampiric Delicacies Café. And then a lot of white tote bags with a stylized red droplet on the front (real subtle there). Laurel was offended at how little there was. At least give her something shiny.

As she picked herself up from below the counter, a light passed above her head. She flattened right back down, heart racing, and waited.

The light lingered on the back wall. That wasn't right. If the maintenance bot had seen her, it would have sounded an alarm. It wouldn't just wait, wondering if someone was there. It didn't sound like it was going to leave. She got on all fours and started crawling back to the cryo-vault.

Moments later, the light shut off. She stilled to listen, straining her ears until she couldn't hear the bot anymore.

Nope. Too weird. One thing she learned very early on when she started lifting was to trust her gut and her gut was screaming at her to get out now. She hurried to the back just as the vault's lock beeped and Juniper was pulling their cord out. Cedar threw open the doors and an alarm sounded.

"Shit!" Clary snapped over the comms. "Not you guys, but a store on a lower level just went off. I don't know why. Nothing's there."

Cedar peered over Laurel's head as she flattened against the wall, out of view from the gated entrance. "I don't like this." He dropped back to his knees and dragged Juniper over with their bag. "Fill it up—now."

Laurel and Juniper dove at the chamber and grabbed as many packs as they could. Ice cold, numbing Laurel's hands, but she powered through it. The maintenance door slid shut suddenly, locking itself. Laurel jerked up, eyes wide. She ran back to swipe the keycard through the reader. It dinged red. Someone had wirelessly recoded the lock.

"Clary? We need another route out."

"I see that." Clary was typing on the other side, frantic. "Out the front gate—Cedar should be able to lift it—there's a door nearby that'll lead right back to the maintenance hall. The stores are starting to lock down. You guys need to jet."

"Got it." Juniper hefted the blood bag over their shoulder and they and Laurel hurried after Cedar.

He'd pushed the front gate up and was outside, peering down the hall. Just as Juniper went to duck under, the gate slammed down. Juniper fell back with a yelp and Laurel tried pulling it back up, but it didn't budge.

"What the fuck?" Clary breathed. "Wait—" The comms fuzzed into static that drowned out all other sound. Juniper clutched at their head in pain and Laurel hurried to cut the feed.

Alarms went off across the entire mall, above and below, and red lights began flashing from the ceiling. Cedar swore and tried to yank the gate back up, but it held even under his vampire strength.

"Blood," he said. "Now." He bent low and shot his hands through the opening in the gate. The bag just fit and Juniper shoved it through. Right as Cedar had it placed beside him, metal shutters crashed down, separating them from Cedar completely. He swore and slammed his fists on the other side, but it didn't budge.

Juniper straightened their back, eyes wide, and their irises flashed white. "Shit! Security's back online. It must have booted Lily." They banged their hands on the metal. "Cedar! Get us out!"

"We were set up," Laurel whispered, her pulse pounding in her ears.

"What?" Juniper stared at her.

"It was too easy." She squeezed her eyes shut. "Shit. Shit. I was having so much fun, I didn't think we could be. No one was supposed to know we were here."

"Cedar? Any ideas?" Juniper called.

No answer. Laurel went cold. "Cedar?"

Gone. Juniper dropped back to their knees beside Laurel. "Cedar?" they called, louder, their voice breaking. "Don't do this. Where the fuck are you?" They pressed a hand to the side of their head and immediately winced. "God, the comms are toast. Cedar! Fucking answer me!"

The lights in the shop came on, blindingly bright. Laurel ducked into Juniper, pressing her palms to her eyes. Juniper dragged her backward by her shirt until they safely were behind an info stand. A few blinks later and Laurel could see, but it didn't help none. They were trapped.

The metal shutters suddenly shook, making Laurel flinch, and the motion eased into a rattle as they were slowly lifted. A row of even brighter lights was lined up on the other side. They were intense in a way that made Laurel's skin feel fuzzy, like natural sunlight.

"Come out now with your hands up!" came a cybernetically-enhanced voice. "No funny business, you hear?"

They both froze. A few heartbeats later and the speaker sighed.

"Put your hands up and come out. I will not ask again."

Laurel's heart was hammering so fast, she was dizzy. Juniper took a deep breath and nodded to her with all the calm in the world. She understood and took a deep breath too. No use pretending they weren't there. Laurel and Juniper stood with their hands raised and faced the bright lights.

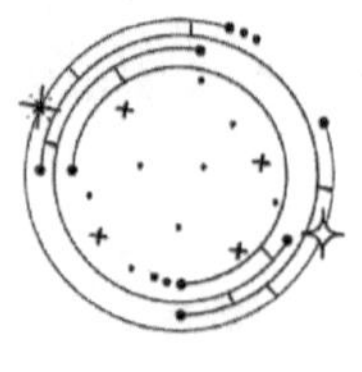

14
JUNIPER

THE WORLD WAS COLD AND DISTANT AS Juniper's footsteps echoed off the metal floor. Two enforcers marched behind them and one in front. Laurel walked woodenly beside Juniper, pulse panic-fast according to their bio-monitor. In contrast, Juniper's heartbeat was normal, even a little slow; rather than panic, they'd gone empty, courtesy of their augments keeping them level-headed. For once, they welcomed the stony calmness.

The enforcers were taking them to the security office beneath the mall to talk. The others were securing the perimeter; didn't need more than three without the vampire with them, apparently. They must have been expecting him too from the sheer number of initial enforcers and sunlamps set to scorch. The lamps were rolled away for now, but Juniper's skin still tingled.

Juniper's cortex computer pinged possible escape routes as they passed them, complete with the moves necessary to get away, but they swiped the suggestions away to think rationally. All the escape routes didn't include Laurel in the equation and Juniper was *not* leaving her behind.

They had the laser knife tucked into their sleeve. The enforcers hadn't patted them down (and why would they? Two underfed teenagers weren't dangerous). Juniper could thrash, make a scene, get Laurel away, but the mall's basements were labyrinthine without Clary's guidance. Laurel had a good memory, but it wasn't *that* good, especially when she was panicking. Better to stick together, but shit.

Shit, shit, *shit*. Cedar left them, just like that. Juniper had hoped he'd hidden himself so he could jump the enforcers once the lamps were gone, but the farther they went into the bowels of the mall, the less Juniper believed a rescue was forthcoming.

They weren't even sure what was worse: that they and Laurel were sloppy or that Cedar had ditched them after pulling the whole parent act.

Deep down, however, it made sense. They and Laurel weren't really the crew. Just a means to an end to shake loose at the earliest convenience. God, Juniper wished they hadn't trusted Cedar. They and Laurel should have just left as soon as Clary offered.

Their arrival at the security room yanked Juniper out of their thoughts. The master desk was near the door, a bank of terminals with screens watching the mall was along the wall, and a table with steel chairs sat in the center. The lead enforcer—the woman who'd flung the orders—told them to sit on the far side of the table, then positioned herself across from them.

Her movements were abrupt and forceful, each done with the precision of cybernetics, not a move wasted. She even had the tell-tale yellow eyes. It figured the one calling the shots was a cyber just like Juniper. Her sandy blonde hair was pulled tightly back into a proper bun, her pale, blemish-free skin looked like she'd had all imperfections buffed away, and she wore the standard enforcer uniform, only in white instead of black as though to denote her tier on the food chain. Pristine and not a wrinkle in sight.

Juniper let their wireless augment send out a feeler into her systems, looking for an opening, but all they found was a wall.

She must have felt it. Her eyes flicked over to Juniper and she gave them a smug smile.

One of the enforcers stood near the door and the other took a stance in front of the terminals. They were basically statues, almost identical beneath all their garb and tech. They'd probably come out of a boarding school like Laurel's. Personality scrubbed away so they'd never question orders.

Juniper's bio-scanner showed that they had scant combat augmentations controlled by some kind of basic cortex computer. That would be enough for Juniper to hack them, but they couldn't risk it if they couldn't take care of their leader first. She was likely watching their systems as well as her own.

Juniper flicked their gaze to the screens. Maintenance robots continued their rounds, but no sign of Cedar. The bastard. They looked away and instead, checked on Laurel. She sat stiffly as she stared at the table, breathing in and out deliberately to keep herself calm. Juniper gently touched her leg and Laurel eased out a more normal breath.

"I'm Officer Rae Forrest. You will address me as Officer Forrest." She gave them both a hard look until they nodded, then gestured to the enforcer at the door.

He unceremoniously dropped their bag onto the table. Forrest dug through their stolen clothes, a predatory little grin on her face, but it slowly slid into a frown. It turned into outright confusion as she uncovered the delicates, and she held up the lacy number Juniper had claimed. She stared at Laurel and received a glare in return, so she turned her gaze to Juniper.

Dutifully, Juniper gave her a bemused look back. "What?"

"You're stealing clothes."

Juniper shrugged. "Shit's expensive." Forrest peered down at the lacy number between her fingers. "I'll have you know: I look hot in that." It wasn't a lie; Juniper was one-hundred percent sure they'd look great in it.

Forrest dropped it and set her mouth into a hard line. She was pissed. Sure wasn't because of the delicates, but rather because neither Juniper nor Laurel was cowering from her. She wanted humility. She wanted them to writhe under her contemptuous stare.

When her glare deepened, Juniper held their hands up in peace.

"Look, we fucked up," Juniper said. "We realize that. Just give us the lifting fine and we'll never do this again." They nudged Laurel under the table with their knee and she nodded. "It was my idea. I just dragged her here with me."

Forrest tapped a nail on her chin, narrowing her eyes. She suddenly smirked, like she was on the verge of laughing, and pushed the bag aside. "I know who you are," she said. "Juniper Austre and Laurel Langley."

There it was. Drawn out in some holier-than-thou tone. Juniper glared at her. "Hey, at least you got my name right."

Forrest chuckled. "I read your file. You get violent

if people don't use that name, and I'm trying to do this as cleanly as possible." She spread her fingers on the table. "You both think you're so good at this, but you're not. We've simply been waiting for you to make a move. All we had to do was be patient."

Juniper's skin crawled. "Here?" They forced a laugh. "You just got lucky."

Forrest continued smiling. If Juniper was anyone else, they might have squirmed, but they were used to this kind of look, like they were a particularly interesting bug under a microscope. Got it all the time before they ran away.

"You think highly of yourself, don't you? You're predictable." Forrest sat back and pulled a palm tablet from her jacket. After a few decided taps, she settled it on the table. A hologram flickered to life, showing a shot from what must have been a security feed.

Tagged this morning. Juniper went numb. It was the vampire's apartment. Juniper was pressed into the futon bed, almost totally hidden by the vampire. No. Any feed near the place had been disabled. He couldn't have had anything in his pad—Juniper had checked. Juniper panicked, trying to think, and then they noticed it was a video primed to play.

Juniper jerked forward and slammed the tablet face down. Laurel didn't need to see that. Hell, Juniper didn't need a repeat of the morning from an outside perspective. Forrest's smile widened.

"There was... a pattern to you on the Lunar Colony," she explained. "Sometimes, you'd show up on feeds when a vampire came through. Not enough for us to know where you were hiding, mind you, and the vampires there were merely visitors." She shrugged and took the tablet back. The screen had shut off, but she turned it back on and flipped to something else. "All we had to do was watch the message boards past Jupiter and bingo, you arrived and immediately sold yourself. What a misuse of your body." Forrest lifted her gaze and eyed Juniper for a reaction. "We paid him a visit, but so sad, you were already gone."

"You killed him," Juniper whispered.

Forrest's predatory grin returned. "Selling restricted items is against the law. He knew that."

And because he was a vampire, he wasn't legally a person, and thus, killing him wasn't a crime. Juniper swallowed past the lump in their throat. The guy was an asshole, but he deserved better than that.

"You were so confident, but all your software is out of date." Forrest tapped her own head. "Makes you stand out. Perhaps you could have prevented this if you'd stayed with your handlers." Forrest turned the tablet back to them and it began displaying images of Juniper and Laurel from the Lunar Colony.

Juniper felt like the ground had swallowed them up. One image was after a hookup—Juniper had actually been smiling—another was when they were talking to Slim in his dock as he worked. And then came the ones with Laurel as she snagged supplies for their escape.

All this time. The feds had known.

The last image settled on Juniper and Slim again. They were hugging. It was the night before the heist. Juniper's throat tightened. That was how they'd known to tap his network for the information at all. That was how they'd known to watch the dealership. It was pure luck the feds had underestimated Juniper, which let them escape this far. But now?

Their lungs squeezed as they tried to keep it together.

"You ruined his life, you know," Forrest whispered.

Laurel squeezed their knee underneath the table, but Juniper was beyond comforting. Forrest's grin grew more depraved, finally getting the reaction she wanted.

"Letting a fugitive with stolen tech hide under his watch? Well, we couldn't leave that be, not when you disappeared. All it took was a twist." She mimed the motion with her free hand and Juniper felt sick. Forced memory dump. "And poof, all the memories of you simply spilled out. Rather indecent, don't you think? Then again, I guess that's what you do." Juniper clenched their fingers into fists under the table. "We retooled him. All of who he was is gone because of you."

No. They couldn't shift the blame to Juniper. It was the Federation's choice. They hadn't needed to touch Slim at all. Juniper breathed out, slow and steady to calm their racing heart, and looked Forrest in the eye. "Eat shit and die," they said.

Forrest laughed and let the tablet grow dark. "Language."

It'd been their dream to go back for Slim once they'd gotten rid of their cybernetics, but now it would never happen. Juniper wanted to rage, cry, pull out Forrest's brain and smash it, but they pushed aside their feelings. They had to stay focused on the present.

"You've got cybernetics too," Juniper tried. "You think what happened to Slim won't happen to you? It's only a matter of time before you're expendable."

"Don't be so dramatic." Forrest's eyes twinkled. "We keep track of investments and nullify aberrations and, oh, you have so many." She faced Laurel, smiling again. "Even you are an investment."

Laurel stiffened and shook her head.

"Why, they called your sister off her tour to help find you. Help keep your parents afloat with all the money they owe us," Forrest said slowly. "All her fans are so sad, you know. Practically the entire system is." There were tears in Laurel's eyes behind her glasses. Juniper felt for her hand under the table and squeezed it. "All you did for her—your poor parents—was waste their time."

She wanted a response, that was clear, but Laurel remained silent and resumed staring intently at the table.

Forrest pouted. "Hm." She rolled her eyes. "I was told you were sparky. Guess that's not true. A speck of space trash simply ruining their lives by existing."

"Shut up," Laurel finally snapped, looking up to glare at her. "It's not my fault. It's yours for expecting an idol to even know where I am when she discarded me years ago. I'm not her property. I'm the Federation's and you guys were the one that lost me."

Juniper would have hugged Laurel for the outburst if they weren't in danger. They bit back a smile instead.

"I have orders to bring you both to your respective parties." Forrest's tone suddenly turned professional. "However, I have been tasked with learning a few things beforehand." She held up her finger. "Who was the blood for? Where is it?"

"No one," Juniper said. "We made a wrong turn."

"You emptied the whole vault. You're clearly working with someone." She tapped the tablet and swiped through a few screens until she found what she searched for. Grainy, hard to make out anything except for Juniper and Laurel holding up their hands in the derelict fed ship.

Juniper tensed. Of course, the enforcers had

gotten good shots of them. Even though that ship was gone—the enforcer bodies and tech with it—their visors must have been sending video feeds to an external source.

"We believe you have obtained sensitive information," Forrest continued as the images flipped through what transpired before Cedar came to their rescue. Juniper couldn't help but wince watching themself get roughed up. Forrest stopped cycling images right before the enforcer met his end. A blurry picture of Cedar. A force in the dark. "I want to know where he is and where it is."

"Yeah?" Juniper replied, voice uneven. "What do we get in return?" Laurel shot them a look, but Juniper ignored it and felt for the laser knife in their sleeve.

Forrest smiled, raising her eyebrows. "I can put in a good word for the two of you," she said. "No punishment; just back to where you belong as though you never left."

Not good enough to even pretend to consider it; the lie was too obvious. "Not a fucking chance," Juniper said. Forrest's face soured, a deep scowl etching deep lines into her face. "We're here alone. You can fuck off."

The room went heavy with silence. The two enforcers glanced at Forrest, as though asking if she was going to sit and take that kind of shit. Juniper laughed.

"I know what this is: you're gunning for some fucking promotion!" Juniper knocked Laurel with their elbow. She tried to laugh, but it was forced at best. "And all you have are two fucking runaways. It doesn't matter what we say." Juniper leaned forward, planting their feet on the floor in preparation to spring around the table. "You'll take us back. Scramble me until I can't even say my own name and give her back to the school's truancy officers to do the same." The knife's handle fell into their hand and they flipped it around. "But you won't take me alive."

The blade ignited and every single one of their systems switched to combat mode. The world slowed around them, letting their systems notice every minute detail for the oncoming fight, and they flung themself over the table, knife raised.

Forrest's expression remained neutral as she held up her hand. There was a small fob in it. She pressed the button before the knife came down.

The world shuttered black and Juniper didn't even feel themself hit the floor.

15
LAUREL

JUNIPER COLLAPSED AT FORREST'S FEET, unnaturally still. The knife bounced under the table. All Laurel could do was watch.

Juniper couldn't be dead... but Laurel couldn't tell if they breathed. Shaking, she slipped off the chair and dropped her head to their chest to check. No one stopped her.

"Juniper?" Tears filled Laurel's eyes. "Junie, please." There was the faint rise and fall of their chest.

Not dead.

Laurel glared up at Forrest. The woman smiled in return as she backed down and folded one leg over the other.

"Relax. They're alive," Forrest said slowly as if Laurel hadn't figured it out. She idly examined the fob. "At least, until their autonomous systems give out." Laurel gasped. "Usually happens within a few hours of being off." Forrest reached her foot lazily forward and toed Juniper's arm. Slack like the rest of their body. "Although, given how little upkeep they've done, maybe less."

She said it all with that smug smile.

"You're a monster," Laurel forced out through clenched teeth.

The smile still stayed. "I do my job very well, Miss Langley." Forrest leaned forward. "Here's how this will go: Juniper will come back with me, and once we have them in restraints, I'll use the reactivator I keep on my ship. No one has to die. And then you?" She inclined their head. "You'll go back to your handlers."

Laurel breathed in. "Don't you care what happens to us? We're dead if we go back."

"Why would I? You're nothing." Forrest shrugged. "I'm personally looking forward to Lola's new single she'll spin about a ghost sister." She leaned back, crossing her legs once more. "I bet they'll hollow you out to prevent another stunt."

Laurel glared at Forrest.

"It starts with the brain," Forrest continued. "Don't need that personality you've developed or all the lies you've learned. Then, once that's all been scrubbed away, they'll fashion you into what you should have been."

No shit, as if that wasn't the reason Laurel had run in the first place. She'd always known when she inevitably stepped out of line, she'd be marked as a danger to society. It was the perfect excuse for the feds to make her into someone like Forrest's underlings; a perfect worker and citizen with no empathy and no personality of her own. The feds always assured everyone this process was done to protect society at large.

It never was. Simply a way to keep people in line.

Forrest glanced at the enforcer behind her. "Pack it up. We've wasted enough time chasing nothing."

Laurel watched the enforcer move, searching for

something in his stoic expression. Nothing. He didn't care. *Think*, Laurel stressed to herself and her gaze trailed under the table. There. Juniper's laser knife.

They wouldn't take either of them alive.

Even her lightning reflexes weren't enough; she'd hardly touched it before Forrest pushed a blaster into her face. She clenched her teeth, freezing, and stared down the barrel at Forrest's smile.

"Leave it," Forrest said.

Laurel pressed her arm to her chest. The ice needle sat right there beneath her sweater. She immediately schooled her expression. One use. She eyed the enforcer, her breaths quickening. Just had to get it out and stab.

As the enforcer bent to collect Juniper and Laurel slowly moved her fingers to the chain, the lights powered off. Everyone in the room froze, too stunned to move. Forrest's eyes, still shining bright in the darkness, flicked toward the dark terminals. A generator kicked to life below them and the screens powered back on. Laurel half-expected the Answer to appear, but each screen only showed static.

In the dim light of the monitors, Laurel peered past the blaster to watch Forrest nod at the enforcer standing over Juniper. He left and slipped into the hallway.

Emergency lights came on next, flipping out of the wall as a pale orange, and the second enforcer attempted to reboot the feeds. The telltale chime of comms connecting echoed from Forrest's ear and she pressed her hand to it.

"Report," she said, her voice clipped.

"Well," came the other enforcer's unsure voice loud and clear, "someone pulled the power cables of the mall completely free."

Laurel's heart skipped.

"What?" Forrest shot a wild glance at Laurel, who stayed perfectly still. "*How?*"

"I'm not a tech. I don't—hey!" He shouted it so suddenly, Laurel flinched. "Hold it—" He made a sound halfway between a shout and a scream. A flurry of blaster shots echoed until there was a gurgle. Then all sound dropped to dead silence.

No one moved. Forrest took in a steady breath, eyes wide, and looked at the remaining officer who stared back in disbelief.

"Go," she snapped and he hurried out.

She kept her blaster trained on Laurel while she switched the channel on her comms with her other hand. Laurel stayed put, trying not to shake. Forrest didn't get a chance to speak into the comms again before one of the feed screens cleared. Forrest stood to look and Laurel craned her neck to see over the table.

The feed showed a wall. Odd... Had it before? The image was grainy, fading in and out, but one thing soon became clear: the wall was spray painted with red. *Not paint*, Laurel realized, her jaw dropping open. Blood.

It simply read: I'm coming.

A warning. A promise. Not at all subtle.

"Secure the docks!" Forrest shouted into the comms, but given how her face twisted, no one had answered. "Hello?" Her voice cracked. "Report! Is anyone there? Status report, now!"

Silence.

Laurel listened to her heartbeat in her ears. One, two, three—then blaster shots echoed down the hall, followed by screaming. Laurel jumped. Forrest spun to the door, eyes wide, and there was a decided thud.

Silence. Laurel gathered Juniper close, pulse pounding in her ears, and Forrest darted for the side of the door. It barely slid open before Forrest unleashed a spray of her own blaster fire. The shots thudded against a body and that was when Forrest made her first mistake.

She paused.

The body was flung aside, dead—*oh shit*, Laurel thought, *definitely dead*—and Cedar pounced. Forrest pivoted to one side, avoiding his onslaught, but before she'd aimed again, he had her hand shoved upwards. The blaster fire slammed across the ceiling and destroyed the fluorescent light above.

Cedar's other hand seized Forrest's throat. Laurel tore her gaze away and jerked herself under the table with Juniper. There was a dying gasp. Laurel buried her face against Juniper, trying to block out the sound. The blaster slipped and hit the floor. A distinct sound of metal on tile. Then a heavy body slumped to the floor after it.

Laurel squeezed herself tighter, refusing to look, and found tears on her cheeks. The shaking didn't stop even when she heard Cedar kneel down. Pupils dilated. Lips dripping with blood. Hands stained completely. Like a horror movie made real.

"Hey," he said, surprisingly soft and at odds with everything. "Are you okay?"

No. Yes. Not after that. Not after leaving them, but Laurel's head betrayed all her interior thoughts and nodded. The squeak in her throat was the only affirmation he was going to get.

It was good enough, he nodded too, relieved. As she pulled Juniper out from under the table, Cedar scooped up the blaster and swung the clothing bag over his shoulder. Laurel tried to lift Juniper with shaking arms, but they were too heavy. She struggled even getting one of Juniper's arms around her shoulder and immediately fell back to her knees. More tears slid down her cheeks.

Cedar bent in front of her again, worried. "What's wrong?" he asked.

"Juniper's out," Laurel cried and Cedar jerked to look them over as though he'd just realized Juniper wasn't moving. "They-They won't wake up!"

Cedar pulled Juniper over to his lap and checked their pulse with bloodied fingers. It left a stain when he took his hand away. "Shit." He wiped his hands on his pants. "I didn't think they'd turn them off."

"S-She had a fob." Laurel started to glance over at Forrest, but Cedar stopped her. "B-But she s-said the reactivator was on her ship."

Not that getting to her ship was within the realm of possibility. Thinking so relit the panic inside Laurel. She had no idea how to wake Juniper up.

Cedar swore again and gently felt the space behind Juniper's ears and then all the way to the underside of their chin and then neck. Juniper didn't react. All Laurel could do was stare, confused.

"They should have a reactivation switch on their body," Cedar explained. "Did Juniper ever tell you where it was?"

"I didn't even know they could be turned off."

As Cedar went to check a few more spots—the wrists and arms—sirens ripped across the station outside. Once more, he swore.

"Thought we had more time," he growled. "We need to get back to our ship. Can you stand?"

Laurel's legs were jelly, but she managed. As soon as she was up, Cedar handed her the bag and flicked the comms on in his ear.

"Clary, I got them." He left Juniper curled up and

pulled a palm-sized black orb out of his coat. "Yeah, I know where to put it. You in orbit? Good." He pressed the center of the device and it made a whirring noise, like it was priming for activation.

"What is that?" Laurel breathed.

Cedar didn't answer and put it on the middle terminal. It took no time at all infecting them; the screens turned red with a smug pixelated cat face dead-center. Cedar bent down and threw Juniper over his shoulder.

"Keep up," he told Laurel and she nodded quickly.

Cedar left the room with quick strides. Laurel meant to follow right away, but against better judgment, she lingered. Forrest had been reduced to a bloody mess. Eyes were dim. Blood gushed fast down her neck, staining her once pristine white uniform an ugly shade of red. Her expression was an emptiness Laurel never wanted to see again.

Then her eyes flickered. Her whole body shuddered, throwing her head to one side while her suddenly bright eyes tracked Laurel. There was a sound from her throat, but no voice. All that came out was a gurgling that invited more blood to dribble down her chin.

Panic kicked through Laurel and she ran after Cedar.

Another enforcer lay on the ground outside, throat ripped out. Not as much blood as there had been from Forrest, but Cedar's eyes were dilated. He'd drank them dry.

Focus! Laurel told herself and pumped her legs to catch up.

"Cedar!" she shouted and he slid to a stop, spinning to face her. She quickly hid behind him. "She moved!"

"Moved?"

There was a scraping noise. Cedar tensed, eyes wide, and Laurel peered around him. Forrest lurched from the room, head twitching violently and one leg dragging behind her. Only when her eyes locked onto Cedar did the twitching stop. She tried speaking again, only half her jaw moving, but nothing came out but a gurgling, drowning sound. Blood splattered on the floor, dripping down from her chin.

"No way," Cedar breathed. "She's fucking dead."

Forrest sprang forward, proving otherwise, and Laurel screamed. It was cut short when Juniper's deadweight hit her. As she scrambled to hold her friend up, Cedar met Forrest head on. He caught Forrest by the neck but jumped away when she shot a fist at his chin. She grabbed his receding arm, digging in her nails and drawing blood, but he gripped her arm in return and swung her into the wall.

The force of the swing made the wall cave in and Cedar let go. Forrest slumped against the pile of rubble left behind, still once more.

Cedar didn't linger. He darted back to Laurel, threw Juniper over his shoulder, and ran. Laurel kept up this time and forced herself not to look back.

But then she heard the scraping sound again and couldn't resist. She peered over her shoulder. With jerking movements, Forrest had picked herself up and set her haunting golden eyes on them in the dark.

The scraping of Forrest dragging herself forward followed them as they ran out into the loading bay. The androids were all gone, thankfully, and Cedar ran for the hovercraft on its side against the ramp. He righted it with one arm and propped Juniper against the side railing.

"Where'd you get this?" Laurel asked as he pulled

her atop.

"Mall enforcers are easy to pick off." Cedar gritted his teeth suddenly and glanced back. Forrest had caught up. She was still twitching, eyes wide and bright. Cedar ripped a blaster out of his coat and Laurel ducked, covering her head. Shots rang out.

Forrest clattered to the ground, a hole in her head and a few more in her chest. Electricity sparked across her skin, making her twitch, but she didn't get up.

Cedar ignited the hovercraft's engine. "Hold on," he said. Laurel wrapped one arm around Juniper's chest and wrapped the other around Cedar's leg. Cedar floored the pedal and the hovercraft shot forward.

She bit back a shout at the sudden speed and huddled over Juniper to keep them both still. As air whipped past them and made her eyes water, she looked back at where they'd left Forrest. She gasped. Forrest stood staring at them once more, her glowing eyes receding into the darkness.

But she couldn't follow this time. She fell back to her knees and stayed there.

"Laurel," Cedar said, his voice almost too quiet to hear over the sirens around them. "I am sorry I was late."

Laurel stared at his back for a moment, tears hot in her eyes. "You didn't leave us," she said. She'd meant to thank him, but those words came out instead, tinged with the betrayal she'd felt when he'd disappeared.

Cedar's jaw tensed. "I don't leave my crew behind. I meant to be back before they got you down in there. I'm sorry. It won't happen again."

Laurel smiled, nodding. "Thank you."

A hum of engines ripped through the air, so

sudden it made Laurel jump, and enforcers' voices followed it up, shouting after them. Laurel shot her attention to the casino lights farther down. Hovercrafts gleamed bright against the darkened horizon as enforcers took chase after them.

"They're trailing us!" Laurel shouted over the sound of the wind.

"I see that!" Cedar shouted back. He deftly swung the hovercraft between two establishments, and they flung out at the other side where alleys snaked between buildings. Hovercrafts were in quick pursuit, but Cedar used Forrest's blaster to shoot at any closing in. Some of the shots hit their mark, careening their pursuer into the walls. There were still too many for comfort. Before Laurel could count and take the blaster to shoot at them so Cedar could focus (how hard could it be?), Cedar sharply turned them out of the alley. She scrambled to hold onto his leg again.

"Hey!" He glanced back. "Reach into my coat. There's a detonator."

Laurel reached up and fished her hand in. There was a small, black device in the interior pocket. The button was beneath a small glass top and she flicked it open. "Wait, what is this?"

"EMP."

Laurel almost dropped the detonator. "But—"

"Juniper'll be fine. This kind of EMP doesn't touch the frequencies cybernetics operate at. Aster made sure of that when he built it," Cedar said before Laurel could voice the immediate thought. He pressed his comms on. "Clary, we're hitting it. Going dark." He didn't wait for her affirmation before turning it off. "Light it up, Laurel."

She pushed the button as hard as she could. It was a tense moment before the shudder of the EMP going off oscillated through the station. Lights died all around them in waves expanding outward from the mall. When the casinos transformed into dark silhouettes against the stars, all fell quiet. The only thing still lit up were the docks.

The hovercraft made a dying noise of its own as its lights flickered off. Laurel hardly had time to scream before Cedar had her under one arm, Juniper over his shoulder, and the craft hit the ground. It flipped, throwing the three of them forward onto the concrete. Thankfully, Cedar cushioned the fall. Laurel felt for her glasses. Still on her face.

Cedar was up in seconds, scooping Laurel under one arm again with Juniper still over his other shoulder, and he sprinted down the dock lane. Not the one they'd used before while the *Gladiolus* was docked, but one for cruisers. Awaiting them was the yellow grappler. The top slid back as they approached and Cedar tossed Juniper into the back, yanked Laurel in with him, and threw himself over her.

Blaster shots pinged off the surface and enforcers shouted at them.

Cedar slammed his hand on the console and the top snapped shut above them. The core systems flared bright, lighting everything up in gold, and Laurel peeked out from beneath Cedar's chest. Enforcers were still trying to shoot them, but none of the shots penetrated the hull.

"They were closer than I thought." Cedar righted himself and pushed his feet into the thruster pedals. "Hold on!"

The ship's engine roared and Cedar gunned it toward the mall structures. Laurel screamed, scrambling to stop him, but he shrugged her off as he shoved his hands into the grappler controls. The arms unlatched from the bottom with a swing, throwing a few enforcers wide and sending the others scrambling out of the way. Cedar forced the grappler hands downward and used them as leverage to propel the ship upward. They spun in the air, thrusters leaving scorch marks along the floor and walls, and the rest of the enforcers scattered for cover. Without anyone else to stop them, their ship soared into the air.

Laurel's jaw hung open; she had to get Cedar to teach her how to do that.

Cedar spun them around toward a public airlock and pushed the engine harder. The airlock doors were stuttering, attempting to close, and Cedar swore. "Lily!" he shouted into the ship's comms. "Keep that fucker open!"

The airlock twitched and froze, half-open, and Cedar turned them sideways. They shot through and it snapped shut not a second later. A dozen hail requests pinged on the cruiser's console, but Cedar swiped them all away as they flew into the stars.

Laurel forced herself to breathe evenly and pivoted to check on Juniper. Still out. She reached back and shook their shoulder. No response still. She pressed her hand against Juniper's bare cheek, hoping to get their cybernetics to react, but nothing. Juniper had grown so cold.

"They doing okay?" Cedar asked.

Thick tears slipped down Laurel's cheeks. "Still off." She tried to wipe them, but more came now that she was out of danger. "What even was that? How can they be fine shutting someone off like that?"

"It's called a kill switch. It's how the feds keep them in line. Already do it all the time to androids. This isn't much of a step up." Cedar turned the ship and swept his gaze over the dark expanse around them. They moved forward again and Cedar reached over, gently patting Laurel's head. He might have been aiming for her shoulder, but Laurel didn't mind; it was comforting.

"Don't worry. We'll get them up."

Everything past the mall's docks was still dark. Any auxiliary power in the station must have gone right to life support. Laurel looked out the front of the grappler. The *Gladiolus* wasn't there. Before she could ask where it was, their ship landed on something solid. The space around them wavered like they'd popped through a bubble and there it was.

Laurel's jaw dropped. "You have stealth?!"

Cedar snorted. "Clary said the same damn thing!" He let go of the controls as Lily pulled the ship in through the lift doors. "Tremaine was wasting my ship's potential."

The ship lowered them into the hangar and Cedar connected the ship's comms to Clary. "Let Lily handle finding a hiding spot, you send out drones as a distraction."

"Got it!" Clary answered.

Once the grappler settled beside the *Maple*, Cedar popped the top and reached over to lift Juniper. Laurel expected Cedar to lay Juniper down on the hangar floor, but he was headed for the stairs. "Where are we going?" she asked.

"Somewhere they know. It'll be disorienting otherwise. Aster always said people like him should wake up somewhere safe. Their room should be fine."

His voice shook as he spoke and Laurel's stomach churned. He was worried. She didn't like it. What if Juniper didn't have an activation switch like Aster had? Juniper was so many years after Aster, it was a possibility. She tried to bury the worry deep as she followed Cedar to Juniper's room.

There was an aroma diffuser activated inside—Laurel hadn't noticed it earlier—and it smelled like juniper trees. Laurel took a deep breath, letting the scent calm her nerves, and Cedar settled Juniper on the bed.

Cedar wiped his hands on his coat, hesitating, and looked at Laurel. "A lot of times, the switches are around where they opened the skin to put in the cybernetics. Check the scars first. Just... make sure to tell Juniper I'm sorry."

Laurel was about to ask why but Cedar's hands were already searching for the button everywhere. Given how much Juniper did not like being touched, the apology made sense. She lingered a moment before she went searching too. It was almost fruitless; most of Juniper's scars were too faint and smooth to see now.

"Aster's was behind his ears," Cedar started speaking, nerves leaking through his voice. Laurel immediately rechecked them, but nothing there. "It was always easy. A lot of them have it near their head-jacks, but of course they'd change that. Come on." He was speaking faster as he gently pressed in on Juniper's ribs. "Please, just wake up."

He suddenly stopped, one hand on Juniper's hip. He pressed again and Laurel helped him roll the shirt out of the way. There was a small depression on their hip bone, right where two faint scars met, and Laurel noticed it on the other side as well.

"There's two," she said.

Cedar pressed his thumbs into the depressions and held them down.

There was a click and Juniper's entire body jolted. Cedar quickly released them as their eyes snapped open, bright and wide, and a gasp escaped from their lips. Multiple gasps, like they were trying to swallow air. They jolted again, violently, hands at their throat. They cried out and shot upright.

Alive. They were alive.

Juniper's gaze jerked to Cedar and their arms shot out to shove him. He immediately stepped back, hands up, and as Laurel attempted to run interference, barely gathering her words to say that it was okay, Juniper shoved her too.

Laurel was not as steady on her feet. The full force of Juniper's arms pushed into her and she hit the floor hard.

"Don't!" Juniper shouted, pulling their knees close and clutching their head. "Don't touch me!"

Cedar helped Laurel back to her feet and Laurel had to stop herself from reaching out again on reflex. Juniper was shivering, rapid breaths wheezing in and out of their throat, and their eyes darted around the room as though trying to figure out where they were. Finally, the trembling slowed and tears slipped out of their eyes. Laurel reached out slower this time, but Juniper flinched away.

"Please." Juniper buried their head in their arms. "J-Just don't touch me."

It hurt and though Laurel found herself stunned, she quickly shook it off and went for Juniper's bag. If she couldn't hug Juniper, she knew something that could. She found it safely wrapped in a sweater. A plush rabbit Laurel had made for them from the scraps of her school uniform. A little ragdoll with uneven stitching and patch-work ears, but Juniper had actually slept with it tucked into their arms many nights because they'd never had stuffed animals before.

She held it out to them. "You're safe."

Juniper stared at the rabbit, wide eyed, and more tears streaked down their face. They took it and buried their face into it, nodding.

Cedar lingered for another moment before he squeezed Laurel's shoulder. "I promise you guys are safe here," he said. "Laurie, watch them, okay? I need to talk to Clary."

He left without waiting for a response.

Laurel watched Juniper as asked. She wanted so badly to pull them into a hug, tell them it'd be okay, but she refrained. No good would come of it, not with the way Juniper had flinched. They'd never done that before when it came to Laurel, even when they'd first met. Something was wrong and a hug wouldn't fix it.

Gently, Laurel sat at the edge of the bed. "Junie?" she whispered.

Juniper dragged in a shaking breath and shook their head. "It-It was so-so cold," they whispered. "I-I... Everything was gone. Everything. At once."

"But you're back," Laurel said. "We got you. It'll be okay."

All Juniper did was nod. Their shoulders shuddered with silent sobs and they curled themself tighter around the stuffed rabbit. Laurel could only watch, wishing she could do more.

SESSION 4

VOICES

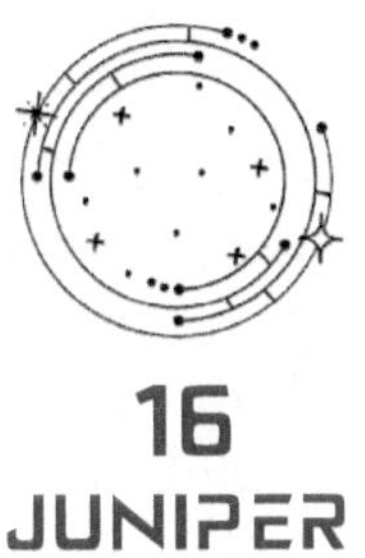

16
JUNIPER

SLEEP. NEVER AGAIN. JUNIPER COULDN'T handle it. The dark. The sound of silence growing between each beat of their heart. The total isolation.

The first night after the mall, they'd desperately tried—even swallowed a damned gummy down—but they'd woken up panicking. It'd only been a half hour, but their self-preservation systems were louder than ever.

No more. Never again. Not after being *off*. How quickly everything had been *gone* had been absolute. Something they couldn't explain without breaking down. Nothing distracted them from the stark emptiness lingering still, and even when they tried to find something, their hands trembled with the reminder: their body was fallible.

And of course, every single one of their systems was on high alert for real and imagined threats now. One process tracked everyone's location, bio-signs, and their voices. At some point, Laurel had said their name, but Juniper's bio-scanner was more interested in how her heart rate jumped when she did so. Then their cortex computer weaved all the information together and gave Juniper a half story about how everyone hated them for letting their sudden nap bother them so deeply. That everyone was just like the scientists in charge of their care and believed their inability to control the cybernetics was *their* fault.

Juniper knew none of that was true, but it was the patchwork story spun to keep them in their room and safe. Too paranoid to sleep. Too paranoid to leave.

What made it all worse though, was that Juniper couldn't find the words to tell Laurel what they were going through. They didn't want to scare her about how everything *really* felt. Juniper had already known someone could turn them off and they'd be powerless to stop it, but they hadn't expected their biggest weakness laid bare so soon. They'd manage to bury their vulnerability deep beneath grand adventures and escape, but now, fear crawled to the surface. Reminding Juniper that people like them never lived long outside fed custody.

Leaving their room beyond bathroom trips late at night wasn't going to happen, so they tried distracting themself with pieces of normalcy. Clary had left the bag of clothes at their door, saying she'd already sorted it for them, so Juniper dressed up in what they'd lifted. They were right: they looked *hot* in the lacey delicates, especially when they added stockings held up by garter belts. Except they had no one to show off to. Took the fun right out of trying on clothes, and Juniper left everything else in the bag.

Days blended together after that. Cedar tried reaching out to them in half-spoken words on the other side of the door, but all it reminded Juniper of was the ghost of his hands waking them up. Reminded them how he'd *left* them with Forrest. Even if he'd planned all along to come back, Juniper hadn't known that at the time. Abandonment wasn't so easily scrubbed away. Juniper eventually told him to eat shit and fuck off and that was the end of him trying to get them out of their room.

Clary, meanwhile, left food every so often and Juniper only took it when they had the stomach for it. Nanomachines kept their body from total starvation, thankfully. Juniper once knew the nuances, but didn't care to dredge up the how. Despite how helpful it was, however, it reminded Juniper how not normal they were. How the very same thing made it easy to be turned off at some asshole's whim. That alone made the food taste like ash in their mouth.

Laurel tried to get through to them the longest, spending hours outside Juniper's door talking about something she'd found while exploring the ship, a new thing Cedar had told her about space pirates, or even a silly sci-fi story from decades ago they'd narrated aloud for one another back on the satellite. Except the satellite was gone, and so too was any comfort Juniper had once had with the stories.

A few days of stories and Juniper couldn't do it anymore. It was simply a reminder of the life they'd sent crashing into the moon. The life they wanted back so everything felt normal again.

"We're back to the Space Pirate Rhys Adventures," Laurel said as she set up today. She sat against the door like always and Juniper pressed their hands to their eyes. "It's your favorite, remember? Very steamy! I think he hooks up with the cool blue space guy in this one." Though Laurel never quite paid attention to that part of the story, it was nice she remembered.

Except Juniper couldn't handle it today.

"Laurel?" they said and she stopped narrating the

opening paragraph. Their bio-scanner picked up her heightened pulse. "Leave me alone, okay?"

The pause was deafening. Juniper knew immediately they should have phrased it differently, but didn't bother trying again.

"Okay," Laurel whispered it so quietly, Juniper wouldn't have heard it if they hadn't been listening so intently.

And it made their heart crack. Made them want to throw open the door to apologize as Laurel walked away, but they let her go. It was easier this way. Locking walls between them because Juniper didn't want Laurel to know how scared they were. Didn't want to add another lie to the pile. Laurel must have hated them for how many they'd already said. From lying to her how safe she was on the satellite with them (she hadn't been), to now lying by omission about how easy it was to simply turn them off and leave them to die.

At least now Laurel had Clary, Cedar, and Lily. She didn't need Juniper anymore.

What they *needed* more than anything in the system right now was one more night with Slim. Physically chasing away the pain and fear would make it right again. Except thinking so simply reminded them it'd never happen again. All because of them.

Juniper could have sneaked out and found someone else willing to help them forget everything on whatever stations the ship docked at for refuels, but fear kept them in their room. At least this way, some sorry sap wouldn't be killed for their indiscretion.

And so, the days continued on, blurring together, and the only solace Juniper eventually found was watching the news and monitoring the crew.

News was entertaining for a time. The mall was

still on high alert after Cedar's stunt; he hadn't been subtle and the heist was all over the airwaves as feds ran damage control. People were angry because the fed's sole promise—protection—was a lie if an entire station's system could go down that quickly from one rogue EMP, letting its occupants asphyxiate if repairs weren't fast enough or if the feds simply didn't care to fix it in time. It'd happened before on older colonies. It could happen again.

What sucked the joy out of listening, however, was the very good headshots of Juniper and Laurel the feds circulated. Probably courtesy of whatever tech they'd recovered off Forrest.

Gossip rags latched onto Laurel immediately. There were already rumors Lola had a hidden sister, and even with glasses, freckles, the shit bleach dye job Juniper had done, Laurel was a dead ringer for her sister. Those rumors ignited in full force as trash TV filled with pseudo-experts talking about how many facial features Laurel and Lola shared. Of course, none of the reports dug deep to expose *why* Laurel had been so hidden. No one actually cared about Laurel. Only how she was connected to Lola. It was all surface deep to find the real reason Lola was going on hiatus.

It must have bothered Laurel a lot—just being associated with her sister again—and Juniper couldn't even be there for her to help her ignore the noise. Some friend they were.

Juniper's face was a blip at most in comparison. Just a dangerous individual the feds wanted apprehended safely. No mention of cybernetics. Couldn't admit to losing one of their prized possessions, after all. The Answer must have *loved* that. Now the whole system was looking out for them. He had a little competition.

When not watching the news and hoping it moved on from Laurel and Juniper (Cedar said he'd plot a course to Pluto once it died down enough, but, at this rate, it felt like that would never happen), Juniper continued keeping watch on the crew. Lily had let them piggyback into her visual systems so they could be 'with' their friends, in a way. Touching, although at the same time, it made Juniper feel lonelier. Life moved on without them there, but it wasn't like they'd given anyone a choice.

Laurel had sulked for a little bit, but with some help from Clary, she'd made herself part of the crew. Juniper enjoyed watching her through the cameras as she trailed after Clary like the eager trainee she was. Cedar, meanwhile, kept to himself. Pacing. Talking to no one, or maybe to Aster's head. Lily had no cameras in anyone's room, so all Juniper had to go on was listening to the hallway outside his room.

Some days—or perhaps it was weeks? Juniper had stopped keeping count of how long—into their self-imposed isolation, Juniper began hearing *another* voice.

At first, Juniper thought it was the Answer. Except his voice was all-encompassing, not this shy drift through Juniper's thoughts. It could have been a hallucination born from lack of meaningful sleep, but Juniper's nanomachines kept those away. Maybe it was simply Juniper's imagination begging for the companionship they were avoiding.

They ignored it, whatever it was, but it persisted. It was harder to detect when everyone was awake, but at night, the meaningless whispers became words and sentences, each one soft and warm.

Except, it didn't sound like it was actively trying to talk to them. Rather, it just wanted to be heard.

One night, when everyone was asleep and nestled in their rooms, Juniper finally had enough. Lily was curled up on their lap, purring away, but the voice was too tempting to ignore. They moved Lily to the bed and she watched Juniper with bright, yellow eyes as they stood.

"I'm exploring," Juniper said carefully. "Don't make a big deal out of this, okay, Lily?"

"Affirmative," came Lily's voice from the cat's speakers. Juniper scratched her behind the ears, earning a soft chirp. "I am glad you appear to be in better spirits. Shall I keep my familiar in here?"

"Sure. I'll be right back."

Juniper slipped out, silent, and went looking in the dark. The voice was clearer tonight. Soft hushed tones, like someone was speaking to their sleeping loved one.

They followed the voice until they saw where it was leading them. Cedar's room. The voice was so clear outside his door. Juniper held their breath, the realization of what it could be keeping them still.

"*Do you hear me, love?*" the voice whispered, muffled words becoming clear this close. "*It's okay if you don't. Maybe I'm not here.*" The voice chuckled sadly. "*Maybe I'm the last memory holding on. I love you. Please don't forget.*"

The words sent goosebumps all along Juniper's skin. It *had* to be Aster—what else could it be? Juniper chewed on their lip and headed back to their room.

It wasn't like they could bust in there now and take Aster's head to examine it. Asking permission was out of the question, too; Juniper had no reason to believe Cedar would let them do what they were thinking. It was invasive and might rip open the hurt all over again.

Tomorrow morning, they'd strike.

Juniper bided their time in their room, imagining scenarios of what Cedar would do if he'd caught them and what they'd say. It helped keep back the dread, although Cedar was a kind of dread of his own. Sometimes the imagined scenarios didn't end well.

Morning finally came and Juniper tracked everyone's movements through Lily's cameras. Laurel was up first, like always, and after a shower and a playful knock on Juniper's door to let them know she was done, she sped off to the kitchen. Sprig rolled in shortly thereafter, a heated breakfast burrito on its back. Juniper took it for sustenance. Food tasted good today, at least.

Clary was up next and joined Laurel in the kitchen after washing up. Cedar was the last, once more lingering outside Juniper's door, but he didn't try to talk this time and simply moved on.

It wasn't long before the three of them moved to the hangar as a unit. Odd. Maybe they were going to teach Laurel how to use the grappler? The thought dashed away when Clary began pulling out what looked like gym mats. *Oh.* Juniper smiled. They were going to teach Laurel how to defend herself. There was more to it than a kick to the balls.

It was tempting to put the plan aside to watch, but Juniper had to stay focused.

"Hey, Lily?" Juniper waited. "I'm heading out. Don't make a big deal about this." They fidgeted when no response came and stood. "I'm going to see Aster."

They slipped out of their room and the cat was waiting for them, her tail swishing back and forth.

"You can supervise me if you want," Juniper hurriedly added. "I won't hurt him."

Lily watched them unblinkingly. Juniper took

that as a yes.

When Juniper stepped into Cedar's room, the rush of cedarwood pushed past them with a faint hint of rosemary. That must have been an Aster thing. Less and less as the days went by with the door opening and closing. Juniper breathed in deep, trying to calm their suddenly racing heart, and forged further inside.

Years upon years lived inside, a never-aging vampire keeping pieces of the time he'd lived. Cedar had decked out the room in shades of reds and purples, making it darker than it really was. On-brand for him, Juniper supposed. Trinkets and old gadgets galore covered the shelves and posters took up the blank wall. Vistas, nebulas, maybe even a place on Earth. Some had been taped over, time and time again, covering a bygone youth. The large bed took up the center, its blankets and pillows left askew, and there were photos taped above the headboard. Old ones of Cedar, of Aster, of them together, pictures of entire crews—even one where everyone was scribbled out but him and Aster—and then a few salacious ones of Aster. Juniper's cheeks flushed and they made themself focus on what they came for.

The container was on the nightstand. Head as ghastly as ever. It was silent, too, no humming and no hushed whispers.

Maybe Juniper was losing their mind.

But they'd come this far; they had to keep going. Severed heads probably needed to sleep. Juniper leaned in and touched the glass with their fingers. There was the softest hum in response, almost like an acknowledgement. Proof enough to continue.

"Can you hear me?" Juniper asked.

Nothing. Not even a click. There was too much echoing activity on the other side of the ship for

Juniper to listen properly. What they needed was somewhere silent.

The bridge. The doors there would hush any sound across the ship. With careful hands, Juniper cradled the container close and headed out. Lily followed closely and kept her silence.

They entered the bridge and Lily immediately took up perch on the pilot's chair. Juniper let the cat act as lookout and headed to the holographic table facing the window. Juniper faced the head toward the view of stars and set it down.

"Want to see the stars?" they asked.

No answer.

"Never thought I'd talk to a dead vampire," Juniper continued, feeling silly. They paused and listened intently. If he was alive, he would have said something by now, right? Juniper felt so silly thinking so. Vampires died when their heads were severed. Everyone knew that.

But this one, he'd had cybernetics like Juniper's. Maybe it changed something. Sure, the systems would have turned off when the vampire affliction took over because to cybernetic systems, a lack of certain vital signs meant the body was dead. No point in running down juice on dead meat. Well, except for Forrest.

Juniper shuddered at the horror story Laurel had told them about what happened. It only served to cement that the feds had found new ways to abuse cybers.

It was almost funny, though; vampirism practically did everything the feds wanted full cybernetic augments to do, and did it better if you didn't mind a diet of blood and staying out of the sun. The high and mighty of the feds would never admit to that, though. They wanted to live forever in a way they could control. Any way they couldn't... Well, they ended up like Aster. A head his previous crew sold because it was easier for them.

Juniper glanced at the back of the head. Cybernetic jack was still intact.

"I got a jack too," Juniper said and settled on the floor beside the table. They took their usual cord from their pocket and held it in front of the head.

"Well? Fancy hooking together? I've really only done it with computer systems and Slim. He was... Never mind that. He was all right with it." They waited, heat creeping up their neck. "I want to see if you're in there. Forgive me for not waiting for a yes."

The first rule of jacking with other people was to always ask first and they hated they couldn't actually get an answer from Aster. Honestly, they'd never considered doing it with anyone until Slim came around. That had been a learning experience for both of them. Juniper had been doing it for the first time and it had been Slim's first time linking with a human. Feds even strictly prohibited androids from doing so, lest they feel human feelings.

Juniper didn't know if they helped Slim feel any more than he'd already had, but they'd enjoyed themselves at the very least.

An ache wormed its way through Juniper's heart as they slid one end of the jack into their head. Never again would Slim be on the other side.

They unscrewed the top of the container carefully, crinkling their nose at the smell of preservation goo, and plunged their hand inside. Ice cold. A tremble danced up their arm, but they managed to push past the discomfort and fitted the cord into Aster's head-jack.

With Slim, there was always the initial, pleasing

jolt and it was the same here. The sensation faded almost immediately and their cybernetics sent a signal to the head, searching for something to pair with. Slim had always been prompt, eager, and pulled Juniper right in. This was a cold emptiness and nothing answered.

Juniper sighed, closing their eyes. "Worth a shot." As they reached in again to retrieve the cord, their cortex computer pinged an oncoming connection and the world went white, disassociating them from their body before they could prepare for it.

When their eyes readjusted to a new, white room, a man dressed in a black body suit was kneeling in front of them. Hand on theirs. His pale skin was splashed with freckles, his soft blond hair was braided over one shoulder, and his eyes were a vibrant yellow. A mirror of Juniper's own.

"Hello," he said, unsure, and let go. "You can hear me? See me?" His voice matched the soft rush of whispers. It really *was* him.

"You're Aster," Juniper whispered. "You're *alive*?"

Aster gave a delicate shrug of his shoulders. "Something like that, I suppose." He smiled so warmly, everything suddenly felt right. If one smile could do that, it was no wonder Cedar loved him. "I've been trying to talk to Cedar, but... I guess I was really talking to you, wasn't I?" He extended his hand. "I am indeed Aster. What is your name?"

17
LAUREL

LAUREL WAS NOT MUCH OF A FIGHTER. WITH stringy arms and footwork that was more like a foot mess, the only thing she'd perfected was kicking a guy in the nads and running away. But by God, Clary was trying to teach her something new. Life of a space pirate had necessary dangers and Cedar wouldn't always be there to protect her. Without the strength of a vampire, she had to fight dirty.

It wasn't like Laurel *didn't* know that, but she just wasn't a fighter. Clary fixed some of her footwork, had her throw some punches so she could correct the angle, and ran Laurel through so many sets ("Go high! Go low! Again!"), she was more exhausted than she'd ever been. She flopped down on the gym mat in defeat.

Clary sighed and toed her shoulder. "Come on, I'm not pushing you *that* hard."

Laurel waved her arms pathetically above her. "Noodle arms tired!"

Clary rolled her eyes, a playful smile tugging her lips, and she lifted her gaze to Cedar loitering nearby.

After being a sturdy punching bag, he'd been drinking some mix of blood and coffee (*bloffee*? Laurel decided it was bloffee and resolved to tell Juniper about it later). Clary pointed at him and he raised his eyebrows.

"Let me show you what you can do to guys like Cedar." Clary beckoned him, and though he looked less than enthused, he placed his mug down and came over.

"Why me?"

"You're big and bad."

Laurel sat up. "I think the enforcers were bigger!"

Cedar pouted at her. "Were not."

"Hush!" Clary faced Laurel. "Now, with most guys, you can just do this."

Laurel knew exactly where this was going. Knee right into the groin. Maybe she should have explicitly said that was what she knew how to do. Cedar didn't react beyond a strained *oof*. Clary balked and put her knee down, confused.

"Well," she said. "Usually gives more of a response."

Cedar rolled his eyes. "Blood hasn't kicked in yet. Can't feel anything without it. Unless you rip off a limb." When Clary gave out an exasperated noise, he chuckled. "'Sides, most enforcers wear cups or have augmentations blocking pain down there."

Clary made a face. "Those augments block *all* feeling."

"Now you know why most of them are dicks." Cedar considered Laurel and pointed at his eyes. "In a scuffle, go for the eyes. You have little nails, use them. Blind them. For vamps specifically, never let one get close to you if you can help it." He tilted his head toward Clary and smiled. "Want to show her how to get out of a hold?"

"Just don't cheat with your vampire strength," Clary said, but she was smiling again as Cedar started explaining.

It was fun watching them. Clary threw Cedar like a sack of potatoes and then dove on him to show Laurel how best to pin someone. It felt more like an excuse for the two of them to work off their own nervous energy. Juniper would have loved to have been either watching or trying to handle Cedar themself. Though Juniper wasn't incredibly strong, they were fast and their cybernetics quickly deduced weak points for them to exploit. Laurel had seen it once on one of their rare visits to the Lunar Colony together; some asshole had come up behind them—probably saw them as easy pickings—and Juniper had him down in seconds.

The same memory soured, reminding Laurel that Juniper could only perform such feats *because* of their cybernetics. The very same ones making them miserable now.

Cedar hit the floor with an *oomph* and Clary made a show of flexing her arms. When Laurel clapped, Clary sauntered over and pulled on Laurel's arm. "You can throw him too! I'll show you."

Before Laurel could weasel her way out of it, the door leading into the ship slid open. Juniper skidded inside and hit the railing, nearly flipping themself over it. They were out of breath, but their eyes were vibrant.

"Hey!" Juniper said, clearly trying to sound relaxed and failing. Everyone stared. "Why are you two hogging Laurel?"

Cedar got off the floor, incredulous. "You feeling better?"

Juniper nodded enthusiastically. Not like Juniper

at all. Especially when they smoothed their hair back in an attempt to look calm. "Let me have some Laurel time." They met her gaze, lifting their eyebrows meaningfully, and beckoned her up.

Perfect excuse to not fold under Cedar's weight, and Laurel was all too happy to oblige. She raced up the stairs, leaving Clary and Cedar to argue about who was going to cook dinner. The instant she was close, Juniper dragged her through the doorway.

All of her excitement to have her Juniper back dropped as Laurel got a good look at them. Dark circles had formed under their eyes. Hair barely brushed. Hadn't even changed out of the tank and lounge pants they usually slept in. They hadn't even grabbed their usual wrap cardigan. This was *not* standard Juniper-fare, and Laurel's worry only grew.

"What's up?" Laurel asked and figured that sounded *too* worried and tried to sound happier. "You up to something mischievous?"

Juniper put a finger to their lips. "Shh! Keep it on the downlow."

"You locked yourself in your room for days." Laurel frowned. "Suddenly reappearing isn't keeping it on the downlow." Juniper waved her concern away and Laurel's face flushed with annoyance. "You told me to go away and now suddenly it's Laurel time?" She hadn't wanted to sound mad, but her voice had other ideas.

Juniper crossed their arms tightly. "I'm sorry," they said quietly. "It's... It's still too much. I just... look! It doesn't matter." Their voice shifted and their eyes practically sparkled. "This is *big*. I'm serious. I need your help!"

It mattered more than Juniper thought, but Laurel bit back from saying so. They were out of their room—energetic, even. She had to let it go. She breathed out and followed Juniper into the bridge.

As she stepped past the pilot's console, Juniper raced around her and slid to a stop in front of the holographic table. Laurel's jaw dropped. Aster's head sat on the table, wires going in and out of his container.

"What the hell?!" Laurel hissed, hurrying after Juniper. The cat jumped from the couch and circled her legs, rubbing them. She nudged Lily off and took Juniper by the shoulders to stop them from bouncing. "Cedar is going to murder you!"

"Not when he sees what I found!" Juniper shrugged off her hands and sat in front of the mess of wires spilling out from the inner workings of the table. Most of them were connected to the head, while the rest plugged into a small frequency device sitting beside the container. "Come sit!"

Laurel was way more weirded out than she wanted to be, but she wasn't going to leave Juniper. Partners in crime to the end. As she sat down, Lily wiggled between them to sit prim and proper like she was helping, too. Maybe since she was here, Cedar wouldn't go ballistic when he found them. Maybe.

The head was still ghastly. Yep. Nothing different about that. The wires just made it worse. Laurel tore her gaze away from it and studied Juniper as they prepped whatever they needed her for. The energy wasn't from them actually feeling better, but rather the distraction of being able to figure something out. Maybe it was a step in the right direction.

"You gonna tell me what's going on?" Laurel asked, trying to sound hopeful.

"He's alive," Juniper said finally.

"*What?*" Laurel snapped around to look at the head. Nope. Still dead. Eyes shut. "How?"

"I don't know!" Juniper bounced on their cushion. "Just that he's *there*. Trapped!"

"That doesn't mean he's alive," Laurel argued. "School said sometimes androids can persist after death as a ghost image imprinted on their circuitry. All they do is repeat the same scenario over and over again."

"He acknowledged my *name*," Juniper stressed. "Besides, I'm sure some of those ghost images are still alive in some fashion..." They affixed electrodes to the head's temple and made sure the wires from them ran to the device on the table. "I'm not sure if I'd trust feds to determine when someone's dead or not."

"Point taken," Laurel conceded. She wasn't sure why she'd blurted that out when she knew Federation policy was to harvest androids for parts mere moments after their deaths. "But this still doesn't make sense. Cedar turned him. Vampirism kills cybernetics—you guys said that. Then he was beheaded and *that* kills vampires. He should be very, very dead."

"That part I haven't the foggiest idea about, but look!" Juniper thrust the frequency device at Laurel. "I'm trying to give him a hologram so he can speak about his alive-or-dead philosophy himself."

It dawned on Laurel why Juniper suddenly wanted her there. "Wait, does his head have a frequency?"

"The cybernetics are giving off something. Just... look, okay?"

Curiosity ate away Laurel's skepticism and she examined the device's screen. This was *her* area of expertise, after all. A lot like adjusting the frequency of keys and fobs, but a bit more complex. To anyone not versed, they'd just see a bunch of wavelengths across the screen and hear steady beeps from the speaker in the back. Whatever was stronger came through clearer. But to Laurel's ears? Distinct patterns she could follow.

Juniper patted her shoulder. "I'll concentrate on setting all the wires correctly and you get the frequency of the table to match his head. It'll be like the time Slim showed us how to make that hologram movie."

Before Laurel could do just that—already hearing two distinct sounds from the device that needed syncing—she paused. Slim. She glanced at Juniper, worried. They'd suddenly grown morose and stared blankly at the table.

"Junie?" she whispered. "You okay?"

Breathing in, Juniper nodded. "Yeah. I just... I miss him." Probably more than they'd ever admit; Laurel didn't know what to do about that. "Maybe we'll meet again someday. He always said he uploaded his self to the net as a backup." They forced a laugh and shrugged. "I-I can't think about it right now or I might cry again." They sniffled and brought their hand under their nose. There was dried blood there Laurel hadn't noticed before. "Let's give Aster's ghost a voice."

Laurel hesitated, knowing Juniper was already pushing themself much too far after everything that happened, but this was doing something meaningful. A perfect distraction from the mall. She nodded and turned her attention back to the device. Even Laurel was glad to be involved, if she was honest. Cooking with Clary, learning the ins and outs on how to refuel their ship and the cruisers without station help, and exploring the ship by herself only took up so much time and mental energy. She'd grown listless. This had meaning.

She plopped her glasses on her head, blocked out all distractions, and focused on the frequencies. The bright line was the hologram table. Easy. It had a steady beat she tapped a finger to as a way to keep track of it. To the untrained eye, that was all the device showed, but an almost faded line rippled behind it. Whatever frequency Aster's head was giving off was incredibly weak, but it was *there*. Visuals wouldn't help her. Laurel pressed her ear to the back of the device and listened intently.

The hologram table remained constant. The second frequency was like a steady, but slower heartbeat. Cybernetics always made noise; Laurel had gotten used to Juniper's when everything around them was silent. Like softly breathing, but mechanical, somehow. Maybe Aster's cybernetics had never been *dead*, merely asleep.

Maybe that was why he'd been such coveted cargo. The feds might not have known why or how it'd happened.

Knowing the second frequency was there let her pick it up more easily. She adjusted the device's knobs. For the movie, all she and Juniper had to do was match the movie's frequency to the hologram emitter. If this was like that, once she finished, the table would display *something*. Hopefully Aster's inner vision of himself.

Juniper's hands were in and out of the head goo, their energy renewed, and it reminded Laurel of the Juniper they first met. It was surreal. A spark was behind their eyes, like they were finally alive again, and all it'd taken was a maybe not quite dead guy.

Laurel hated that it made her jealous, but she did her best to brush it aside to focus.

Slowly, Laurel matched the table's frequency to that of the one coming from the head. The sounds were finally melting together as one steady beat, and she grinned.

Laurel pulled herself out of the zone to check the wavelength display. Piece of cake. "I think we're golden, Junie."

The bridge doors opened. She and Juniper froze, eyes wide.

"God, can you believe it?" Clary said and Laurel and Juniper whipped around to face the door. Clary had two pizza boxes in hand, oblivious to their mess.

"The delivery guy from the station legit could *not* find us. I had to go out and fucking meet him. Should've made Cedar do it. Ordering out was his idea of cooking." She smiled at them, but her gaze drifted right past their stunned looks and landed on the head. Her jaw dropped and she threw the pizza boxes into the pilot's seat.

"Holy fucking shit!" she hissed. "What are you two doing?"

Lily's tail perked up. "I am supervising."

"Like hell you are!"

The bridge doors slid open again and she froze. All the blood drained from Laurel's face as Cedar came in.

"Hey, have you guys seen—" Cedar immediately stopped when he sighted Aster's head. Confusion and fury darkened his face. Clary tried to run interference, but he shoved her away and stomped toward them.

Juniper reached around Laurel for the table's controls, undaunted. "Got a surprise for you, big guy," they said and flipped the switch.

The bridge darkened and the table buzzed on. Instead of the usual holo-map these tables typically displayed, the bust of a man began to materialize. A reverse cascade of pixels in soft orange hues resolved into the distinct image of the man in the container. Aster. Tension eased out of Laurel with a breath. She wasn't expecting it to work on the first attempt. The movie had taken three.

Aster smiled, eyes bright, and peered up toward Cedar. "It's been a while." Aster's image moved his lips, but the sound came out of the table's speakers, creating a dissonance between image and sound. Laurel had also expected a computerized AI voice, similar to Lily's, but this was surprisingly soft and smooth. "Hasn't it been, Cedar?"

Cedar collapsed to his knees in front of the table, mouthing a dozen or more words. He tried to touch the hologram, but his shaking hands moved right through.

"He's been trying to talk to you since we found you." Juniper settled back down. "No one else could hear him, so I fixed that." Cedar stared at them in shock. "He's alive, Cedar. He's not dead."

"Alive," Cedar repeated, a meek whisper. Tears filled his eyes as he snapped his gaze back to Aster's ghost. "Alive."

Aster's face flickered as it softened. This hologram was rudimentary at best. Movies were one thing— predictable pictures—but a person must have been too much to be fluid. Laurel was surprised it let him emote at all.

"Something like that," Aster said.

"How?" Clary came up behind Cedar, eyes wide. "I thought your cybernetics were dead."

Aster glanced in Clary's direction and Laurel wondered if he could actually see them. "I don't believe we've officially met," he said.

"Uh." Clary glanced at Cedar. "Yeah, I'm new." She raised her hand in greeting. "Hi. Clary Sage. Pilot. Sorry I took your job."

Aster laughed; it was so warm and good natured. "Well, I'm a little indisposed. I don't mind."

"But seriously." Clary edged another step closer. "*How?* You're dead. Beyond dead. Doubly dead. The feds can't even make themselves persist past death with their selves attached."

The look flickering to life on Aster's image reminded Laurel of a teacher faced with an interesting question. Newer teachers in the boarding school once had the very same before the grim reality got to them. This was rather endearing.

"Does anyone know the true aim for cybernetics?" Aster swept his gaze across the four of them and when Juniper eagerly raised their hand, he chuckled. "I know you're raising your hand, Juniper, but I *know* you know."

Laurel had her guesses, but stayed quiet to wait for the real answer. Cedar smiled goofily. "He loves teaching," he said. "God, Aster, I miss you so much."

For a moment, the hologram paused. Laurel worried about a glitch, but then it flickered again and Aster had glanced away with a shy smile. He cleared his non-existent throat. "Their end goal is transhumanism. Escape from the mortal coil. Androids live an incredibly long time—maybe forever—if given regular upkeep, and can come back after years of dormancy so long as nothing happens to their memory core."

Made sense. Everyone knew the elite of the Federation wanted to live forever and recent android advances were steps in that direction.

"Of course, the Federation doesn't believe

androids are even alive—not like humans." Aster rolled his eyes. "Not with a soul. I think they're vastly underestimating an android's capability, but I digress. What I believe happened to me is what they've wanted to achieve all along."

Clary straightened, jaw dropping again. "Wait, really?"

Aster nodded. "Essentially. As you can see, I am quite dead, even by vampire standards. My cybernetics have ceased their primary function and all that's really left in there of any use is that dreadful datacrypt." He considered them all again, raising his eyebrows. "Somehow, something was preserved when I lost my body and that something *is* the quintessential me. I'll never know what the soul is—whether it's a bundle of preserved memories or nerves we tricked into feeling the sublime—but I *know* I'm still here. My complete self. I have persisted in the face of my death."

Laurel frowned. "But they don't count vampirism as transhumanism," she pointed out. "They believe as soon as you agree to be turned, you give up your soul. And that you can still die and lose yourself... but..." She fixed her glasses back on her nose, sudden excitement coursing through her. "But you got around *all* that!" Her cheeks heated as Aster faced her with a smile that urged her to continue. Was this how it felt to be recognized by a teacher for doing something good? "Did you—your soul or whatever—imprint on the datacrypt? Is that how? Did it make a backup of what was considered the most you?"

"It's probable," Aster said, nodding. "But then why? No other datacrypts have shown this pattern of behavior as far as I know. I was no one special."

Juniper's face lit up. "What if it was because of the

vampirism?"

"Perhaps," Aster murmured, "but we know beyond the shadow of a doubt vampires do *not* persist after their heads are torn from their bodies. Feds have performed many gruesome tests to prove this."

Juniper threw their hands up, still smiling. "Does the how and why really matter?" Aster pursed his lips. "You are alive!"

"Yes. I am indeed some variation of alive."

Cedar chuckled. "You always did get lost in the details, love."

Aster smiled sweetly at him. "But as you can all plainly see, I am rather... stuck."

Juniper was already prepared with a suggestion—Laurel knew that look on their face. "Androids can upload their selves into new bodies," they explained. "I bet we can do the same for Aster."

Cedar's jaw dropped. "Seriously?" he whispered. "You think we can?"

"Holy shit." Clary jiggled Cedar's shoulder. "We just need a body."

Aster nodded. "We do! Love, do you remember that job we had before? Well... Before all this?"

Cedar perked up. "We were transporting parts to the android facility near Saturn."

"We can use their facility," Juniper blurted out. "Make a body tailor made for him with their bio-android tech." They were bouncing again and Laurel had to admit she liked their energy.

"The manufacturer and museum?" Clary asked.

"Yeah, that one!" Cedar nodded, oblivious to Clary balking. Even Laurel cringed, knowing exactly how expensive it was. "We were lugging old parts there to be recycled. Was supposed to get good cash for that too..."

"That place is *elite*." Clary made a face. "We don't have that kind of cash."

"Who said we'll pay for it?" Aster winked.

Cedar laughed. "You haven't changed!" He reached over and clapped Laurel on the shoulder. "You and Laurel will have so much in common with your sticky fingers."

Stealing a whole android body? Never would Laurel have thought she'd even consider the prospect, but it was a thing she could do now. She vibrated with renewed excitement, as bouncy as Juniper, and a plan was trying to form in her head.

While Clary headed back up to the pilot's chair, Lily quick at her heels, Cedar kept watching Aster, his expression right back to awe. He really looked like he'd hug the hologram if he could. He finally drew his attention to Juniper.

"Yes," he said. "I like this idea." He hesitated and smiled gently. "Can I hug you?" he asked and Juniper's eyebrows went up. "This means the world to me."

Though Juniper looked a little flustered, they immediately nodded. "Yeah, of course."

Squeezing himself between Laurel and Juniper, Cedar wrapped his arms tightly around Juniper. A shy smile danced across Juniper's lips and they easily relaxed into him. Laurel was happy to see it. Of course, when Cedar finished with Juniper, he turned expectantly to Laurel. She wasn't about to say no either and let him wrap her up too. It was a delightful bear hug and she squeezed him just as fiercely back.

Bouts of incredible violence aside, the man was a giant marshmallow deep down.

"Thank you both so much," he whispered as he drew back. "If we hadn't found each other, I wouldn't be here. Aster wouldn't be alive."

Before Laurel could get all misty-eyed, Clary broke the touching moment by bringing the abandoned pizza boxes down. "Okay, pizza's getting cold. We've got some eating and planning to do."

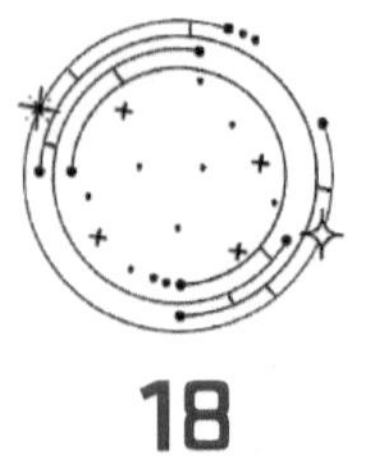

18
JUNIPER

HAVING AN OUTLET MADE EVERYTHING better. A real distraction from the nights where everything buzzed too loud for Juniper to sleep. And, most of all, Juniper had someone who understood what they were going through. Sure, Aster's understanding was buried under years of memories after vampirism had quieted everything, but he *knew*, and talking to him kept Juniper from disappearing into their own head.

Of course, Juniper let Cedar have the bridge when they were supposed to be trying to sleep (they promised Aster they'd *try*). It was sweet, hearing how happy Cedar sounded whenever he sat down with Aster. Though the temptation to eavesdrop was there as the night rolled by, Juniper refrained, and Lily helped by cutting the feed. Cedar and Aster deserved their privacy.

The ship was en route for the android facility near Saturn and while it was a detour from Pluto, it was practically on the way. Getting Aster a body took precedence; Juniper didn't want him stuck in his dead head any longer than he had to be. While they traveled, they had time to hammer out the plan. It boiled down to: sneak in, bake a bio-android body, and not get caught.

The closer they came to the facility, the more Juniper let Clary and Cedar handle the finer details while they focused on giving Aster a way to come with them. Lugging the container and hologram emitter wasn't ideal, and it wasn't like Aster could *see* through his hologram anyway. The only way he knew where people were in a room was because Lily shared some of her space so he could see the way she saw (Aster couldn't quite describe it beyond bio-signatures).

Sharing her space also meant Aster could connect to their comms like Lily could, but it still didn't let him *see*. Juniper felt wrong trying to build his body without him being able to see it. No matter how many photos Cedar threw onto a drive for them to use to get him right, Aster should have been able to decide the details himself.

All they'd found useful in the *Gladiolus'* storage was an old tech watch with a usable jack. Android pilots once used them to interface directly with the ship's internals. Maybe there was a way to reverse it so Aster could see *through* the watch safely from the ship.

Syncing it to Lily was easy. She remembered the watch from a long time ago before Cedar found the ship and paired with it easily. Aster connected to it and it let his voice come out of the watch's speaker. That was as far as Juniper got before they felt like they were too far in over their head.

"You're hooked into the ship, right?" Laurel asked when they were both well into their respective projects on the bridge. She'd started hanging out there more, especially if Juniper was already there, and

Juniper was embarrassed it'd taken them so long to realize why.

With the whole Aster thing, they hadn't really sat down and done anything with Laurel. It wasn't that Laurel hadn't tried including them—snack runs, taking a break to make dinner, et cetera—but Juniper had declined each time. Maybe this was her way of bringing her presence back to Juniper when Juniper refused to be in hers. It was nice, almost like they were on the satellite again.

Except, of course, Juniper was growing agitated at the project and thus, their bio-scanner honed in on Laurel's shifts in mood in case Juniper was affecting her or vice versa. She was growing just as agitated over the trip and they knew why without asking.

They were a duo. Something Juniper was throwing aside to talk to this dead vampire they hardly knew. Explaining all the reasons why sitting with Aster was helping whereas sitting with Laurel would not, however, sounded too dickish in their head. So, instead of making excuses, they kept it to themself and let her simmer.

It'd be right soon.

"What do you mean?" Juniper asked.

Laurel glanced at them over her glasses. She was working on a stolen keycard to make it act like a skeleton key like they'd done at the mall. Except Laurel was insistent she could make it fuzz all fed-sanctioned locks. Lily was sitting with her, the cat's eyes scanning the card after each round of tinkering to test it against the locks she had on file.

"You're linking the watch to the ship which Aster is already linked up to," Laurel explained. "If you jack into it yourself, would it let Aster sync with you? That's what androids do sometimes when they link, right?

Maybe he can see that way."

Aster's hologram brightened with a smile and he nodded. "I believe she's correct," he said and Laurel beamed at the praise. "Theoretically, with a stable uplink between the watch and the ship, I should be able to come along inside your own augments. As long as you don't mind, of course. I promise I'll be quiet."

As if him being loud was the problem. Thinking of someone else in the mess that was their head truthfully made Juniper's skin crawl. Slim was different. He'd seen Juniper at their worst plenty of times and was used to the mess. In contrast, Slim's mind had been orderly and comforting. What Juniper always needed whenever they linked together. There'd be none of that this time, but it was a plan.

"It doesn't hurt to try."

Between Laurel's insistent help and Lily remote connecting the watch to Aster in her systems, they finished before anyone shuffled them off to sleep. Laurel helped Juniper hook their usual cord into the watch, taped it to their arm all the way up, and tested hiding it under a sleeve. Definitely workable.

"Ready for a test run?" Juniper asked as Laurel helped thread the cord out of Juniper's collar. They took the end and Aster nodded. "All right. Hooking in."

The usual full body fuzz and shudder washed over Juniper upon connecting and they waited. This time, they weren't mentally going anywhere; they were inviting someone in.

Aster's hologram disappeared, and just as a little panic set in, Juniper felt a gentle tap against their cybernetics. It was *weird*, feeling something they were not in control over inside their own head. Juniper focused on the tapping until Aster bloomed in the corner of their mind. It was similar to hook ups, but instead of the merging sensation, Aster stayed exactly where he was with a clear divide.

"Well?" Juniper asked, nervous.

"I can see!" Aster's voice came from the watch and echoed in Juniper's head. "I almost feel like a thought. Oh! Let me see Laurel. I want to memorize people."

Juniper faced Laurel and she waved, smiling awkwardly.

"Well, aren't you adorable?" Aster said.

Laurel bit her lip to stop her smile from widening. "Thank you," she said and glanced back at Juniper. "Think you can handle it, Junie?"

"I can deal," Juniper said and felt Aster leave. A hole was left, but in a microsecond, *they* filled it again. Spooky, but if it worked, it worked.

Aster's hologram reappeared on the table, smiling.

"Well..." They grinned at Laurel. "I guess that's figured out. You think *you're* ready to heist a whole ass body?"

There was a twinkle to Laurel's eyes. "Do you really even have to ask?"

IT WAS A RESTLESS TWO MORE NIGHTS before they arrived. Once in orbit, Clary and Cedar brought everyone together for the plan they had finalized.

The Android Manufacturer and Museum Facility of Saturn was the cornerstone of the colony on the artificial satellite orbiting the planet. The facility existed first and a colony had taken shape around it sometime later, even though the androids taking care of the facility always insisted they never needed human supervision. Feds simply wanted assurance against any android uprisings and encouraged people to populate the colony. The colony itself was lit up like a cluster of stars pushed together in the dark, providing a variety of things like the pretty swanky College of the Arts and Cybernetics, but the biggest draw was the android facility.

Most android bodies could trace their origins here. There was another facility near Mars, but this one had more technologically advanced tools, and, as such, was lauded as more elite. Its specialty was its state-of-the-art bio-androids—an advanced android body comprised of more organic tissue and material. The closest thing to a human body the Federation could create. The best way to bring Aster back to the life he had before.

Since the staff of the facility consisted of androids and a single human curator who was hardly there, Juniper and Lily made a new code injection to fuzz their bio-signatures once the heist was in motion. It meant androids wouldn't be able to detect them on scans (although staying out of view was still a must).

"We're going in like we're with the tour." Clary had loaded the facility's itinerary on her screen. Lots of tours at all times of the day. "There's one at the end of the day. I already ghosted us in. We'll dress nice, act expensive, and when it ends, we head to the bathrooms and wait. Our ghost will disappear from their system and they'll believe everyone is gone when they show everyone else out."

Cedar didn't look enthused. "It's too subtle," he grumbled. "Are you sure you want me waiting here on the ship?"

Clary rolled her eyes. "I don't think going in fangs first will do us any good."

As Cedar moped, Aster snickered from below. "You never did like the quiet jobs, love," he said and then addressed Juniper and Laurel. "While you're down there with Clary, Cedar will direct you from the ship."

Truth be told, Juniper also didn't like the idea of leaving their muscle behind. However, if subtlety was the game, it made sense. He stuck out.

"No bitching!" Clary clapped her hands together, grabbing everyone's attention. She pointed at Juniper and Laurel. "Us three gotta get dressed in something nice. Lily's going to get us cloaked and hidden so no one sneaks up on the ship while we're gone."

It wasn't hard to look good, especially with all the clothes they'd lifted from the mall. Juniper dressed in a sharp button-up black shirt beneath a midnight blue vest and paired it with tight pinstripe pants. The shirt had long sleeves to hide the wire and a collar high enough so no one would notice a cord feeding into their head-jack. Juniper filled the vest's pockets with a small drive of Aster's photos to help with the body building and a hand-sized stunner for protection.

They slicked their hair back with some hair product Laurel had also nabbed and smiled at themself in the bathroom mirror. Blue dye still held up, although their black roots were beginning to show. All in all, though, decidedly more masculine today. For good measure, they added the blue lipstick Laurel found from forever ago. Totally their color. Last to go on were Cedar's sunglasses to hide the gold in their eyes. Look completed.

They finished threading the cord through the top of their collar and slotted it into place. The fuzzy feeling was less this time and, like before, they felt Aster nestle himself inside.

"Getting easier?" Juniper asked him.

"Indeed," Aster replied. "Finished dressing?"

"Yeah!" Juniper grinned at themself in the mirror. "Can you see?"

"I was waiting for permission." There was a subtle shift in their visual augments before it felt like Aster smiled. "Oh, all of that really suits you."

"Damn straight it does!" They raised their voice so Laurel could hear them through the bathroom wall. "Hey, Laurel! We should have done this sooner. I look real fucking good. Even Aster agrees!"

They were glad when she giggled on the other side. "Good!" she said. "If you're done, can you help me? I can't reach the zipper."

Juniper's augments shifted again as Aster's presence dulled. They wanted to tell him he didn't have to do that, but it was sweet he made sure they and Laurel still had a little privacy while he was connected. Juniper quickly headed over and peeked into her room.

She'd really made the place her own. Her old, sheer multicolor tapestry she'd had since before boarding school was hung from the top of the window and reached to the ceiling light. Her room was still a little messy, too, as expected. Juniper had gotten used to her little controlled messes in the satellite and was warmed to find them here too. Unused gadgets for her to tinker with were left in piles, some of her new clothes were still folded together with the tags attached, and then her closet was overflowing with what she'd already gone through.

Laurel stood in front of the floor length mirror hanging from her closet door and she struggled to reach the zipper in the back of her dress.

The top half of her dress was black with layered

floral lace that extended across her arms to make short sleeves. The main skirt was a bright orange and fell to her knees while another sheer and sparkly skirt was layered atop it. Definitely cute and fit Laurel well. She'd paired it with a pair of neon-yellow tights and little black flats. Clary must have done her nails at some point—they were freshly bright yellow—and Juniper was a little hurt Laurel hadn't asked them to do her nails. She always had in their satellite.

Juniper brushed the hurt away and zipped her up. "Pretty as a flower," they said. "You remember the pinwheels Cedar gave you?"

Little devices resembling pinwheels, except once thrown, the pinwheel petals turned into sharp propeller blades. Small enough to hide and useful in a pinch. Laurel patted her thigh. "Got them here! You got your stunner?"

Juniper patted their vest. "Good to go."

Laurel snagged her palm tablet from her bed and pulled Juniper next to her in the mirror. Without needing to be asked, Juniper posed with her. The palm tablet flashed with a photo and they devolved into giggles. Just like they used to do back in the satellite.

"I knew that lipstick would suit you!" Laurel said, saving the photo.

It was easy, superficial commentary and Juniper was glad for it. It let them forget everything else.

"Want me to do your makeup?" Juniper asked, hopeful.

"Yes, please!"

Juniper had all of Laurel's usual colors spread out on the vanity in the bathroom in seconds and dolled up her face with precision and practice. They'd spent years alone, learning how to make their own face pretty or handsome, and had applied that knowledge to Laurel when she came into the picture. Though Laurel wasn't much of a makeup person beyond winged eyeliner, she loved whenever Juniper did her makeup. It was cathartic.

There was the usual sheen of sparkles to highlight her round cheeks and eyes, and then they used her favorite color—yellow—on her lips and on the edge of her eyes. When they finished, Juniper leaned back to consider it.

"Lola eat your heart out," Juniper said and Laurel giggled. "Well, Aster? What do you think?"

His presence fully came back like a practiced dance. Once more, Juniper fought from smiling as he smiled. "You both look lovely," he said.

Laurel looked away, suddenly bashful, and slipped her glasses back on. Everything framed itself well together.

"Let's show off to Clary," Juniper said. "Bet we look better!"

Laurel eagerly hopped up. "Let's go!"

Juniper was wrong. Clary blew them out of the water. While she kept her usual stoicism, she'd made up a look that rivaled most idols. Her hair was wrapped in a messy bun, but it felt more calculated than random. Keeping it in place were two hair sticks and Juniper wondered if she was hiding knives in those. Her makeup looked like an expert had done it. Perfectly contoured cheeks, every blemish and mark softened from view, and she'd painted her lips a shocking red. Eyeshadow made the dark blue of her eyes pop and she'd even drawn razor sharp wingtips off the side.

Out of the three of them, she'd dressed the most adult in a little black slip dress showing off curves Juniper hadn't even noticed she *had*. She'd paired it with her velvety black shawl tied in the front for modesty. If that wasn't enough, she also had sheer stockings up the length of her legs with garter belts holding them in place, and an impressive set of heels making her almost as tall as Cedar.

Aster whistled in Juniper's head and Juniper found themself stuck on words, unable to force out even a shy compliment. Laurel stared slack-jawed at Clary, starstruck.

"Perfect." Clary smirked. "I'm the best dressed." She handed Laurel an orange and black clutch and a set of comms. "I put a palm tablet in there to keep track of everything, and it's pretty roomy, so swipe to your heart's content." She slipped her own comms into her ear as she shuffled them down the hall. "Cedar, we're about to head out."

"Really?" Cedar sounded like he pouted on the other side. "Don't I get to see how you all look before you go and mess it up?"

Clary sighed heavily. "Lily! Get a good shot of us!" As she pulled Juniper and Laurel close, Juniper noticed the camera sliding down from the ceiling. Laurel fully leaned into Clary with a wide grin making her cheeks sparkle, and Juniper managed an awkward smile.

It was another moment before Cedar whistled. "Okay, yeah, I can't compete with any of that," he said. "Good luck down there. Don't take too long; I'll get bored and sneak in myself."

THEY SNEAKED INTO THE TOUR FLAWLESSLY and it was actually rather informative. Juniper acted as a potential buyer with as many oohs and ahhs as they could muster, and hastily whispered nonsense to

Clary and Laurel like the three of them were considering their options. The other fabulously dressed groups were definitely made of money and ignored their trio outright, like they could smell they didn't actually have any cash.

The android tour guide was unfortunately attentive. The internal network shared between the androids was also harder to grasp than Juniper wanted to admit, not to mention the security android network. Lily and Juniper decided to leave it alone after glancing at it—too complex on short notice and if the plan went well, no security would be called.

It was near the end of the tour before Juniper managed to crack into the internal network and they quickly injected their code. Soon their names would disappear from the tour, androids would be compelled to stay on the ground floor and ignore their bio-signatures.

For good measure, Clary had them slink off one at a time to the bathroom near the back of the ground floor. Laurel went first, clutching her bag tightly as she went. The tour guide completely ignored her. So did the other groups. Perfect.

Once Laurel flipped her comms off and on, indicating she was in, Juniper leisurely went after her. The guide was finishing his presentation about bio-androids and the tour politely clapped for him.

"That was rather informative," Aster murmured in their head. "The terminal the display showed off looked complex, though. I sort of wish we could have seen it."

"Don't worry," Juniper replied subvocally. "Can't be much different than the diagram we found on the net."

They made it to the bathroom without being

caught and slid into the same stall Laurel had taken over. She sat on the toilet tank, her back pressed against the wall, and Juniper balanced on one side of the toilet bowl. Laurel had Clary's tablet on her knees and clicked through the steps in their plan. Juniper craned their neck to peer into the open clutch on her lap. Already swiped two cred sticks. Juniper bit back from chuckling.

"Third floor," Laurel whispered, peering up at Juniper. "That's where they have the bio-android terminals. I found the schematics on their network."

Cedar sighed over the comms. "Come on, I sent you schematics."

Laurel pouted. "They were out of date—I found updated ones!"

Cedar continued grumbling on the comms and the stall opened. Juniper and Laurel jumped, almost slipping, but it was only Clary. She crammed herself in and got her feet off the floor the same as them. None of them looked dignified and Juniper had to bite back a snort at the ridiculousness of dressing up so nice only to perilously balance over a toilet.

Clary made a face. "This is stupid."

"It shouldn't be much longer," Laurel said. "Five to ten minutes for the tour to end. Then another fifteen to thirty as they do a final sweep, then a little longer to give them time to delegate the cleaning bots."

It felt like way longer. Juniper's legs started cramping, and given how Clary's face twisted, so were hers. Laurel kept her eyes glued to the tablet, even as the bathroom lights went off from lack of detected movement. As soon as it was off, Juniper connected into the light's network and disabled detection.

It wasn't too long after that did Laurel pick her

head up. "Phase three," she said.

"Stairway nearby," Cedar directed over the comms, totally sounding like he enjoyed it. "Right behind the maintenance door to your left as you get out. Your keycard should get you in and out."

Clary took the lead, her shoes somehow silent despite the heels. The lights across the facility had been set low to preserve power, leaving the hallways lit in soft golds like candlelight. Juniper swept their gaze across the floor, letting their cortex computer scan for anyone nearby. Nothing. Androids were busy elsewhere.

Their new skeleton keycard worked on the maintenance stairwell doors, and they hurried upward. While the ground floor had scant activity of robots disinfecting and cleaning the public areas while the androids finished routine checks, the third was empty.

On the far side, there was the grand staircase the public used to access the other floors. A balcony extended from there and wrapped across the third floor so anyone could peer down. Hanging in the center above everything was a glowing digital art piece Juniper couldn't make heads or tails of. It was pretty, especially in the dim light, and cast a haunting golden glow across the balconies. Also gave them enough light to see.

A carpeted walkway followed the balcony around and led to different offices with glass walls so anyone could peer inside and see android creation in action. Right now, most of the rooms lay dark as no production was in process, except for the suite marked for bio-androids.

Inside was a row of terminals with corresponding glass tanks beside each one. The tanks in use were lit up in orange with a body being programmed and prepped. Each terminal listed a time it'd be done and even where the body would be shipped once finished. The only terminal not in use was one at the far wall near another set of large doors leading back into the balcony. Juniper hurried over and immediately got to work.

Juniper and Aster had researched how the terminals worked on the transit over, but even with that knowledge, after the startup, the commands and options were daunting to look through.

Helpfully, their cortex computer pinged what to do first: slot in the drive with the photos. Juniper did so and the computer dinged. The photos flew by, bits and pieces lit up as though trying to capture Aster's features exactly. Hopefully, it would get close enough and all Juniper would have to do was tweak a little here and there according to Aster's specifications.

As the photos continued cycling, creating a 3D image of the android to be, the terminal brought up a prompt, asking about specific programming and internals to use. Juniper quickly declined the fed programming and selected only the operating systems to make the body work. Didn't need any of that fed spyware. If there were any gaps, Lily had a plan.

Once the prompts were cleared, the tank buzzed and filled with liquid. According to the terminal, the ETA was roughly around two hours. Not bad.

Clarry huffed behind them. "I expected more action."

"It's better this way," Juniper said.

"I guess..." Clary rolled her eyes and switched her comms on. "Hey big guy, you listening? How's it out there?"

"Stars," Cedar said. "Few ships are starting to

leave, but then just stars. I'm really bored. How do you even do this, Clary?"

As Clary gave him suggestions—paint his nails, do a facemask if he wanted to brave her room for one, play a game with the cat because she needed the exercise—Juniper tuned them out. Laurel was hunkered down beside them, working on hooking a few things up to the palm tablet to help erase Aster's data once the body finished.

"Good to go here," Laurel said.

Juniper nodded and let Aster's ghost into their head. "All right," they said. "You ready to make the body yours, Aster?"

Aster smiled and Juniper's lips made to follow the motion. "We can start with tweaking the face," he said. "I'd love to keep my vampire teeth. Cedar *really* liked them."

19
LAUREL

THE SPEED AT WHICH JUNIPER ENTERED ALL sorts of details Laurel would never have thought about concerning a body left her a little stunned. A coral pink substance quickly filtered into the tank as the tweaking continued and lasers began molding it into an android framework. The screen Juniper hadn't taken their eyes off had a readout of the entire process, and while the technical jargon flew over Laurel's head, Juniper easily answered every prompt. Before Laurel knew it, the frame was finished and bones began to form.

Laurel was fascinated, especially as the system moved on to the muscular structure and the somatosensory programs, allowing androids the capability to physically feel as humans did, but then Juniper began frankly asking Aster more personal details. Like dick size.

Juniper's entire face went red as soon as the question was so confidently asked, especially when Aster's awkward laugh echoed out of the watch; they must not have meant to ask that aloud.

Although, the question wasn't a surprise. Bio-androids were incredibly lifelike, sexual characteristics included. It also wasn't unheard of for androids to enter into relationships with other androids (humans less so because the feds heavily frowned upon it).

Then again, coupling may not have been what the feds intended. They'd never give something they believed as lesser the ability to find pleasure through the goodness of their heart. No, Laurel guessed it was closer to what Aster had said before: transhumanism. The pleasure was for eventual humans in those bodies, not androids.

In any case, Juniper had Aster handled and Laurel made herself useful elsewhere. It hurt a little that neither of them noticed her slink away, but she tried not to dwell. Aster was focused on his body and Juniper was absorbed in the shininess of a new friend. They weren't ignoring her on purpose.

Laurel just needed to clear her head. No dwelling. No worrying. Just filching it all away.

A misplaced keycard there. A whole ass tablet here. Anything she could fit into the clutch went in. Although she didn't dare go into the other locked offices or what looked to be the curator's office, she found enough along the balcony walkway and all the open seating rooms on her circuit.

She finished too soon, unfortunately, coming right back around to the bio-android suite, and found her gaze drifting outward for another distraction. There wasn't much activity below, just sweeper bots doing their rounds and the occasional android helping one that was stuck. No one looked up; Juniper's code made sure of that. What drew her attention the most, however, was the digital art installation hanging in the middle. It twinkled gold, lights glowing within like stars, and when the light pulsed, it reminded Laurel of a nervous system firing off.

Clary was leaning on the balcony just outside the set of double doors nearest Juniper. They'd been left open, probably to reduce the sound of them opening and closing if one of them left the suite. Not that Juniper was doing that; they'd grown quiet, likely deep in a mental conversation with Aster. The body looked way more solid now, at least, with the muscular system finishing. More organic substance floated in the tank as lasers made quick work to fashion it into the next step.

Too squeamish to watch more, Laurel turned away. Frame and bones were one thing, but anything fleshy was another. She stayed with Clary and leaned beside her on the railing.

Clary eyed the clutch and smirked. "Nab anything good?"

Laurel let Clary dig through it. She immediately went for the tablet, an *ooh* from her lips, and checked it. Password encrypted. Didn't bother her none; she pulled a small flash drive from her bra and slotted it in.

Laurel snorted. "You just carry around flash drives in your bra?"

"You never know when a decryption injection will come in handy." Clary winked. "Gotta use my girls for something." She let the program load and a bar appeared on the screen. "Curious for what's on here. Maybe it's something we can sell. We need the cash. Someone's gonna start noticing a pattern when our ship comes in and shit starts going missing."

Laurel grimaced. Clary wasn't wrong. She also regretted she hadn't thought to carry anything similar on her person. Granted, she was nowhere near as well-endowed and doubted she could've smuggled it in her shirt. Still, she had so many skirt pockets she'd left empty. She could have brought something. Been useful for a change.

Without meaning to, a sigh made its way out of her lips.

"Hey," Clary whispered. "What's wrong?"

"All I've really done is open doors." Laurel glanced at Juniper over her shoulder. They probably still hadn't noticed Laurel wasn't beside them. "You and Lily could have done that."

Clary shrugged. "I mean, sure, but you had it handled. I wouldn't take that away."

"Then what good am I?" Laurel gave her a look. "Everyone has something they want and can bring to the crew. I don't. I'm just here."

Clary wrapped an arm around Laurel's back, bringing her closer. "Pirates don't need to know what they want. They just have to be willing to go. You're on the run because if you go back, well, you're dead."

"It feels like I should have more."

With an exhale, Clary peered out at the twinkling art. It had started another pass of pulsing light. "Sometimes, life is the simple act of living until tomorrow and then the next day and then the next. It has no rhyme or reason, just the continued existence of you."

Laurel frowned. "That's a little depressing."

"A bit." Clary chuckled and tapped a dialog window on the tablet. It was more than halfway finished now. "But life isn't some grand adventure until your brain ceases. It's the little things." Her face lit up with an idea and she turned a smile on Laurel. "I like reading. You like reading. Let's start a book club on the ship."

"You think anyone else will join us?"

"Lily will," Clary said. "She's always into my

antics."

Maybe it'd be nice. "I'd like that." Laurel giggled when Clary pumped a fist, triumphant. "Is this what you wanted to do? When you were younger? Just be out in space like this?"

"Oh, hell no," Clary said. "I thought I'd have some cushy desk job. I gave my life to the feds thinking that would get me there, but I should have known better." She shook her head. "Even now, I have no idea what the hell I'm going to do five years from now, much less a month. I'm directionless, but I like it this way." Her smile softened. "And sure, Junie has this impressive end goal that I'm not even sure we can do and now so does Cedar, but us normal people? We don't need some grand goal. I think living is enough."

"I like the simplicity," Laurel said.

Clary leaned in closer and dropped her voice. "Don't tell Cedar I told you—I can't believe he hasn't spilled it himself—but he was trying to think of a way to sneak you into seeing the Smashing Coffins when all this is over."

Laurel's entire being brightened and she clapped her hands over her mouth. "Really?!"

"Yes!" Clary grinned. "He told me all about how your face lit up when he mentioned he knew them. He wants to do something to see you smile."

"He's really just a big softie deep down, isn't he?"

Rolling her eyes, Clary leaned back on the balcony. "Yeah, when he's not shredding the feds."

"Do you want to see the Coffins too?" Laurel asked.

"Fuck yeah, if we can get in for free," Clary said, nodding. "I'll just be in the back. Too old to be any-where near a mosh pit full of vampires. They hurt."

Laurel stifled a laugh. As Clary interacted with a

new popup on the tablet, Laurel's gaze drifted below. There was new activity. The cleaning bots were being hurried out of the way and the tour guide had returned, ordering two more androids to see to the door.

Odd. She leaned over on the railing to see what was going on. A beep from the tablet distracted her and she looked at it. A spreadsheet was already pulled open.

"Bingo," Clary said. "Let's see..." Her eyes went wide. "There's an after-hours tour. Shit!" She immediately ducked and turned her comms on. "Cedar?!" she hissed.

No reply. Laurel adjusted hers. Just static. Fuzzed like the mall had been. The main doors opened below and Laurel's legs went weak seeing who was striding inside.

Lola Langley. Idol of the stars. Her sister.

Long chestnut brown hair tumbled in waves down her back and she had the same twin buns up top because that was the style she and Laurel had agreed upon when they were little. It was her signature look. She wore her usual yellow trench coat, highlighting the warm hues in her skin, and had large tinted glasses failing to hide her identity. Flanking her were her usual two androids with duo toned hair of yellows and pinks with snazzy suits to match. They were her backup dancers and bodyguards in one.

No paparazzi trailed after her, so likely, this was being done even under their watchful radar.

"Miss Langley!" The tour guide greeted her with a low bow. She removed her sunglasses and tossed her hair back. Trained perfection always ready for a photo. "It's an honor to see you on such short notice. What will we be looking at today?"

"I'd like to inquire about new bodies," Lola said, her speaking voice as smooth as butter.

"Of course. Is your agent here with you tonight?"

"No. I gave her the night off. I wanted to see everything for myself, if that's all right?"

"Of course it is! Right this way and I'll give you a tour of our newest models in the showroom upstairs."

Lola stepped after him and paused. She inclined her head upward and Clary yanked Laurel down, covering her. No way. She couldn't have known Laurel was there. She was just looking at the art piece. Not toward Laurel stupidly watching when she should have already been hiding.

"Is..." The tour guide's voice returned, followed by a few cautious steps across the floor. "Is there something amiss? The art was graciously donated—"

"It's fine," Lola said. "The piece is pretty. Solven, yes? He's done work for my concerts. Nice man."

Clary dragged Laurel into the bio-android suite as the guide began speaking at length about what the art symbolized. Juniper was watching them, wide-eyed.

"We have a problem," Clary hissed as Laurel pulled herself upright. "Someone's here."

"My sister."

Juniper swore. "Is she coming up here? We're not done yet."

It was definitely almost there. The face was completely finished, a near replica of the ghastly head in the container back on the ship. Even the hair was done, leaving soft blond strands wisping around his head. The machine's lasers were adding the finer details and the programming was performing updates to the somatosensory system and the main nervous system program as it finished applying skin grafts.

"I don't know." Clary swiped through the tablet.

"All it says is the tour, not an end time. We need a distraction to make them evacuate her."

Laurel straightened with an idea. "What if we blow the fuse for the place?" she suggested. "Androids always evacuate humans first and foremost, so they'll be concerned with getting her to safety before they figure out why the lights went off. We'll have time to jet."

Juniper glanced between their terminal and the one next to them and crawled over. They popped the side paneling off with deft fingers and nodded. "The terminals look to be on their own grid." They left the panel on the floor and came back. "Sounds good to me."

"Where the hell is the breaker room?" Clary asked.

Before Laurel could check on the tablet, Juniper's eyes glowed white. "Ground floor," they said, gaze tracking an unseen map. "Right off the maintenance stairs is a small maintenance closet with the breakers."

Releasing a tense sigh, Clary kicked off her heels and headed off. Laurel pivoted so she could get back to the balcony railing. She couldn't see her sister. As she craned her neck to look, the tour guide's voice echoed from the floor below and Laurel froze.

"Shit!" Juniper snapped. "Are they already here?"

"I didn't think they'd go up to the showroom so fast." Laurel chewed on her lip. "She wants bodies. He'll probably want to show her the terminals soon."

Juniper swore again. "We've got ten minutes left."

Distraction... distraction... Laurel patted down her dress, looking for anything, and found the pinwheels. She pulled one out and nodded. "I can distract them until Clary gets the lights." Juniper stared at her, unhappy with the idea, but Laurel shook her head. "I'm small and fast. I can do this."

Juniper nodded. "I'm finishing this as quick as possible. Good luck. Be smart."

Laurel pushed herself to her feet and ran for the maintenance stairs. The floor below was dedicated to the museum side of the facility and had a showroom of ready-to-go android bodies. There were stands showcasing android models throughout the years, and thankfully, those were easy to hide behind.

The tour guide had stopped Lola while he spoke at length like he'd done before. Lola was hardly a rapt audience; Laurel knew it with the way she was holding herself. She was bored. Her androids were still beside her, backs ramrod straight. Gossip rags always wondered if she was closer to androids than people, but every time Lola made a friend, her *fans* went ballistic about it. So, she'd carefully constructed her public persona around the androids being the only ones for her.

Laurel wondered if it made her lonely.

No. Laurel shook it from her thoughts. She couldn't feel sorry now. It wasn't like Lola had ever felt sorry for her.

"Tell me more about the bio-androids," Lola interrupted and Laurel jetted out from the stairwell and hid behind one of the display pillars. "My other backup dancers have been stiff even with proper maintenance. Would upgrades to your newest model be worth the investment?"

"Of course!" the tour guide said. "Current gen bio-androids have greater capability for movement, and we've been making them so their parts and internals can be easily upgraded. We have chambers for a few in progress upstairs if you'd like to see the customization. Each one is made to order." He chuckled.

"Even yours truly. I was given the privilege to make my own body when I upgraded."

"I can see the care that went into you," Lola said. "Is it possible to transfer my androids here if I choose to make an order?"

"Unfortunately, no," the tour guide said. "The curator took me to Mars to get it done. Federation policy, you know."

"I understand."

"Right this way then, Miss Langley."

Laurel swore. She'd spent too long eavesdropping. They were headed for the grand staircase and that would lead them right to the bio-android suite.

She opened the pinwheel device. If anything, the androids would see the danger and maybe start evacuations early. She tossed it toward them as hard as she could.

The blades spun so fast, they became a blur, and the pinwheel cut through the space between Lola and one of her androids. Laurel covered her mouth to smother her gasp. She hadn't meant to get it that close. One android jerked Lola aside, out of harm's way, and the tour guide snatched the device from the air.

Shit. His reflexes were good. He stared at it, eyes gleaming, and Laurel sped for the first door she could hide behind.

Bathroom. Dead end. She scrambled into a stall and just when she'd scrunched herself from view, someone followed her in. The lights were still on. They'd know someone was here. She covered her mouth and a careful step echoed off the tiles.

"Laurel?" came Lola's voice, barely above a whisper.

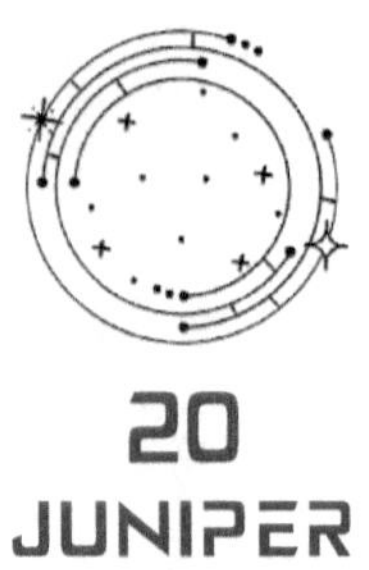

20
JUNIPER

JUNIPER WAITED, STRAINING THEIR EARS TO listen to everything around them. Distraction was taking too long—both of them. Juniper counted the beats of their heart, willing it to calm down before their bio-monitor did it for them. When enough numbers had gone by, Juniper tried forcing a connection to Clary's comms.

It clicked, surprising them. Whatever was jamming the signal to the *Gladiolus* must not have been short range. It just jammed communication to the ship.

"Clary!" Juniper hissed and heard her startle on the other side. "What's the hold up?"

"I'm working on it!" Clary snapped. "Breaker switches are locked by a passcode."

Shit. Juniper looked at Aster's body. Didn't need much longer; he was *there*, down to the little details only he knew, but not ready yet. Taking him out too early might unseal the skin and ruin everything. There had to be another distraction; Laurel was a sitting duck down there with the lights on. They shouldn't have let her go alone.

Another terminal in the suite dinged, making them jump. It was done. Their cortex computer slotted another plan into place not a moment later. Another body was a better distraction.

The terminal reminded Juniper of a morgue drawer as they pulled it open, although with a lot more fluid. Whatever juice was in the machine spilled out at their feet, making them gag, but they held it together. They looped their arms around the inert android's chest. It was just a shell, thankfully—no brain activity yet, according to the screen. With a lurch, Juniper dragged it out. The limbs made such uncomfortable squelching noises as they hit the tile.

And it was *heavy*. Juniper's arms strained as they dragged the body over to the balcony. They forced their augments to give their arms strength and with it, managed to toss the body over the railing.

At least, they tried. The shell hung, one half over and the other half on their side still. Pale pasty ass in the air.

"For fuck's sake," Juniper growled, catching their breath. They braced themself and pushed the body as hard as they could. Slime terminal goo helped and the body cartwheeled downward like a ragdoll.

It smashed the side of its skull against the second-floor railing, splattering pieces of its head across the tile. Lola shrieked from somewhere below, her bodyguard androids practically flew over to protect her, and the body simply continued cartwheeling the rest of the way down until it hit the ground floor with a sick thud.

Juniper's stomach flipped as they glanced over after it. "Well." They swallowed. "Aster, it seems like your blood is going to be blue."

"Oh, joy."

Lola jerked out from beneath the balcony and lifted her gaze. Juniper threw themself away from the railing to hide and ended up tripping backwards.

The lights finally turned off. Would have shuttered everything into darkness if not for the bio-android terminals still in use. Juniper wiped their hair back, breathing out, and scrambled up on their knees to listen. It was only a matter of time before *someone* broke through Juniper's code and checked on the terminals. They were sure to notice something amiss in their systems by now.

"All off," Clary said breathlessly into the comms like she was running. "Look, pretty boy better be done baking—we gotta make tracks."

Juniper tuned their cybernetics to reach out for Laurel's comms, but paused as dim auxiliary lights turned on. Too fast. Frantic footsteps hurried across the third floor; it wasn't the sound of the bare slaps of stockinged feet, but actual shoes. Not Clary and too heavy to be Laurel. Juniper flung themself to the other side of the terminal for cover and noticed too late they'd left Clary's discarded heels beside Laurel's tablet.

An android ran up, dressed the same as the tour guide. Her eyes shimmered white as she took in the space.

Juniper fumbled trying to connect into the android's network. Rising panic made everything buzz, too loud to concentrate correctly. The android was clearly intrigued by the shoes and the rogue tablet, but that only led her gaze to the terminal she probably *knew* wasn't supposed to be in service.

"When did this one start?" she murmured. "No. No. What *is* all this? How much was used? Ugh... He's going to have our heads."

If connecting to the network was out of their reach, Juniper had one more trick. They pulled the stunner from their vest and turned it on. It gave an audible whir and the android lifted her head. Juniper force-started their combat reflexes, feeling the adrenaline shoot through them, and whipped themself around the corner. The android wasn't fast enough to stop them; Juniper drove the stunning prongs into her neck, right at the base of her skull.

The voltage overpowered the android's systems, making her eyes even brighter, and her body went limp. She collapsed, all her systems inert. Thankfully, the voltage wasn't enough to permanently disable her, giving Juniper some piece of mind. The power surge only forced her systems to restart. Bought them time.

At least she *would* restart.

The thought was too sobering, too fast. Their heart rate spiked and their bio-monitor blared a warning in their head. A cooling sensation rushed through their limbs, making them dizzy, and Juniper gritted their teeth to fight against it. Not the time. It was making the panic worse.

Everything was still, pressing in on them, and it was getting worse and worse with each heartbeat they measured, until they felt a gentle presence. A ghost of a hand soothingly drawn through their hair.

"Hey," Aster whispered it so quietly, but his voice drowned out the warnings. "Juniper? It's okay."

Sucking in a deep breath, Juniper tore their gaze away. It'd have to be. Maybe with Aster, it could be.

The android had swiped away whatever the terminal had been trying to say, but there was a green checkmark. Juniper breathed out. "I think you're done baking."

Juniper twisted the drawer's handle and this time, let the chamber drain. Vents inside the enclosure opened next, blasting air all across the body, and once it finished with a ding, Juniper pulled the drawer out.

And realized they couldn't carry Aster alone. As they turned, connecting to their comms, a dark shape ran into them. A squeak of panic came from both parties. Juniper's hand with a death grip on the stunner was thrown wide. Before Juniper changed tactics, their bio-scanner pinged who had run into them.

"God dammit, Clary," they said, trying to relax.

Clary gripped Juniper by the shoulders. "Where the hell is Laurel?"

"Lights took forever; she went to make a smaller distraction," Juniper said. "I thought she'd come up with you."

"Damn it." Clary wiped a few strands of hair off her forehead. "M-Maybe she was smart and went to get the ship ready. Let me grab our sleeping prince— see if you can connect to Laurel." She slipped past Juniper and bent over, delicately checking the body for wires.

Juniper connected back to the comms, but stopped when their optics sharpened and honed in on a shade of red illuminating the suite. Heart thumping hard in their chest, they turned to find the source.

The security android. A hulking shape in the dark with eyes red and bright. Completely free from Juniper's code. Shit. It wasn't supposed to go belly up so fast that they'd send in security. Without warning, the android charged.

Juniper twisted out of the first grab, combat reflexes already spry. As the android tripped over Clary, making her gasp, Juniper drove the stunner into his arm. There was a spark, hot and white, but it did nothing. Before Juniper could pivot and attempt to drive it into the head-jack, the android caught their arm and yanked them close. The stunner clattered on the floor and Juniper drove their fist into the underside of his jaw.

He let go, Juniper's whole hand smarting with pain as they danced out of another attempt to grab them, but it led them out against the balcony with nowhere to go. The android caught them this time with fingers tight around Juniper's neck.

All he'd have to do was squeeze and Juniper's neck would have broken, but he didn't. The android pushed Juniper so they were halfway over the railing. He must have been programmed not to kill humans, but dropping them? Perfectly fine. Threat would be eradicated one way or another.

Juniper scrambled to hold on, the world moving in slow motion as their cortex computer flashed failed scenario after failed scenario for breaking free. Ninety-nine percent chance to fall. Break their neck. Nanomachines couldn't fix that; it was too absolute.

Clary was standing, but she wouldn't be fast enough.

Their bio-scanner pinged an oncoming shape.

There was another shock, right into the back of his neck, making the android buzz, and the stunner drove deeper. His eyes lit up white like a smoldering star and his arms convulsed until his fingers entirely let go.

Leaving Juniper halfway over the railing. Slipping. Their mind went blank as their body tipped backward with nothing to catch them.

Arms clapped around their waist, jerking them forward, and Juniper was swung back to the balcony floor, right on top of Clary. All of Juniper's systems caught up and they took in hurried gasps as they were reminded to breathe. Clary hadn't let go yet; her grip was ironclad like she thought if she did, Juniper would keep falling.

All in all, not dead. Juniper's heart calmed, some rush of nanomachines flushing through their body again to do the trick, and Laurel knelt beside them.

"Are you okay?" she asked, breathless.

Juniper nodded. "Good shot."

Laurel's smile made Juniper melt. "Thanks, I love you too." She held out her hand. "I got the back bay doors unlocked. Once Lola's safe, they're going to start searching. We should scram."

Leave it to Laurel to make sure they had an escape. With Aster's body secure on Clary's back, Juniper collected the shoes and tablet, and Laurel took point.

Juniper lingered a moment near the two unmoving androids. They mouthed an apology and hurried after everyone. The androids were just doing their jobs, after all. Deep down, Juniper knew they wouldn't have cared so much if those had been enforcers and they weren't sure if it should have bothered them or not.

The three of them hurried down the maintenance stairway and left through the back doors just as power returned to the facility. The lights flickered on across the landing bay, but thankfully, it was deserted save for a few shipping containers waiting to be picked up. The *Maple* was exactly where they'd left it hidden in the back.

By the time they were in the air, alarms kicked on across the facility and colony both. A news broadcast connected to their ship, immediately describing the theft and sabotage. Juniper was a little impressed; reports weren't usually that fast. At least they were out of immediate danger and no one had a good look at their faces. Juniper rested their head against the back of the cruiser where they'd been shoved with Aster's body, exhausted.

"Cedar!" Clary snapped into the ship's comms as she turned the ship to line up with the colony's highway so they could blend in with other late cruisers. Juniper slid, hitting the seats, and Aster's body rolled over onto them. The comms picked up on the other side and Clary huffed. "The fuck? *Now* you pick up?! Are you up there or not?!"

"What?" came Cedar's voice. "You guys have been *dead* silent." Juniper picked their head off the cruiser floor, confused. "I thought it was going well! I made y'all dinner!"

"Shit!" Clary ripped the comms from her ears and tossed it to Juniper. They tried looking it over, but it was too dark to see what was wrong with it.

"Long range must have been fuzzed," Laurel said, readjusting her glasses. "But *why*?"

"Fuzzed?" Cedar grumbled something incomprehensible on the other side and Lily answered. "Shit, was Tremaine not upkeeping *anything* the three years I was gone?"

"Not my fault!" Clary said and switched the cruiser's systems into space flight. They were almost out of the colony, no one the wiser. "We got the body!"

"Oh!" Cedar sounded like he was smiling. It made Juniper do the same, but they wondered if it was because Aster was smiling in their head. "Good! You make him hot?"

Clary sighed and glanced back at Juniper. "Well? Junie? He hot? Inquiring minds want to know."

Juniper flipped her the middle finger. "Not like I can see back here! I followed the photos!"

"Okay, then he's hot." Cedar said, snickering. "What else happened down there?" His voice grew serious. "Did you guys come out with all your limbs attached?"

"Would Lola have fuzzed the comms?" Laurel said slowly, absorbed in her own thoughts. She'd curled up on the seat and Juniper couldn't see her. "She somehow knew I'd be there. She was expecting me."

Clary tilted her head. "Idols do sometimes fuzz communication to prevent any unsanctioned photos from going out at press releases. But she was alone, right?"

"Wait, idols?" Cedar asked.

"One idol." Laurel sighed. "Lola Langley. She's my sister."

Cedar whistled. "Shit. You guys *do* have the same nose, huh? But she's *just* an idol, right? No covert spy or whatever? Probably just being careful."

"Maybe." Laurel's voice continued to grow quieter and Clary reached over to rub her shoulder before Juniper could untangle themself from Aster's body to do the same. "Maybe it's nothing. It's just... weird."

"I wouldn't worry about an idol out here," Cedar said. "Lily's got a handle on the sensors coming out of the place, so it's safe to fly back. Did I say I made y'all dinner?"

"That's really sweet of you." Laurel's voice warmed. "What'd you make?"

It was the right question. Juniper could just imagine how Cedar's face lit up as he rattled off a list of ingredients right off the box. Definitely one of the foods they'd lifted from the mall, but he sounded so proud putting it together. Too endearing. Even Laurel sounded happier, giving him the requisite oohs and ahhs.

He was still rambling when Juniper decided to rest their eyes. It'd be a dozing kind of sleep, but with the continued awareness of everything going on around them. They hoped it would take some of the edge off.

Aster's presence bloomed, catching their attention.

"Hm?" Juniper whispered so quietly, only he probably heard them.

"Thank you for hearing me," Aster whispered in Juniper's thoughts. "I can't wait to be in my new body."

Juniper smiled. "Yeah," they said. "I can't wait either."

SESSION 5

FAMOUS LAST WORDS

21
LAUREL

THERE WEREN'T ANY OBVIOUS ANSWERS. Laurel flopped into her pillows with a long, drawn-out sigh in an attempt to push all the worry out of her. Didn't work; still festered. Once more, she held her tablet above her face and cycled through everything she'd gotten her hands on concerning the recent affairs of her sister.

There was no way she'd publicly announce a hiatus and then go all the way to Saturn to pick up new bodies for her dancers. One: Lola never did that unannounced; she liked showing off her support of android advancements. Two: she'd said Laurel's name. It wasn't a fluke, but she'd been dragged away too fast and Laurel hadn't dared to answer her then.

What if Forrest was right? What if Lola had gone on hiatus to search for Laurel?

But that didn't make sense. Laurel had been officially missing for an entire year and Lola kept on singing. Her hiatus even began before Laurel's face showed up anywhere.

Besides, none of it answered why Lola knew it was

her who'd flung the pinwheel and hid in the bathroom.

And so, once more from the top, she went through everything.

Gossip articles in order of appearance with official sightings interfiled within. Biggest sighting was on some billionaire playboy's private cruise ship near Jupiter. She'd been with a mysterious woman. Dark skin, fluffy hair in a thick headband, and a smile to die for, but no one knew who the woman was. Lola seemed to really like her; there was a genuine smile on her lips in their pictures together. Then there were loads of speculation about Lola's sexuality, but nothing concrete. After that, Lola kept a lower profile, only being seen with her bodyguard androids or agent. Then she announced her hiatus. Rumors blamed the unnamed woman, but Lola had cited family reasons.

More than likely, family reasons were a kind of truth. Laurel was considered an investment by the Federation. When she'd gone missing, they must have hounded her parents for the money that had gone into her supposed rehabilitation. Not that her parents would have it any more; they would have blown it immediately, living lavishly above their means, or gambled it away. One of the two. Which meant they must have been in a bind.

Laurel doubted pulling Lola away from touring was really going to help that.

Beyond Lola's sudden appearance at Saturn, Laurel still wanted to know who fuzzed the comms. First thought was Lola's androids, but it wasn't local. It had only jammed long-range comms. Then came the whys. Why did Lola have a hunch Laurel would be there? Why were the comms fuzzed? Why, why, why and no answers.

Laurel wasn't sure what bothered her more though: the lack of answers or everyone else's lack of caring. Lola was the idol of the stars, beloved by most of the system, so it should have been a huge red flag she'd shown up like some common bounty hunter.

It was equally possible, however, that Laurel was biased. Lola was her sister. It was easy to say that was the reason why she was obsessing and it would be better for all involved if she dropped the subject.

With another sigh, this one of defeat, she rested the tablet face down on her chest and let it darken.

They'd docked at some backwater vampire station that had a tech who owed Cedar a favor. Lily was getting a much-needed update on her internal systems. Hopefully, that meant no more fuzzing.

They were definitely out of the fire, for now, even with all of Laurel's apprehensions. Unfortunately, she and Juniper were under explicit orders not to leave the ship on their own. This was a skeevier station than the one in the inner system. Laurel sort of wished she could have gone out to clear her thoughts, but she didn't dare on her own.

Juniper, meanwhile, was attempting to get Aster into his new body (thankfully, now clothed courtesy of Cedar). They'd eschewed everyone's offer of help, insisting they could do it with just Lily. It made sense; too many people working at once cramped Juniper's style and it really was only a job for one person.

Aching eyes and tense shoulders meant Laurel should have gone to sleep already, but she resolved to look over everything one last time. Find a reason Lola had willingly gone so far out of her way. A reason the comms fuzzed. Even something small and inconsequential would stop the buzzing in her head. All she wanted was proof Lola wasn't actually looking for her.

She had everything reordered, color coded, and noted with how reputable the sighting was, when her door swished open. She jumped with a yelp as Juniper stormed inside, face scrunched in annoyance. They flopped into the bed and released a big sigh.

Laurel joined them, laying down so their heads were beside each other.

"Not going well?" Laurel asked. When Juniper made another face, Laurel did too. "It's the middle of the night. Maybe you need a break." She tilted her head and studied Juniper. The circles under their eyes had only darkened. She couldn't remember the last time Juniper slept. "Maybe sleep?"

"No." Juniper sat back up and ran their hands through their hair. "Don't need it."

Laurel crawled over to sit beside Juniper. "We all need sleep, Junie. Can I do something to help?"

"Drop it, okay? I do not. Not now."

The urge to shove Juniper off the bed and tell them to get out raged through Laurel. She bit it back, though, swallowing the frustration. It was Juniper's life, not hers. She couldn't make her friend sleep and yelling was no help. It'd just stress them both out.

"Then what's up?" she said instead, trying to even her voice. Sound curious instead of pissed off.

Juniper took her hand. "Check my work? I think I'm missing something."

Laurel let Juniper drag her off the bed and to the door, but they stopped abruptly and glanced back when Laurel tossed their tablet back on the bed.

"O-Oh. Were you doing something? I-I didn't actually think you'd be awake. M-My bio-scanner said you were, but..."

Then why immediately come in? Laurel bit the question back and exhaled. "Just looking at intel on

Lola. Something's been bugging me."

Juniper waved a dismissive hand and Laurel resisted shutting the door in their face. "Probably just idol things, right?" They tugged on her hand. "Come on, she's already gone. Thinking about her too long always makes you grumpy."

Maybe that was true, but Juniper didn't have to say it like that. Laurel bit back another reply, knowing anything she said would have sounded too mad. Instead, she shrugged.

Silence pushed between them, a sudden wall building up like before. It was awkward, poignant, and Juniper must have felt it too. They frowned, glancing away, but instead of apologizing, they continued on.

Fine. Totally fine. Laurel was being silly, after all. Everyone else had already dismissed her fears and she wished she had. Besides, she'd wanted out of her head. Maybe this was the way to do it.

The bridge had the easiest access to Lily's super computer and it was where Juniper had brought Aster's body. If the plan had any chance at working, they needed major computing power and Lily had happily offered her services. The cat's interface and cybernetics were updated with the very same computer, so theoretically, it should've worked.

Panels of the floor had been pulled aside near the hologram table, allowing Juniper access to the computer ports below. All sorts of wires fed out of it, either connected to Aster's head or to his body resting like a sleeping prince on the couch. Juniper also had multiple tablets connected into everything laid out around the stolen couch cushion they'd been sitting on. The screens listed diagnostics, percentages, and a string of code constantly updating. Aster's hologram shimmered on the table and he looked deep in thought.

Juniper stepped over the wires, adjusted a few looking a little slack, and sat on their cushion. "Here we are." Laurel squeezed in beside Juniper and studied everything. "Every time I do the final tests, the lights on the bridge warble and the program fails. There's an error I can't parse and it boots me out so I have to recompile everything."

"Everything looks fine on my end," Aster said. "Since we're in uncharted territory, we followed the way androids perform uploads and downloads to the letter."

Laurel frowned. "But you aren't an android."

"Well, yeah," Juniper said. "But it's the only template we have for what we're trying. Androids are a lot closer to—"

"No, I mean..." Laurel scrolled through the updating code. It was way too much even if it had been for an android. "Androids have a data limit, right?" Juniper nodded slowly. "Humans don't. This is trying to track everything that's Aster and he doesn't have a limit or an end. The only reason it works on the cat is because cats are simpler than people, android or otherwise. Lily might not have enough power."

It was the simplest reason the test was failing. Her android class at boarding school liked to use a similar scenario in word problems. The more complex the android, the more power needed. Juniper stared at the code, chewing their lip. Laurel sat back and looked around for the cat.

"Lily, have you ever done this on something other than the cat?"

"Negative," Lily replied from the intercom. The cat was asleep on the pilot's chair. "I apologize. I thought we'd have enough. It hadn't occurred to me otherwise."

Juniper groaned, running a hand through their hair again. "Goddammit."

"The brightest minds in the Federation can't even do this," Laurel reminded. When Juniper just shook their head, she sighed. "We should grab Cedar."

"Why?"

"So we can brainstorm another plan," Laurel said. "You're at a dead end. We heisted a body we can't even use. Maybe in all the years he's been alive, he'll have another idea." If they didn't start brainstorming now, Juniper would grow despondent and mopey. Laurel did not have enough patience to deal with a mopey Juniper tonight.

"Fine," Juniper sighed and stood. "I'll grab him. It's my fault I jumped the gun. Stay here."

Laurel couldn't volunteer to go instead fast enough to get out of helping. Juniper was already gone. She fidgeted, trying not to look at Aster's hologram or the ghastly head still in its container.

"Have..." Aster began slowly. "Have you and Juniper known each other for a long time?"

Laurel shook her head. "Just two years," she said.

Aster waited. He probably wanted more of a backstory, but Laurel didn't want to give one, especially when she didn't really feel like she knew Juniper at all lately.

He frowned. "You don't like me, do you?"

"No!" Laurel said quickly. "No-No-No—I like you!" God, she hadn't meant to mess that up. "It's just... I don't know you and I'm not good with new people."

Aster's face lit up. "Ah! Shall we fix the 'don't know me' part while we wait? Cedar sometimes takes a moment to rouse." He chuckled. "We can even start with something silly."

"Something silly…" Laurel gave it some thought and shrugged. "H-How about your favorite color?"

"Purple, although pink was growing on me. I had my hair pink before I died."

Laurel eyed the android body. Blonde hair, not pink; the machine must not have been tooled for weird hair colors. Maybe she could find some dye for him when they got everything sorted.

"You?" Aster prompted.

"I like yellow. *Vibrant* yellow." Laurel smiled and brought her knees to her chest. Her nails were still vibrantly painted. Toes too. "What's your favorite food?"

"Oh, that's tough." Aster's hologram became thoughtful. "You know, I think I miss this one spicy noodle egg drop soup the most. We used to get it all the time. I hope the place is still there when I can taste again." His gaze flicked back toward Laurel's general vicinity. "You?"

"When I was younger, my sister and I used to visit my grandmother on Mars. She always took us to get these fried sweets glazed in saffron-flavored syrup." When Aster's eyebrows went up, curious, she shrugged. "I think they were a local thing. I've never found them out here."

Aster's curious look melted into a smile. "I used to cook. Perhaps we can find the ingredients and make some together. I'd love to learn."

"I'd like that, too." She cleared her throat and tried to ignore the pang of regret welling in her chest. She didn't realize how much she'd missed food from home. "Did you get on with your family?" she asked.

The hologram shook as Aster frowned. "Not really," he said. "My father was a researcher and before I ran away, I started a chain reaction that blew up half his lab. I like to say it was payback for agreeing to make me a cyber, but it was honestly an accident." He hesitated, looking sad, and Laurel wished she'd thought of a different question. "Were you and your sister close when you were little?"

"We were, actually," Laurel admitted. "Once, when we were younger, I convinced her to put on a little concert in our home and invited all my schoolmates. I got yelled at for exploiting her." She rolled her eyes and scoffed. "Isn't that what my parents were doing? At least my schoolmates weren't lecherous old men evaluating her sex appeal."

Besides, Laurel still remembered the glee on Lola's face as she danced across their couches, singing her heart out. She got to be a silly kid again with no expectations.

Laurel cleared her throat. "Did you have siblings?"

Aster looked taken aback and pondered a moment, but never answered. Laurel frowned. "You don't remember?"

"That's the thing about living a long time," Aster admitted slowly. "You start to forget. Squishy minds weren't meant for this. Androids can upload old memories to the cloud to make room for new ones, but humans... well, unless they are considerably rich, can't." He looked apologetic. "I'm sure I had one, which is why my father was so quick to wash his hands of me, but they must not have made any lasting impression."

That was humbling and made Laurel fidget again. Memories were fickle, sure, but she couldn't imagine them fading the older she got.

"Do you remember how you and Cedar met?"

"It was a formative memory." He paused, chuckling awkwardly. "It might not be appropriate."

"Oh, come on. I can handle it. Tell me."

Aster pondered another moment, like he was deciding just how much to tell her, and began speaking. "As I said, I ran away and well, all I had going for me at the time was that I was pretty." He said it slowly and Laurel nodded, understanding the insinuation. "I made my way from ship to ship, port to port, trying to find a home. I happened across Cedar's ship and he was..." Aster paused again, a shy grin playing across his lips as he glanced away. "Well, he worried about me leaving, so he said I could stay as long as I needed and insisted I didn't need to sleep with him or anyone else to have a spot on his ship. Although, I really could not resist his charms." Aster rolled his eyes and Laurel bit back a laugh. "We were attracted to each other and got along. That's all people really need. The crew also accepted me as one of their own even though I was a broken cyber who was mostly useless."

Laurel smiled. "That must have been nice, though. Being accepted you like that."

"It was much better than the other ships who saw me as someone to use," Aster said and nodded. "You would have liked Maggie. She immediately took me under her wing like I was her little brother. Large lady, she could squash skulls with her thighs if she really wanted to. She was our muscle and cook. We still have all her recipes."

"Are you saying we'll be officially saved from pre-packaged food?"

Aster nodded. "It's one of the reasons I told Junie to give me the entire somatosensory system. Taste is included. At least now I won't have to guzzle blood beforehand."

"That does sound like it'd get in the way," Laurel said. She peeked at the bridge doors, but Juniper hadn't come back with Cedar in tow yet. Another question popped into her mind and she indulged her curiosity some more. "Why'd you become a vampire?"

"I didn't want to grow old without Cedar," Aster said, sounding embarrassed. "I know it sounds a little rubbish, but after we'd spent five years together, I couldn't imagine leaving. I was scared of dying, scared of my cybernetics running out before I was ready, and I wanted to be with him." He glanced away, sad. "Cedar goes through these stages. He lets his crew go because they either grow too old to keep up or die. I didn't want him to be left alone if he did that again."

"It's not rubbish," Laurel said. "I think it's sweet. You found the person you wanted to be with for the rest of your life, no matter how long it is. Did it ever get boring?"

"Cedar keeps things interesting, but I'm sure you don't want the details," Aster said. "I don't regret asking Cedar to turn me. If I can be with Cedar until the heat death of the universe, I'll consider it a life well-lived."

Laurel rested her cheek on her knees, turning her gaze to Aster's body on the couch. "It sounds nice to know you have a home with each other. I've never felt at home, even when it was just me and Juniper. Sometimes it was lonely."

Aster considered her in silence for a moment. "For what it's worth, I think you will always have a home here. Cedar's already practically adopted you both."

Laurel raised her eyebrows. "Seriously?"

"He would have kept you at arm's length otherwise. He's accepted you as his new crew. As his family."

The thought put a smile back on Laurel's lips, but

it waned just as fast, remembering what Aster had said about memories. "In a hundred years, he won't remember two runaways."

Aster scoffed. "Oh, don't sell yourself short, love," he said. "I believe you have made an impression that will transcend lifetimes. You certainly have with me."

"Well, you'll cheat," Laurel teased. "You'll be able to upload your memories."

Aster laughed and nodded. "Yes, but I think I'll keep these ones always near. I promise."

The bridge doors finally slid open again and Cedar came in dressed in a robe and boxer shorts. Juniper followed him in, frazzled—probably hadn't expected the view. Clary also padded inside, yawning, and was wrapped in her black bathrobe like she'd also got up from whatever racket Juniper had made.

Juniper was motormouthing a way too technical explanation of the problem and Cedar was making a face trying to keep up. Clary ignored them and picked up the sleeping cat to plop herself into the pilot's chair.

"Shush!" Cedar stressed, holding up a finger at Juniper. They stuttered the rest of the words as Cedar came over to kneel beside Laurel. "Okay, you tell me. Spare me the technical terms. I haven't had coffee."

"Not enough processing power," Laurel said. "Er. Ship not strong enough." She simplified it further when Cedar narrowed his eyes. "Need more juice." Juniper groaned loudly and looked ready to throttle him.

"That's what I was saying!" they insisted. "I—"

"I get it," Cedar said, gazing at the screens. He grimaced at the diagnostics and shook his head. "Can't believe we found something Lily can't do."

"I apologize," Lily said over the intercom. "I am shocked too."

"Not your fault."

"What we need is a legit transfer terminal," Laurel said. "Something that androids themselves would use, but hopefully one with the potential for more juice."

Juniper grumbled and sat at Cedar's other side on the floor. "The only terminals I know of are back near Mars."

"Too risky." Cedar scratched the underside of his chin, thinking. His face lit up after a moment and he faced Aster's hologram. "Hey, we're going to Clyde's facility for Juniper, I bet he has a transfer terminal there too."

Aster was nodding before Cedar had finished. "Yes! He even made his own androids there, remember? We had to smuggle him some extra drives once."

Up above, Clary tilted her head at the name and opened a screen on her console. She was typing a search query, but before Laurel could ask what it was for, Juniper spoke.

"We don't have cash," they reminded. "How are we gonna be able to pay him to fix me *and* Aster?"

"I've done work for him in the past," Cedar said. "What's another month or two of smuggling shit the feds won't let him have access to?" He gently nudged Juniper and when they didn't look convinced, Cedar faced Aster's hologram. "Back me up here, love."

"I think he liked us," Aster said. "I'm sure we can trade services if we explain the situation."

"Uh." Clary cleared her throat and everyone looked at her. She was craning her head around the console. "Clyde? Do you mean Clyde Lowell? That's the Pluto plan?"

Cedar inclined his head. "Uh... yeah? I told you, right?"

"Just that we were going to Pluto." Clary pivoted

the screen to face everyone. An obituary. Laurel's jaw dropped, reading the name. "Clyde Lowell died ten years ago. No one's been able to get into his lab since."

Everyone was stunned silent until Cedar spoke. "Well, shit."

22
JUNIPER

JUNIPER DIDN'T THINK IT WAS POSSIBLE TO fume so much. They wanted to explode on Cedar. The one thing he promised them was a memory. He hadn't even known the guy had died. Lab effectively lost because without Clyde, it wouldn't open. Leaving Juniper screwed. Trapped. At the mercy of the feds if they crossed paths again. Juniper squeezed their nails into their palms, the soft pain keeping them from hyperventilating as the worst-case scenarios flitted to life in their thoughts.

There had to be another plan.

Clary gathered them in the den with a mini-documentary she'd found on the intrasolar net to get them up to speed. It wasn't what Juniper wanted to do, but maybe learning a bit more about Clyde Lowell would help spark another plan because they were out of them.

Knowing the documentary even existed and Cedar still hadn't realized the man had died, however, made Juniper fume more. Their bio-monitor tried coaching them through breathing exercises to calm them down, but Juniper wanted to hold onto their rage. It was valid.

While Clary set up the video, Cedar tried again and again to apologize, saying that he'd had no reason to keep up with fed news and then he was iced. Juniper tuned him out. He eventually trailed off. Good. Less chance Juniper actually snapped and yelled at him.

The room darkened with the video primed to play and Clary took the only position left on the couch—the armrest on Laurel's side. Juniper was unfortunately sandwiched between Cedar and Laurel. They held themself tight to not give their bio-scanner any reason to ping anyone's emotional state and focused on the documentary.

Clyde Lowell was lauded as the system's finest mind with untold years of technological advancement under his belt. While the announcer spoke at length about the man, the video showed various shots of him from galactic meetings, visiting an android facility, or simply giving the camera a tight-lipped smile. All of them showcased a serious man with snow white hair and tan skin. High cheekbones, a thin face, and a long nose. In every shot, he wore shaded glasses and his outfits were of regal fare.

What drew Juniper's immediate attention, however, was the golden signet ring on his middle finger. Even Laurel noticed it, tilting her head when it showed up in frame.

The ring had a symbol engraved on the face that was a slim crescent moon with a bident emerging from the center, while an orb balanced above it. Not any symbol Juniper knew offhand, but their cortex computer focused on finding the origin of it on the local net.

"Look, I'm really sorry," Cedar tried again during

a lull in the video. Juniper folded their arms tighter, refusing to look at him. Petulant, sure, but maybe he'd get the hint to stop talking. "I had no idea how much time had gone by. I was busy figuring out my crew."

"It's fine," Juniper said, knowing their voice definitely didn't sound fine. Cedar exhaled deeply with a strained frown.

As the document discussed Clyde's relationship with his androids, Laurel looked at Cedar over Juniper's head. "How old was he when you last saw him? He doesn't look different in any of these shots."

Cedar waved a hand toward the screen. "About as old as he looks here. Figured he'd live forever that way."

"A lot of people thought that," Clary said. "My moms sure did. I still remember how shocked they were when the news broke."

Juniper tuned them out; they weren't looking for apologies or ruminations on Clyde's age. That ship had sailed. Guy was dead. What they needed was a way inside the lab.

Clyde was a hermit and never let the feds into his facility, but he'd made visits frequently throughout the Solar System and always had an android accompanying him. Never more than one and it always changed. From what Juniper could tell, there was no discerning the make or model of the androids, but they looked more complex than what the feds could make at the time. Probably too much to find one to let them in. Knowing Juniper's luck, all the androids were the same person, just upgraded models.

The moon bident symbol reappeared on the androids. Be it a tattoo emblazoned on a bare hand or attached to a golden necklace—each one wore it. Was probably Clyde's mark then.

The documentary soon moved on to Clyde's accomplishments. There were many, but the biggest was the cybernetic system adopted into the Prodigy Program. Juniper grimaced, thinking about his hand in their own predicament. No wonder he had the tech to undo it. Although, according to the documentary, he hadn't intended for it to be used as it was. The feds only had it because he liked to publicly release his research when he was through. When the Federation expanded the Prodigy Program—beginning to use the tech on children—he'd vehemently protested its use. The feds and this documentary, of course, spun this as the first signs of his mind going with age.

In addition to that accomplishment, his other major one was the first bio-android interface and he was also responsible for the somatosensory system used in androids and cybernetic limbs. It was a little impressive how much he'd made while remaining out of the Federation's claws.

Of course, all that changed with his death. The next shots were sweeping ones from his funeral. Curiously, while it was crammed full of supposed contemporaries, none of Clyde's androids were in the crowd. The documentary didn't even mention their absence; it simply moved on to the eulogies old researchers gave. Juniper doubted any one of them cared about Clyde Lowell as a person. Their eulogies were about the loss of what other technological advancements he may have had in his mind. Typical. Grieve the opportunity lost instead of the person who was behind it.

Juniper chewed on their lip as the camera focused on Clyde in his coffin. The ring was still there, a glimmering gold beneath a bouquet of white lilies. He still looked the same, too, even in death. Almost like he was asleep.

The final scene was a forlorn image of the supposed opening of his lab under a squall of snow. It looked more like an obsidian obelisk than an entrance. Juniper's cortex computer pinged the symbol engraved in the obelisk. There had to be more to the symbol than simply his mark.

"And we may never know," the announcer's voice boomed over the somber piano piece, "what secrets Dr. Lowell left behind with his death. His lab has been lost since with no way inside. Today, his body resides with in the Orbiting Cemetery of Ganymede."

As the credits rolled, Juniper sunk back into the couch. "What was the procedure to get inside his lab?" they asked. "Was it the obelisk opening?"

Cedar shook his head. "Nah, that was for knowing where to land," he said. "When you land, his lab's AI forces a connection to your ship. If you don't give the right passcode, you get zapped. I was gonna use our old code when we went there."

"And after you give the code?" Juniper asked.

"There's this lift under the snow," Cedar explained. "Once you get all the way down—it's a pretty big elevator shaft—Clyde was there to greet you in front of the real door to his lab. Couldn't get in without him 'cause the door wouldn't budge. We beat him down once and nothing Aster could do opened it." He slowed, watching Juniper like he was trying to figure out what Juniper was digging for.

All at once, his jaw dropped. He reached across Juniper and Laurel to get the remote from Clary. She yelped, almost throwing at him from how fast he'd shot his arm out, and he fumbled with it to rewind the documentary. He paused at the shot of Clyde in the coffin, ring in view.

"A door with that symbol," he breathed.

Laurel gasped, eyes wide. "The ring was the key."

"It has to be," Cedar said. "He'd wave his hand in front of the door and it'd open."

Laurel adjusted her glasses. "Why did the feds bury him with it? If it's obvious to us, they must have noticed it too. It would have had a frequency."

"Clyde was a genius," Cedar said. "He probably has it masked. Must have just thought it was his mark."

"Why did they bury him, anyway?" Juniper asked. "He never gave them anything willingly and even decried their practice."

Clary slid off the armrest and plucked the remote from Cedar's fingers. "They like collecting dead heroes." She switched the screen off and tossed the remote back with the game systems. "They wanted to own him and finally got their chance when he died."

Morbid, but fit the Federation's MO.

If they wanted into the lab, they needed the ring. Assuming the AI inside hadn't gone rogue since his death, everything must have still been inside, even if years out of date. Given Clyde was the reason the feds made as many technological advances as they had, it was probably still sound.

Laurel jerked upright. "We can grave rob it!"

The last place Juniper wanted to go right now was a cemetery, but it *was* the next logical step. They could hold it together and nodded.

"I'm not opposed," Cedar said, like he'd done it before. He probably had.

Clary shot them both an incredulous look. "This is a terrible idea."

"No one ever visits that cemetery," Cedar argued. "The feds are scared of dying. Hell, they put it near Jupiter for a reason. I'm sure we'll be fine."

"There's security," Clary reminded.

Juniper held up their hand. "Lily and I can deal with that," they said and Clary audibly exhaled a sharp breath. "I doubt it's as advanced as the android facility. Do you have a better idea?"

Clary glared at Juniper. "We don't even know if Cedar's code for the lab still works."

"So, we should just give up?" Juniper asked, raising their voice unintentionally.

"This is better than chancing the inner system." Cedar interjected before Clary replied. "If we get in and find the place trashed, then we can brainstorm on another idea, but right now, I'm out of them." He stood up and glanced at everyone, hopeful. Clary folded her arms tightly. "Look, if this seriously bugs you, I can find a safe place to drop you off at with some starting cash. No hard feelings."

"Please. I'm too valuable and you know it." Clary dropped her arms. "I just figured one of us should point out the obvious."

Cedar smiled and glanced up. "Well, Lily? How long until we can get moving?"

"The updates are almost finished. I estimate as soon as the clock strikes galactic morning, I'll be able to disembark," Lily said over the intercom.

"Good." Cedar stretched his arms over his head and headed for the stairs. "I'm going back to bed in the meantime. Wake me up when we move out."

"Affirmative."

After he left, Clary gave it a moment's thought before she was heading after him. "You know what, me too, Lily! I didn't realize it wasn't even morning yet." She paused at the stairs and looked at Laurel and Juniper. "You guys try to rest up a little too. You'll be doing the legwork."

Sleep was the last thing Juniper wanted. Waste of time; they'd rather brainstorm a backup plan with Aster in case this one went belly up. Something useful to keep the brain occupied out of the downward spiral waiting for it if they shut their eyes.

As they stood, thinking, Laurel did too and touched their hand. Juniper hated how their body immediately flinched with panic, especially because Laurel looked hurt every time.

"You should rest," she said softly. "You've been up for a while."

"I don't need to." Juniper took their hand away. "I'm fine. Stop acting like I'm not."

In all honesty, Juniper knew that was the wrong thing to say as soon as they'd said it. Laurel frowned deeply and Juniper hated themself. They'd never been this snappish at Laurel before. She was just worried; it was and always would be endearing.

So why couldn't they just apologize?

Laurel didn't end up replying—not that Juniper blamed her—and headed up the stairs.

Juniper trailed after her, trying to find the words to apologize and not have it sound like a kiss off, but the words never materialized. They were at the door to her room before Juniper finally dragged their voice out of their throat.

"Laurie," they said and she hesitated. "L-Let's just work on something together. Like we used to."

Laurel looked at them. "I was already busy, remember?"

"Let me help."

"You won't."

"What?"

There was a low sigh, pushing the wall between them. The door swiped open as Laurel touched her hand against it. "You already dismissed it."

Juniper glared at her. "Oh, come on."

"No." Laurel whipped around. "You come on, Juniper. I'm not someone you only talk to when you need a distraction or a critical eye for you to then dismiss me out of hand. I'm actually going to go to sleep, like you should too, so just leave me alone."

She stepped inside and the door slid shut between them, leaving Juniper in the dark hallway. They stared at the door longer than they'd meant to, a million replies ranging from sad to angry fuzzing their mind, but nothing came except a sudden emptiness.

It never used to be like this. They were supposed to be attached at the hip. A duo.

Juniper's mind scrambled to find when exactly this started. It was more than just their cybernetics, they knew that at least, but cybernetics made it worse. Extrapolating Juniper's emotions and making them into what Juniper didn't mean to think and do.

No. That sounded pathetic.

It *was* their fault.

They'd been pushing her away ever since they got here, thinking it'd be easier for her and them. Then they'd dragged through their sloppy plans where they'd almost gotten killed too many times. Lied about how much danger she'd been in. Even stopped being there for her once others were in the picture. There was the perfect opportunity to fix it too, and they'd even fucked that up being so laser focused on something else.

Juniper blinked, their vision blurring. They were so tired of everything.

"I'm—I'm sorry," they whispered too quietly for anyone to hear and let their feet guide them back to the bridge. Sleep wouldn't help now.

Aster's hologram awaited them in the bridge, a sad smile on his lips as Juniper came down to the table. "Welcome back," he said as Juniper sat on their forlorn cushion.

He sounded worried. Juniper sighed and rubbed their eyes. "You heard all that, didn't you?"

It was obvious. If not from his voice, it was the way he was watching Juniper, like he was waiting to be a willing shoulder to lean on if he'd had access to his shoulder.

"Yes," he said. "I apologize, it was not my intention nor Lily's to eavesdrop... but we did." He paused, thinking. "You're both at a volatile age with different goals that sometimes will not align and I—"

"I don't want a pep talk." Juniper drew their knees to their chest.

Aster hesitated. "All right," he murmured. "We can watch the other ships take off out of the station, if you'd like. We have a nice view from here."

"You can't even see it."

"No, but you can," Aster whispered softly. "Would you describe it to me? I remember it was pretty."

The view actually was nice. Would have been better if they hadn't fucked up so bad with Laurel so she could have been here too.

The dock had glass doors, showing the glittering expanse of space beyond it. Ships thundered off, leaving a trail of jet fuel behind which lit up against the distant stars as a blend of colors.

Juniper described it haltingly, struggling to find the words, but Aster listened intently.

Juniper was only glad Aster couldn't see the silent tears running down their cheeks or mentioned how their voice was breaking with each word.

23
LAUREL

THE ORBITING CEMETERY OF GANYMEDE was exactly as named: an orbiting cemetery. There was some schtick about lifting mortals to something immortal, although Laurel was pretty sure whoever named the place misunderstood the old Earth myth.

Laurel flicked through the informational brochure she'd downloaded while Cedar piloted the *Maple* toward the cemetery. Truth be told, Laurel wanted to pilot—do anything, really—but he'd already had all the systems engaged by the time she'd worked up the nerve to insist. Instead, she sat beside him while Juniper was in the back.

Silent.

They hadn't really spoken since Laurel sort of slammed the door in their face. Laurel had gone to bed angry, but by morning, she'd felt bad about it. Except what she'd said was true to what she'd been feeling and she couldn't find it in herself to apologize.

Without it, however, there was a newfound silence. Laurel hated it. It was somehow worse than before; the wall between them had become a chasm.

Friends were supposed to talk things out, weren't they? Yet when Laurel wanted to give it a shot, no words came.

She threw her attention back to the brochure. She had to focus on the mission, not interpersonal problems she and Juniper would deal with like rational people.

Eventually.

The cemetery resembled other stations with its large glass dome where incoming visitors could peer into it. Below were various circular disks where the landing bays were located. No private docks here. Laurel's gaze was drawn to the large tree visible at the top layer of the cemetery. The brochure boasted it was there so heroes could think of Earth as they slept.

Charming, except the heroes weren't asleep. They were dead.

There was also a light rail system taking visitors from the docks and through the entire cemetery above. The choice must have been deliberate; it forced visitors to see everything and be wowed at the lengths the feds went to preserve the bright minds and heroes they didn't burn. Everything was all about pomp and circumstance and it bugged Laurel.

When she was little, her grandmother died unexpectedly. Even with fed care and medicine, she was just gone. There was a celebration of her life and accomplishments as a beloved educator, but then she became ash in a pretty urn. No matter how much she meant to her loved ones or all her students, it wasn't enough to be immortalized like this. Ash and dust she became. Some of that had been sprinkled across space to return her to the stars. Laurel's parents kept most of the ashes and Laurel wished she'd taken some herself.

The whole thought made her sadder than she

realized; it wasn't like she and her grandmother had ever been super close, but part of her wanted to believe if her grandmother had been alive, maybe things would have been different. There would have been someone who cared.

Except then she'd never have met Juniper. Wouldn't have been here.

Laurel shook the thoughts free, letting them go. What mattered was now. The present.

"Going in," Cedar told Clary over the comms.

He wasn't a bad pilot; his steering was smooth and so was his acceleration and deceleration. He was also better at tracking the information on the console. Years of experience, no doubt.

As they neared the airlock along the lower deck, a hail came from the cemetery's AI system. Cedar answered it only after Juniper had jacked into the console to be ready with the injection they and Lily had prepared.

"Welcome to the Orbiting Cemetery of Ganymede," the AI chirped and showed the facility's logo on their console. It was an orb with a tiny meteor going around it. "What is the nature of your visit?"

Cedar cleared his throat and Juniper gave him a thumbs up. Their injection was in. As soon as they left, any evidence of their visit would be wiped from the cemetery's internal systems.

Laurel checked it off the list on her tablet. They were on phase three now: find Clyde Lowell's grave. Juniper retrieved their cord and sat back.

"Paying respects to Dr. Gellar," Cedar answered.

Dr. Gellar was the woman responsible for syncing up time management throughout the system. It was something small, but helpful in many respects. No one probably visited her except primary schools when they got to her name in the history books.

"Thank you for your visit." The airlocks hissed open in front of them. "Please dock your civilian class cruiser inside and board the light rail at your leisure. Thank you again for visiting the Orbiting Cemetery of Ganymede. Please enjoy your stay."

As Cedar took them through the airlock, light sparkled to life, showing him the way to the correct docking bay. All the while, silence continued. Cedar flicked glances at both Laurel and Juniper in turn, an eyebrow lifted, before he returned to the task at hand. Laurel was sure they both looked miserable. She felt like she was sitting with a stranger behind her. Like she and Juniper had forgotten how to be friends.

They left the *Maple* locked up on the landing bay and they followed the glowing floor arrows to the lift in the center. There were benches facing outward around it with vending machines with various picnic-like packaged food, and chutes for trash on the far sides. The place was spotless too, not a speck of misplaced dirt like Laurel expected being a cemetery, and the tiles gleamed beneath the fluorescent lamps.

There were no other cruisers, but it was night across the system. Almost everything was dim with a perfect view of Jupiter looming in the distance. The lift was in contrast to the dimness, an eye-searingly bright white which was made worse when the glass doors shut them inside. Laurel's eyes adjusted soon enough, letting her look out of the glass, but the lift went up agonizingly slow.

It would have been a good time to try and talk to Juniper, but the words still stayed stubbornly out of reach. Juniper had closed in on themself anyway; arms drawn protectively across their chest and eyes cast anywhere else. Laurel left them alone.

The rail was short with two cars attached together and it was sleek and white. Enough room inside for at least two school classroom field trips; no one else probably visited in droves. The inside was just as white, but at least the seats along the walls were a dark gray. Gave Laurel's eyes a bit of a break.

As soon as they were aboard, the rail chimed and shut them inside for the full tour of the cemetery.

If this had been before Laurel and Juniper forgot how to be friends, Juniper would have immediately dragged Laurel over to the control panel flush against the front windows and had her open it so they could peek inside. All Juniper did now was stand there, tightly gripping one of the standing poles. Laurel almost thought to suggest it, but the spark of adventure really wasn't there for her either.

The gulf between them must have been growing more obvious; when Cedar sat down, he was glancing between them, worried.

"So," he said, breaking the silence. "Is everything all right? You two are usually chatty."

"I'm fine," Juniper immediately said. "I'm just... tired, I guess."

Cedar shared a worried glance with Laurel. "Sleep not helping?" he asked.

"I haven't been."

The way Cedar's face fell made Laurel's stomach twist. She must have been the only one who actually knew.

"At all?" Cedar asked.

"It's fine," Juniper snapped. They let go of the pole to wrap their arms tight around themself again. "Nanomachines, remember? I don't need to. Not really."

"Hell, I don't need to either, but it helps," Cedar

argued. "Juniper—"

"Stop it!" Juniper spun to face Cedar. "We already talked about you not trying to be a parent. I can still do cyber stuff just fine, so just stop it."

Cedar frowned deeply, but before he could snap back, Laurel cut in.

"Junie, he's only trying to help," she whispered. "You can tell us what's wrong."

Juniper finally looked at her, incredulous. "Nothing's wrong!" they said, their voice breaking with the obvious lie. "I just don't want to. It's cold. It's dark. And it's a waste of my fucking time."

Oh, Laurel thought, realization dawning on her. It made sense now. Cedar blinked and the same realization must have come over him. Juniper tensed and twisted to look away from them.

Laurel wanted to reach out and be comforting, but she froze, remembering how Juniper had flinched from her touch numerous times since.

"It's because she turned you off," she whispered.

Juniper's face twisted. "Yes! Everything was gone. I was dead!" Their voice broke even further as they raised it. "Everyone says I just need to fucking rest—fucking sleep—but it's just like I'm dead again! What if it happens again and I don't wake up?"

Laurel's heart sank. It didn't help they needed the gummies to sleep, too. Knowing those *would* kill them if their cybernetics went lax for one moment... no wonder Juniper had forgone sleeping altogether.

"I'm scared of dying, okay?" Juniper whipped back around to look at Cedar. "And it feels so much like dying if I actually manage to fall asleep. So, I just don't. There's only so many distractions I can find to not think about it."

More and more slotted into place. Juniper's

moods, their sudden manic energy to bury everything awful, and how snappish they were when it didn't work. Their lack of sleep drove them to do anything they could to not ruminate on their mortality.

Knowing Clyde was dead and so too the assurance they could stop their cybernetics must have been another crack. And now, being here with the dead must have made it all worse. What once could have been a fun adventure, was now a reminder to Juniper that they would die too, just like all the heroes buried here.

Laurel wanted to kick herself for not putting two and two together before coming, but it wasn't like Juniper would have stayed behind if anyone had suggested it.

Tears were slipping down Juniper's cheeks. "I'm sorry. I know I've been a dick." They flicked a quick glance at Laurel and immediately jerked it away like they were ashamed it took them so long to apologize. "It's just been so overwhelming. I can't think. I feel sick. And it fucking sucks." They squeezed their eyes shut and pushed their hands to their ears like they were blocking something out. "And we're here. W-What if all of these people aren't dead? What if they're like me? Trapped?"

Laurel had to do something other than watch her friend spiral downward and pulled Juniper into a hug. Juniper flinched, but instead of pushing her away like they had been, they dissolved into her arms and wrapped her up just as fiercely, burying their face into her shoulder. Laurel couldn't fix anything—they were both aware of that—but hugs always helped.

She was so focused on holding Juniper, she hadn't noticed Cedar standing beside them until he'd wrapped them both up himself.

The three of them stood together and it felt as timeless as it was warm. Until Juniper picked their head up and squawked a laugh. Laurel couldn't help it and giggled too. She peered at Cedar; he had the silliest grin on his lips, teeth and all.

"Did you want a hug too?" she teased.

Cedar loosened his grip. "You both just looked like you needed a big one."

Juniper leaned into Cedar, bringing Laurel with them, and closed their eyes. "I think I did." They actually smiled genuinely this time, especially when Cedar tightened his arms around them again. Juniper giggled. "You give very nice bear hugs."

Though Laurel wanted to stay there until she absolutely had to move, Cedar let them both go. "I won't let anyone do that to you ever again. And I know it might not make it all better," he said slowly, watching Juniper especially, "but my offer is still there. If none of this works out."

Vampirism.

"Yeah. I know," Juniper whispered. "Thank you."

It was the only way Cedar could fix it himself, but Laurel hardly found herself fine with the idea even as he looked at her like he expected an answer from her too. Guess he figured if Juniper was ever turned, Laurel would be too. They were a package deal. She couldn't truly imagine living forever, though. Fear of death aside, having none scared her almost the same. Still, she nodded and hoped it didn't come to that.

Juniper turned, tugging Laurel with them, and nodded at the window. Right back to old times, then. Laurel didn't mind and eagerly stood next to Juniper to stare out the window.

The rail was twisting around the main cemetery plots along the top now. Sad, empty, but lit with soft orange lamps that surrounded the large oak tree in the center. Massive in person, Laurel was surprised the tree thrived at all.

The rail chimed and began to slow, the brakes like quiet whispers. The doors slid open, letting them off, and an android grave keeper awaited them on the other side. As expected, but Juniper and Lily had planned for it. Juniper jerked ahead and pressed a chip to his hand. The program within was an upgraded version of one they'd used in the android facility.

The android blinked and hesitated, before looking right past Juniper. He checked the rail up and down, not even acknowledging Cedar or Laurel, before shaking his head.

"AI's taking the shit again." He sighed and turned. "Whatever. Back to my shows."

He ambled off, grumbling to himself, and Juniper smirked.

"God damn," Clary said over the comms. "Didn't think you two could make an android ignore you while staring right at you."

"Me and Lily are gonna be unstoppable—just you wait," Juniper said and Laurel found herself grinning at Juniper's confidence. "Feeds stable?"

"Got them all loaded and looping. You two geeked for some grave robbing? I know Cedar is."

Laurel nodded. "Totally the type."

Cedar scrunched his face. "I am not! This is the first grave I've ever robbed."

Juniper covered a snort and Laurel grinned at them. First step to remembering how to be friends and sharing a silly laugh? Check.

"I'm ready," she said, hoisting the bag of supplies over her shoulder. "Let's go!"

Maybe she was a little too geeked, but she'd always

wanted to go graverobbing after watching one too many heist films as a kid late at night. A lot of them had graverobbing as a focus for some reason, and many times, she'd gone to sleep imagining reasons to do it herself. Digging up a signet ring to unlock a research facility orbiting Pluto had unfortunately never been one of them.

After checking the holographic map of the cemetery in the small common area outside the rail, they found Clyde Lowell's resting place on the lower Evergreen Shelf in Sector Sigma. Not important enough to sit underneath the oak leaves, then. Cedar took point and led everyone toward the slope heading to the lower shelves.

Solid white headstones marked the graves and the ones nearest the tree had flower wreaths or grave blankets draped across them, creating bright pops of color against the grim monotones of the grass and tombstones. Every time they passed a grave too closely, a hologram came to life of whoever was buried within. The first few times, Laurel and Juniper had both jumped, scrambling to get behind Cedar, but he was never surprised.

The holograms showed the heroes in the prime of their lives. Sure, they stood in a single stiff pose and didn't look at all alive like Aster in his hologram, but there was an attempt made. All in all, though, a hollow reminder of who was buried within.

The flower wreaths and grave blankets became less and less as the path sloped downward. Many of the graves here only had a single lily resting atop them.

Clyde Lowell's grave was as unassuming as the rest with its single lily. His hologram flickered to life as they stepped near, showing a man of indeterminate age, but older with soft creases around his wizened eyes. Definitely looked the same as he had on the documentary.

"Sorry Clyde," Cedar said as he took the shovel out of Laurel's pack. "But we need your ring. You understand me, right?"

If he hoped for an answer, it wasn't forthcoming. He simply nodded and stripped his coat, leaving it on Laurel's head, and got to work. She eagerly threw it on, realizing how cold she was.

She and Juniper watched him dig for a moment before he stopped and glared at them both. Immediately, Juniper grabbed the other shovel from the pack and got to helping while Laurel kept watch. Only had two shovels, after all. She and Juniper traded places every time one of them got tired, but Cedar never did. Vampire stamina.

Surprisingly, it wasn't long before Cedar's shovel hit something wooden. He and Laurel dusted off the dirt and found the top of the coffin. Clyde wasn't buried deep. Small miracles.

Laurel took the crowbar from her pack and hooked it beneath the lip of the coffin. It took her and Juniper to upend the nails and they pulled the top open.

Clyde Lowell lay within, although Laurel wasn't sure why she thought otherwise. He wasn't as decayed as she'd figured he'd be after ten years. Didn't even smell like death. Just cemetery dirt.

"This kinda weirds me out," they said, laughing weakly. "He's not even rotting." They took the crowbar as Laurel went in search of the gold ring. "All yours, Laurie."

Cedar snorted from above, his back turned to them as he kept watch. "They pump corpses full of shit for their funeral. Can't look *too* dead," he said.

"Probably just hasn't broken down yet." He jerked his head to one side so suddenly, Laurel froze and listened.

There was a distant sound, but Laurel couldn't tell what it was. Cedar inclined his head the other way, crossing his arms. "Must have been the grave keeper." He glanced back at them. "Come on, get the ring. We've been here too long already, I'm getting antsy."

"Yeah, yeah." Laurel scrunched over Clyde's body and looked at his hand. He didn't have anything in his pockets anyway. The gold ring still glistened despite being buried for ten years and she tested turning it. Loose, so they didn't need the wrench after all.

She twisted it free with minimal effort and held it above her head. "Got it!"

A hand from below latched around her collar and yanked her close. She might have screamed. Juniper was probably screaming too, but Laurel's mind went completely blank as she was face-to-face with the man who should have been dead.

But Clyde Lowell's eyes were wide open. He snarled at her with a mouth full of sharp teeth.

He was a vampire.

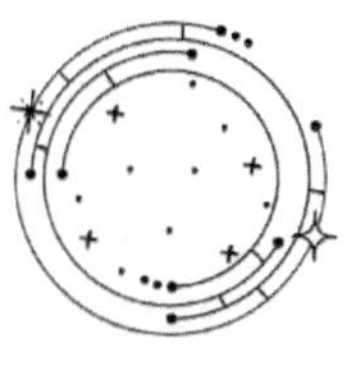

24
JUNIPER

LAUREL WAS SCREAMING. SO WAS JUNIPER and they were pretty sure the vampire in the coffin was too. Their combat systems shot adrenaline through them and they smashed the crowbar down on the vampire's arm. He let go, snarling, and before he could do anything more, Cedar swooped in. Cedar's arm collided with Juniper's chest, sending them flying out of the grave. They thumped some feet away, losing their breath from the impact, and watched as Laurel fell on the other side with the selfsame thump.

Clyde got out from beneath Cedar and launched himself at Laurel.

By the time Juniper forced themself upward, panic ringing in their ears, Cedar had sprung out of the grave and had Clyde tackled to the ground. Laurel scrambled away, hyperventilating, and dodged the vampire limbs flying in every direction. Cedar wrestled Clyde still, although not for lack of trying on Clyde's part.

Juniper dropped back to their knees, standing very short lived, and breathed in deep to slot themself back together. Their bio-monitor calmed and a soothing chill rushed through their limbs. Imminent disaster over.

"H-Holy shit!" Laurel spat out, her voice still high with panic.

No time to sit there and catch their breath. Juniper forced themself back to their feet to get between Laurel and the vampire struggle. She was still trembling when Juniper came over and hauled her up. Unharmed, at least, and the gold ring was still tight in her hand.

"He's a vampire?!" Laurel asked.

"How did you not know, Cedar?!" Juniper edged in front of Laurel as Clyde made another effort to escape.

Cedar gave them both a withering look. "I just didn't!" When Juniper glared at him, Cedar scowled. "You don't just go up to people and say 'hey let me see your teeth', for fuck's sake! Fangs aren't always big!"

Clyde threw his head back, smashing Cedar square in the nose. Juniper readied themself to bolt with Laurel, but Cedar held on with a growl.

"Junie," he said between gritted teeth, "there's a flask in my jacket. Get it in his mouth. He'll get the picture."

It took Juniper and Laurel patting the jacket down before Juniper found it in one of its many interior pockets. The flask was a stout steel bottle and upon opening it, Juniper caught the whiff of blood. They scrunched their nose.

"He's hungry—it doesn't matter how old it is," Cedar said. "That's why he's like this. I'd let him go to do it myself, but he'll go right for Laurel."

Clyde had gone still, sniffing the air, and focused on Juniper with a stare they couldn't believe had once belonged to the man responsible for all of the fed's technological advancements. There was no one there behind the hunger for blood.

Juniper left Laurel an arm's length away from the vampires and slowly crept closer. Clyde held frighteningly still as Juniper bent down and shoved the flask opening at his mouth.

He got the picture. He tipped his head to one side and Juniper poured the contents in. Once the flask was emptied, Juniper withdrew back toward Laurel. Cedar waited, not even breathing, and finally, a long sigh eased out of Clyde.

"You can let me go now," he said, his voice gravelly with disuse.

Cedar's shoulders remained tense. "If you go after either of them, I will rip your head off. You get me?"

"I only wish you'd already had."

Juniper kept Laurel behind them, ready to run as their cortex computer gave them options for the best direction to go, but as Cedar slid off Clyde and stood, all Clyde did was sit up. The mania was gone, some color had flushed his pale cheeks, and he looked more like the regal man he'd been in the documentary.

He was so obviously a vampire looking back at the signs. Why he'd wore the shaded glasses—hiding the dilation of his eyes if he'd recently fed. Why he'd been a hermit on Pluto of all places—less chance to get caught as a vampire. And why he'd never aged. Sure, Cedar wasn't wrong, Juniper barely saw Clyde's fangs as he spoke, but all other signs literally pointed to vampire. Cedar should have known.

Laurel suddenly gasped. "They were starving you," she said as Cedar helped Clyde stand. "That's why it was so easy to unearth your grave. They needed you close so they could get to you."

The thought gave Juniper a powerful shudder. Yet another reason to hate the feds. Burying a man alive.

Clyde smiled gently at her. "You are correct, my dear," he said and paused to wipe the blood tricking down his chin on the back of his hand. "I apologize for my outburst. Their intent was to get information from a raving, starved, vampire. Never got much."

Cedar frowned. "Why didn't you ever tell me you were a vampire? I could have kept better tabs on you."

"I wouldn't have wanted tabs." Clyde paused and squinted at Cedar. "It's... it's Cedar Woods, right?"

"Still kicking," Cedar said and Clyde's lips shifted into a warm smile of recognition. "These two are Laurel and Juniper. My new crew."

Somehow, hearing it aloud made Juniper warm and fuzzy. A sense of belonging. Clyde gazed at them and their cortex computer shot them another plan of escape. They swiped it away.

Clyde's mouth tightened. "Cybernetics. I see now why you want my ring. For once, I'm glad the feds are so high in their ivory tower, they never thought it would grant them access."

"Can we have it?" Laurel asked, still holding it tight. Juniper bit back a sigh—marshmallow to the end. Now that he was alive and being shit on by the feds, she felt camaraderie with him.

Clyde raised his eyebrows and chuckled. "You were willing to steal from a dead man. You hardly need my permission at this point. I'm still dead to the world."

"We can take you back," Juniper offered.

"No." The answer came so sharp and quick with bared teeth, Juniper and Laurel flinched.

Cedar folded his arms. "Start from the beginning. What the hell happened?"

The answer didn't come immediately. Clyde was still rubbing his wrists, gaze searching Cedar like he expected a trick of some kind. Sometimes he glanced at Laurel and Juniper, but he always looked back to Cedar. Finally, with a slow exhale, he began.

"I chose a death day for myself," he said quietly. "I uploaded pertinent memories to my lab's AI so my last android wouldn't feel alone and I set out to see the sun one last time." He closed his eyes and Juniper expected a tear to slide out with how shaken his voice was. None came.

"I don't know how, but the feds found out and seized my ship. When I refused to tell them how to get into my lab, they put me in a heavy slumber and masqueraded my death to the masses. No one knew I was a vampire, thus no one had any reason to think it anything but my death. Then they were starving me, hoping I'd talk. I never did. So, they buried me in this shallow grave only to dig me up every year or so to see if I'd finally cracked. To the world, I am but one of their greatest minds gone too soon, and, to them, the greatest mystery they have yet to crack."

Nausea rolled through Juniper, making them tremble. Clyde was literally trapped, going mad from starvation, and no one had known. Laurel's hand pressed against theirs and Juniper took it to hold.

"Why'd they want your lab that badly?" Cedar asked.

Clyde shrugged. "They are convinced I made some damning breakthrough and that's why I wanted to die. I had simply exhausted my will to live. Their desire to live forever is not one I aspire to. My research was simply to answer my questions and when I found a suitable answer, I gave it to the public. They want all my half-truths to simply confront their own mysteries.

All they'll find is more questions."

He cleared his throat and stood straighter with realization. Suddenly, he was not the starving vampire, but the researcher he'd been before his supposed death.

"You." He made eye contact with Juniper and they stilled. "You wish to use my lab to fix yourself."

Juniper exhaled, nodding. "That's our plan."

"I do have the technology," he said and Juniper's heart soared, replacing the terror. "There were a few before you who have done the selfsame procedure, one being a good friend of mine. Though I cannot promise it will work the same, as your cybernetics are more evolved than theirs ever was, but it is yours to use."

Laurel was tugging on Juniper's arm, excited. They resisted the urge to tug back. It was really going to happen.

"As long as you destroy my lab once you're finished."

The good spirit escaped like an exhale, leaving Juniper and Laurel frozen. "What?" they said in unison.

"One day, the feds *will* get inside," Clyde explained. "If they find my tech and use it to learn where the weaknesses are? They'll close all loopholes and the process will be completely irreversible."

They'd be dooming others in need of a reversal process. Juniper shook their head. "No. We can protect it. More people like me deserve to be fixed."

"You can't protect it," Clyde said and Juniper shot a look at Cedar, begging him to step in. He was resigned, however, looking away. "I could barely do so, even with my death." He stepped forward, hesitant, and stopped an arm's length away from Juniper.

"Cybernetics were meant to aid and improve human life." He gently touched Juniper's shoulder and they resisted flinching. "The feds twisted it for their own aim and you are the end result. A possible weapon they can control on a whim when the time comes." He dropped his hand. "When they get my research, the kinks will be ironed out. While they continue their fruitless search for immortality, they will keep everyone they believe lesser tethered under their one will. It'd be the end of humanity as we know it. My research cannot be used as a door to this end."

So what if all that was true? Juniper still shook their head. "The feds can find other people who can replicate your research," Juniper said and Clyde scoffed at the notion. "People like me can't. If we bury it now—we're dooming them all."

"Burying it now buys everyone time." Clyde tilted his head, expression hardening. "If you go in without my blessing, my remaining android *will* kill you on sight. You do it my way or none."

The option was either to doom humanity or doom humanity. Juniper glared at Clyde, but the will to fight him fizzled. Nothing Clyde said was wrong. One day, the feds would finish fixing the Prodigy Program and cybernetics would become ironclad. Burying the lab made it so it wouldn't happen right away. Humanity was doomed, with or without the lab's help.

"Fine," Juniper whispered and Laurel's fingers tightened around their hand. "Fine. We promise."

Clyde smiled, relieved. "When you arrive, tell my android—his name is Morus—tell him Clyde is buried beneath the mulberry tree. He'll know then I sent you."

Laurel nodded. "Clyde's buried beneath the

mulberry tree," she repeated. "Got it." She slid the ring securely on her thumb.

"I've one more request." Clyde faced Cedar. "Kill me. Let this nightmare end. I know you cannot take me to the sun, but dying here in my grave will be enough."

For what felt like a lifetime, Cedar was silent. Juniper slowly stepped closer to him and touched his arm for solidarity. He breathed out and nodded.

"I will," he said quietly.

Clyde needed help getting back into his grave and Juniper and Laurel guided him in. His legs were weaker than Juniper had given him credit for; muscles atrophied from starvation and disuse. It was a wonder he'd stood as long as he had. He sat in his coffin and tilted his head back against the bottom of his tombstone. His hologram appeared above them, sheathing everyone in gold.

Their cortex computer helpfully gave them the surefire way to kill a vampire: separate the head from the body. Cedar didn't need telling; he'd taken up the shovel. With enough force, it would do the trick. Juniper turned Laurel away; she didn't need to see that.

"Thank you," Clyde whispered as Cedar positioned the shovel's spade at Clyde's neck. "I always liked you."

Cedar hesitated. Maybe he couldn't do it. Just as Juniper reached out to offer to do it for him, Clyde's eyes snapped open. He gripped Laurel's ankle, jerked her into the grave, and did the same with Juniper. Before Juniper found their voice to ask him what the hell he was doing, their aural augments pinged the sound of a blaster priming.

"Put your hands up and don't make any sudden

movements."

A voice they knew even without their cortex computer finding the match. It was as smooth as honey, sending a shiver down Juniper's back like it always did.

The Answer had found them.

25
LAUREL

CEDAR DIDN'T MOVE, BUT HE SETTLED A piercing gaze on Laurel and Juniper. Laurel knew that look; he wanted them to stay put. Not like she had a choice. Clyde's grip was ironclad, keeping her against his chest, and Juniper was in similar straits on his other side.

What made everything worse, though, was Laurel recognized the voice. Even if she hadn't, the pure panic on Juniper's face would have told her everything.

The Answer in the flesh.

Slowly, Cedar raised his hands, the shovel still tight in one of them. His gaze bored into Laurel—practically begging her to stay down—but he needed help. There had to be something that she or Juniper could do.

"Turn around. Slowly," the Answer said.

With one last burning look, Cedar slowly turned. He lifted his chin to stand tall and faced his back to the grave.

"Ah. Cedar Woods." The Answer chuckled. His voice this close had the aftereffect of static. "I should have known you'd be here mixed up in this. All the evidence said as much."

Clyde's grip relaxed, his eyebrows folding in confusion. Maybe he recognized the voice too. Laurel gently pulled away and when he didn't immediately snatch her back, she peered over the edge of the grave.

The Answer had his faceplate focused on Cedar and it oscillated scan lines. His blaster was primed and glowed gold. He looked the same as he had back on the vampire station—dark trench coat over a shirt and vest combo, now paired with dark pants and boots.

Cedar snorted. "Why you gotta say it like that?"

The Answer tilted his head and the screen on his faceplate cleared, becoming a blank void. "It's curious... Three years ago, you disappeared and when you finally reemerge, it's everywhere Juniper Austre has been."

His faceplate flickered and switched to show a reel of images. All of them were of Cedar and Juniper. From Cedar bending down to kiss Juniper's cheek at the motel, to their dock on the Mars Transit Station where they'd shared the eggroll, sitting at a bench at the mall, and then to Cedar carrying Juniper out after they'd been shut off.

Even their hug on the train. Goosebumps prickled Laurel's skin; he'd never been far.

The Answer twitched his head and the faceplate went blank. Laurel flinched downward, hoping he didn't notice her. Clyde latched onto the back of Laurel's coat and pulled her in again. His lips were moving, like he was trying to piece a plan together silently.

"And," the Answer went on, "you've been rather... quiet compared to who you were before." He waited, like he expected a reply, but when Cedar stayed silent, the bounty hunter continued. "Beyond, of course, the few instances where I assume you were protecting your new wards. Grisly. Shades of who you used to be. What happened to the Red Bandit? Who painted the stars red with blood? I'm curious."

"He got tired," Cedar said. "Happens sometimes."

"Well." The Answer gave a little exasperated huff. "I suppose the boring explanation will do. Although, your proclivity for violence dulled quite some time before then, hadn't it? You didn't *just* become tired. You found someone. I looked it up, made some inferences, but where is he now? He's absent from all your recent adventures."

Juniper moved on Clyde's other side and Laurel glanced at them. They tapped their ear. Laurel fiddled with her comms and connected to Juniper.

"I can't get a hold of Clary," Juniper said sub-vocally over the commlink. "It's like what happened at the android facility. Long range communication is toast, but not short range."

Laurel bit back a sharp breath. The Answer must have been there too. Watching. Waiting for an opportunity to intercept them. She shot her gaze back to Cedar, worried. The Answer was probably trying to goad him into moving. End the standoff so he could get to them in the grave.

"So, what?" Cedar snapped after the long pause. "You gonna turn me in for graverobbing?" The Answer chuckled. "That's not your style."

"I agree," the Answer said. "It's really not. A little boring. Especially for you."

"You also don't turn in vamps," Cedar reminded and the Answer hummed. "Hey, actually. I got a question about that."

The Answer laughed. "Oh?"

"Yeah. Why don't you go after vampires? You got a soft spot for us?"

"Perhaps."

"And you know what? One more thing." Cedar's voice was running faster, moving right into motormouth territory. "I thought you'd be taller."

The Answer paused. "Yes," he drew the word out. "I get that more than you'd think."

And Cedar kept going on and on with trivialities. Laurel wasn't sure why the Answer hadn't shot him yet. Unless he expected Laurel and Juniper to make their move and was content to wait.

Clyde pulled her closer. "He's buying time," he whispered and Laurel bit back from saying duh. "Promise me again."

"What?" Juniper winced as Clyde held them tighter. "Fine—Fine. I promise I will personally blow up your lab."

"And get your android out first," Laurel hastily added.

"His name is Morus, don't forget." Clyde eased out a slow breath. "He's a good sprout. When I let go, grab Cedar and run. Do you understand?"

"What about you?" Laurel whispered.

"Just focus on running."

Juniper's eyes widened. "We can't leave you here with him."

"Cedar can't kill me—I saw it in his face." Clyde let them go. "But this one will."

He was a blur all at once, springing himself out of the grave like he'd never been starved. The Answer gasped and Cedar charged him with the shovel. The blaster went flying. Too far to grab.

Juniper moved just as fast, augments audibly humming, and dragged Laurel out of the grave. Clyde was on top of the Answer with strength only a vampire had. They wrestled, Clyde smashing the Answer's head over and over again into the ground, but after what must have been shock keeping him still, the Answer measured the vampire's movements and swiftly gained the upper hand. Very soon, Clyde was against the ground and the Answer on top of him, holding his head tight.

Cedar looked like he wanted to intervene, but he steeled himself and before Laurel realized it, she was lifted off the ground under one of Cedar's arms and Juniper's wrist was tight in Cedar's other hand as he ran.

Against sense, Laurel looked back. There was a crunch and she regretted looking. Blood gushed everywhere as the Answer crushed Clyde's heads between his hands.

Clyde Lowell was dead like he wanted.

She lost sight of the Answer as they raced up the incline. They were passing a row of graves when shots rang out. It missed them entirely, but chunks of headstones spewed across them. Warnings. Cedar didn't flinch, even as Laurel and Juniper did, and she jerked to look behind them again. The Answer wasn't far behind, blood stark against his hands.

His speed was no match for Cedar's head start however; the vampire halfway carried Juniper and Laurel all the way to the rail and threw them inside. As he jumped in himself, he ducked low. Shots pelted the doorway and over his head. They only ceased when the doors snapped shut. The car sped forward, easing them into the glass tube enclosure around the tracks.

"How the fuck did he find us?" Juniper asked as Cedar paced up and down the car.

"He's *been* following us," Laurel said. "The fuzz

was the same as the android place, you said it yourself. It must have been him. He's never been far behind."

Juniper scowled. "But why not interfere then?"

"Too many potential witnesses and variables," Cedar growled. "Since it's just us—"

Glass shattered above them, cutting Cedar off, and the pieces spilled over the train car, plinking down the sides. Then something heavy thumped down. The Answer must have come through the railway tube. Cedar swore, gritting his teeth, and the three of them raced for the front car.

The AI warned them to remain seated as Cedar forced open the doors and let Laurel and Juniper through. Laurel pivoted to the control panel flush against the wall and popped it off with her fingers. Juniper immediately saw her plan and linked into it. A holographic keyboard buzzed to life and with quick keystrokes, Juniper initiated the unlocking sequence.

The latches holding the cars together disconnected. Without the front, the rear car slowed immensely. By the time the Answer managed to force himself inside and reached their end, there was a large enough gap between them that jumping would end up with him on the rails.

He hesitated, looking like he was going to try the jump anyway, but stopped instead and watched Cedar take up the entire doorway. They stared at each other, Cedar baring his teeth, but the Answer stayed put. He probably could have made it, honestly; Laurel was sure he had propulsion in his boots. All he did, however, was fold his arms and lean against the rail's doorframe. Almost mockingly.

"Shit." Cedar flipped him off and the Answer laughed, covering where his mouth would have been underneath. Cedar ushered Juniper and Laurel further in. "He must know where we parked our ship. He knows we have to take the lift down. He'll catch up."

Juniper paled. "What do we do?"

"Go down faster than the lift."

"How?"

Cedar threw up his hands. He didn't know. Laurel perked up, an idea coming to mind.

"You saw the garbage chutes earlier, right?" she said and they looked at her, confused. Of course, they hadn't. No one ever does. "They're around the lift—they're big. They probably go straight down to the dock to wait for a garbage barge." She paused and made a face. "Wait. No. It'd be a straight shot down. We'd break our legs."

"No," Cedar breathed. "We won't. Just follow me."

At least he picked up the plan, even if Laurel had no idea what he was going to do with it. The AI announced their arrival and Cedar was already forcing the doors open against the AI's warning against destruction of property. Cedar jumped off, holding Juniper and Laurel close, and hurried them toward the lift in the center. All Laurel had to do was point and he turned to take them to the garbage chute along the side.

It was industrial sized to keep debris from getting jammed regularly. Big enough for the three of them if they squeezed together. Cedar effortlessly yanked the whole chute door off and Laurel peered inside. Straight shot down like she thought. Her stomach flipped thinking about it, but Cedar was nodding. He had Laurel wrap her arms around him on one side and had Juniper do the same on the other.

"Hold on tight," Cedar said and dropped the three of them inside.

Air whipped by, stealing Laurel's unwanted

scream away, but then the three of them jerked still. Cedar had pierced his fingers into the wall from vampire strength alone. Once they were stable, he began climbing his way downward as fast as he could reasonably go.

Laurel's comms connected to the *Gladiolus* halfway down, making her flinch.

"Where the fuck are you three?!" Clary screamed.

Laurel picked her head up. "It's working!"

"I have been hailing you for the past—fuck! I don't even know! What is going on?" Clary asked. "Another ship docked inside and you all stopped answering me!"

"It was the Answer!" Juniper snapped. Clary gasped on the other end. "When he catches up, it'll fuzz again. Gotta be something on his person. Get ready to head back to the transit gate. We have to lose him!"

"For fuck's—" The rest of Clary's words were lost to fuzz and Laurel looked up.

The static of the Answer's faceplate shined brightly at the top. "You think this will work?"

Cedar swung his foot into the wall and dislodged the bottom chute. He threw them through just as the Answer threw himself in after them. The three of them clattered over one another on the docking bay floor.

Laurel got her wits about her first. She dragged Juniper over to the trash terminal and Juniper immediately got to work.

With practiced hands, Juniper jacked into it and initiated emergency eject procedures. All of the chutes sealed off, the sound echoing across the cemetery, and Laurel stepped back.

Maybe it was a little cruel, but the Answer was

going out with space trash. Juniper smiled shakily at her and she returned it. A team once again.

A second ship had indeed joined theirs in the landing bay and it was as black as the reaches of space. Larger than their cruiser, it was big enough for a single person to live aboard with minimal comforts. It had to be the Answer's.

Juniper peeled away from Laurel and Cedar as they were passing it and slapped a chip on the underside of the hull.

"Disrupter!" Juniper said as they caught up. "It'll keep him grounded for a little bit!"

"Good idea!" Cedar shouted back.

Once they reached the *Maple*, Laurel threw herself into the driver's seat while Cedar and Juniper checked the chassis to make sure the Answer hadn't done anything to it.

"I think we're clear!" Juniper said.

Laurel started the *Maple*'s systems. "Then get in!"

Cedar tossed Juniper into the back and slotted himself in the copilot seat. Laurel felt safer with the three of them inside and the crystalline top protecting them. She pressed her feet into the thrusters to take off.

Then the whole thing nosedived. A tether had connected to them, yanking them downward. The front hit the ground, busting a headlamp, and a body flung itself onto the hood.

The Answer.

Laurel screamed and slammed her foot on the thruster pedals to shoot back up, shake him, but he held on. Trash was sliding off him, his faceplate was blank, and it was all Laurel registered before his fist smashed through the glass.

He was strong enough to break crystalline glass

with a punch.

Cedar slammed his fist on the top's disengage button and it flung back. The Answer's fist was stuck in the hole he'd made and the top flung him off. He landed hard on the landing bay.

Laurel engaged the top again and froze. It had a hole in it. Her mind went blank—it wasn't safe to fly—and Cedar pushed his foot over hers to ignite the thrusters. The ship jerked upward just as blaster shots grazed the thrusters in the back. They all flinched, but the ship was still airborne.

"Wait!" Laurel shouted as Cedar reached over to steer them toward the public airlocks. "There's a hole!"

"For fuck's sake!" He opened a screen on the center console that had been blinking and tapped commands faster than Laurel could read. "Next time: I'm flying!"

A nozzle shot up from the front of the ship and sprayed the broken top with a shimmering mixture. Of course. Every cruiser was built so if the top was ever breached, there was a quick drying crystalline fluid inside to patch it in a heartbeat. Her cruiser driving class had gone over that, but she'd forgotten.

Not that it would have done them any good if they'd been in space.

Didn't matter; it patched the top, although now Laurel had a glaring blind spot. Cedar was still reaching over her, turning the wheel, and guided them upward toward where the airlock must have been according to the pings on the console.

As they neared it, a lockdown announcement peeled across the cemetery, and Cedar swore.

"I got it!" Laurel pressed harder on the thruster pedals.

They got out before the airlock shut entirely and

sure, she might have dinged the side of it with the wing, but what mattered was they were outside. The AI's announcement continued echoing out of the *Maple*'s speakers. Good. That would keep the Answer even more occupied unless he managed to punch a hole in something else.

They were well on their way back to the *Gladiolus* before she and Cedar shared a collective sigh of being in the clear. They sagged in their seats.

"What a way to go," she said, a weak laugh bubbling out of her throat. She glanced toward Juniper, hoping it made them smile too, but her face fell.

They were still. Too still. Their silence should have been the first clue something was wrong, but Laurel hadn't even registered it until now. Their eyes were bright and wide, staring at absolutely nothing.

"Junie?" she whispered, her voice breaking.

Their hands slowly and mechanically reached into their hair, eyes somehow growing even wider. Cedar flung himself into the back just as Juniper started screaming. Juniper thrashed, but Cedar had them wrapped up too quickly to have done any damage to themself.

"It's okay—it's okay," Cedar whispered. "We'll get out of range soon. I promise."

Range. Laurel's stomach dipped. It was the Answer; he'd reached into them again. Laurel turned back to the controls and found the ship moving on its own. Lily had already connected. Good.

Laurel reached around to pry Juniper's hand off Cedar's arm before they clawed through it. Something about Laurel's touch must have helped; Juniper's hand went slack, letting her have it, and Laurel held it steady.

"We're here, Junie," she said. "Don't worry."

Only when the *Maple* landed on the *Gladiolus'* deck did Juniper stop thrashing. They slowed into a full-body tremble and blinked. They darted their gaze around the *Maple*, searching, until they saw both Laurel and Cedar with them.

Cedar relaxed his grip and slumped against the side of the ship, exhausted. Juniper stayed where they were in his lap and covered their mouth. They were still catching their breath.

"Are you okay?" Laurel asked as Lily rolled their ship into the hangar lift.

Juniper dropped their hands to their neck and nodded. "Y-Yes," they said. "He-He's just never done that before."

"What did he do?"

Tears slipped down their cheeks. "It-It felt like he was reaching inside me. Opening me up." Their hands trailed lower, resting at their collarbone. "All I could feel was him." Their breathing came out in erratic bursts, panic revving back up. "A-And he wouldn't let me go."

Darkness shut over them as the hangar lift drew them downward and Juniper flinched. Laurel found Juniper's hand again and held it tight. Juniper squeezed back.

"He won't get you," Laurel said. "Okay? We won't ever let that happen."

It was all she could say, even if promising it felt like a lie.

SESSION 6

BLOODY TEARS

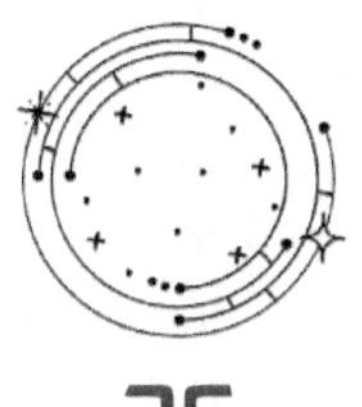

26
JUNIPER

THE ONLY WAY TO FIGHT THE AWFUL feeling left crawling its way through Juniper—the way the Answer had reached inside squeezed their lungs still, telling them to give in—was to do something mundane. Normal. Like dyeing their hair with Laurel.

They had time, at least. After their close call, everyone wanted a breather and it wasn't like the Answer *could* follow them, at least not right away. Not after the chip Juniper had put on his ship. It would screw his diagnostics as soon as the engines engaged. Besides, he also had to wait until the cemetery's lockdown finished, which likely required in-person Federation approval. He *could* break out, but mass desecration of Federation satellites wasn't his style, so he'd probably wait like a good dog. By the time he shook the red tape and took chase, they'd be gone.

Right now, the *Gladiolus* idled in dead space. Clary had sent them through a pirate transit gate, so they literally could have been anywhere. Nothing but stars as far as the eye could see.

Except Juniper *hated* waiting. Pluto was right

there—figuratively—but when they'd complained, Clary said she had to make a specific route to Pluto. Not as easy as inner system travel and Juniper took the hint. Patience.

So, they'd dug out some old hair dye, accosted Laurel with what color she'd like the morning after. They didn't admit to their continued lack of sleep (although, now for yet another reason). They were glad when Laurel agreed to the silly idea.

Maybe it wouldn't help keep them under the radar, but it would feel good. Like friendship.

Hair dyeing had always been a quiet bonding experience between the two of them since they'd officially met. Laurel's fingers were soothing as they combed through Juniper's hair even now, laying another color atop the blue because they didn't have bleach to strip it away. She was always careful and it almost felt normal. Like nothing had happened. Like Juniper could open their eyes and find themself back in the satellite with Laurel and none of their problems.

It would have been nice.

Once Juniper was done, hair wrapped in a quick-drying towel to seal in the color, they considered their choices for Laurel's hair. Always a work-in-progress. They'd bleached it so many times and honestly, was surprised it hadn't fried off completely. No bleach this time, unfortunately, but Juniper had a plethora of other colors to mix with the faded red down below. Laurel wanted to keep the sunshine blonde, so they'd trapped the top of her hair in a shower cap to keep it safe.

They were well into melding blues and purples into the red to make some kind of mermaid-looking gradient when they found themself smiling, a sense of calm settling over them.

"This is nice," they said.

Laurel tried peeking over her shoulder. "Hm?"

"Doing this again," Juniper said. "I missed dyeing your hair."

Laurel smiled. "Me too. It makes everything simple again." She fidgeted, readjusting her knees underneath her, and waited as Juniper ran water through her hair to wash away the extra color. It stained the tub as it swirled toward the drain. "I'm..." She swallowed and Juniper paused. "I'm not good with friends."

"I'm not either," Juniper admitted, snorting. Laurel did too. "I've been a colossal dick too. For a whole year, it was just us and a daily routine. It was easy. And now, we have so much more than that and... it's been stressful making sense of it all. I... I should be better."

"I feel bad for snapping."

"Don't." Juniper leaned forward to look at her worried face. "I deserved it." They pulled themself away and considered Laurel's newly colored hair. Gradients were a lot harder than Juniper thought, even with a cortex computer giving them tips. Probably not what the feds had in mind for that particular augment. "We'll get through this. Pinky promise."

Laurel giggled. "I have to believe it, or else I'll just worry all the time and cry."

"Are *you* okay?" Juniper combed her hair back with their fingers. "This is a lot of ride or die shit going on here."

That got a bigger laugh out of Laurel. "I'd have it no other way! It's feeling alive. Scary, sure, but living in a way I wouldn't be back there."

The bathroom door swiped open. Juniper yelped, Laurel nearly hit them as she flung her head back to look, and Cedar grumbled from the doorway. Still wasn't dressed beyond a robe and red boxer briefs Juniper recalled grabbing from the mall for him. And of course, with no imminent danger or anything to be frustrated with, their bio-scanner honed in on how barely dressed he was. Juniper's entire body heated up.

God, Juniper wished they could shut it up right now.

"That's gonna stain," he said, quickly drawing his robe shut. "I ain't cleaning it."

Juniper snickered. "You have your own bathroom." They leaned toward Laurel and dropped their voice into a stage whisper. "Aster told me Cedar's tub is jet-black." Laurel giggled, covering her mouth, but Cedar gave them a look.

"He did *not* tell you that," he said. "'Sides, this is the tub I fit in. Clary uses it too, so you'll have to deal with her being pissy. Not me. I don't care what color it is."

Laurel pushed her hair back. Her hand came away tinged with blue and Juniper handed her the towel they'd been using.

"It's not like it stained that bad," she said. An outright lie and Laurel's eyes bugged out as she looked at her hands. She quickly hid them under the towel. Not helpful when some of her forehead was blue now.

Juniper ran interference and pulled the towel off their hair. They ruffled the now dry strands. Feather soft and smelled like lavender from the dye. "Like it?" they said. "It's nightshade."

"Looks black."

"It's purple under most lights!"

Cedar snorted. "Fine. It's nice."

Killjoy. He'd been distant since Clyde asked him for a mercy kill, but Juniper had been hoping to get him to crack a smile, just so they'd know the Cedar they knew was still in there. They had Laurel turn her head and drew their fingers through the new colors. "I'm giving her a mermaid look to replace the red. See? Starts bluish up at her roots and ends up very purple at the ends!"

Truthfully, the gradient wasn't... *good*, but anyone could tell Juniper had given it their best shot. Laurel was a fan and that was what mattered.

Cedar turned away, but a gentle smile did crack his lips. Success. Before he commented any further, the intercom across the ship crackled on.

"Hey guys?" came Clary's voice. "I'm just about done plotting a route! Get your butts in here!"

"So much for a bath..." Cedar grumbled and rolled his eyes. "You heard the lady. Hurry it up in here. Got places to be before he catches up."

The door stayed open, letting the aroma from all the dyes escape into the hallway as a medley of scents chasing after Cedar. Juniper watched him go, fully brought back down to the reality they were ignoring and the lingering creeping sensation the Answer had left behind.

They'd always been scared of him, but it'd been distant before. Now, it was real, and it didn't matter how far they went. He'd always been closer than they'd thought.

They must have been too deep in their head, scrambled with fear and what ifs, because they came back to Laurel holding their hand tightly. Their bio-scanner picked it up late, but when it did, the sensation felt like a fuzzy warmth. Friend-shaped. Both their fingers were tinged with blues and purples now. Juniper smiled sadly at her.

"You'll get dye on your hand," they said.

Laurel shrugged. "It washes off." She pulled off the shower cap, revealing blonde hair still wrapped in its usual twin-buns. "We'll get through this."

Juniper leaned into Laurel and was happy when she leaned back. "I'm sorry for being a dick. I'll be better."

"I know."

Their bio-scanner pinged another shape nearby and Juniper glanced at the door. A blur of black shot inside and shortly, Lily was wiggling her way between them. Laurel let go and happily petted the cat with the dyed hand. Juniper winced, Laurel froze, but Lily didn't react.

"Are you two finished?" Lily asked through the cat's collar. "Clary believes she didn't quite express the urgency." The cat looked between them as Laurel hastily wiped the dye from the cat's back with the towel. "She'd like *everyone*'s vote. Even trainees."

"Yeah, yeah." Laurel tossed the towel into the laundry hamper near the door. "I smell purple, so I think we're done here."

Juniper laughed and helped clean what they could. "What does that even smell like? Purple soda? Grapes? Plums?"

"I don't know. Just... purple, I guess!" Laurel devolved into laughter and Juniper couldn't help but do the same.

They had to leave the tub in the sorry state it was in with the blue and purple dye staining the usual off-white color when the cat herded them out. She even took them all the way to the bridge before they could get sidetracked, like they were lost kittens.

The bridge had been cleaned since Juniper had been there last. While Aster was still hooked into the hologram table, someone had carefully unhooked everything from Lily's super computer, leaving the bridge how it had been before. Probably a good thing someone else did it so Juniper didn't have to confront yet another failure. Aster's body was still on the couch, like the sleeping prince he was.

In contrast, Clary's pilot console was a mess. Multiple screens were opened in front of her and a few tablets had been spread around her, each one detailing different transit stations.

Cedar was already there too, leaning over her chair, thankfully with a shirt and pants on this time. His face was pinched like he had a headache and he sipped from his mug. Some concoction Laurel had explained was *bloffee*. Sounded gross and Juniper kept their bio-scanner from giving them the details.

Once the cat had Juniper and Laurel inside, she hopped into Clary's lap, immediately rolling onto her back for a belly rub.

"Stop making faces at me," Clary said, looking at Cedar. She moved the screens around in front of her and Juniper's gaze bounced from set to set. They were displaying pirate transit gate locations and activity. "This is the best way to chart a course."

"I know," Cedar grumbled. "Aster just did it without all the bitching."

Aster's hologram chuckled. "And I had *years* of practice. Maybe when I have my body, I can teach her some of my ways. I certainly can't see anything as I am."

Juniper glanced at him and pointed to the watch they'd kept on their wrist. "I can hook you back in if you'd like."

Aster smiled at them. "It'd be easier with hands."

It was weird enough letting him see through their own eyes; thinking of him controlling their limbs sent a shudder through Juniper.

Clary groaned, catching Juniper's attention, and batted the cat's paw away from one of the screens she'd swiped out of formation. Laurel intercepted the next attempted sabotage and picked the cat up.

"I have a system!"

"Then why do we have to be here?" Cedar asked.

"All you were doing was brooding."

"Was not."

Grumbling, Clary ignored him and brought two screens together. "I have two potential routes. We should decide which one to use as a team."

The first one was shorter. It took the backchannel gate they'd used to come here, but sent them to Saturn instead of Jupiter. Then, it piggybacked off the Saturn Gate, giving them more range, and launched them to another backchannel gate before finally arriving at Pluto. The other was a much longer route and bounced from backchannel gate to backchannel gate, never coming close to anything official.

"Why does that one take so long?" Juniper said.

"All the ETAs are guesswork," Clary said. "Backchannels are maintained on stolen tech and pirates with the audacity to ping off real gates for coordinates. The Saturn route will take us at max, three or four days. The backchannel route will take a little more than a week." Even Clary made a face when everyone else did. "I know. I'm also factoring in a stop for supplies because with that route, we'd *have* to."

Juniper didn't like the idea of stopping. Not when the Answer was so close.

Clary pointed to the route going toward Saturn. "I'm worried about this one since we'd have to sit at the Saturn Gate long enough for Lily to hack in our real destination so we end up at a backchannel gate, then we'd have to wait for our turn. Sitting ducks."

"It will be fine," Aster said. "We shouldn't be out of the gate long enough to be detected."

Clary frowned. "You sure? The Answer's gotta have a scanner in all the transit gates. It must have been how he found out we'd gone back to Jupiter."

Aster shook his head. "He'll expect us to take the safest route—the longer one—because he'll believe we'll want to avoid that very thing. I bet he's watching those more closely because he has to by virtue of them being backchannel gates. Besides, if we stop to resupply, he *will* catch us. I'm sure of it."

Spoken like someone with years of expertise outrunning those chasing him. Cedar was smiling smugly behind his mug like he'd known Aster would know exactly what to do. Clary still looked uneasy and he patted the back of her chair.

"We haven't been quiet," he said. "I was listening to the fed channels overnight. We're not the hot topic right now, but I still heard our basic descriptions. I'd rather not chance having to stop and resupply in a place we don't know. Saturn's station is huge. Our ship will blend in with all the others."

Clary sighed. "All right, but if we get snatched running up near Saturn, I'm blaming you guys."

She swiped away all the screens, leaving only the one with their planned route, and positioned herself to pilot. The diagnostic screens from the ship popped up on either side of her console. Everything was good and ready. She pressed her foot on the thruster pedals.

The entire ship jostled. While Cedar caught himself on Clary's chair, Laurel bumped into Juniper, catching them off guard, and they both clattered to the floor. The cat bounded out of Laurel's arms and rushed up Clary's chair to stand on the back of it.

"The fuck was that?" Clary asked and threw open the viewports around the sides of the ship. "I did *not* hit anything! Nothing's even there!"

"Danger." Lily's voice sung over the intercom. "We've been snared by a tractor beam."

"From *where*?!" Cedar pushed past Clary to get to the feeds, slamming his mug down on the console to get it out of the way. Juniper pulled themself up to look too, but there was nothing as far as the eye could see.

"Signature was suppressed. They snared us as soon as we attempted to move. My guess is they were watching us." Lily opened another screen showing the starboard side and there was a glimmer.

A ship bigger than theirs unfurled from the dark, like it had been waiting for them to look their way for the grand unveiling.

Sparkling gold, the ship was shaped like an oversized shuttle. There were multiple decks at a glance with the bridge at the top—front and center—and a myriad of smaller ships hanging on like extra living spaces. Cedar went frighteningly still.

"They are hailing us," Lily announced. "Shall I patch them through?"

"Yes. Answer them," Cedar said.

Clary frowned as she opened a channel. It was asking for a video hail and as Clary set herself up, trying not to look as underdressed as she was, Juniper pulled Laurel out of focus. All they'd see was Cedar and Clary in the shot. Once Clary finished fluffing her hair, she let it connect.

A new screen popped up to show the hailer and it was fuzzed with static as the ships connected. When it cleared, a woman with dark skin was on the other side. She smiled wide, showing off impressively white teeth. Her black hair fell in ringlets around her head, only kept at bay with a black hairband.

Juniper's gaze shot right back to her teeth. She was smiling big for one reason: to show off her two distinctive golden fangs. She was a vampire.

"Hey!" Cedar said, suddenly friendly. Juniper snapped a worried look at him. "Franny! You repainted your ship gold, I see. Gotta live up to your name, huh?"

The woman scowled. "Oh. Cedar. Didn't see you lurking. Heard you went and got yourself fucking iced. Guess you're back. Also." She leaned closer to the camera, baring her teeth. "It's *Francesca*. Not Franny. Don't call me that around your fucking crew!"

Cedar cleared his throat. "I see you've snared my ship." Francesca sat back and nodded enthusiastically, the motion making her hair bounce. "You wanna let us go? For old time's sake?"

She threw her head back and laughed like it was a joke. "Oh, honey. Old time's sake means I don't blast you without warning for trespassing." She steepled her fingers together and leaned forward. Cedar was looking less and less enthused. "Here's what we'll do: y'all are gonna come aboard my ship so I can shake yours top to bottom and see what falls out. And I do mean all of you. It's no use hiding anyone, I know all your hiding spots. You will do so quietly, without a fuss, or I *will* blast you. Clear?"

Cedar swallowed. "Clear."

She leaned back. "Can't wait to see your ugly mug in person again."

The call ended and Francesca's ship maneuvered itself closer at a leisurely pace. No one spoke for a tense moment until Cedar eased out a long sigh.

"Where *are* we, Clary?"

Clary was already pale from the hail and somehow, turned paler. "I. Uh... I piggy-backed off the gate near Ganymede and flung us through this route Tremaine made a long time ago." She looked through the log, eyes growing wide. "Although, some of these backchannels are configured differently now." She drummed her fingers on the controls. "Where are we, Cedar?"

Cedar released another sigh. "Right in the middle of Francesca's territory."

"Who's that?" Juniper asked. "She knew you, right?"

"To pirates she's Francesca the Golden. She's one of the most notorious space pirates between Saturn and Uranus," Cedar explained. "She *hates* trespassers."

Laurel frowned. "No way a single person can own space this big."

"She maintains all the backchannels out here like a hawk. If she catches you lingering, she definitely *can* own space. She or her coalition is always watching." Cedar closed his eyes and pinched his nose. "God damn it. I did not want to deal with her today."

Juniper leaned toward Cedar. "But you *know* her."

"We were sired by the same guy and pirated together for years after he died. None of that will do a lot of good if she's in a bad mood." Cedar watched her ship draw closer on the feeds. "And we're on her turf." He patted Clary's shoulder and faced everyone. "Get dressed before they board. I'd like us to look somewhat presentable."

27
LAUREL

PRESENTABLE. THE DRESSES LAUREL HAD snagged from the mall were too fancy for a presentable pirate, so instead, she grabbed an inoffensive striped yellow sweater and new jeans. She threw a button-up beneath the sweater, just to dress it up a little, and nodded at herself in the mirror. Presentable. Even if she looked so far removed from a space pirate. More like she was going to school. *Ugh*.

She brushed and tied up her new hair back into its usual style. Honestly, the new colors were cute. She liked the contrast between the blonde and the mermaid color below.

Getting back on task, she pulled on her boots and shoved the ice needle beneath her sweater. Just in case. Cedar certainly trusted Francesca enough if he agreed to this, but there was unease gnawing at Laurel's stomach.

Francesca was *familiar*, but Laurel had no idea why.

She was deep in her thoughts, wracking her brain, as she came out of her room and bumped into Juniper.

They'd dressed in their button-up and vest paired with the same pinstripe pants as before. Hair was still a little messy—not suavely pushed back this time—but they looked presentable too. Juniper looked her up and down and gave her a sheepish smile.

"I should have dressed a little more down," they said. "I bet you're comfier. I don't know even what a presentable pirate is supposed to look like."

Laurel snickered, pushing their shoulder and they pushed back. Little levity didn't hurt, but it only lasted until they made it to the airlock door Francesca's ship had attached a walkway to.

The same one Tremaine had been pulled through. Didn't help the unease in Laurel's stomach one bit and she blocked out the memories by looking out the windows beside it.

Not much of a view. Francesca's shimmering gold ship loomed in every single one from being so close.

Cedar and Clary were already waiting. While Cedar hadn't changed beyond grabbing his red coat, Clary had gone for an oversized sweater, probably hiding a blaster underneath it, and had leggings tucked into her usual boots. Instead of her ponytail, she'd gathered her hair suspiciously into a messy bun with two long hair sticks keeping it together. Laurel hoped those were knives.

Upon seeing them, Clary immediately pressed herself close while Cedar stayed between them and the airlock door.

"Plan?" Juniper asked as the walkway pressurized to match both ships. The door at Francesca's end swiped open.

"Do what she says until I say not to." Cedar crossed his arms. "Got it?"

Not a *good* plan by any means. Laurel bit down

from saying so and nodded.

Their airlock door swiped open and three vampires came through, crowding the hallway. They were all dressed in black thermal gear paired with sturdy black gloves and boots. Juniper's eyes glimmered even though they'd kept their gaze downcast. Cybernetics must have been telling them what tech the vampires had on them. All Laurel recognized were the visors along their heads. Standard fed wear, but probably cannibalized for pirate use. It dinged information as the vampires looked at them and one locked their gaze on Clary.

The visor probably pinged the weapons she had stowed in the sweater.

The vampire in the center, the one with the side of her head shaved and the rest left in fuzzy curls around her head, looked Cedar up and down. "Long time no see, Ced."

"Yeah, hi, Bethany," Cedar said a little less than enthused.

Bethany beamed at him, showing her teeth, before facing everyone else. "Annie: go check what that one's packing." She pointed at Clary and before Clary could insist otherwise, Annie—the vampire with the shocking orange hair in twin braids—was already patting her down. Clary huffed as Annie immediately found the two blasters and the stunner.

Bethany whistled. "I like this one. Spicy."

The third vampire paused, settling a hand against his ear. "Francesca wants to know how many fleshies." He scanned them and counted, briefly pausing at Juniper.

"Three," Cedar said.

"Three fleshies aboard. Two kids." The vampire paused and nodded at Bethany who'd come over to

Laurel and Juniper.

"Didn't figure you for picking up kids," Bethany said, studying them until her comms chirped. "Here's how Fran wants this to go. The two kids come with me and Annie first." She was undaunted as Cedar turned a dark scowl on her. "Billy stays here with you two. When Annie comes back, she'll bring you aboard and Billy heads the shaking down." She paused as Cedar flicked a glance at Billy. Laurel did too.

Definitely scrawnier than Cedar, but they were about the same height. Cedar could probably take him.

"No fighting," Bethany said. "You get me, Cedar? Fran likes him, so if he comes back all busted up, I can't be held accountable with what happens to your kids."

Cedar rolled his eyes. "We can go together. The airlock's big enough."

"No can do. Fran's orders." Bethany beckoned to Laurel and Juniper and though Laurel had all intentions of staying put, Juniper gently eased her forward. "Assurance you will behave, big guy. We know how you roll."

Cedar looked at Laurel and Juniper, worried, but all emotion dropped from his face as he nodded toward Bethany and Annie. As good an order as any. Juniper held Laurel's hand tightly and they walked after Bethany while Annie took up the rear. Laurel tried to appear as impassive as Juniper, but she doubted she looked any different than a frightened mouse.

It wasn't long before Juniper's hand began trembling. Laurel peered at them and realized it wasn't from nerves. Their augments were revving them for a fight. Not that Laurel knew if they could do it. One cybernetically enhanced human against two decidedly beefy vampires was not good odds. Plus, the small clump of other vampires awaiting them as they stepped into Francesca's ship.

Laurel avoided their gazes as Bethany continued down the hall. The ship looked darker than theirs on the inside, perpetually low light with graffiti of self-expression along the walls and some of it even glowed. Laurel couldn't stop to figure out what exactly was painted; as soon as she tried, Juniper was pulling her along.

The farther they went, the more the ship felt like a small living structure than a hardened pirate ship; Laurel heard partying chatter from the halls they passed, and saw some of the crew milling about like normal people. Only a few gave her and Juniper a glance, but none of them approached. Laurel had expected to be demoralized somehow, but was pleasantly surprised everyone left them entirely alone.

Bethany took them to a lift near the center of the ship and the four of them squeezed aboard.

As they began their steady crawl downward, Annie glanced over at Juniper. "You can relax, kiddo."

"I am relaxed," Juniper snapped.

Bethany grinned, showing her fangs. "Not with that tone." She leaned closer to Juniper. "We ain't gonna eat ya."

"I'm sure vampire pirates say that all the time," Juniper said.

Bethany shrugged. "Word is, we're not to touch a hair on your heads. Fran runs a tight ship. You're safe as long as she wants ya safe."

Laurel wasn't sure how much of a relief that was, especially as Annie looked at her, gaze flitting over her hair.

"Kinda wish I *could* touch your hair, though. Needs a better dye job." She lifted her hand and without meaning to, Laurel flinched into Juniper. "Just saying! Could actually do a real gradient instead of… whatever the fuck you ended up doing."

Bethany snorted. "Stop it. It's no use terrorizing the fleshies."

"It is a little bit if you lived once and a while."

"Seriously," Bethany stressed, showing her teeth. Annie held up her hands and stepped away. Bethany looked back down at them. "Fran wants to eat dinner with you guys."

Juniper eyed Bethany. "She threatened us."

"She and Ced have a history," Annie cut in. "Threats used to be their way of showing affection. They go too far back to bury it all like that." She paused, Bethany eyeing her with daggers, and shrugged. Maybe she'd said too much.

Laurel perked up anyway. "How far back?"

"Guess it wouldn't hurt to say so…" Bethany peered at the light indicating what floor they were on. They were almost there. "Fran and Cedar used to pirate together, so *way* back."

"Together?" Juniper asked and Annie snorted.

"Not *together*, together, if you get me," Bethany quickly added. "Just terrorizing space on the same ship."

"Why'd Cedar leave?" Laurel asked.

Bethany and Annie exchanged another look over their heads. "Beats me," Bethany said. "Sometimes people drift, I guess. Once a fearsome duo became two equally fearsome pirates once he found that ship, but then Cedar faded out." She grew quieter. "Everyone— Fran included—thought for sure Cedar was done doing *anything*, but then all these stories that keep reaching us lately? Big guy was never subtle."

"What *have* you heard about us?" Juniper asked.

The lift reached their floor and the doors twisted open to a dim, but immaculate hallway. A far cry from the vamps and graffiti from before. The floor was buffed to a shine, curtains covered the walls (for aesthetics, if Laurel had to guess), and it was empty. Must have been the deck for esteemed guests.

"Heard he took down a whole fed ship inside the inner belt. Fucking ballsy to pull that off." Bethany led the way forward. "That's not on official channels, mind you. Feds tried to scrub it clean—it's embarrassing—but a few of us are circulating the report. Then that fucking captain at the mall? Grisly sight he left there, but she'd been terrorizing everyone out here. Hoping she stays dead." Bethany slowed and eyed Laurel and Juniper behind her.

It was then Laurel realized Annie hadn't followed them off. She quickly glanced behind herself and watched Annie take the lift back up.

"The big guy was laying low for literal *years*," Bethany continued. "Just not when it came to you two. So, some of us just wonder if he's back."

Laurel glanced at Juniper. Clary had called him the Red Bandit when they'd met, but Laurel had been too nervous to look up the name on the net. She wasn't sure if she could handle his past exploits. Juniper was giving her the same worried look, although they probably regretted not looking it up.

Bethany faced the hallway ahead of them. "But hey, he's not my captain so what he does or doesn't do don't matter to me. Come on. Fran's gotta be restless waiting for y'all."

Laurel stayed deep in her worrying thoughts until they passed another hallway threshold halfway covered by a curtain. Two androids were walking away together. Familiar models with dual toned hair styled in such a meticulous way.

No way. Laurel slowed. *It can't be.*

Juniper tugged her elbow just as Bethany peered back, noticing they both had slowed. Laurel hid her expression. Those two couldn't have been Lola's androids. Androids enjoyed styling themselves after the pair to feel fancy. No way in a million years would she be here on a space pirate's ship, so far from the inner system. Idols didn't do that.

Bethany took them into the large room at the end of the hall. It was flush against the side of the ship with a huge window looking out over the side. It must have been made specifically for entertaining guests. Blood red curtains were drawn across the walls, the electric chandelier above twinkled like real candles, and a large wooden table sat bolted to the center of the room. There was a centerpiece atop the table with real candles and an ivory white table runner going from one end to the other. At the far end of the table, toward the large double doors in the back, was a high-backed wooden chair that absolutely screamed vampire.

Everything did, actually. Juniper must have realized it too with the way their face twisted in amusement.

They both turned at the same time to accost Bethany, but the vampire had already left them and closed the doors to the hall. Definitely locked. Laurel didn't even have to test it to know.

"Well." Juniper giggled and faced the room. "This is a statement."

Laurel covered her smile. "Yeah. Boldly stating: I am a vampire!"

It stole the tension out of them both and they

leaned into each other, laughing. As it petered off, Juniper began snooping. Drawing curtains back and forth only to find more doors. All locked. They even tried the double doors at the end, but those didn't even have a terminal for the lock. They came back, shaking their head.

"Definitely not risking jacking into their systems," they said.

Laurel nodded. "Even if we got out, I'm not sure if we'd make it back to our ship without being found." She gazed toward the large window and noticed an airlock door right beside it. She lifted her eyebrows and peeked out.

There was a short walkway attached to the airlock and headed into a ship Laurel hadn't noticed before. Larger than a cruiser model, but not by much. Minimal comforts at best.

"I wonder what that's for."

Juniper came over and craned their neck to look. "Maybe extra storage?" They grimaced and stepped away. "Too far away for my scanners to pick anything up." They stalked back to the table and sat in the high-back chair. As Laurel covered another laugh, Juniper hopped back up. "On second thought, I shouldn't piss her off."

"You're not vampire enough for that chair," Laurel teased and Juniper rolled their eyes as they passed her.

They sat down in one of the wooden chairs across from the lone one and Laurel settled beside them.

"Guess we're waiting, huh?" She pouted. "Should have brought something to do."

She hated waiting and given the way Juniper went from easygoing to on edge, they weren't enjoying it either. Together, they listened to the groan of the ship and the distant intercom chatter too garbled to hear. The least Bethany could have done was leave them some elevator music. Would have killed some of the monotony.

Soon enough, Juniper had grown deep in their thoughts, brow furrowed. Their eyes had gone back to bright, glowing in the dim light. Classic Juniper scanning the feeds look. Laurel waited before speaking.

"Hear anything?" she whispered.

Juniper released a low sigh. "Not enough," they said and their eyes dimmed. "There's a lot of chatter, but nothing substantial. Cameras are too ironclad for me to peek inside wirelessly. All I can gather is Franny has special guests, but I don't think it's us."

"The feds?"

"Can't be. Too many vamps," Juniper said. "And I doubt it's the Answer. He would have already snatched me." They shuddered. "I can still feel Lily's network, so I can check in on the ship once they start shaking it down."

Laurel didn't know how she felt about other special guests. A big unknown. She stewed on the half information, and soon, the doors behind them swiped open again. Cedar and Clary strode inside like they owned the place, some practiced precision between them to look dangerous, and as soon as they were past the threshold, the doors went right back to being locked. Clary flipped the doors off before speeding over to kneel between Laurel's and Juniper's chairs.

"I think I can undo the lock." Clary plucked out one of the sticks from her bun and showed Laurel. Not a knife, then. A chip was at the end of it, likely loaded with unlocking programs. "As long as you guys promise to run right back to our ship—"

"Stop it," Cedar said. "We're not doing that." He

pulled out the chair next to Juniper and sat down, undeterred when Clary straightened to glare at him.

"Too many vamps. You start running, one's bound to be hungry and give chase. Predators, remember?" He waved his hand toward the last chair. "Just sit down. If Fran was gonna hurt us, she would have."

"Fine." Clary shoved the stick back into her hair. "Fuck all this, but *fine*." She took the seat on Cedar's other side and crossed her legs and arms, looking as closed off as possible.

And the room went right back to silence. Murmurs across the ship reached them, people moving beyond the doors, and Cedar was looking more and more ready for a fight. Completely calm, barely breathing, and hands flat on the table like he was going to propel himself upward.

One of the side doors opened, making Laurel flinch. An old gen service android came in with a dining cart. Without speaking, the android set the table faster than Laurel could track and very shortly, the mixed aroma of everything made her stomach growl.

The largest dish was in the center, covered with a gleaming steel top, and side dishes were carefully arranged around it. Salads filled with vibrant greens, juicy red tomatoes, and cucumbers; roasted potato wedges covered in sour cream and cheddar; a bowl of fried green beans with shallots; and a plate full of buttery steaming rolls.

Before Laurel could tell the android thank you, he'd already slipped out with his cart. Someone else was coming, however; their strides were long and purposeful as heels clacked against the hard floor.

The candles and lights went off with a breath and

the doors at the far end swooshed open. Before Laurel could snort at the sudden theatrics, the lights blazed back on with a flash. Confetti even rained down from the fake candles above, flickering like embers before they disappeared.

It was another moment before Laurel realized the high-backed chair was taken now by Francesca. She was grinning wide at them, showing off her golden vampire fangs, and was clearly proud of her entrance.

Everyone was silent, however, even Bethany and Annie who had taken posts at the far door. Laurel meekly applauded.

"Aw, aren't you a sweetie?" Francesca smiled at Laurel, looking too familiar and Laurel still didn't know why. "Take a hint, Cedar. Was the best I could do on short notice as far as entertainment goes."

Cedar snorted. "You could just let us go."

"You know the rules, big guy. Idle and ya get searched."

Francesca gazed over everyone, studying them, and Laurel took the time to do the same to her. She was actually rather short on second glance compared to all the other vampires, but her presence certainly made up for it. Her dark ringlets shimmered beneath the flickering candles, as did the gold chains and baubles she'd strewn across her black hairband. Her skin was a rich, warm brown and practically glowed, although it might have been either from blood recently drank or the golden dusting of makeup she'd applied. She wore a blood red bustier pushing up her chest and had a handful of glittering golden chains hanging across her neck. A vibrant yellow sash hung across her black leggings which she had tucked into her leather thigh boots. Definitely dressed to impress.

"Well?" Francesca flicked her bright brown eyes

from one person to the next and steepled her fingers together. "Introduce yourselves." She pointed at Laurel.

Laurel squeaked and straightened in her seat. "L-Laurel!"

Francesca nodded and looked at Juniper, raising her perfectly made eyebrows.

"Juniper."

She snorted. "God, and what's *her* name?" She nodded at Clary while staring at Cedar. "Fig?"

Clary bristled. "It's *Clary*."

"Close." Francesca hardly hid the snicker in her voice. "Aw come on, Cedar. You've never done brooding well. I'm feeding y'all, ain't I? Stop looking like you're going to a funeral."

"You're accosting my ship," Cedar grumbled.

Francesca shrugged and snapped her fingers. Bethany and Annie made quick work of passing out glasses, and after everyone had one, they took the top off the center dish to reveal what was within.

A hunk of meat drenched in red, garnished with what Laurel could confidently say was cilantro. It smelled divine like the rest of the dishes, but the presentation threw her thoughts in all the wrong directions. Juniper's eyes had gone wide, face pale, and Clary recoiled.

Cedar sighed. "It's not human flesh," he said. "That isn't blood."

"Killjoy. I almost had them tricked." Francesca pouted as her vampires snickered. "Pork drizzled in... oh, I can't remember the sauce. It was the reddest we had on such short notice."

The android from before had slipped back inside with his cart, so silently he was already at Francesca's side before Laurel noticed him. He filled her deep wineglass with something red. Blood. Probably blood. He came over to their side next, starting with Laurel, and gave her and Juniper something sparkly and fruity. Cedar got blood and Clary got champagne. Clary instantly took a big gulp and stopped the android to fill it up again before he left.

Laurel gingerly sniffed hers. Lemon and cherry. She took a sip and the bubbly taste pleasantly slid down her throat. Not bad.

No one had gone for the food. Laurel wanted to, her stomach was grumbling, but she was too enthralled watching the vampire stare down between Cedar and Francesca. Cedar hadn't touched his blood, yet, while Francesca nursed hers.

Clary finally sighed, bringing all eyes to her, and held out her hand toward Juniper and Laurel. "Gimme your plates. I'll load you both up."

Juniper jerked out of whatever they had been scanning and handed Clary their plate and Laurel did too. It was a little awkward with the way Francesca and Cedar still watched one another while Clary loudly and gleefully sliced the pork. She settled back into her chair once she'd served the three of them and dug in. Juniper did too, although they gave it more tentative bites, and Laurel followed suit.

Vampires could do their stare down. Laurel was hungry and the food was good. *Fresh* good. Nothing out of a package here. Pork was tender, vegetables were crisp, and rolls were perfectly done.

"This is really good," Laurel said after she'd eaten a forkful from everything.

It broke the stare down. Francesca beamed at her. "Why thank you. Marshall—that android—is one of the best cooks I've ever had." She tilted her head. "Cedar not cook for you?"

Juniper bit back a snicker. "He tries. It's got heart."

"What are you doing, Fran?" Cedar asked and she took a slow deliberate sip from her blood.

"I'm just trying to feed you before I blast your ship. It's polite of me."

"You're not going to blast it," Cedar said. "Drop the pretense, they ain't buying it." Francesca pouted and set her glass down. He frowned at his blood. "And I know you laced this. What do you want?"

Francesca released a long, drawn-out sigh. "It'd be easier if you just drank it. I didn't want you going ballistic." She flicked her gaze toward Laurel and Laurel stilled, another bite halfway to her mouth. "Someone asked me to keep an eye out for y'all and we got a tip you'd be here. Surprise, against all odds, you're *actually* here."

Wait. Laurel set her fork down and stared intently at Francesca's face. She tried seeing it without all the makeup and shimmer. She'd seen it in tabloid photos, she was sure of it.

Laurel grew cold. "Who was looking for us?"

Francesca's smile returned, fangs and all, and Laurel's chair suddenly jerked backwards. Bethany had snuck up behind her to pull it out. Laurel's entire body began trembling.

"Why don't you go see for me?" Francesca said. "Beth will show you the way." She nodded at the airlock leading to the ship below.

Laurel broke into a sweat, feeling the color drain from her face. Cedar had his hands flat on the table again, ready to charge, but Francesca dropped her smile to glare at him.

"Stay there," she said. "No one will hurt her. I promise." She smiled at Laurel again, but Laurel wasn't fooled. "Go see her for me. Maybe she'll want to eat too. She's been waiting."

She. Laurel's heart leapt into her throat as she slowly extracted herself from the chair. Bethany led the way to the airlock and showed her through. Laurel's body didn't feel real as she followed. She didn't want to believe the obvious. She had to see it with her own eyes. Except, she didn't want to go alone.

By the time she thought to voice it, she was already at the other ship's airlock and Juniper was too far away. Bethany was right behind her. Laurel swallowed as the airlock opened into the small ship.

The ship's bridge awaited her on the other side. Ships of its size only had a bridge and a small loft for sleeping. Wasn't made for long distance, but definitely more suited for it than Laurel's broken cruiser back in the *Gladiolus*.

The bridge was awash with bright lights, and everything was an austere white like it had never been touched A pastel-colored couch was the only pop of color and it sat pushed against the column holding up the pilot's console.

Two androids with duo-toned hair sat at the pilot's console above, absorbed in tracking what was on their screens, and Laurel's gaze darted back to the couch where a woman waited.

Tears flooded Laurel's eyes as the woman placed a tablet down to stand. Laurel didn't need to see through the tears to know who the woman was or what she looked like. With her long brown hair pinned back in the selfsame twin buns, the same round face and wide nose, and the same brown skin. She looked every bit the idol she was.

"Lola," came Laurel's voice, barely above a whisper.

28
JUNIPER

WHAT JUNIPER WANTED TO DO, ESPECIALLY when Bethany led Laurel away and didn't immediately return, was to toss the table and run after her. Just letting her go was asinine and Juniper couldn't believe they'd let it happen. That Cedar had let it happen. It could have been anyone in that ship.

The food soured in Juniper's stomach, making them sick, and they glared at Cedar, wanting a real plan, but his eyes never left Francesca.

Instead of meeting anyone's glares, Francesca politely served herself and happily ate her pork in delicate bites. She was chewing slow on purpose. Juniper's knee bounced under the table from pure agitation watching her soak in their discomfort.

"Who's over there?" Cedar finally asked and she rolled her eyes at him. "You're not usually this secretive. Who set you up?"

"God, a gal can change in twenty years, can't she?" Francesca said. "You sure did."

"Have I?"

They sniped back and forth. Not useful. Francesca

artfully dodged the question, giving no real answers, and Cedar kept falling for her goading him into talking about something else. Clary watched them with the same annoyance. Even she was able to see what Francesca was doing. Yet, Cedar never did. *Siblings*.

Juniper had enough. They tuned them out—the entire room—and worked on connecting their wireless augment to the *Gladiolus'* systems. It took a moment to feel out for something friendly among the sea of an unknown ship, but once found, they easily connected. Their body became a distant presence while the familiarity of their ship washed over them. They were greeted by a gentle touch, which they knew right away was Aster. Without the watch, Aster's presence was faint, just like a ghost among Lily's systems.

"How'd you even know I was coming?" Juniper asked.

They got the sense Aster shrugged. "Lily says your presence hums when you connect and she's right."

The *Gladiolus* feeds weren't loading for Juniper; they were a dark haze of black and they bit back from physically frowning. "I can't see anything."

"Lily disabled the feeds so Fran's people couldn't peek in," Aster said. "Lily can still see though. Nothing to write home about. What's going on over there?"

"Bethany led Laurel into this ship that's attached. Cedar's convinced there's more at play here," Juniper explained. "I agree, but he's being dense about it."

Aster chuckled. "He's rather hardheaded when it comes to Fran. I am also inclined to agree. Fran's crew is rifling through the place, but curiously, they haven't taken anything."

"Really?"

"Perhaps this is just for appearances. Lily has all your items accounted for and nothing has left your rooms."

Whatever was going on must have been related to the *other* guest Francesca had. Everything else was a distraction. But who was the other guest and why take Laurel of all people? Agitation sparked throughout Juniper's thoughts from all the unknown variables.

"It'll be all right," Aster said soothingly. "Fran and Cedar would never actively try and hurt one another or their crews. Posturing aside."

"Did you ever meet her?"

"I've had the pleasure," Aster said. "She and Cedar were used to be friends. They both had a hand in killing their sire."

"Really?"

"Cedar doesn't talk about it much, but the man was not a good person. He put them both through a lot. It was probably why they pirated together as long as they did. Waiting for wounds to heal."

"Why'd they separate? Even one of Fran's vamps said they were a good team."

"I'm unsure. Although, they're both touchy about it, I'm sure. Best not to pry." Aster hummed and Juniper felt the sensation of them crossing their arms. "When I met Fran, we were collaborating on a job where we smuggled a whole colony to another. Her ship was the only size we knew that could do it."

"Why would you smuggle a whole colony?"

"They asked nicely." Aster smiled and Juniper felt their lips twitch to try and smile too. "Some of the residents were sick and the colony was breaking down. Instead of risking infection, feds decided to let them all die. It pulled at Cedar's heartstrings and he asked her for help. With a crew of vampires, she and them wouldn't get sick and she had room. We found a pirate colony who took the risk of accepting them. Afterward, Cedar and Fran ceased speaking."

Still wasn't much of an answer to what was going on now. "All right, not much bad blood then... but why all this pretense? Couldn't Fran have just asked us if she wanted something?"

Once more, Juniper felt the sensation of a shrug. "No idea. Could be more posturing. One of her vampires came into the bridge briefly, but as soon as he saw my ghastly head and the body on the couch, he immediately left and pretended he hadn't seen anything." Aster chuckled. "I suppose I spooked him."

Juniper couldn't help but snort as they imagined it and realized the vibration in their thoughts from the motion meant they'd physically snorted. *Shit.*

They disengaged from the *Gladiolus* and rushed back to their head. It was dizzying and as they settled in—the room blurry and sharp at the same time—they saw Francesca staring at them, wide-eyed.

"Oh." She spat the word out with venom. "That's what you are."

Juniper pounded their chest. "Sorry. Swallowed something wrong."

"You weren't eating." Francesca's face hardened. "You're a cyber, aren't you?"

As if the bright yellow eyes hadn't already given it away if Francesca bothered to look. But no. Juniper had just been some human fleshie Cedar had taken a liking to. They should have played it safer. They shrugged. "What of it?"

"You peeking into my ship?"

"No."

Cedar placed a hand on the table. "Fran, leave them alone."

"Are you talking to your ship?"

"Yeah?" Juniper snapped, even more incensed. "What is your deal? You led us away from it and don't expect me to check on it? It's *our* ship—our home that you've threatened."

Francesca's nostrils flared. "You're ungrateful. I'm fucking feeding you this feast Cedar's never gonna give you and you're talking back to me?" She crossed her arms tightly. "Cybers are pricey. I bet I could make up for it and send someone to turn you in."

"Is that how it works in *your* space?" Juniper asked, their mouth moving before they thought better about fighting with Francesca. Their pulse roared in their ears, rising faster than their bio-monitor could calm it down. "Just take from a friend, isolate one of their crewmates with who knows what, and then threaten another crewmate?" Cedar's hand found their leg under the table and squeezed it. A warning for them to stop, but Juniper did *not* care. "Threaten to *sell* one of them just because they're mouthy? Screw being grateful. Go fuck yourself."

Admittedly, Juniper should have left off the last bit, but they'd already spat it out before their rational thoughts caught up to their mouth. Francesca blinked, her face somewhere between fury and shock, and Annie shoved a fist in her mouth to keep from laughing.

Francesca breathed in. "Cybers are dangerous," she said coldly. "Everyone knows it. No good comes from one aboard our ship. I am simply looking out for my people."

"Cedar's not your people," Juniper shot back, even as Cedar's fingers dug into their knee. They shoved his hand off. "I haven't done anything. All I want is for Laurel to come back. I know you're just roughing up our ship with no intention to take anything. Stop it with this charade."

With a huff, Francesca sat back and considered Juniper. Without breaking eye contact, she pulled a small black device from her bustier. Juniper's entire body went cold, the fight immediately bleeding out of it. It was the same device Forrest had used in the mall.

A kill switch.

Cedar stood, knocking his chair back. "Don't you fucking dare!" he roared.

"Or what?" Francesca snarled. "You'll attack me on my own ship? You'll lose, you ungrateful fuck!"

"Juniper hasn't done anything to warrant that," Cedar stressed. "Please. Don't."

Francesca settled the device down on the table in full view. Only when she took her hand off it did Cedar slowly right his chair and sit back down on the edge, like he was ready to spring up again.

But Juniper could barely breathe, eyes glued to the device. Clary set her hand back on the table; she must have been reaching for something Annie hadn't found. Helpful. Except nothing helped Juniper's heart calm down. Helped Juniper forget the dark awaiting them.

"I won't," Francesca said. "Unless they talk back again."

Cedar scowled. "Why do you even have that?"

Francesca stared at him, incredulous. "Did your three-year nap make you dense?" she asked and his scowl deepened. "I've seen the writing on the wall. We need protection."

"Against me?" Juniper asked, their voice breaking.

A sigh eased out of Francesca's lips, but she didn't reach for the device. "Not *you*. You're malnourished and neurotic." She dismissed them with a hand wave.

"Ced, you haven't seen what they can do now. Look how young this kid is. I didn't even suspect it. If I had, I wouldn't have brought them on my fucking ship."

Juniper bit down from sniping at Francesca.

"Cybernetics are making people on par with vampires without the drawbacks," Francesca continued. "The strength, the speed, the wherewithal. Feds are going to sic cybers on us and I need to defend my people." Her voice was breaking, like she was pleading with Cedar to listen. "I am doing what I need to do. When are *you* going to do the same? Teeth and brawn will only get you so far."

Cedar didn't answer. Juniper glanced past him and at Clary. She'd grown still too, eyebrows folded in worry. It wasn't like Juniper didn't *know* about other cybers. Forrest was the prime example. Clyde even saw the writing on the wall. Cybernetics were all about controlling the masses if you weren't one of the elites. When it was rolled out to the population at large, there'd be no escape.

"You ever see one get up when it should have been dead?" Francesca whispered and Juniper's skin prickled. "How their eyes glow as their cybernetics force them to keep fighting through the pain just to kill you? While their body breaks down?" She paused, drawing the silence out. "I have. And I will not subject my crew to it ever again."

If Juniper *had* been that kind of cyber, they could have already wrecked their way through her crew and it would have been Francesca's fault because she hadn't looked close enough. None of her people had. If Juniper's cybernetics weren't years out of date and they weren't underfed from years alone on a satellite, they could have done so much more. What Forrest had been was probably what the feds had planned for them if they hadn't run.

And if feds got a hold of Clyde's complete research, they'd make it even harder to escape. Nigh impossible. Rendering anyone with cybernetics imprisoned against their will despite everything the augments were meant to do.

Juniper peered up at Francesca. "Why won't you help cybers? I never wanted this. I can tell you there's hardly a cyber alive that really wanted this."

"Does it matter when the feds brainwash them?" Francesca shot back. "I'm a pirate. I protect my own. I will not stick my neck out for someone who willingly let themself be duped into thinking the feds had their best interest at heart."

"I never had the choice," Juniper choked out. "I was a literal child."

"And I don't care," Francesca stressed. "The younger they get you, the more entrenched your brainwashing is. Better to just wipe the whole lot and start over. It's the only way I can protect my own. It's how we *have* to operate out here. I trust the wrong one with a pretty face and it's all over."

The will to argue died and Juniper looked away. Cedar touched their arm; it wasn't a frantic squeeze to get them to shut up, but gentler in support. At least Cedar wouldn't kill them for something they never had a say in. They blinked back sudden tears welling up, nodding, and Cedar took his hand away.

"Cut the games, Fran," Cedar said. "For old time's sake. Why were you looking for us? Who wanted to see Laurel?"

Francesca held his gaze for a moment and then let out an enormous sigh before dramatically flopping back in her chair. All vulnerability locked away.

"This was supposed to be fun," she grumbled.

"Scare the lights outta ya, feed you something nice, and hell, get you high off your ass and parade you around my ship while they talked." She blew air out of her lips.

"Who?" Cedar asked.

Another moment went by before she straightened back up. "I was asked very nicely with oodles of cash that if I found a one Laurel Langley, I'd bring her aboard for a one Lola Langley. And what luck, we got an anonymous tip saying you'd be right here."

Juniper sat up straight, eyes wide. "What?!"

Francesca put a hand on her chest. "Lola and I are friends, you know. How could I ever tell her no?" She grinned, letting her golden fangs glimmer. "What I wouldn't give to be a fly on the wall for *that* reunion."

29
LAUREL

LAUREL WAS NEVER QUITE SURE WHAT SHE'D do if she stood face-to-face with her sister again like this. With nowhere to run or hide. Part of Laurel begged herself to turn back and walk out—this wasn't worth it—but the other part, the squishy center overriding sense? It made her tremble as tears welled up in her eyes. Her sister *had* come to find her. The reasons why didn't matter.

Even more tears came when Lola swooped forward and gathered Laurel in a tight hug Laurel hadn't even realized she'd missed until she was already within its capture. What happened between them— what didn't happen between them—became the quietest whisper and Laurel fiercely hugged her sister back. Perfume smelling of jasmine rolled off Lola like it always did back then, reminding Laurel of home. Staying up with Lola in the darkest nights talking about absolutely everything until their parents separated them. Of hidden smiles and silly faces when no one was looking.

This was Lola, the sister. Not the idol singing to the

stars.

It felt too soon when Lola parted and held Laurel's at an arm's length. She was always taller, but Laurel found herself inclining her head less this time to look at her. Lola's gaze stuttered, like she equally realized Laurel had grown taller, but then she studied her completely, like she wanted to memorize this new Laurel she'd only caught a glimpse of before.

"What are you doing here?" Laurel asked.

Lola looked hurt. "I'm looking for you, silly."

"With a vampire?" Laurel sniffled and removed her glasses to clean them. It let her step back and listen to the voice at the back of her mind telling her something was amiss. When she set her glasses back on her face, Lola's expression had hardened.

"She's my... friend." Lola's expression shifted with practiced ease. It was softer this time, the face she deployed when wanting to appear impassive, but still vulnerable. "When I'm performing near Jupiter, I ask her to keep an eye on my concerts. Someone crashed one once and she happened to be there to help." There was a small smile on her lips and she glanced away, attempting to hide it. "That never made it to the news, somehow. Maybe she had something to do with it." Her smile dropped and she sighed. "Tabloids have seen her, but they always make inferences and they're never right. She's not like that."

Them being friends was why a vampire was willing to let a human dictate what she did. Cedar wasn't the only one with soft spots for humans.

"We're friends," Lola stressed. "In as much as a human can be with a vampire."

"And you did all this for me?"

Lola's hesitation came as a practiced breath. Would fool reporters. Not Laurel.

"I mean, *yes*," Lola said. "I received a tip you'd be at the Saturn Android Facility. It was right. Then I received another tip from the same source that you'd be out in this area and told Fran." She tilted her head, a soft incline of her mouth in a careful smile. "If one tip was right, then the other had to be too. I just needed help with the scouring. Space is vast and so are your machinations."

Laurel forced a chuckle to cover her unease. The only person she knew who knew about their activities was the Answer, but then why send an idol a tip about her sister? Unless he was hoping Laurel would leave Juniper, isolating them further.

Never going to happen.

She cleared her throat. "W-Why did you want to find me?" The more reason trickled back into her thoughts, the more she noticed the androids carefully watching her.

Sisterly warmth cracked just a hair from the question alone and Lola tensed. "Because you ran away," she said like it was the most obvious answer.

It *was*, but with the way she'd said it, she didn't understand why Laurel would ever do such a thing.

"Out here with those people is no place for a sister of mine." Lola scrambled to piece the warmth back together, but Laurel wasn't going to be tricked this time. "It doesn't matter. We can escape. Go back."

Panic snared Laurel. "Wait," she whispered.

Lola scowled at Laurel for a brief moment before she smiled again. It was distinctly absent of warmth. "We can bury this chapter with no one the wiser."

Laurel's heart was racing now. "My friends are back there."

"They are *not* your friends." Lola's face twitched. "Maligned fringe pirates are not friends. They kidnapped you. That's the story." The smile turned mean, rueful. "I blow those ships to the stars, bury everything with them, and return with my wayward sister." Laurel sucked in a sharp breath and darted her gaze to Lola's hands. There was a small device she hadn't noticed before. A detonator.

"We go back together and I become an idol again."

"No," Laurel whispered, feeling sick. "No. No. You can't do that."

"I will not have this haunt me," Lola whispered, her smile finally collapsing. "I know Fran will ask me for a favor and I just can't indulge it. All this will ruin the me everyone loves. I will blow that ship before I'm ruined. Before *we're* ruined."

We. She emphasized it, but Laurel was already ruined in all the ways that mattered to the feds.

She stepped back, putting space between her and Lola. Cedar's tips for fighting rolled over her thoughts; don't be in range of anyone's arms and keep her distance.

"She's your friend, Lola, you can't seriously want to blow her up."

"She is... she is a stepping stone," Lola argued, but the words had no belief in them. Repeated phrases said throughout her career to get ahead, all because she was more concerned with how the feds used her rather than what *she* wanted. The perfect idol. "I am not stupid enough to believe vampires are ever friends with humans. They forget. We're so miniscule in their forever lives. She will not remember me." She gazed at the detonator in her hands, shaking her head. "What kind of pirate is she even, if she didn't even notice my androids setting everything?"

The reunion was over. Everything good Lola had meant to Laurel once upon a time was buried by who she was now. So far gone appeasing the feds just to keep doing what she loved. She wasn't wrong, though; if word got out she'd made a deal with a vampire, her idol days would be over. Idols didn't *do* that; they were good starlets staying within fed regulation. Lola could be so much more, but it was the life she'd been given to.

Laurel should have known better. She'd been so lost in just *having* her sister back—the sister she fondly recalled when they were inseparable—she forgot who Lola really was. As soon as their parents convinced her Laurel was a parasite, she bought it completely and abandoned Laurel just like them.

"Where are you going to take me?" Laurel asked with another gentle step backwards.

"We're going home," Lola said.

"I won't."

Lola's mouth twitched into a mean scowl and her eyes hardened, letting her entire façade drop. "Yes, *we* are," she stressed.

"No!" Laurel shouted louder. One of the androids up above paused and looked down at them. Good. Maybe he wouldn't launch the ship.

"I am never going back there—out here is *my* home. With them is *my* home! You are *not* my home!"

"You're fucking with me," Lola sneered, dropping her arms.

Yep. There was the Lola that Laurel knew. A petulant woman too used to getting everything she asked for.

"Is this all this is about?" Laurel asked. "To bring me home so you can be the good daughter?"

Lola propped a hand on her hip. At least she wasn't holding the detonator with both hands like a lifeline anymore.

"You running away screwed over our parents. I had to bail them out of all their debt, but the feds want more and more because *you* leaving inspired a bunch of copycats. The feds spent so much money finding them and you're the *only* one they haven't found yet!"

Laurel blinked, eyes growing wide. "Copycats?"

"That's what you care about?" Lola scoffed at her. "What about Mom and Dad? You were an investment! They're on the fucking hook for you and everything you caused and all you care about is the other fucking deadbeats in that school?"

"I was sold!" Laurel shouted, angry tears welling up. "You know that! They got rid of me!"

Lola gave her a pitying look. "No one was *sold*. Stop being dramatic."

"Yes, I was," Laurel breathed, her entire body shaking. Lola rolled her eyes. Another tantrum from her dear little sister. "So were you."

"I was *not*," Lola whispered as her face pinched into outright contempt.

Laurel threw up her hands in exasperation. "You're so full of shit, you don't even see it!" Her words came out uneven and breathless. Everything burning to explode out of her at once, struggling to be first. "You were their golden child and had the world handed to you when you sang! What did our parents do, then? Sold you to who paid the most! Except, you kept getting sick so they had another kid to use as replacement parts!"

Lola took in a deep breath, rage making her tremble the same as Laurel. "Shut up," she snapped. "You don't get it. You had everything. Freedom. My fucking face! God, your face showing up on all the feeds and leaving me to deal with those interviewers wanting to ask me why this little bitch was running around with my face?!"

"And that's *my* fault?!" Laurel shouted back. "I didn't have freedom. They sold me the moment your first album went big. I was no longer needed!" A few more paces back and she'd be at the airlock door. "Our parents never loved me and they sure as hell never loved you beyond what your fame brought them. They're bleeding it dry because that's all they've ever known."

"Shut the fuck up!" Lola cried.

"You know I'm right!" Laurel hesitated, flicking a glance up at the androids. One of them moved, but he was staring at Lola worriedly. Like he debated about stepping in to calm her down.

Laurel forged on. "How many times did you cry to me in the middle of the night because of how horrid people were before you got your break? And how Mom and Dad told you that you just had to take it and smile? Then you made bank! Made them so proud of you!"

Lola scrunched her shoulders tighter, dipping her head down so she wasn't looking at Laurel.

"You don't even *care* about me," Laurel continued, her mouth moving all on its own. "All you care about is getting Mom and Dad set to rights because they made you feel responsible for them. All they want is money, no matter what happens to us. You die from a drug overdose? They'll cry crocodile tears and rake in royalties from your songs and from a sad documentary they'll sign off to be made.

"*You* can go back to that," Laurel whispered, lungs starved for air. "I won't. I won't ever go back. I took my life back. They deserve whatever hell they get."

"Shut up," Lola screeched. "Shut up. Shut up!"

"No!" Laurel cried. "We both lied to ourselves

thinking they loved us. They never did and still don't!" There was realization there, suddenly stark, and brought on hot tears. "And *you* never loved me. You buried it so far down, it suffocated because it was easier than admitting you cared for someone you knew the feds would hollow out. And now you're going to blow up the family *I* made on my own and maybe the only friend you're ever going to make."

Lola went strikingly still as she picked her head up. Panic and anger wiped clean off her face. Compartmentalized into a scary blank expression. She made a hesitant step forward.

"Stop acting like this," she said, attempting to be the level-headed sister again. Laurel knew better this time. "Come with me. Let's start over."

"I already started over," Laurel said, squaring her shoulders. "My life's out here."

Laurel's one mistake upon reaching for the airlock door was turning her back on Lola. Immediately, nails dug into her hair and ripped her back. Laurel threw her elbow backward. Wheezing, Lola let go. As Laurel turned—some sudden fear she'd hit her sister too hard—Lola's hand cracked across her face.

The force knocked Laurel sideways, but she caught herself, setting her feet just like Clary showed her. Her ears were ringing, the room was spinning, but she buckled down on her knees and sprang at her sister.

Her head smashed into Lola's sternum, hard, and Lola toppled backwards, shouting. The android that had been watching them closely jumped down from the pilot's console and Laurel immediately retreated, letting him handle Lola.

"Tell them I'm dead! I don't care!" Laurel ran for the airlock before the other android stood to stop her.

"I am never coming back!"

She ran as fast as her legs could carry her. Maybe those androids could get through to Lola someday. Laurel's speech certainly had an effect on them if they hadn't launched the ship. But it wasn't her problem right now. She had to warn everyone.

She pumped her legs and flew past Bethany pacing down the airlock walkway.

"Hey!" Bethany shouted and was upon Laurel in seconds, stopping her. The whole walkway shuddered as an AI's voice announced Lola's ship was disengaging. "Hey, hold on, kiddo!"

"No!" Laurel swung her arm at Bethany and the vampire let her go. "No! I have to warn Fran! Lola wants to blow up her ship!"

Bethany stammered, eyes growing wide, and she overtook Laurel with longer strides. They made it to the end of the walkway and as Bethany threw the airlock doors open, Laurel shoved herself inside. She didn't bother stopping and charged into Francesca.

The vampire's wineglass went flying as she yelped in surprise, catching Laurel.

"Lola is going to blow up your ship!" Laurel shouted.

There was beeping. Loud and shrill, over and over again as it echoed through the halls, and Laurel tensed, pressing into Francesca. But then nothing happened. The beeps distorted and slowed until they'd outright ceased.

The room remained still until a hand patted Laurel's head. She looked up, finding Francesca smiling sadly at her.

"I know, sweetie," she said. When all Laurel did was stare, dumbfounded, Francesca fished a palm tablet out from the sash across her waist. She entered a code, shaking her head.

"Noticed them as soon as she placed them. Didn't think she'd have the heart to do it, but I already had my people disable them. Forgot about the beeping. Girl always *was* overdramatic."

Laurel's strength gave way and she dropped to her knees. Bethany had moved to Annie in the back, whispering to her, and Annie hurried out. Everyone silently watched Francesca as she tapped at her tablet with both thumbs.

"Little diva ain't so smart." She leaned down and pulled Laurel back up, letting her settle over the side of the chair just to get her into the tablet's viewfinder. It was making a hail call.

Another moment of tense silence rolled by before the other side answered. The static cleared and it showed Lola's frantic face on the other side.

Lola's eyes widened and her jaw dropped.

Francesca smiled wide and tightened her arm around Laurel's shoulders. "Hey, Lola!" she said, showing her teeth. Lola started shaking, despair contorting her face. "I like your moxie, but don't come back." She turned and pressed a kiss to Laurel's temple. "I'll take real good care of your lil' sis out here, though!"

The words were noise. Pure noise as Lola disconnected the hail without verbally responding. The AI announced Lola Langley's ship was speeding away. All Noise. Laurel was distant, realization eclipsing everything else.

Her sister was totally willing to destroy the ship—blow *her* up—instead of letting her simply live free. It was either die or go back to the feds. Never did Lola consider the third option.

And Laurel started crying. Large tears streaked

down her cheeks, fogging up her glasses, and she couldn't stop them. Sobs wracked her chest as she slid to the floor, half-dragging Francesca down with her.

"Hey—Hey—" Francesca awkwardly smoothed her hair back. There was another movement, somewhere else in the room, but Laurel's vision was too blurry with tears to parse it until the wash of lavender scented hair dye rolled over her. Juniper had their arms around her, pulling her close.

"I won't shoot her ship," Francesca continued, just as awkwardly. Her hand removed itself from Laurel's head as Juniper gathered Laurel closer. "I promise. She can leave. She's just a speck of stardust in the end."

Laurel couldn't find her voice to explain that wasn't why she was crying and instead, cried harder despite herself. Everything's she'd kept dammed inside finally released as a flood.

Another body came over, stronger arms squeezing her and Juniper together in a way only Cedar could. Laurel let them both hold her tight because she wasn't in any position to hold herself and tell herself it would be all right.

Because it wasn't. She'd fooled herself into thinking her sister loved her, that it really *was* different. She'd let herself hope for one moment, but she'd been lying to herself.

Lola would have killed her rather than let her be free. Just like that.

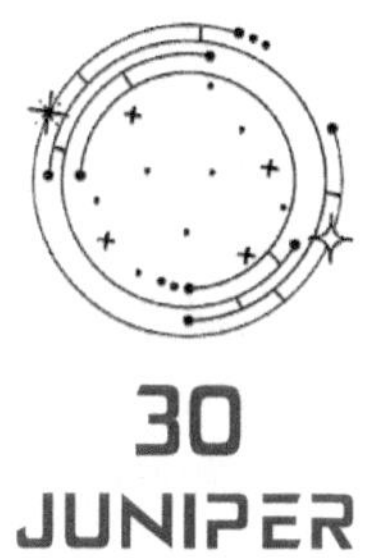

30
JUNIPER

FRANCESCA GAVE LAUREL A FEW MORE
gentle head pats, clearly too perturbed at the crying,
and inched away from her once she saw Juniper and
Cedar had Laurel covered. She wiped a hand on her
pants and drew her mouth tight.

"Humans cry a lot," she murmured.

Juniper glared at her, happy to find Clary doing
the same as she moved around the table to join them,
napkins for Laurel in her hands.

Francesca ignored them and stood, waving a hand
over Cedar. "When she's done with her waterworks,
get off my ship. Bethany will escort you in pairs."

Cedar blinked and looked up at her. "That was it?"
he asked. "You knew she planted fucking bombs on
your ship and let her take Laurel anyway?" His voice
rose with anger. "Fran—"

"I liked that little diva," Francesca growled, baring
her teeth as she met Cedar's gaze. "I thought maybe
she'd have a change of heart after seeing the sister
she'd been searching for." She looked away, shaking
her head. "Too bad I was wrong."

There was real regret in her voice, giving Juniper pause. Maybe she wasn't as aloof as she tried to make herself out to be. Francesca narrowed her eyes as though realizing it herself and snarled.

"Get off my ship, Cedar."

"Franny," Cedar whispered and she rolled her eyes.

"I don't know what the fuck you're doing with a dead cyber's head or this mouthy one, but a collection will kill you." Her expression softened, suddenly looking older and wiser. "I'll tell you one more thing about this debacle: the Answer gave me the tip that you'd be here. Don't know what the hell he wants with you or your fleshies, but it's nothing good."

Juniper stilled hearing the Answer's name. It made sense, though; if anyone was going to give a tip about Laurel to anyone, it would have been him. Juniper held Laurel tighter.

"You trusted that bounty hunter?" Cedar growled.

Francesca shrugged, unbothered. "Doesn't really matter since I'm a vampire with a vampire crew, does it?" She had a point; the Answer wouldn't go after her. Juniper scowled. "With him sniffing around, the feds are sure to follow, especially after that stunt with Lola. Whatever shit you're in, I want nothing more to do with you and yours, Cedar. Get out. Don't come back."

She sounded more worried than angry. Deep down, she must have still cared about Cedar and carefully kept it buried. Cedar nodded.

"All right," he said quietly. "Nice seeing you, Fran. Despite everything."

"Glad you didn't die in those three years," Francesca whispered and headed out.

By the time the doors closed after her, Clary had taken advantage of Juniper's distraction and gathered

Laurel closer to herself, being sisterly about it. Something Juniper couldn't be and they appreciated Clary filling the hole Lola left behind.

Laurel's sniffles had died down; she was mostly dealing with snot at this point. Bio-scanner noted her pulse returning to normal parameters and her breathing had evened.

Bethany cleared her throat and stood in front of their sorry huddle on the ground.

"All right," she said. "Cedar and the girl first."

Juniper squeezed closer to Laurel. "I can go back with her."

"Fran wants Cedar off the ship first and foremost." Bethany pointed to Laurel and frowned. "And well, I figure she wants off the ship too. No hard feelings, kiddo."

Cedar exhaled and Bethany watched him, tense, like he would attack. He simply stood, squeezing Juniper's shoulder as he went, and helped Laurel to her feet. Arguing wouldn't have done any good, but Juniper hated seeing Laurel go without them. Again.

The agitation must have shown on their face; Clary had come closer and put a gentle hand on their sleeve. Bio-scanner was softer around her too, just pinging that she was there. Sort of friend-shaped.

"You good?" she asked.

"I didn't just have my sister try to blow me up."

"I know," Clary said. "I just meant about what Fran said about *you*." She crossed her legs and leaned forward as though to get a better look at Juniper. "Look, I know we haven't really bonded, but that cyber stuff was out of line."

"But she's right," Juniper said. "What she saw? That'll happen more and more. Hell, didn't it happen at the mall?" Clary's face went grim. "It's only a matter of time and we're going to blow up the only lab that can free those people."

Clary looked away. "It sucks, but if this keeps the feds from making it ironclad? We gotta." She blew out a slow sigh. "When we get back, I want you and Laurel to take it easy. Let me and Cedar handle the day-to-day shit."

Being part of the crew with day-to-day shit would have been a nice distraction, except Juniper couldn't gather the energy to argue. After being on such high alert seeing someone who wasn't fed with the kill switch, they were exhausted.

It wasn't long before Bethany returned and led them out the way they'd come. Leaving was a lot faster than arriving. The hallways were hushed, the previous groups milling about absent. Maybe the potential for explosions spooked everyone. It certainly had Juniper.

Their ship, of course, was ransacked. Thoroughly. Piles of their junk strewn across the hallway floors. Cedar's voice echoed from the open bridge doors as he asked about a status report from Lily. Nothing missing. He didn't sound perturbed. Just resolved. Maybe it was something he and Francesca had done often to one another. A way of siblings to annoy each other.

Clary gave Juniper's shoulder a squeeze before she ran off to go help him and Juniper headed to Laurel's room. Francesca's ship disengaged, drifting away from the windows, and Lily announced their own departure.

Laurel was wrapped in a blanket that wasn't hers as she sat curled up on her bed. Smelled like Cedar, though. He must have put her here and dragged something off his own bed to wrap her up. It was touching. Silent tears glistened down Laurel's cheeks as she stared vacantly out the window.

Juniper slowly lowered themself beside her. She took in a shuddering breath before she leaned into Juniper's shoulder.

"Hey," Juniper said.

"Hey," Laurel squeaked.

"Are you okay?" Stupid question, but Juniper was grasping at what to say.

"I think so." Laurel sniffled and ran her sleeve under her nose. No more snot, at least. Just sniffles. She exhaled and looked at her lap. Her palm tablet was beneath the blanket with all the articles on Lola pulled up. A few of them were missing. She must have been deleting them.

"Sometimes, at boarding school," Laurel began speaking softly, "I'd dream that my sister would come save me. By the time I left, I knew it'd never happen. I made myself hate her for selling me out just like my parents did." Her face scrunched and Juniper rubbed her back.

"In her ship, though? I thought she loved me after all. Except... she never did. She tried to blow Fran up—knowing I was there, too—just to save her image. I want to hate her still, but I think I'm more sad than anything else."

More tears slid down her cheeks, unimpeded with her glasses on her head. She pushed the damp napkins against her eyes. "I thought I was done crying."

Juniper leaned Laurel into their shoulder and gently drew their fingers through her hair. "I don't think the crying ever stops," they said. "Sometimes I still think about my parents and wonder the same. Wonder if they ever actually loved me."

"I don't think mine ever did." Laurel peered up at Juniper. "You never talk about your parents."

"They were scientists." Juniper didn't remember their faces well. Just the fed uniform they wore. How white and clean it always was. "The fed's best and brightest. When I showed signs of being gifted, they signed me up for the Prodigy Program and I got all my cybernetics installed." Their voice went uneven without their intention. "Then they disappeared from my life and never came back. It was easier, I guess. I wasn't their kid anymore. I was an experiment.

"When I ran away, I looked them up." Juniper breathed in, finding the motion shaky, and Laurel was rubbing their back now. "They had another child—a normal child—and retired from research."

Laurel grew still, thinking, and then snorted. "God," she said. "Our parents suck."

Juniper snickered and was happy to hear laughter trying to bubble its way out of Laurel, too. "No fucking kidding." They squeezed her closer. "I like our new family. Two dads, a big sister, a cat, and even a dog!"

"A dog?"

"Sprig, clearly."

Giggling, Laurel rested her head against Juniper's shoulder. "Oh, of course."

"Want me to sleep in here tonight?" Juniper asked.

"I do miss cuddling," Laurel said.

"Me too." Maybe their bio-scanner would be chill about it. Juniper extracted themself from Laurel and smiled. "First though, let's find something to eat and then load up a movie. Clary told us to slack. Gotta listen to our big sister, right?"

Laurel smiled, crinkling her nose. "Right. Didn't fill up on all that pork, then?"

Juniper rolled their eyes and stood, holding onto Laurel's hands. "We need something with a boatload of sugar. I think I remember how to make chocolate rolls and Clary's gotta have a chocolate stash. Let's just be silly and normal. None of this bullshit, okay?"

Laurel squeezed Juniper's hands and stood. "I'd like that."

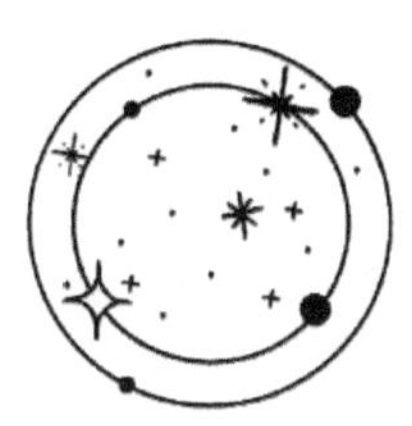

SESSION 7

ENJOY THE
SILENCE

31
LAUREL

LOLA'S FACE BUBBLED UP IN LAUREL'S MIND— her frantic, desperate stare—and jerked Laurel out of what was supposed to be a sound sleep. It'd been two whole days. She wanted to be over it. Lola *never* mattered. Would never matter again. But if she'd never matter *again*, it meant she had mattered, a little bit, and Laurel trapped herself in circular thinking.

She rolled over to her back and sighed. The night after Francesca let them go, Juniper and her were like old friends again. Something tasty shared between themselves (Juniper did not, in fact, remember how to make chocolate rolls, but they were still good), and then they fell asleep curled up with one another as an old movie played. It really *had* been like they were back on the satellite, but it didn't last long.

At least Juniper waited until Laurel was up before they slinked off, too far in their own head to hold onto whatever solace they'd found. Then they locked themself off again. Laurel didn't blame them, especially once Aster let her listen to what went down while she was on Lola's ship. He'd wanted Laurel to understand why Juniper was out of sorts, although it was a little embarrassing their strained friendship was so obvious.

Laurel couldn't help Juniper in a way that mattered. If Juniper closed off from mundane day-to-day things, Laurel couldn't force it. Hopefully Pluto would bring them back.

Clary tried to give them distractions while they were en route to Pluto. Over the three days in transit, everyone had a routine and something to be in charge of. Laurel's was easy. Find some dusty spots and set Sprig loose. After that, Laurel had wanted to try fixing the *Maple,* but Clary was too busy making bombs (with plenty of direction from Aster) and everyone else was too distracted. So, Laurel concentrated on the routine.

At least it was easy. So easy Laurel's thoughts listlessly went right back to her sister.

She desperately needed out of her head.

It was still nighttime when she extracted herself from her blankets and slowly made her way to the bridge. The ship was hushed, all the lights turned to a low ember setting to help facilitate sleep, and it felt empty without anyone else flitting about.

The bridge was dark with only the strung fairy lights and the pilot screens keeping back total darkness. The screens outlined their route to Pluto and they were almost there. Ahead of schedule, but Laurel wasn't complaining. Lily's cat was asleep on the chair and though Laurel had the urge to pick her up and pet her to soothe her worries, she drew her gaze across the rest of the bridge instead.

Juniper was down below, their head laid on the hologram table, and there was a blanket draped across their shoulders. A cable fed from their head-jack and into Aster. They didn't move beyond a soft rise to their shoulders as they breathed. Laurel braved her way closer and stopped when Aster's hologram flicked a glance upward toward her.

"Shh," he said. "I convinced them to sleep. Cedar brought the blanket."

Laurel returned the smile. "Really? They're actually sleeping?"

"They needed the gummies, but I promised I'd watch their vitals," Aster said. "I figured it was the least I could do before we reached Pluto."

"I'm glad they listened to you at least."

Aster considered her sadly. "Laurel..."

"No, it's fine. I didn't mean to sound sad," she cut him off. "I understand I can't provide everything for Juniper. No one friend can. I'm just glad you can cover what I can't." She breathed in a practiced breath to keep back a sudden onslaught of tears. "When every-thing's settled, we'll be friends like we were before."

"I know," Aster said softly. "Juniper misses being Juniper with you too. Try to sleep. I don't want anyone heading out sleep deprived."

"Yes—*Dad*," Laurel teased and Aster chuckled.

She left them be, but didn't intend to go back to sleep. If she tried, her sister's face would be waiting for her. Instead, she made her way to the den. Maybe she could catch something to watch on the net. Sometimes signals reached through transit travel.

The den was awash with flickering blues, a contrast to the ember her eyes had become accus-tomed to. Cedar was on the couch, one foot propped up on the table with his body halfway under a blanket, while a movie played. The volume was so low, it was a mere hum at best. Laurel lingered, contemplating, and before she made a decision about coming down, Cedar tilted his head toward her.

When he'd dropped her off at her room after the whole Lola business, he'd been incredibly softspoken and caring. It'd taken Laurel by surprise, given she wasn't used to it from anyone but Juniper, but she couldn't deny how safe she'd felt. Especially when he wrapped her in a blanket straight from his own stash in an attempt to make her feel better. He'd been awkward and dodgy ever since, though not just with Laurel. He'd been that way with the whole crew.

Maybe something got to him too.

"Hey you." His lips shifted into a smile. "Can't sleep?"

Laurel shrugged and came down. "No. Guess you can't either."

"Don't really *have* to," Cedar said. "I'm just thinking." He peered back at the screen. It was some children's animated flick from way back with a cat in the shape of a bus.

Laurel waited to see if he was going to elaborate and when he didn't, she decided to hell with it and sat beside him. He pulled the blanket over to her and before she could protest, it was mostly over her lap instead of his. She was the fleshie, she supposed; the cold would bother her long before him.

"Are you..." Cedar started until Laurel looked at him and he stammered off. He made a face and scrubbed a hand down it. "Are you okay?"

"Yeah," Laurel said, like she'd said countless times to Juniper, Clary, Aster, and Lily already. Although, she wasn't sure if she really was deep down, but she didn't want to admit that aloud. Everyone probably saw through it anyway.

In an attempt to move the conversation off her, she blurted out the first question that popped in her mind.

"Since you and Fran were sired by the same guy, does that mean you were like siblings?"

Cedar grimaced. "Uh... no?" He laughed nervously and covered his mouth. "Well, kinda? But—uh..."

Laurel read between the lines and sank into the couch. "Bethany said you guys weren't together like that."

"We weren't, not by choice." Cedar looked uncomfortable, but before Laurel could change the trajectory of the conversation, he continued. "Being with our sire was a lot of drugs, blood, and sex. Believe me, you don't want to know the details. I barely remember half of it."

"Was that normal?"

"Sometimes. It's fallen out of fashion. Most of the really old vampires who forced it on their spawns are dead now," Cedar said. "Fran and I were taken advantage of a lot, so I'm glad it's different now."

"I'm sorry for bringing it up," Laurel said.

"Years in the past." Cedar smiled at her, quick reassurance, but it fell just as fast as he tipped his head back against the couch. "'Sides, we're free vampires now. Can make our own friends and shit. Fran's made more than me."

"Have you've only made Aster?"

"Yep," Cedar said. "Fran was always friendlier, if you can believe it. No one's seriously asked me like Aster did, anyway."

"What do you have to do to make a vampire?"

Cedar hesitated for longer than Laurel wanted him to. School never quite said *what* vampires did to make more of themselves and she was honestly curious. Until he looked uncomfortable at being asked. She couldn't take it back before he started speaking.

"You basically have to die," he said haltingly, eyes darting back and forth like he searched for the words somewhere in the room. "Some vampires prey on people who are desperate and already dying, but other times, we drink just enough blood and hope it's not too much." Cedar drew his hand up and looked at his wrist. "Then you have to drink the vampire's own blood."

Laurel adjusted her glasses, trying to see what he saw on his wrist. Nothing but smooth skin. "How does drinking a vampire's blood do anything?"

"You got me." Cedar shrugged. "It's not something I liked doing."

Especially since he'd only done it to Aster. The love of his life.

Cedar didn't continue and Laurel left it be. Turning someone sounded harrowing and she didn't need to know more. Instead, she focused on the movie and leaned against Cedar. He draped an arm around her and squeezed. It felt like family.

"Any plans after Pluto?" Laurel asked.

"Got feelers out for jobs, but not really," Cedar said. "Might need to heist a casino for some quick cash. You know how to count cards?" Laurel shrugged. "They'll spot Junie and Aster in a heartbeat."

"Juniper tried teaching me," she admitted. "They're really good at it."

"Yeah, well, cybernetics make it easy. Eyes are a dead giveaway though, and casinos would check for augments." He rubbed his chin with his free hand, thinking. "Maybe Clary could come with. The three of us can do it, I bet."

Laurel grinned. "I *did* like dressing up for the android heist," she said. "You got something fancy to wear to go with us?"

"Hey! I'm sure I got something buried in my closet and I clean up good. Just ask Aster."

The thought made her smile. As she opened her mouth to ask for more details, brainstorm to keep her thoughts occupied, the ship jostled. Cedar held tighter to Laurel, making sure she didn't roll off the couch, but he didn't look too worried. Once the jostling finished, the ship hummed. Lights eased on, ridding the den of the soft ember glows of nighttime.

Lily's voice came on over the intercom. "We've exited the transit gate. Proceed to Pluto?"

"Ah, wait." Cedar heaved himself up, cracking his joints as he went. "Let me do some maintenance on the gate first. Pretty sure no one's done it in a bit if it was that rocky leaving."

"Maintenance?" Laurel sat up.

Cedar grinned at her. "Yeah, want me to show you how? It's what pirates do for the backchannel gates. Get to use the grappler ship for actual detail work."

Laurel's mood instantly lifted. "Yes! Let me at it!"

PILOTING A CIVILIAN CLASS CRUISER WAS one thing; the controls were easy to understand without much guidance. Cedar's grappler ship—the *Honeycomb,* as he called it—on the other hand, was a little more complex, especially once the grapplers were involved. There were the standard pedals and console, but then holes where she had to slot her hands into to control the grapplers. Between keeping the craft stable and doing little tweaks on the gate massively dwarfing them and the *Gladiolus,* Laurel was a little overwhelmed. Cedar was crammed in beside her as copilot and he gently adjusted her if she looked like she might mess up. All in all, though, not a bad teacher. Very patient.

"Squeeze it just a smidge," Cedar said, eyes unblinking as he watched.

"Got it." Laurel squeezed her fingers around the soft handles within the controls and on the outside, the grappler fingers tightened around the loose bolt. She didn't overdo it or underdo it, and breathed out. Cedar watched it intently and she rotated the arm to turn the bolt.

When they'd done the other side, Cedar had done it much faster and motormouthed while doing it. This took all of Laurel's concentration to not slip and lose the bolt in space. She was learning at least. Hopefully, one day, she could motormouth like Cedar through the process.

She honestly liked Cedar as a teacher. He peppered the silence with compliments and affirmations and remained calm even when she did something poorly. Compared to boarding school, it was a breath of fresh air.

She finished with the bolt and grinned at Cedar. He snickered and patted her shoulder.

"Don't get cocky," he said. "They aren't usually *this* well maintained. Next one's gonna be a mess, I bet."

"So, why'd we fix it?" Laurel asked as Cedar showed her the commands to retract the grappler arms. They slotted back into place along the sides of the ship and locked with a snap.

"'Cause there's no Federation maintenance crew doing it for us," Cedar said, directing her back to the *Gladiolus*. "The only way the backchannels remain in use is if we all pitch in." He leaned back and slid his hands behind his head. "Otherwise, if a far gate goes down, we'd be stranded."

Laurel shuddered at the thought, remembering learning about just how long it took to travel before transit gates were installed. Hardly anyone went past Mars or Venus back then and even those treks took longer than humanly necessary. There was always talk about the Federation developing hyperdrives so ships could essentially travel at gate speeds without the gate, but those were only rumors as far as Laurel knew.

She pressed on the thrusters and they leisurely made their way back to the ship. "So, since we've reached the point you'll never be able to shake me..."

Cedar snorted. "You think so?"

Laurel nodded. "Make sure you keep teaching me," she said. "I like being useful."

He reached around and ruffled her hair. "You already are."

By the time they'd returned, Clary and Juniper were up and dressed. Clary was busy inputting the final course to the artificial moon orbiting Pluto, while Juniper was down below unhooking Aster from the table. As Cedar went to collect Clary's bombs, Laurel helped Juniper finish up. The hologram was gone and everything looked as it did before they'd set him up. Lonely without his kind smile watching them.

"Aster ready?" Laurel asked as she approached.

Juniper finished rolling a spool of wires, nodding. "He said he is, but I think he's nervous." They smiled at Laurel. "Did you have fun piloting the grappler? I was watching."

Laurel grinned. "Maybe when we fix the *Maple*, we can give her grappler arms too." Clary barked a laugh from up above. It was probably way harder than it sounded. Laurel gently nudged Juniper. "You sleep okay?"

"I think so. I'll definitely sleep better when this is all over." They inclined their head to the couch where Aster's body still lay. "Want to help me lug that to the hangar? It's surprisingly heavy."

It actually was; Laurel wanted to give up halfway there and convince Cedar to carry it, but she and Juniper persevered. The cat, of course, made a nuisance of herself, constantly jumping over the body like it was a game. Laurel was only glad when they had the body safely curled up in the back of the *Honeycomb*. It'd be a tight fit inside with all of them, but doable.

Before they reconvened on the bridge, Laurel shuffled Juniper back into their room to get them decked out for cold weather. Laurel had already bundled herself up with a sweater thrown over a set of thermal wear to stay warm, leggings and socks over that, Clary's coat, and a scarf and glove set to keep her warm on the grappler. She wasn't about to let Juniper go out in anything less. The *Honeycomb* regulated temperature well, but it was still chilly.

Thankfully, someone had already grabbed them a better coat than theirs. It fit a little loose around the shoulders and had a small aster plant embroidered on the breast pocket. They'd also dressed in their own set of thermal wear underneath a cowled sweatshirt, and had long socks underneath black jeans.

"I'm going to overheat in this if we don't get moving soon," Juniper complained as they headed back to the bridge.

They wouldn't have to wait long; when they reentered the bridge, Pluto was fast approaching and more importantly, the fake moon orbiting the planet. Cedar waited near the pilot console with Clary, not any warmer dressed beyond long sleeves, but being a vampire, maybe it didn't bother him as much. Aster's head was safely back in its bag across Cedar's shoulder and at Cedar's feet was the duffel bag of bombs.

Clary gave them all their commlinks, promising Lily fixed them so the Answer couldn't fuzz them. Even Juniper had one in case they lost a link to the ship after messing with their cybernetics. Once they all had them slotted and tested, the fake moon loomed in the windows. Shrouded in white squalls covering the surface, it reminded Laurel of a snow globe.

"One more time, from the top." Clary finished setting commands on the pilot's console and pivoted her seat to face them. "You three head out in the *Honeycomb* with all of the bombs, even that nasty antimatter one I found in Aster's old workshop. What do you do upon setting a bomb?"

Laurel shot her hand up eagerly and her cheeks blazed realizing she didn't have to. "We tell you which bomb—you numbered them all," she said meekly. From Clary's end, she'd keep track of the ones they used, prime them, and detonate them when everyone was back.

Juniper cleared their throat. "Aster's bomb is the last resort," they added. "Don't use it unless we feel we absolutely *have* to."

"Perfect," Clary said. "I've never worked with antimatter, so I'm not even sure what all it's going to do except decimate everything in its path. Aster couldn't remember either."

Laurel and Juniper peered at Cedar and he shrugged. "Don't look at me," he said. "I did the biting. He did the blowing. Up. Blowing up."

Juniper snorted, slapping his arm, while Laurel groaned and rolled her eyes. Clary sighed heavily and everyone looked back at her.

"What else is everyone bringing?" Clary asked,

right back to the plan.

"Stunner!" Laurel opened her jacket; she'd stowed it in a pocket right beside her hip. She patted her chest next, where the ice needle sat beneath her sweater. "And my ice needle."

Clary smiled, nodding, and looked at Juniper. Likewise, they opened their coat and pointed to the interior pocket. "Stunner," they said and then pointed at their wrist. "And a few pinwheels. Aster had a slot for them in the sleeve."

"Good, good." Clary faced Cedar, raising her eyebrows.

"Blaster." Cedar patted the holster on his leg. "Laser knife." He patted the pocket on his long coat and his eyebrows shot up. "Oh!" He bent forward and showed his teeth off. Laurel had to choke down a laugh. "And my teeth."

"Very funny," Clary said and Cedar grinned. "And the order of operations?"

"Aster's body first," Laurel said, some burning desire to ace the pop quiz. She'd never been geeked for them back in school, but here was different. "Juniper's cybernetics second. Grab anything not nailed down that looks important and plant explosives in-between all that. Then, we leave and you detonate everything once we're safely home."

"And then it'll all be gone," Juniper whispered, distantly.

What remained of Clyde Lowell's great mind would become stardust in the vastness of space. Truthfully, Laurel hated it too, but they'd promised. Laurel fidgeted with Clyde's ring on her thumb. Better gone than in fed hands.

"There is no response from the lab," Lily announced, interrupting them. "Be careful. With all the snow, I cannot get an accurate reading of the surface."

Cedar gazed out the window. "Didn't used to snow like this."

"Think you can pilot in it?" Juniper asked.

"We'll find out." Cedar shoved his hands in his pockets and turned. "We're moving out. Watch our asses, Clary."

"Can do. Just don't do anything stupid." She faced her console. "I'll lower the ship toward the shadow of the moon and follow its orbit. We'll be hidden so long as nothing sneaks up on us. Got drones zipping around keeping an eye on everything too. You guys go fix yourselves."

While Cedar piloted the *Honeycomb*, Laurel made herself the dutiful copilot and Juniper sat crammed in the back with Aster's head and body. Though Laurel had wanted to fly a bit more, get used to the grappler, she was glad she wasn't when they descended through the artificial atmosphere. Squalls of snow pushed their ship back and forth and frosted the front windows completely. If she'd been driving, she would have panicked. Cedar, on the other hand, was undaunted; he righted the ship each time it veered and with a few quick commands he made sure to point out to Laurel, the top melted the snow right off.

The surface wasn't altogether different from the uninhabited areas of the moon. Barren, craterous, but with the addition of snow blowing everywhere. Not all of it seemed to stick; there were areas without, but there were just as many dunes where it piled up. The diagnostics on their ship read off an absolutely chilling temperature, but it wasn't as cold as Laurel expected. Clyde's lab must have been generating heat.

They sped through squalls, drawing lower and

lower to the ground with each pass as they searched for the landing pad. Dark shapes jutted out of the white snow, but most of it was debris. Cedar grew more and more frustrated with each pass; he must not have been able to see much more than Laurel. Juniper was leaning between their seats to look out the front, eyes gleaming, but it wasn't until the third or fourth pass when Juniper finally pointed.

"There!"

Cedar eased on the brakes, slowing them down, and they flew by a black obelisk almost buried in the snow. Only the top stuck out, and even it had been frosted over, making it appear almost as a white spire instead. Cedar swung them back around, going even slower, and had Laurel draw the ship's searchlight across the area.

One side was a mound of snow, burying the obelisk, while the other sloped until it revealed the bottom of the structure where Clyde's bident symbol was emblazoned. The *Honeycomb's* scans finally picked up metal beneath the snow and Cedar pulled back around to settle their ship down.

Once they landed, their ship was immediately hailed.

"Welcome," came an AI voice sounding almost like a digitized version of Clyde himself. "Please enunciate your code now."

Cedar had already positioned himself so he could smash his feet on the thrusters at a moment's notice and Laurel and Juniper braced themselves. He rattled his code off, clearly enunciating each letter and number, and they waited. And waited. An agonizing amount of time. Just as Cedar looked ready to shoot them back into the sky, a set of locks hissed them, letting out clouds of steam which melted the snow.

"Welcome, Cedar Woods," the AI said. "Stay aboard the lift or you will be locked out."

The metal below shook and made the ship buzz. Cedar looked tense, like he was still very willing to fly off, but then the entire platform began descending. As soon as they were down far enough, fluorescent lights buzzed on and another metal gate closed above them, sealing them in.

Cedar finally breathed out. "I thought we were gonna fry." As Laurel shared a pained expression with Juniper, he flipped on his comms. "We're inside, Clary."

"Got it." Her voice was washed with static, but still understandable. "All quiet out here."

The descent was long, delving deep into the core of the fake moon, and with each level down, the temperature rose. Much more livable by the time they reached the bottom. The walls here resembled black stone, polished to a sheen, and steel beams stood tall in each corner. When they officially reached the bottom and the shaft gave out a soft chime, Cedar gave it another moment of acceptable readings before he disengaged the top.

Everything was hushed around them with no indication there was anything here other than them. They waited another moment before Cedar hopped out and cast his gaze over the place slowly.

Laurel and Juniper took it as their cue to get moving. They both helped get Aster's body out of the ship and onto Cedar's back. Once it was secure, Laurel took the bag of bombs and Juniper took Aster's head in their arms.

The only door was the one flushed against the wall. The moon bident symbol was emblazoned in gold across the center. There was also a small console against the wall beside it with thin lines reminiscent of a circuit board leading away from it.

"Put the ring near that." Cedar nodded at the console. "It's what Clyde always did. Might as well let ourselves in."

Laurel hovered her hand in front of the console and felt an electric arc reaching toward her from inside the mechanism. It wasn't painful, simply a friendly buzz, and she held still like Clyde must have done. Before long, the locking mechanisms within the wall hissed, letting out a plume of warm air smelling like an old archival room, and the door slid to the side.

"Welcome home, Clyde Lowell," the AI warmly announced. "We await your command."

An immense pang of guilt struck Laurel as she drew her hand to her chest. He'd never come home again. Juniper gently touched Laurel's arm and Laurel tried to let the guilt go.

Lights beyond the door flickered on. Most of them, anyway. Some were dim, others bright, and then any that weren't, remained dark voids in the tunnel. Mechanical gears whirred within and the walkway inside began inching forward.

They stepped on as a group and though Laurel was ready to keep going to get everything over with faster, Cedar stopped her. Probably better *not* to rush, on second thought. Especially when she noticed the glint of a gold light passing over them.

"It's scanning us," Juniper whispered.

"Figured that's what it did," Cedar said. "Probably to check for threats. Bet it's pinging what we brought with us."

Laurel frowned and adjusted the bag on her shoulder. "I hope it doesn't mind the bombs..."

The walkway ended shortly before a set of frosted

glass doors lined in gold. Cedar took the lead and Laurel and Juniper stuck close.

The doors slid aside upon their approach and more lights attempted to flicker on. The room resembled what Laurel always imagined the waiting rooms in pristine fed labs looked like. Smooth white walls, fluorescent lights, and a set of screens to one side. It looked like it should have had a schedule displayed, but instead, it showed a starry vista.

Juniper gripped Laurel's arm suddenly and she noticed an android coming through the glass doors at the other end of the room. He stopped dead seeing them, his expectant expression falling into something close to panic.

His brilliant yellow eyes widened, the noticeable white rings within spinning like he was scanning them. He had disheveled black hair, styled to one side crookedly like someone had haphazardly cut one side and gave up on the other. His face bore heavy resemblance to Clyde's own, with his sharp cheeks and nose. He wore a pristine white button-up tucked into black trousers and had his sleeves rolled up like he'd been working on something.

Laurel's gaze lingered on his arms; an intricate network of black floral tattoos covered his tan skin. Some of the linework was shaky, but others were smooth as though by a trained artist. She'd never seen androids tattoo themselves and suddenly wondered if this really was an android.

He must have been, though, with the white rings inside his irises. They turned as he considered them and his eyes grew even wider with panic.

"Oh," he spoke, his voice young and soft. "Oh." It sounded higher the second time. "I thought... oh. Oh no. No. No." He sucked in an audible breath as though to calm himself.

He'd been expecting Clyde. Laurel squeezed the ring; he must have been Morus.

"I suppose that makes sense. Clyde never used that dock…" Morus dropped his arms and his glances between them became frantic. He shook his head and stepped back. "No. No, it doesn't. You can't be here. No. He told me no one is allowed in. He said—"

"We don't mean you any harm!" Laurel shouted and the android's gaze fixed on her. On the ring. His face fell and she held it out. "Clyde's buried beneath the mulberry tree. He said we could come."

A soft gasp lifted from Morus' lips as his entire body stilled. His eyes dimmed, the rings all but hidden in the milky shade of yellow, and after a moment of stillness, a sigh followed the gasp. His eyes lit back up. "He must be. If you have his ring."

He came over slowly, like he was expecting someone to strike him, and stood before Laurel. He was barely taller than Juniper and was made of lanky limbs he kept close as though to make himself look as small as possible. Up close, Laurel noticed freckles carefully arranged across his cheeks. They reminded Laurel of constellations.

Morus gently took the ring with shaking fingers and for a long time, he didn't say anything. He stared at it like he expected an answer it wasn't giving.

Juniper cleared their throat. "You're Morus, right?"

"Yes. I am." Morus clutched the ring in his fist and lifted his gaze. "Would you care to introduce yourselves? I haven't had guests in years."

Juniper gave him a shy smile. "I'm Juniper—they/them—she's Laurel." They nodded toward Cedar who hadn't moved. "And he's Cedar."

Morus's gaze flicked between them. It lingered on Cedar, then on Aster's sleeping body over his shoulder, to the bag in Juniper's arms, and then finally to the bag of bombs Laurel held. His eyes narrowed and he stepped back.

"You're here to bury his lab."

"Yes," Laurel said slowly, parsing his response. Morus didn't react. His expression was empty. "Clyde asked us to."

The silence was heavy between them. Morus watched them so intently, like he wanted to believe something else and not the reality in front of him. Finally, he gave them a grave nod.

"I know. It's the only way he'd give someone I don't know the passcode. Well? What else?" A sad smile stretched across his thin lips. "I see you have an empty android body, a container with a vampire's head inside—please, don't feel the need to cover it, I've seen ghastlier. And you." He stared at Juniper so clearly, they tensed. "You with cybernetics going haywire. I am Morus, the last living witness to Clyde Lowell's greatest works and warden of his memories. I am here to serve his final guests, so please: what do you need?"

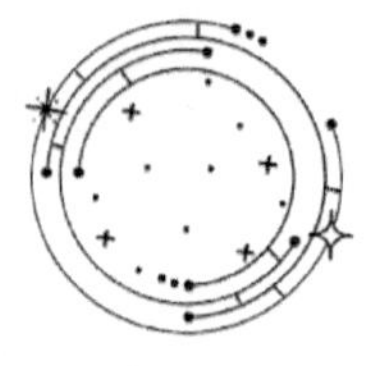

32
JUNIPER

CLYDE'S FINAL GUESTS SOUNDED TOO FANCY when they wanted to blast the entire place to stardust. Juniper kept the thought to themself as Morus took the three of them up the stairs past the glass antechamber doors and to the only room lit up in the lab. A lounge with the perfect vantage point to look at everything down below. If it hadn't been dark, anyway.

Before Morus led them up, he ordered the AI to prepare two rooms. One for a transfer program and the other, for cybernetics. Juniper's body shuddered hearing it, their pulse buzzing. It was really happening after dreaming of it for so long. They tried to stay calm as Morus let them into the lounge room.

Vinyl red couches hugged both walls of the lounge while a nebula patterned glass table sat in the center. Near the door was a small kitchenette complete with an old red fridge, cabinets, and a small stove. Wrapping around the wall from the kitchenette to the back of the far couch was the window overlooking the lab below. Juniper tried to peer out, but all they ended up seeing was themself. Tired and pale.

They immediately turned away and sat with their back to the window. Nothing to see anyway.

Laurel eagerly sat beside them while Cedar gently set Aster's body down in a sitting position and sat next to it across from them. Feeling incomplete, Juniper took Aster's head out of its bag and rested it on the table. Still ghastly. Somehow more so.

Morus glanced at it, but no emotion crossed his face. He fussed with the kitchenette instead and had a kettle full of water quickly on the stove. It boiled in seconds and he poured its contents inside a black teapot he'd hardly glanced at as one hand prepped the tea leaves. A precise and practiced hand on autopilot like he'd done it many times before.

"I honestly wasn't expecting anyone," Morus conversed, breaking the silence. "I've been making tea out of my flowers lately. It's been... a long time since I had a shipment of *actual* tea." He came over and handed out teacups. Each one was black with a red interior and had a handle of gold. "It's all I have. I hope this is acceptable."

Laurel smiled at him. "It sounds lovely," she said. "What kind of flowers do you grow?"

Morus' face lit up and he told her with life so clear in his eyes, Juniper couldn't believe Clyde had left him all alone. Morus had *no one* and likely never would have if they'd never gone to rob Clyde's grave. At least when Juniper was in their satellite, they'd had an out. If not a quick visit to the Lunar Colony, there was chatter. Something to get lost in. As Juniper concentrated, there was nothing around them for their wireless augment to connect to. No soft murmurs on airways and no real net. Just a heavy silence.

It was no wonder Morus immediately warmed to Laurel as soon as she'd shown interest in something he clearly adored.

As Morus continued talking about his sunlamp grown botanicals and Laurel remained a rapt audience, Juniper glanced at Cedar. His mouth had grown tight as he watched them interact. Juniper saw suddenly why. Laurel would definitely *not* want to leave Morus—although, leaving him wasn't in the cards—and she'd also definitely want him to join their crew so he wouldn't be alone.

The feds would just scoop him up otherwise and tear him apart to learn how Clyde had made him.

Juniper jostled out of their thoughts as Morus leaned close to grab their cup. He'd already filled Laurel's and she held it with both hands, taking in the aroma. Morus actually smelled like flowers up close. Slim had always smelled like an android. It was hard to describe, but definitely unique to androids. This was endearing.

Juniper thanked Morus as he drew away to give Cedar the same treatment. The perfect host.

"Did you..." Juniper paused as their gaze drew back to his arms. "Did you draw your own tattoos?"

Morus nodded and considered the lines of lavender down one arm. "Yes. I did. I was... bored one night. Clyde already tattooed me with his signature— it's on my stomach—so I figured, why can't I do something myself? Calibrating the lasers to follow my sketches was the hard part. Although, I think they turned out nice."

"They did!" Laurel piped up. "Did it hurt?"

"Well..."

As Morus tried to answer her, Juniper thought about what he'd just said. Androids were *never* supposed to express boredom; it wasn't in their capability because the feds never wanted idle androids. Slim always had *something* to occupy his time with and he was always content with it. Fed programming at work. Morus, on the other hand, clearly wasn't a fed android. He was something else.

"Oh, right!" Morus suddenly picked his head up and looked at Cedar. "You're a vampire." Cedar stopped from drinking his tea and raised his eyebrows. "Would you prefer blood? I still have some. I can mix the two. Clyde always preferred it that way."

"Sure." Cedar held out his cup and Morus took it with another smile that could have melted ice. He happily went to the fridge built into the counter.

Upon opening it, his smile waned. "Oh." He chuckled. "I suppose I could give all this to you. He won't be needing it, will he?" He freed a small blood pack and squeezed it into the teacup. About as appetizing as bloffee and Juniper avoided looking at it.

When Morus returned, the smile was back on his lips, no hint of the previous sadness, and he happily handed the mixture over.

Juniper sipped on their own non-blood tea. It was delicious, its soft floral taste revitalizing them. Made them warm and at home, but they wished they were actively doing something else but waiting.

Morus must have sensed Juniper's apprehension; he paused, watching them, and drew his gaze out the window. Everything was still dark. Morus fidgeted with the teapot.

"It shouldn't honestly be *long*," he admitted. "The systems need time to synchronize since they've been dormant." He settled the teapot on the coffee table, but still fidgeted. Laurel scooched closer to Juniper, making room for him, and he only sat when she patted the spot.

"Do you not drink?" Laurel asked.

Morus shook his head. "I don't have to. I just like the way it smells."

Juniper raised their eyebrows. "But you could? Like normal bio-androids?"

"Of course." Morus peered at Juniper. "If my energy is depleted, food and drink is arguably better than electricity. Bio-androids like me and your soon to be friend have systems that change all of that into energy, leaving behind no waste. I am glad to see the Federation using the tech finally. It's been around for over ten years and this is the first bio-android I've seen with a system so similar to mine." He chuckled and crossed his legs. "You could feed us literal garbage and it'd work, but that's rather cruel. We do have taste buds after all."

Cedar was slowly nodding, like he was taking mental notes. They didn't have a manual for Aster's new body, after all, so that probably wasn't a bad idea. Juniper glanced at the container with Aster's head, attempting to reach out to get his opinion, but forgot they weren't connected.

"Well?" Morus asked and dropped his hands tight in his lap. "How is it? No one's tried my flower tea and I'm quite biased."

Laurel jumped, almost spilling what was left in her cup. "It's wonderful!" she said and Juniper nodded eagerly in agreement. "I actually have a question for you, Morus." She placed her cup down. "How old are you?"

Morus looked taken aback. He blinked a few times, like trying to parse why she was asking. "Likely not much older than you two." He nodded at her and Juniper. "Although, bio-androids ages are a little weird. I was never mentally a child, even at a year fresh out of the tank. My mind and pieces of me are also countless years old."

"The tank?" Juniper asked. "How did Clyde make you?"

"My siblings and I began as a cluster of cells in a tank," Morus explained slowly. "As we grow, we're fitted with cybernetics and the cells take the shape of an android frame. I've never looked much into the specifics. Clyde shut it all down after I was finished." He glanced down at himself and had a lopsided smile on his lips. "Although, given I'm rather thin and not as tall as my siblings were, I wonder if he rushed my process."

Different than the terminals at the Saturn facility, then. Juniper watched him, hoping he'd say more, and he grew nervous.

"It's not a way the feds would want," he finally said. "It's more organic in nature and makes us *too* close to humans for them. It also takes a rather long time. The way feds do it also has less chance of failure."

"Where are your siblings?" Laurel asked. "We watched this documentary about Clyde and we didn't see any of them at his funeral."

"You wouldn't have," Morus said slowly. "Any funeral would have been a way to capture them, I'm sure. Besides, not all of them left happy. Clyde wouldn't have held it against any of us for not appearing, anyway. He didn't even *want* a funeral."

Laurel frowned. "And he left you here while he decided to die."

"Yes." Morus grew still and kept his gaze down-cast. "I-I'm sure someone was supposed to come get me, but he never did." His voice grew quieter. All pretense of energy and jubilation over tea gone. It'd been a mask. "Clyde made me, helped me grow, only to leave so soon. Why did he even bother if he was going to choose to die? He must have known when he made me." He closed his eyes and his shoulders trembled. "He gave me nothing but a lab to keep hidden. How many fed ships have I fried because they weren't allowed inside?"

It explained the scattered mounds of metal buried in the snow. The wind must have knocked them from the landing platform once the rider was dead and then the snow buried it.

Juniper was unable to respond and Laurel watched Morus, her eyes wide.

"Could you have left?" Cedar asked.

Morus shrugged. "It never truly occurred to me to try until you spoke those words, although it's not like it would have mattered. Clyde's own dock is empty and after a ship gets fried, it won't fly again. I never truly considered leaving. I just... stayed silent like I was supposed to."

Laurel shot a piercing look at Cedar and Juniper matched it. They *had* to take Morus with them—no ifs, ands, or buts about it. He was alone in the universe and no one deserved that. Cedar sputtered on his tea as he caught them staring and wiped his mouth.

"Okay, okay. You two can stop staring at me like that," he grumbled. "You think I'm heartless?" Morus glanced between them, confused. "You know we're blowing this place to stardust, yeah?"

Morus slowly nodded. "Given the number of bombs... I had an inkling."

"Obviously not with you in it."

"Well, yes... I would hope not."

"What do you want to do after you leave?"

It wasn't a bad way to frame it. Cedar wanted to

give Morus likely one of the first few choices he'd make completely independent of Clyde's wants. Except it had left Morus stunned. The white rings in his eyes turned brightly in thought for what felt like a long time. Finally, he shook his head.

"I don't know," he whispered. "I don't know anything beyond this lab."

"Come with us," Laurel spelled out. "We have a spare room on our ship. You don't have to go into the world alone."

Morus shot Cedar a wide-eyed look and clamped his hands to his mouth. "You'd truly take me?"

Cedar shrugged. "I'm in the business of picking up kids. Plant-named kids." He snickered and Juniper bit back their own laugh. "I can't in good faith leave you here or dump you at the nearest station."

Morus settled his hands in his lap again. "Thank you," he said, genuinely smiling. It made his eyes delightfully bright. "C-Can I bring some of my plants? Please? They won't take up much room."

"Of course," Juniper cut in, grinning. "We need more greenery anyway."

"We can take all of them!" Laurel cut in.

"There's quite a few..." Morus said.

Juniper grimaced. "The grappler's not *that* big, Laurie."

"Oh."

Cedar groaned and dipped his head back, thumping it against the wall. "The logistics of keeping those alive."

Morus laughed softly with a shy grin. It was strangely adorable.

A ping echoed across the facility and the lights in the dark below slowly eased on, revealing rows of research rooms and glass doors in the snaking hallway.

Screens across from the research rooms fuzzed on and displayed a pictorial landscape on a loop. What drew Juniper's gaze the most, however, were the floating plant trellises hanging from the ceiling. Morus wasn't kidding; he had a lot. Greenery hung down like curtains and some of them were dotted with flowers. It brought color to the sterile white.

"The transfer terminal for your friend is finished." Morus stood and faced everyone, right back to business. "I've honestly never done this, but the AI is installed with Clyde's mind and knows what to do. Your friend will be in good hands."

As everyone mobilized—Laurel helping Morus collect the tea cups and Cedar gathering Aster's body—Juniper took a moment to plug into Aster's head. The fuzzy feeling was an old friend by now and the connection was faster than it had ever been. The white room flickered into focus and Aster was there waiting for them.

Juniper grinned and his worried expression melted into a smile.

"We're about to start," Juniper said. "You're in good hands."

Aster looked outwardly nervous, giving Juniper pause. He'd hidden it so well before. He breathed out an audible breath, shaking out his arms.

"All right," he said. "I'm ready. I swear." He chuckled, realizing he did not sound it. "I promise."

"We'll be here when you wake up," Juniper said.

"I know. Juniper..." Aster hesitated and then shook his head. "Thank you for everything."

"Save that for when you're up!" Juniper grinned. "I'm disengaging now."

Aster waved at them. "See you soon."

Laurel was waiting for Juniper when they

disconnected. Morus and Cedar were already heading into the lab with the body.

Smiling, she asked, "Aster ready?"

"Ready." Juniper stood and gathered his head close. "I hope this works."

They had to air it out. Just to get it out of their head. It *would* work. They had to have no doubts. When Laurel reached out and squeezed their hand, they really believed it would.

The transfer terminal room wasn't far, just down the walkway beneath candle-like orange lights covered in what appeared to be ivy. The room was small and compact with a single sparse bed in the center, a diagnostics screen looming above it, a computer terminal to one side, and a basic nightstand on the other. As Cedar gently laid Aster's body on the bed, Morus took wires from the drawers underneath. There was a lot. Morus handed some to Cedar, but he balked, clearly out of his element, and Juniper handed the head to Laurel to help instead.

It was the standard procedure of transferring android bodies. Exactly what they'd tried to do on the ship. Between them and Morus, the bed soon resembled a bed of wires. The body was connected to the head and the head was connected to the main terminal.

Morus initiated the process on the terminal without any fanfare. The lights dimmed in the room so only the diagnostics screen glowed, and the AI made another announcement over the facility.

"Diverting power to Transfer Terminal Alpha. Please standby."

The diagnostics screen above shifted, showing an outline of Aster's body. All the programming therein was on one side, while the other side had scrolling lines of code. Everything ran too fast for Juniper to read and shortly, it finished its test much faster than Lily's supercomputer had.

And when it reached the end, it didn't fail.

Cedar tensed beside Juniper and they gently squeezed his arm in lieu of any meaningless spoken platitude.

"The initial test was successful," Morus spoke as he read over the terminal. "The actual process will take a little longer, but this is a good start." He typed in a final command and the diagnostic screen started up again. A thrum of power shuddered through the room and Aster's body's braincase whirred with a fan deep inside as if in response.

Morus faced everyone. "Now, we wait."

33
LAUREL

THE HUM OF THE ROOM SHOOK LAUREL down to her bones. Fans whirred to life in the terminal and Aster's body both, but his severed head remained still as always. Laurel picked her eyes up to the diagnostics and tried to parse it to do something other than stand there and fret. Nope. Couldn't read it. Too fast and her eyes weren't focusing.

She dropped her gaze to Aster's android body again. There was a glow across his head now, fine lines beneath his blond hair.

Laurel's vision continued wavering, making her dizzy. She couldn't tell if it was from the hum or the sudden anxiety that everything might fail. She'd wanted to be a steady pillar for Juniper, but she couldn't stop thinking of the what ifs. All at once, she wanted out of the room to exhale all the worries invading her mind.

Morus peered over, curious. He glanced at Cedar and Juniper and so did Laurel. At some point Juniper had taken Cedar's hand, but otherwise, they were as still as statues. Juniper watched the screen, eyes flitting back and forth across the information, but Cedar kept his eyes on Aster alone. Cedar wasn't even breathing. Nothing was affecting either of them.

Morus cleared his throat. Cedar broke his steady gaze and raised an eyebrow at him. "Sometimes the process is disconcerting for the living and those without cybernetics." He waved his hand across his head. "The vibrations."

"Oh!" Juniper faced Laurel. "I didn't even think..."

"As the process is more or less handled by the AI, I am not needed here." Morus gently came over to stand beside Laurel. "I'll show her where my plants are before she vomits. Stay with your friend. The AI will tell me when it's finished."

Juniper watched Laurel sadly. "I'll be here," they said. "Go get some air."

Stepping into the hallway was an immediate relief. The dark a break from all the information and the silence a reprieve from the sudden anxious thoughts. Nothing nauseating here. The vibrations and the hum were contained to the room. Laurel took a deep breath.

"Better?" Morus asked.

"A little bit. I never thought it'd feel like that."

"It's the power required," Morus said. "Thankfully, Clyde structured his lab in such a way, the rooms are fitted with material to contain most of the vibrations from the calibration."

Laurel's mood lifted. "Does that mean it's working?"

"Humans always worked until the very end," Morus said slowly. "It's the disconnection from their original bodies that ends up killing them. Your friend has already done the disconnection, in a sense, and survived anyway. I have faith in the process."

It wasn't a resounding yes, but good enough. Laurel nodded. "Faith is good. Have you seen it done often before?"

Morus gave a tiny shrug. "Not in person, no. Clyde keeps impressive records, however, and they include video footage, so I know about as much as one can from those. Most of the time, it was my siblings going from one body to the next when they outgrew a previous one. All of them came out with their souls attached."

"Would the same process work for a human without cybernetics, if you tried?"

Morus hesitated and crossed his arms. "I don't believe so. What makes us who we are is very much attached to *what* we are. It's why the Federation fails when they try to live beyond the needs of their mortal body. The only thing they can do is cram someone so full of cybernetics, it forgets itself, and attaches to whatever tech was inside. To the point of your friend in there: the datacrypt within."

"Do you think that helped Aster live despite losing his body?"

"It's a guess." Morus stretched the words slowly. "The vampirism probably had something to do with it, too. Whatever he is was already unattached and imprinted on the datacrypt. The very same process would not have worked with Cedar, I'd imagine. With no tech, if he'd lost his whole body and effectively died, he would have given up the ghost. It happens the very same with humans."

"And people like Juniper?"

Morus made an uneasy motion with his hand. "It really depends. Federation experiments into this have largely failed. It's just so hard to convince the part of the human brain responsible for you—the soul, or whatever it is—to let go of the body and persist. The body is all you know, after all. Androids know tacitly they can be upgraded, so while there may be some resistance with older androids and bio-androids, the process is doable with minimal failure."

At least Juniper wasn't getting a whole new body, Laurel supposed. Though she couldn't wrap her head around the logistics, she wanted to trust Morus' assessment. He wasn't worried, so she wouldn't be either.

If only it was that easy to push away worries.

Morus smiled at her, circles in his irises spinning, and she urged him on to show her to the plants for grabbing.

As Morus led her to another set of glass doors blocking another hallway, she was struck once again by the silence. An entire lab for one android.

"Did you ever meet your siblings?" Laurel asked.

Morus shook his head and drifted his hand in front of the door's locking mechanism. It came apart and he took her through. "None of them have come home, so no. Clyde only made another android when he was lonely. I'm sure they are still out there some-where doing something with their lives, but I haven't the foggiest idea where."

He sounded lonely admitting it and Laurel put a new plan into the back of her head: try to find his siblings. Maybe they could reconnect. Probably better chance than her and Lola.

The corridor beyond the glass doors was cozy, draped in more plants than Laurel could count. Morus insisted he knew those weren't coming with them; they were too big. At one end of the hall, where ivy crawled downward across the wall, was a large terminal. Likely the interface for the supercomputer.

Its screen was divided into a dozen and most of them showed simply snow. Only two displayed anything of interest: one was the transfer terminal room with everyone else inside it, as still as statues, while the other was the room Juniper would go to next.

To fix their cybernetics. Laurel's heart clenched. It was what Juniper had wanted since they set out from the Lunar Colony. It was finally happening and Laurel could mentally check it off their list.

The screens blipped, darkening, and though Laurel startled, Morus continued on.

"The snow interferes sometimes," he said. "My room's this way."

Morus turned her to a small hallway across from the supercomputer terminal. There were a few more doors here with another set of glass ones at the very end, blocking passage to the dark lift beyond it.

"That leads down to Clyde's personal dock," Morus said when he noticed Laurel lingering to look. "His ship's gone, so there's nothing worth taking down there." He took her through the nearby door.

A rush of plant smells hurried out, free to fill the sterile air around them. It reminded Laurel of when she visited her grandmother; she had plants all over her place just like this. Laurel breathed in, hoping to memorize it. Maybe they could fill up the *Gladiolus* like this. Greenery at every corner.

The room was small, barely bigger than her room on the *Gladiolus*, with sunlamps casting a pleasant warmth over the rows and rows of shelves overflowing with different plants. Flowers and leaves of all kinds fought for space and hidden beyond them was a cot carved into the wall with dresser drawers beneath it. Morus' whole life contained to a single room. Still, there was a proud smile on his lips staring at it all. He'd found happiness no matter how small it was.

"I know you won't have room for all of them." Morus eyed the bag across Laurel's shoulder. Before she could figure out the logistics of fitting *all* his plants in their grappler—space be damned—he spoke again. "I'll choose my favorites and set them aside for when you've made room in your bag."

"I feel bad we're blowing it all up," Laurel admitted as Morus bent over his plants to look at them. Her gaze shot to a few books laying forlorn on the side table. She quickly slid them into her bag.

"Don't be," he said. "Clyde deserves rest. His ideas included."

As he fussed with a plant's drooping leaves, Laurel peered around the room again for anything else to pack. Nothing at first glance.

"So," she said and he peered over his shoulder at her. "Who was supposed to come for you? What you said earlier sounded like you had someone in mind."

Morus looked away. "He hasn't been by since before Clyde left. He was the only person allowed to use Clyde's dock." He freed a pot from the others. Purple and white flowers dotted the inside, practically overflowing as a blanket of colors. "He would have been the only one who knew I was alive in here."

Laurel inclined her head and sniffed the flowers. Lilacs. "Who was he?"

"He was..." Morus set the pot down on his bed, thinking. "Clyde's sexual partner, I guess. I wouldn't call them anything more romantic. He came by, they caught up, disappeared into Clyde's chambers, and then the next morning or so, he'd leave." Morus gently pet the lilac and turned for another plant. "His name was Wilhelm. I had a crush on him." He made a face. "Is that the correct term?"

"Were you infatuated?" Laurel asked.

"A little bit?" Morus thought a moment. "Moreso, I wanted to know him. Be like him. He was someone I found inspiring. I don't know."

"Really? You just saw him and went yes, this is who I want to be?"

Morus chuckled. "I'm not really sure. I just had this desire I hadn't felt before. Maybe crush *is* apt. I was too shy to tell Clyde about it."

Laurel considered Morus. "Why would you be shy?"

Morus freed a small urn of succulents from the others. This one had a red flower blooming like a hat. "How would you tell someone who is essentially your father that you find his partner sexually attractive?"

"Right..." Laurel cringed. "Sorry, that's a really obvious answer."

Morus chuckled. "Although I think I was more awed than aroused, in the end. I don't think Clyde would have known what to say had I told him."

In any case, he definitely sounded smitten with the man, albeit sadly. "I'm sorry he never came."

Morus set the succulent with the lilacs. "Do you get crushes?"

Laurel shook her head. "Not like that. Just friend crushes, I guess. I'm not really interested in relationships beyond that."

"I see." Morus eyed her, hopeful. "Do you think we can be friends?"

Laurel smiled at him. "I would hope so!"

"Me too." He turned and pulled a third plant free. A bushel of yellow chrysanthemums spilling over the side of the pot with a few shoots of white buds in the center. "Wilhelm always called me his seedling and liked seeing my flowers. Whenever he visited, he'd bring me a packet of seeds and some soil from Earth." He placed the mums with the other three. "I don't think the soil truly made a difference, but it was kind. Giving me something no one else but the elite has touched for such a long time."

Laurel was already reaching forward to do just that and Morus let her. The dirt felt like regular old soil. Nothing life changing. She withdrew her hand, feeling silly.

"What do you want to do with your life?" she asked. "Your siblings seemed to have found something, right?"

Morus' smile dropped. Eventually a weak chuckle worked its way free and he folded his arms tightly. "Like I said before, I don't know," he said. "You aren't wrong. All my siblings wanted to change the system in some fundamental way and could not do it by being a hermit's assistant. I don't think I have that selfsame spark." He gazed at his chosen plants and touched a petal.

"Sometimes, I wonder if Clyde made me wrong, but he said some people are quiet. Their sparks but embers that simply need time to grow into a fire." He suddenly eyed her, raising his eyebrows. "How about you? What do you want to do?"

"I'm not sure either," Laurel admitted with a shrug. "I just want to be free to live the way I want to. I don't know doing what, though. Maybe just being a space pirate."

"And thief," Morus teased and glanced at the bag. "I see you like my books."

"Ah!" Laurel's cheeks blazed. "I just—I was, uh..."

Morus laughed, covering his mouth with a hand. "I don't mind. It's nice you want to take them with you. I hadn't considered it. I've memorized them by now."

Laurel eased out a relieved breath. "I have more books on our ship. We can trade."

"I'd like that." He considered the three chosen plants on his bed and nodded. "These will do. They've been with me the longest." He sadly considered the others. "I am sorry friends, but we have to part ways here."

It was sweet the way he murmured to them one last time, touching each petal and leaf in goodbye. By the time he finished, he'd found his packets of seeds and a small jar of dirt straight from Earth. He sat them by his chosen plants and as he bent to look through his clothes, the lights flickered.

"Morus," the AI called over the intercom. Somehow when it spoke Morus' name, it sounded warmer. Maybe Clyde programmed it that way. "Please return anon. Your experiment is almost finished."

Laurel's heart wound itself back up, but it slowed when Morus took her hand. He wasn't worried and Laurel tried to have as much faith as he did.

Morus' professionalism slotted back into place, hiding the unsure young man he was, and they returned to the transfer room. There were prompts waiting for him and Juniper instantly made room as he came up behind them. Juniper set themself back to Cedar's side—he definitely hadn't moved—and Laurel stood beside them, taking Juniper's hand.

"All the readings look good," Morus said and glanced over the slumbering body. He nodded and clicked to accept the final prompt. "It's time to open your eyes, Aster."

As the diagnostics screen cleared, the lights in the room whined back on. A stillness descended across everyone as they waited. Slowly, very slowly, a hand twitched. Then the face shifted. Juniper held Laurel's hand tighter, eyes growing wide. Aster—because it *had* to be him—slowly opened his eyes, revealing the soft green he'd asked for because that was what they were before his cybernetics. They tracked the ceiling a moment and he blinked a few times before he looked at the three of them.

A small smile graced his lips as he tilted his head, eyes locking onto Cedar. "Oh, Cedar," he whispered, his voice crisp and clear now, "I can finally see you again."

Cedar was shaking, his jaw working to make words but nothing verbalized. Morus gently maneuvered around the bed, undoing all the wiring. It didn't take long. Aster's smile widened, showing off the vampire teeth he'd asked for, and he propped himself up on his elbows.

"I've missed you, my love," he whispered.

Cedar swooped down so fast, he was a blur. He wrapped his arms across Aster, lifting him off the bed to simply hold him. It really looked like Cedar wouldn't ever let go and Laurel's heart soared seeing them so.

Their lips met next with soft kisses, like Cedar feared breaking Aster. He broke away first and simply stared at him like nothing else in the system existed. Aster drew a shaking hand through Cedar's hair.

"Oh, how I've dreamed of your lips again," Aster said and pushed Cedar in again. More passionate kisses this time and definitely hungry. Especially when Cedar pressed Aster back into the bed.

It felt wrong watching, but Laurel was rooted in place, unsure what to do. Reminding them they had a plan and bombs to place felt wrong, especially when they had three years of kisses to make up for.

"Uh." Juniper gripped Laurel's shoulders and

turned her away, barely biting back a snicker. "Let's give them a moment." They steered Laurel out of the room and Morus followed them. The door swiped shut once they were in the hallway and by then, Laurel had to bite back her own snickering.

Morus glanced at the door, eyebrows folded in worry. "I feel I should tell them that transferring to a new body elicits a period of adjustment. He might not be ready for much more."

Juniper swatted at Morus. "Just let them kiss it out," they said. "I'm sure they won't keep us waiting long." They raised their voice with the last bit, but no reply was forthcoming.

"I'm sure. I'm happy to see it worked." Morus watched Juniper expectantly. "You're next, am I right?"

The words stole the smile off Juniper's lips. Laurel wrapped an arm around their back for support.

"I am," they said, a little weakly. They fidgeted and after another silent moment, drew their gaze back to the door.

Laurel couldn't hear anything beyond it, but maybe that was a good thing.

"Okay, how long are we giving them?" Juniper huffed. "I'm impatient."

34
JUNIPER

WAITING BECAME AWKWARD FAST AND Juniper was happy when Laurel pulled them and Morus away to do a little of what they came to do. Their bio-scanner had immediately tried to parse what was happening in the room and thankfully, failed. Soon it'd be silent.

Soon.

They set and primed three of Clary's bombs, made a pit-stop for Clyde's blood packs, and grabbed Morus' clothes from his room. At least, what he had by way of clothing. They needed to get rid of more bombs before the plants came. Once his clothes were packed away, they rounded back to the transfer terminal.

By the time they'd returned, the door was open and Cedar and Aster were coming through together. Aster wore Cedar's coat, being absolutely dwarfed by it, and held his own head in his arms. There was a dried bite mark on Cedar's lip, but he was smiling too proudly for it to have hurt much. He looked like a big dork, grinning wide with his arm tight around Aster, and Juniper couldn't help but smile too.

They'd finally done something they'd set out to do.

Morus studied the way Aster moved as he and Cedar came closer. "Aster, could you move all your limbs for me?" he asked.

Aster peeled away from Cedar and did just that. Every limb moved stiffly. Though Juniper was worried, Morus was nodding like he expected as much.

"Typical range of movement this soon after. How are you feeling?"

"Honestly?" Aster stopped and grimaced. "Weird." He laughed with a shrug. "I'm not quite used to everything. My limbs feel like phantoms, but at the same time, it's not. Thankfully, the interface reminds me of my cybernetics, so I'm not too lost." He gently touched Cedar, squeezing his hand, and smiled up at him. "But I feel whole."

"The phantom feeling is a common phenomenon among androids," Morus said. "After an hour, your mind should finish making its connections. I'm happy to say this is a resounding success."

"I'll say," Cedar said. He still hadn't taken his eyes off Aster.

Juniper cleared their throat before Cedar saw fit to steal Aster back into the transfer room. "What are you going to do with that?" They pointed at the head.

Aster glanced down at it like he'd forgotten he was holding it at all and his smile dropped. With hardly a glance, Cedar gathered the head out of the container for him. The preservation goop dripped all over the floor as Aster considered it. His once face. Once head.

And he cracked it in half, like he was pulling apart a pomegranate.

It happened so fast, even Juniper was slow to

realize the head was split open. Laurel had recoiled behind them while Morus simply stared, eyebrows high. All the blood had congealed, so nothing ran down the head or the exposed skull within. Still grisly. Especially when Aster delicately pressed his fingers through the skull.

Juniper finally had to look at their feet. Even the sounds made them squeamish. Laurel had fully turned away now, leaning her back against Juniper's.

"Ah. There it is." Aster's teasing voice made Juniper glance back up. The head was back in the container, now way ghastlier than it had any right to be, and Aster was holding a small chip to the light. He gasped and nearly dropped it.

"Oh! I am so sorry. That was rather ghastly of me, wasn't it?" He cringed. "I should have said something."

The weak laugh out of everyone but Cedar was his answer. Aster gave them a sheepish look and let Cedar take the head back into the room. While he did that, Aster showed Juniper the chip. Small, barely bigger than his thumb, it was a pale yellow with circuitry running along one side while the other had prongs that must have been what kept it in the brain.

"I wanted to retrieve my datacrypt."

Juniper lurched closer to look at it. They'd expected something grand, given how much the feds wanted it and the corresponding cyber back, but it was uninspiring. A simple chip.

"Seriously?"

"Lily will find out what's on it." Aster wiped it on his shirt and gave it to Laurel to inspect. "For now, keep it safe. We'll be set for a bit after we sell what's on it. There's always a buyer."

They *did* need funds. Laurel slipped the chip safely into the bag and Cedar returned without the head. He immediately looped his arm around Aster's waist, pulling him close again.

"Well? We good?" he asked.

Aster nodded. "I'm eager to start anew." He flexed his fingers slowly. "It's already feeling more like me."

Everyone softly fell silent and glanced at Juniper. Their bio-scanner made their thoughts buzz as it tried to parse everyone's expressions at once. Juniper forced a breath into their suddenly starved lungs. When had they grown so nervous? They shouldn't have been.

"My turn." They nodded at Morus. "Lead the way. I'm ready."

Morus watched them—everyone did, actually—like they were about to bolt. Their augments certainly wanted them to, given how suddenly scared they were. For years, nothing had changed. They got by, ignored everything the best they could by locking themself away. Now faced with the decision to change every-thing they'd ever known? They wanted their simple satellite back. The empty days solely focused on existing until tomorrow.

Except *this* was what they'd wanted for years. *This* was their tomorrow. Juniper forced their legs to follow Morus into the other room. Their life from here on out would be under *their* control. Not to the whims of their cybernetics.

As Juniper stepped inside, their legs jerked still, refusing to go farther. Sleek white everything, like the room Juniper had been in during their childhood when all this mess started. Even the smell was the same. Some disinfectant that made Juniper's nose wrinkle. The bed was sparse with wires on every side. God, it really was just like the cybernetic priming room. They could imagine the nurses flitting around the bed, preparing them.

Their mind went numb, their body faraway and steeped in some other place. Everything grew distant as the only thing reigning in their thoughts was panic. Dread replaced the warmth they'd found watching Aster move and now *they* couldn't move. Their cortex computer latched onto the burgeoning panic and directed them how to escape. How long it would take to get back to the *Honeycomb* and fly away.

Until a friend-shaped presence took their hand. Their unmoored mind found its way back to their body and they breathed in. Laurel stood beside them, worried, and had taken their hand. Morus returned and gently took Juniper's other hand. With careful steps, he led them through the doorway.

"It's okay to be scared," he said.

"I'm not scared," Juniper snapped—a reflex.

"It's okay not to be scared," Morus amended. Juniper was a few paces inside now, right in front of the bed. Laurel ever-present beside them. Grounding. Even if she made the room smaller.

Juniper's heart sped as another scenario of escape flashed through their thoughts. They dismissed it.

"It's only naturally because your cybernetics will be as complex to change as they were to put in," Morus explained.

Juniper's fight or flight was so firmly on flight, they thought their legs would do it of their own volition. Especially with the way Morus spoke. The soft tenor of his voice like he was talking someone down. Their bio-scanner picked out the minute changes in his face and their cortex computer spun it as a trap.

No, it couldn't be. They'd come so far.

"Why do you say it like that?" Juniper asked.

Morus let them go. "The longer those cybernetics are inside a person, the more the body relies on it and it forgets how to live on its own."

Like when Juniper couldn't wake up after being forced to stop. Their body stiffened, squeezing all the air out of their lungs, and Laurel held their hand tighter. It wasn't like it was unknown, but it felt too real out in the open.

"It's why the Prodigy Program begins younger and younger," Morus continued. "A child's body adapts to the cybernetics and nanomachines within like both were part of them all along. Technological marvel it is, it's also terrifying because of the clear violation of consent." He spoke slowly, like he was giving a lecture. No warmth, completely detached. "Because of that, I cannot ever truly delete its functions, which is what I think you want." He held up a hand as Juniper opened their mouth to argue. "But we can *change* it so you're in control. Turn off or on the augments at your whim."

The sudden pause was deafening, threatening to swallow Juniper up.

"But changing how it operates can very well leave you dead."

Distantly, Juniper expected the warning. Hearing it aloud as a fact, however, still chilled them to their very core. Laurel gasped and failed to cover it in time. Maybe she was the only one who hadn't put it together. Cedar and Aster were silent in the doorway. No gasps. No panicked sounds from them.

"What?" Laurel faced Juniper. "Junie..."

Juniper couldn't look at Laurel. "What's the chance of failure?"

Morus studied Juniper before answering. "That largely depends on you. If what makes you, well, *you* imprinted on the cybernetics as you grew, I cannot guarantee you will wake after the necessary changes."

Laurel dropped her hands. "Is it like how Aster was saved because he imprinted on the datacrypt?"

"Yes, only we're hoping Juniper did not," Morus said. "You are still maturing as far as humans go, so there's a chance you are still between your two halves."

Juniper swallowed. "Tell me the chance of failure."

Morus eased out a deliberate sigh. "I don't know the actual chance. It could be one percent. It could be ninety-nine percent. All I know is there is a *chance* you could die." He turned his gaze to the room. "The only comfort I can give you is you'll be in good hands. Clyde has impressive records and I can follow exactly what he did when he performed the same procedure."

Wildly different chances and Juniper could hardly breathe as they repeated the numbers in their head. It wasn't supposed to be like this. There was never supposed to be the sliver of doubt whether Juniper lived or died. They were just supposed to live.

Except now doubt became not a sliver, but a hemorrhaging wound. It was all they could do to shut up their cortex computer as it outlined the reasons why Morus was intentionally trapping them.

Morus slowly continued. "There were four who attempted this before. Three were older and had their cybernetics installed in adulthood. Only one of them lived after turning them off. She was caught and torn apart by the feds to learn *how*. They never did." He twisted his hands together. "For the fourth, I don't know how long he'd had cybernetics, but Clyde changed them to be what I am going to do with you. He lived, if that makes it better."

Juniper swallowed. "How does the choice work?"

Morus tapped his head. "Internally, it'll feel like a switch. I can't quite explain it any simpler than that. They'll do what they should have been doing: aiding and augmenting. Just as easily, you can switch them off." He smiled gently. "This has the least chance of failure, but it's still largely unknown because every subject is different."

"Junie," Laurel stressed, her voice quivering, and they finally looked at her. Her eyes were full of glistening tears. "Junie, there has to be a safer way. You aren't supposed to die doing this."

"I'm not going to get another chance like this," Juniper whispered. "We're destroying it all."

Laurel was shaking her head and Juniper looked away again. If Juniper didn't do it now, then they'd be ruined the next time someone brought out a kill switch. While Francesca hadn't used hers, anyone else would. Cedar couldn't always save them. They had to protect themself, so they could also protect Laurel no matter the chance of failure.

They pulled her into a tight hug. "Believe in me," they whispered and leaned back to commit her to memory just in case. Her face scrunched up as she attempted not to cry. A marshmallow through and through.

Juniper nodded at Morus. "I'll do it."

Silent tears ran down Laurel's cheeks, slipping out from beneath her glasses.

Juniper pulled her in again, squeezing her tighter. "I'll be fine," they whispered, their own voice breaking. "One of us has to say it, right?"

Laurel nodded into their shoulder, fingers digging into their back in an attempt to bring them closer. They were as close as two people could get, but Juniper wanted the same. They kissed the side of her head.

"I promise: I'll live."

"Not allowed to break promises," Laurel said into their shoulder and pulled back. She looped their pinkies together. "You'll live."

"Pinky promise." Juniper shook their pinkies together and smiled at her.

Morus cleared his throat; while Juniper and Laurel had babbled, he'd started the terminal. His hands worked fast across the digital keyboard.

"I do suggest it only be me and Juniper when the process begins." He paused and glanced at Aster, the white circles in his eyes turning. "And Aster, perhaps seen as Juniper is fond of you. Laurel and Cedar will have to wait outside."

Juniper frowned. "Why?" Well, there was the obvious. If Juniper *did* die, Morus probably didn't want Laurel to see that.

"Brainwaves," Morus settled on, albeit awkwardly, but it was so subtle Juniper was sure they were the only one to notice the shift in tone. "Human brainwaves— yes, Cedar is included in that—can disrupt the process."

Cedar tilted his head. "How'd Clyde do it then?"

"He always had androids," Morus explained.

Juniper squeezed Laurel once more. "You go plant some bombs," they said and parted to push some of her hair behind her ear. "I'll catch up for the mayhem soon."

"You don't want to miss it." Laurel threw her arms around Juniper one last time before she left without looking back.

It was easier that way. Especially with the way Juniper's heart raced thinking it might be the last time they'd see each other. They breathed in deep, trying to push those thoughts away, and their bio-scanner flashed a warning of an incoming pair of arms. Cedar, this time. He held them close and Juniper breathed him in.

"See you soon," he said when he parted.

"Yeah. Watch over her, okay?" Juniper asked.

"Don't say it like that."

He slipped out and the door swiped shut after him, leaving only three of them in the room. A little easier to breathe.

Morus had returned to the terminal, shoulders tense, and Aster came up beside Juniper. He hesitated, watching them like he waited for permission, and Juniper enveloped him in a hug. Might as well get one in, just in case. It wasn't like their cybernetics could surprise them with information they didn't know about Aster; they helped make his body, after all. Already friend-shaped.

Aster held them tightly, but they exchanged no words when they parted. Didn't need to.

"Were you lying?" Juniper asked Morus. "The brainwaves thing?"

Morus paused. "Is that an unwanted trait?"

"No, it's fine." Juniper tried to smile, but felt tears creeping into their eyes. "Thank you."

Juniper faced the bed and all the wires and cables laid across it. They felt like a child again. How alone they were in the world when they'd awoken. A buzz between their ears and an ache following each and every muscle as they acclimated to their cybernetics.

Except this time, they wouldn't be alone when it was all said and done. They breathed in again, held onto the thought, and let Aster help them out of their coat and into the bed.

Morus' touch was softer than the scientists had

ever been, even Aster's was when he volunteered to help. Electrodes stuck to Juniper's skin in various places to monitor their vitals. The diagnostic screen above lit up with the racing panic Juniper was trying to hide. Aster combed Juniper's hair back, letting Morus fit a few electrodes to their temples. A wavelength soon appeared on the screen with their vitals. Brainwaves. At least it was active. The last to connect was the cord into their head-jack. There was a tiny jolt as usual, but nothing to immediately connect to.

All the while, their augments were more alert than ever. Their cortex computer flashed them scenarios about everything that could go wrong if they were intent to see this through. Their bio-scanner searched for any deceit in either Aster or Morus and even tried to guilt them about how Laurel must have really felt. Juniper squeezed their eyes shut, willing it to just shut up for once.

When they opened their eyes again, the room had softened. An aura glowed around everything. Pretty, all things considered, but it struck Juniper as odd. Not the usual blinding auras that came before cybernetics induced migraine. This was... gentle.

They were distracted from it when Aster ran his fingers through their hair again. A sensation they could honestly get used to. Thinking so made their heart lurch, bare for all to see on the screen above.

"You good?" he asked, smiling warmly.

"I am." It was a bold-faced lie, but Aster didn't comment on it. He simply took their hand between his and held it tight.

"I'm almost ready," Morus said. The screen was pouring out code, scenarios, and so much more Juniper couldn't catch. Something beyond what any human could read. "There is one thing I can tell you to help." As he spoke, the room became increasingly soft and sleepy. "The feds ruined their cybernetic program. What was once to help and serve humanity was changed to make humanity slaves to their will. As such, cybernetics are implemented so they have control. What you want is your soul—your humanity—to have control back. Do you understand?"

Juniper swallowed. "I think so."

Why was the room fuzzing around the edges? Juniper thought it was some sleeping injection through their jack, but their scanners didn't detect anything coming in yet.

"Follow what makes you the most human," Morus said.

"What do you mean?"

"It's different for everyone." Morus tore his gaze away and though Juniper couldn't see it through the sudden haze at the edge of their vision, they heard him typing a chain of prompts into the terminal.

"Deep down, is there an event, a person, a thing that made you feel the most you? Latch onto it and follow it no matter what."

"How will I even know?"

"Humans always do." There was the ghost of a smile on Morus' lips as he glanced back, the rest of him too washed out to read. "It's simply if you can keep up with it in spite of your cybernetics. Your body has to remind itself to live on its own. What do you live for, Juniper?"

"Laurel." Her name slipped out of Juniper's lips without hesitation. They had no life, no future without her.

Admitting it aloud slotted something into place, a realization, and they breathed out. If she'd never been there, they never would have left. They would have been caught eventually. None of them would have been here alive like they were without her. A little lynchpin holding them together. Aster smiled at them, like even he'd known.

"Then focus on her," Morus said. "The terminal will focus on your neural pathways and remake connections that is the most *you*. While you're under, I will also take care of the frequency for the kill switch so no one can use it ever again."

Juniper nodded. "I understand." Going under. It must have been why everything was fuzzy. They held Aster's hand as tight as they could, focusing on how real it was. "I'm ready."

A calming sensation rushed through Juniper, letting the world melt away. Everything silenced but the sound of their own heart. Juniper counted the beats, one after the other, until even it quieted. The world and everything in it was silent now.

Until someone whispered through it. A voice made of honey they'd always known. One who shouldn't have been there.

"Hello, Juniper." The weight of the Answer's hand pressed into Juniper's shoulder. "You will not get away this time."

35
LAUREL

POSTURE HAD TO COUNT FOR SOMETHING. Laurel didn't start sobbing until after the door slid shut. She resisted running back in to beg for another way. Juniper's life had value, too much value to throw away for a risk.

Laurel swallowed her frustration. It was Juniper's choice. Not hers. She had to respect it. Deep down, she knew that.

But it still felt like her heart was torn in two, now faced with the possibility of living without Juniper. The first person who'd accepted her for who she was.

The facility's lights dimmed and diverted power like before, except the whole place seemed even darker this time. Laurel wiped her cheeks, breathing in deep to stop crying, and turned. She ran right into Cedar behind her.

"Hey." Cedar gripped her shoulders to help steady her. "Hey—"

"Don't ask me if I'm okay," Laurel said and took off her glasses to clean them. Distract herself.

"I won't," Cedar said and let go. "Laurel—"

"No. No platitudes or whatever you're going to say," Laurel said, turning away. She slotted her glasses back on her nose, but everything was still blurry. "I'm trying not to cry." She wiped her nose with the back of her sleeve, resolving to apologize to Clary later for leaving snot on it, and Cedar stepped beside her.

"What do *you* even do?" she asked suddenly, if only to get out of her head. "When people die on you?"

Cedar didn't answer right away. They stood together in silence, but while Laurel watched him, hoping staring alone pried an answer out of him, even as she started to regret asking, Cedar looked out at the screens showing the snow-ridden stars outside, eyes distant in search of what to say.

When she was tired of waiting and dug out a bomb to at least do something useful, Cedar finally spoke. "You don't get used to it."

Laurel fidgeted with the bomb. Clary had drawn a cat on it. "Will you miss us? Will you even notice?"

Cedar watched her sadly. "Of course I will."

Laurel looked up at him, more tears threatening to spill over. "If-If—*when* Juniper comes out, when we're both old and gray, what will you do with us then?"

Cedar tilted his head. "What is this about?"

"I don't know what I want to do with my life," Laurel said. "Beyond this? Juniper doesn't either. And—and—everything is just a lot and I don't know why I'm asking—and—and—"

Cedar pulled her into a sudden tight hug, catching her off guard, and she cried again, burying her face into his chest. She didn't mean to blurt it all out. Especially not when it maybe didn't matter. What mattered was Juniper. Yet her thoughts immediately tangled with everything else in their future. They'd age. Cedar and Aster wouldn't. Hell, she didn't even know if Juniper would age like she did or if she'd be the only one.

"Junie's all I got left," Laurel cried. "If they die, it's just *me* and I just—"

"Shh. It's okay." Cedar gently stroked her head. "We're here. All of us. You don't even ever have to leave if you don't want to."

He began motormouthing words that became noise. It became strangely soothing and she fully leaned into Cedar, hoping to hear and feel it with her entire being. Eventually, when he rattled off something about concerts, she started laughing and wiggled to escape. He trailed off and looked down at her sheepishly.

"Sorry," Laurel said, trying to smile despite the weakness in her voice. "Everything was a lot."

"Humans *do* cry a lot," Cedar teased and Laurel slugged him in the arm. He grinned at her in return and beckoned her to follow as he headed down the hall. "Planting bombs will cheer us up."

It gave Laurel something to concentrate on, at least. Planting bombs was easy, even if she had to bury the regret of all what they'd be destroying. By the third bomb, the one they placed along the super computer near Morus' room, Cedar began talking again.

"There was one human who stuck with me and Aster a long time," he said. "Her name was Maggie."

Laurel brightened. "Aster told me about her. She could squash skulls with her thighs."

"That was a talent of hers!" Cedar snickered. "What she loved most of all, though, was cooking. She dreamed of owning her own restaurant at the end of the Solar System and when she started getting old, Aster and I put money aside for her so she could have that. It was a little place orbiting Jupiter—not quite the end of the Solar System, but it felt that way." A distant smile slotted itself on his lips. "She's gone now, but every year after she retired, we'd visit her and regale her with all our adventures. She was always happy to see us and kept a bottle of blood around just for us. When she died, it hit us hard. It *always* does." He breathed in and scratched the back of his neck. "You get attached no matter what."

It already felt that way to Laurel. A whole whirlwind of an adventure starting with Cedar threatening to steal their cruiser to now, with Laurel genuinely attached to the vampire. He must have felt the same toward her and Juniper. It really was a family she'd found on her own.

"I'm sorry I put you on the spot."

"We had to have this conversation someday," Cedar said. "I don't know if I'd ever turn either of you, so I know you won't be forever like me."

Cedar took a bomb from her bag and they peeked into a dark room flanking Morus'. Nothing was in here but old circuitry not even in use. He set it down and waved away the dust rising at their intrusion.

"Why'd you offer vampirism so quickly back when we met, then?" Laurel asked.

"It was an option and I was desperate to get you both on my side," Cedar said. "And I knew what Aster had gone through."

Laurel frowned and followed Cedar out. "What happened with Aster?"

"It wasn't like Juniper, but he'd say his cybernetics itched," Cedar said as they found another spot for a small bomb. Laurel gave Clary its number and the light on it glowed as it primed. "And well, he'd scratch at it until it bled. It was involuntary, but in some way, it showed him he still had control. As you can see, that thinking is dangerous."

Laurel slowed and nodded.

"So, when he asked me yet again after so many years together, I'd run out of reasons to tell him no." Cedar shrugged. "'Sides, I liked having him around."

Laurel smiled up at him. "You like us."

Cedar gave her a look and shook his head. "You don't want vampirism. Not right now." She expected him to elaborate, but he just beckoned her to follow. "Come on. More bombs."

Laurel was happy to do so. She felt better knowing she and Juniper had a home with the *Gladiolus* for as long as they needed. Meaning in life and reasons to go on could come later. She had a space pirate life ahead of her (whatever that entailed) and it included Juniper by her side.

She gave Cedar a handful of bombs to place on his own to make room in her bag and returned to Morus' room for the plants. She breathed it all in once more and let the scent of plants calm her mind further. She headed to his chosen plants and jar of dirt.

"You'll be on the ship soon." She gently slotted everything inside her bag with Morus' clothes wrapped around each pot for cushioning. "Hope you don't mind the bumpy ride, though."

Once she had everything nestled inside, she checked a few more drawers in to make sure Morus got everything. He did. A small life already packed up. She stripped the quilt atop the bed and folded it to take too. She and Juniper had their own blankets when they'd arrived on the ship, after all, the least she could do for Morus was make sure he had one of his own.

She zipped her bag and lugged it over her shoulder. Heavy, but she could deal. She fished one of her last bombs out and placed it at the back wall of his room.

Before she had any second thoughts, she left. Cedar had returned too, finished with his own armful. There were little lights in the darkness from all the bombs priming and she distantly counted them. That was all the smaller ones, then.

"Only Aster's bomb left," she said.

Cedar stilled so suddenly, Laurel flinched. Goosebumps flushed her arms as she held her breath to listen. Just a soft wash of static. She and Cedar turned to the supercomputer terminal nearby. The screens around it once showing the planet had fuzzed. Laurel's heart skipped. It stabilized in seconds, but dread pooled in Laurel's stomach.

"What was that?" Laurel asked.

Cedar pressed his hand to his comms. "Clary? What's up there?"

"SHIT!" Clary yelled and Laurel jumped. There was a clatter on the other end and Lily hissed. "Shit—fuck!"

"Clary!" Cedar shouted. "What's wrong?"

"A fucking fed ship came out of nowhere! It's a juggernaut!" Clary was typing something on the other end. "It's the biggest ship I've seen in my life. Lily, how the fuck did that come out of nowhere?"

"I suspect advanced stealth," came Lily's voice. "It's focused on the moon, not us. I'll keep our channels clear."

"Shit," Clary breathed. "You guys gotta scram. Probes are going out. I'm safe, but I don't know how long you guys will be."

Laurel swore. The feds must have found Clyde's very dead body and decided to force the place open, regardless of what was destroyed in the process. Cedar had already pivoted to return to everyone, but as Laurel stepped after him, Clyde's dock down the hall activated. She stumbled to a stop and yanked Cedar's shirt to stop him. He slowed, eyes wide.

It was coming up. Someone had docked without anyone noticing. Someone who'd known where Clyde's dock was.

The lift finished its ascent and the door swiped aside, revealing the Answer. His blaster was already drawn and primed, the barrel aglow with gold. He tilted his head mockingly.

"So, we meet again, Cedar Woods."

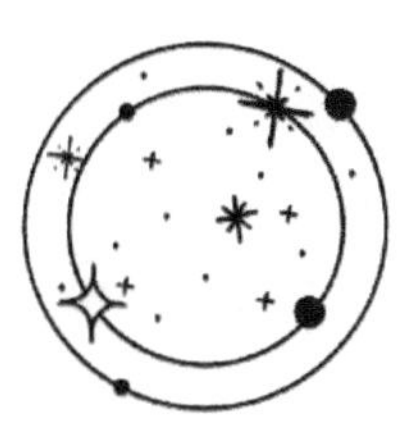

SESSION 8

VAMPIRES
DON'T DIE

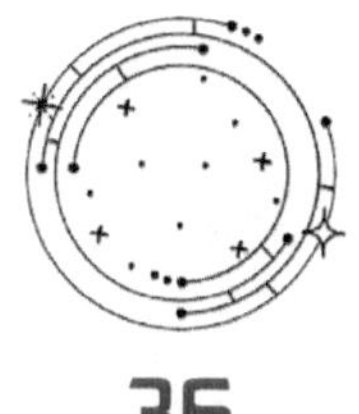

36
JUNIPER

EVERYTHING MELTED WITH LIGHT SO bright, Juniper's eyes stung. When they could see again, Aster and Morus were gone—so was the entire room—and what replaced them was an empty world, hollow in all corners. The Answer's voice echoed around them, but his presence was all but gone if not for the deep ache his fingers left on their shoulder. Alone. All alone.

Not new. They'd been alone before.

Juniper steadied their breathing, willing their chest to expand with each breath to prove the air wasn't constricting them. Their labored breathing resounded like a steady pulse.

"Laurel?" they spoke into the empty corridors on all sides. Their echo played back, morphing into the Answer's honeyed voice. They scowled. Of course, it wouldn't be that easy, especially if he was here. Or something like him; if it *was* the Answer, he'd already have been there in the flesh. Then what was it?

Juniper gasped with the realization.

Virus.

Questions of how drowned their thoughts. Had Clyde known him? Had he followed them through the gates? Had Morus let him in?

Juniper shook the paranoia from their thoughts as soon as it took hold. They squeezed their eyes shut to concentrate. There wasn't anything they could do about him now; they had to deal with themself first. It wasn't like Juniper knew how to wake themself up and worried trying it at all. They might really die if it came to that.

They had to trust that everyone else could deal with the Answer. They exhaled and opened their eyes.

Still fucking empty. They clenched their fingers. What if it was already too late? What if their soul or whatever Morus was talking about had already become reliant on their cybernetics?

No. Juniper—their very self—had to still be here. Somewhere.

As if responding to their defiance, the emptiness oscillated like a wave of water. It rippled outward, pushing the haze as if it was a thick fog, and a room took shape, bit by bit.

First was an office window letting in golden sunlight. It was so bright, Juniper had to look away for a moment. When they were able to see again, a desk had appeared. Reports and folders were neatly stacked across it, each with their old name on it. Juniper's stomach sank. This was the office of the researcher who headed the Prodigy Program on the Lunar Colony.

He sat at the desk now, his face hazy because Juniper couldn't exactly remember him except for his self-serving smile. That came through clearly, like it always did, with his brilliant white teeth only the feds could manufacture.

Juniper turned as the rest of the room made itself. Harsh white walls shot upward, decorating themselves with his research breakthroughs and doctorates hung in frames. The shelf of self-serving knickknacks to paint him as a good man (that he wasn't) folded out next. The last to materialize was the doorway behind Juniper and two figures stood there with a third between them.

There Juniper was. A shy kid of barely eight-years-old with their mother and father behind them. Still wearing their school uniform with the tie they'd made sure matched the ones their parents had so they could feel like the three of them were a team. A family. Juniper blinked back unwanted tears. Tears they'd cried so many years ago for the parents who'd given up their child to the Federation in the name of research.

Their faces wouldn't focus, but it was Juniper's fault. They stopped trying to remember their features long ago. Their mother put her hands on their child self's shoulders and squeezed them tight. Little Juniper continued looking at their polished shoes.

"Here we are," their mother said, her voice still so real to Juniper despite the years between then and now. All the nights she hummed Juniper to sleep rang clear and true despite everything Juniper had done to forget.

"They prefer they pronouns, by the way," she added in a hurry. "I know the form was already filled out, but I hope—"

"Forms can be amended," the researcher said, waving a dismissive hand. "I'm so glad you've come."

"We're excited you chose them for the program," Juniper's father said. His voice was always quiet and clear. He'd never once raised it in anger.

Little Juniper nodded shyly, refusing to look up.

It wasn't shyness. No. It was fear. They'd been scared. Their parents had told them this was the chance of a lifetime, but Juniper had read between the lines even then. Their parents had no choice but to volunteer Juniper once the Prodigy Program recruiters met with them. All their explanations of what the program meant was always full of vigor and excitement, but Juniper never quite felt comfortable. Their parents probably knew what would happen to their child and all the fake excitement in the world couldn't hide it.

And yet, knowing this, their parents still willingly let them go.

The researcher's predatory smile at Juniper then had been anything but warm because he saw Juniper not as a person, but as a test subject. Juniper wanted to punch it, the whole scene, but as they moved to do so, the researcher's gaze shot up, meeting theirs with such clarity, Juniper stuttered to a stop.

His neck twisted unnaturally to one side. Juniper jerked backward and the man's entire face melted and reformed into the Answer's faceplate. Juniper threw themself farther back, falling through the memories behind them, and heard another voice.

"Hey, Junie?" Laurel's voice plucked through the memory like a song, making it tremble. "Want to listen to this album I found? It's old shit! Your thing!"

Juniper spun around and found Laurel peeking at them through a door from their satellite. A stolen palm tablet in her hands with all her songs already downloaded onto it. She'd found new ones every day on the underground net and subjected Juniper to each and every one. She'd still had her natural brown hair then, but they'd lopped off the messy ponytail she'd come with.

All the dread and fear washed away and Juniper smiled. "I'd like that," they said.

Laurel grinned mischievously and darted into the blooming haze behind her, leaving the echo of the Smashing Coffins in her wake. Juniper raced after her.

As they slipped through the satellite door, the music stopped. Their foot caught on the doorway and they stumbled into a room that was *not* their satellite.

The same impersonable golden sunlight streamed in from all windows and shined on a younger Juniper sitting alone on a sterile white bed, crying. Their hair had been shorn off for the cybernetics surgery. The stitches piecing their skin back together after the operation were in full view across their scalp. Bandages covered the ones on their arms because Juniper had picked at the stitches until they bled.

They raised their hands to wipe the tears, straining the IV port. Juniper's skin prickled with phantom pains along scars long since faded with time.

A nurse ghosted through the room, trying to placate Juniper. Her face was obscured with a surgical mask and her hands were covered in gloves. There was a huge risk of infection shortly after the procedure and the hospital never took chances. The children were, after all, an investment first and foremost.

Juniper felt their wrist, feeling the scar only they could still trace. The burn the stitches once made seared into their memories.

The nurse gently touched Juniper's head, checking the stitching. She'd always been gentle, if distant. She gave a little nod of her head, muffled words lost to the memory floating around them, and left the room, likely searching for something to help the itching.

Tears found their way down Juniper's cheeks as they stared at themselves so alone on the bed. The sobs had quieted. They'd wanted to be a good kid for the nurse since she was nice, but it was only achieved because Juniper had buried their face into the blankets.

"Mom and Dad aren't coming back," Juniper whispered. Their younger self didn't look up; it was a memory replaying itself, trying to make a connection. "You know that, right? I did." Juniper's body was trembling. "The nurses promised us, saying again and again they'll come back, but it was a lie. You weren't theirs. You didn't even belong to yourself."

Little Juniper snapped their gaze up, sobs cut off, and stared through Juniper with haunting yellow eyes glimmering as their cybernetics revved up. Juniper turned and jerked away.

The Answer stood in the doorway, a stiff shadow that shouldn't have been there at all.

He didn't move.

Which meant he wasn't really there. Not physically or mentally. A virus like Juniper thought, but it wormed panic into Juniper's chest. If he still wasn't here, then what was he doing out there?

"Junie?" Laurel's voice echoed past his form and chasing after it was more music. All music she'd added to Juniper's life. "You back? Where'd you even go?"

Juniper opened their mouth, but didn't get a word out before their own voice answered from somewhere down the hall.

"I went to see Slim! I brought back chocolate!"

"Welcome home!" Laurel's voice was so bright and sunny every time she'd said those words.

Guilt clenched Juniper's heart; it had always been

that way whenever Juniper left Laurel all alone in the satellite. They never realized how unfair it really was every time they'd done that to her.

"We can have that for dessert! I made pizza," Laurel continued. "Well... I think that's what it is. It smells good!"

The Answer disappeared from the doorway and Juniper looked back at themself. Their face had been replaced with the Answer's faceplate, twitching like cybernetics gone awry, and Juniper headed through the doorway to chase after Laurel's hum.

This time as they went through, darkness encroached the haze and Juniper stopped to let their eyes readjust. The music had softened to the general hum and chatter of a station beyond thin walls.

The room was a cramped pad lit with an orange light above the bed. Always small, everything within reach. Androids typically never received much else when they were dock workers like Slim. Juniper's eyes darted past all the projects Slim left in organized piles and then to his bed beneath the loft. Juniper was curled up with him, covered in his many blankets, with their head tucked under his chin.

Sadness squeezed Juniper and held them tight. They'd ruined Slim's life. Their little meetings were never supposed to mean anything, but it was such a small measure of comfort being out of their own head for once and engulfed in someone else so completely.

One day, Juniper had been so touch starved, craving for someone they *knew*, they'd bluntly asked Slim if they could sleep together. He'd been confused and Juniper had quickly backpedaled. The second time, maybe a month later when the embarrassment had time to soften, Juniper had asked with a little more tact. Slim had said yes.

Even though he should have said no.

And because he didn't, because Juniper kept coming back, all his softness and understanding was gone. Fizzled like an ember because the feds had found out. If Juniper had been more careful, kept their distance like they'd initially meant to, Slim would have been left alone.

Tears slipped down their cheeks again as they watched themself kiss Slim's jaw to wake him. The way he roused, though, he probably wasn't actually ever asleep around Juniper.

"Good morning," Slim said so softly. His voice still sent a delightful shiver down Juniper's spine. "Do you feel better?"

Every time, Juniper *had*, but never had the words to truly describe what Slim had meant to them. Now they'd never be able to tell him. The Slim they knew was gone, maybe a spark of memory running wild and free across the net, but with no way for Juniper to find him unless he reached out first. Hell, they'd already said their goodbyes.

It shouldn't have hurt so much. Yet, their heart ached in so many ways they hadn't believed possible.

They ripped their gaze away. Slim had made them feel human, yes, but he was gone now. They needed to focus on Laurel. She was still there. A constant in their life reaching deeper than anyone else ever had. The catalyst which had changed the trajectory of Juniper's sorry life.

They turned and found a ladder leading up into their satellite. It was just like the chamber the shuttle from the moon docked into. Music trickled downward, inviting them to follow.

They ran for it, hearing Laurel's distant voice humming with the punk tune. Arms suddenly clutched Juniper from behind, holding them tight. Juniper spun around, ready for a fight, but froze upon realizing the arms were *hugging* them. Slim was there dressed in his station threads. He held them close, like he always had every single time. It must have been a piece of memory lingering from the last time they'd linked. The cord was even there, entwining them together.

Slim kissed their cheek, his lips warm. "I'll let go," he said and gently pulled the jack free from Juniper's neck. "I just wanted one last hug. One I couldn't give."

And just like that, his phantom was gone. A whisper of memory growing dormant. Juniper breathed out. "I love you, Slim," they said. "I'll miss you."

A mocking laugh answered their sincerity and the room warped along with it. Juniper flipped it off, hoping the Answer saw it somehow, and ran after Laurel's voice.

They climbed the ladder as fast as they could and into a bright light. As they stood, a door swiped open behind them.

Laurel stood there haloed in light, a duffel bag slung over her shoulder, her dark brown hair tied back in its messy ponytail, and her eyes wide with worry. She paused, tilting her head, like she was trying to match the real Juniper up to the photos they'd given her. Some of them had admittedly made Juniper look a lot hotter than they probably were, but it was meant to be that way on those boards. Laurel had looked exactly like she had in hers. It had been immediately endearing.

"It's me," Laurel said, sticking out her hand. "Laurel."

Juniper smiled, relief washing over them, and

they took Laurel's hand. "And it's me: Juniper."

The touch of Laurel's skin was electric, connecting into Juniper, digging down into the core of themselves.

Time bled by quickly. Pieces of Laurel's hair chopped away into the mangled bob she had now and loved. There was another lurch where the brown ran from her hair as bleach stole it away, leaving red dye to bleed into the strands. Then, she and Juniper were lying in Juniper's bed in their loft, looking out of the skylight above them.

They were watching the ships take off from the moon, sometimes coming precariously close. Juniper never minded. They always left a glimmering trail of colors in their wake.

It was the night before they'd heisted the cruiser. Before Juniper left the only world they knew to crash down on the surface. They'd been scared, pulse racing so fast, their bio-monitor wouldn't shut up about it. At least, until Laurel gently had held their hand.

In that single moment, the world was right. Juniper was simply there, existing with their friend.

"Hey, Junie?" Laurel spoke into the dark.

"Hey, Laurie?" Juniper remembered responding, leaning their head against Laurel's.

"Do you regret meeting me?"

Juniper faced Laurel, as incredulous now as they had been then. "Why would you think that?" Juniper found themself saying, following the thread of memory instead of simply saying no.

Laurel wouldn't look at them. She had her eyes trained on the looming vastness of space. "I'm making you leave. I-I don't want to force you to do anything you don't want to."

"I want to leave." Juniper propped themself up on

their elbow to look down at Laurel to catch her gaze. "I want to be bold. I want to run through all the stars with you." They smiled as Laurel did, relief softening her face. "I wouldn't have let you into my satellite if I didn't want to change."

It had been a big deal. Alone for years, only going down for a quick romp with someone—mostly Slim—and then locking themself back in the cage they'd made. Even Slim had never been inside their satellite. Then, they'd accidentally met Laurel.

Words could never describe how much Laurel had made the world real. They'd loved leaving messages for her, waking up to messages from her, talking late into the night until Laurel fell asleep and how comforting it'd been simply staying with her until the link timed out due to inactivity. And then Juniper invited her to run away to their satellite. Giving her the escape she had unknowingly given Juniper.

And then she was here. Chasing away the damning loneliness. It was never perfect, but life seldom was.

Laurel smiled wider and happiness bloomed in Juniper's chest. As they reached in to bump their foreheads together, fingers gripped Juniper's scalp from behind.

They were wrenched backwards, away from Laurel, and the satellite's loft faded into darkness with nothing tangible to be seen. The Answer pulled himself out of the black hole, hand gripped so tightly in Juniper's hair.

But Laurel was still there. She stared, frozen in time, horrified, and Juniper ripped themself away as hard as they could and wrapped their arms and legs around Laurel. They folded into the dark with her and they were falling.

"This is my body!" Juniper yelled, holding Laurel tighter as the darkness tried to rip their arms away. "I am in control of what's inside of it! No one else!" Their heartbeat sounded stronger, surer in their ears and rang in the silence. With it came music beats they knew so well. The perfect victory music: *Ode to Joy*.

It drowned out the mechanical whir of their cybernetics. All the doubt and apprehension still lingering. The touch of the Answer's hand in their hair softened. He would not get in. They would never succumb to him or their cybernetics.

"I am Juniper Austre and this is *my* life!" they screamed, squeezing their eyes shut. "So get out of my fucking head!"

All at once, Juniper fell on their back, like they were spat out of the dark, and they sucked in a deep breath. Their heart raced, but their bio-monitor didn't warn them with how fast. They opened their eyes wide. A ceiling. Bio-scanner silent, not pinging the hand holding theirs. Not scanning the room for dangers. The world felt starkly different. Real. Within reach. Not something to be quantified behind a veil of cybernetics.

Juniper blinked hard, reaffirming that they were really here, as themself, and relief washed through them just as tears slipped free. They'd done it. Fuck that chance of dying. They were free.

The room violently shook, ripping away the relief. A yelp escaped their lips and Aster threw himself over Juniper to shield them. Nothing came free from up above, but there was a crack along the edges of the ceiling. The lights warbled and a siren pierced across the facility.

Aster quickly pulled himself off Juniper and noticed they were awake. He smiled gently. "Hey you," he said. "Doing okay there?"

Juniper nodded and let him unhook everything. His hands were like lightning as they moved. Definitely used to his body now.

"I'm fine," they said, voice weak. Their head hurt, like nails really had raked across their scalp.

The pain—the reason for it—made them gasp. They shot upright, the motion making Aster and Morus jump. "The Answer's here! He's in your systems!"

Morus shot them an alarmed look. "Who?"

"A bounty hunter. He spoke to me—he must have hacked into your AI." Juniper yanked the rest of the cords free—it was all going up in the end, no need to be delicate—and Aster helped steady them as they tried to stand. Their legs folded and they hit the bed again.

"That explains the subtle abnormalities," Morus whispered, eyes flitting across the terminal screen.

"Why didn't you say something?"

"It was... familiar. I thought it was something Clyde had done to help the process."

The room quaked again and the lights died a moment before blazing back on.

"The fuck is going on?" Juniper asked.

"*That* is the Federation." Morus typed away at the terminal. No longer was it showing the cybernetic screen it had before, but a long string of command prompts. "They're attempting a breach. It was bound to happen once they gave themselves a reason. I'm stopping the main AI and wiping it so they can't hack it." He paused before hitting confirm and the power died down to the absolute minimum. "Auxiliary power will last a few hours, giving us time to escape."

Juniper looked across the room and they jolted.

Laurel and Cedar weren't there. They forced themself up, ignoring all the pain igniting across their body. "If the Answer's not here, then he's found Cedar and Laurel!"

37
LAUREL

LAUREL WAS THROWN BACK, CEDAR'S ARM jutting into her, and she hit the ground rolling. Blaster shots sprayed where she'd been, but Cedar had already charged the Answer. The shots changed trajectory, riddling the wall beside them with holes and then into the ceiling lights as Cedar pushed the Answer's arm upward. The lights shattered into dozens of pieces, twinkling down around Laurel, and she covered her head until the shooting ceased. The gun went flying past her, skidding across the floor, and she lifted her head.

There was already blood. A long streak of it on the ground. Cedar's arm was soaked and the skin was twisting to repair itself. Out came his own blaster, but the Answer was faster. He mirrored Cedar's own movements. He threw Cedar's arm upward and disarmed Cedar with a well-placed smash to the face.

Cedar stumbled back, scowling, and lost hold of the blaster. The Answer dove after it, but wasn't fast enough; Cedar yanked him back by his collar and wailed on the Answer with his fists. Whatever the

Answer's head was made from, it refused to crack beneath Cedar's frenzied blows.

Unfortunately, the Answer didn't just take the blows—he began to give them back just as much. The few Cedar landed, the Answer returned in kind. Neither needed their blasters.

But Laurel did. Her gaze darted toward the Answer's weapon. Not far. Much closer than Cedar's. She picked herself up and ran for it. She'd barely bent down to scoop it up before a body collided with hers. They went rolling, Laurel screamed, smelling searing android circuits as she breathed in, and despite attempts otherwise, she ended up with her back on the floor while the Answer pinned her down.

She spat in his face. He paused, his screen blanking out, and he remembered himself as Cedar's shadow loomed. He jerked to the side, yanking Laurel with him. Cedar's fist hit the ground, smashing the tile, but before the Answer could use Laurel, Cedar had his fingers around the Answer's head and ripped him upward.

Free, Laurel rolled out of the way to reorient herself. The bounty hunter hadn't resisted, but his hand had shot into his jacket. Laurel caught the flash of metal from within. She gasped.

"Cedar!" Laurel screamed.

He dropped the Answer, jerking to one side, and the pinwheel blade shot by, merely grazing his cheek. It was enough of a distraction, however, and gave the Answer an opening. He tackled Cedar, throwing him off-balance. They wrestled on the ground for mere moments before the Answer was on top of Cedar, pinning him down.

The research facility rocked then, shaking every-thing, and Laurel covered her head as debris shuddered free from above. Some of the plant trellises came down, catching on wires and making them spark over the hallway.

The Answer looked up. "No, they aren't supposed to be here yet."

Which meant the feds weren't with him.

The distraction cost him; Cedar slammed his palm into the Answer's chin, throwing him sideways, and Cedar dove on him again.

There was nothing dignified about the fight. Each hit viciously found its home, and though Cedar had brute strength, the Answer had finesse. Cedar simply couldn't keep him down. The Answer repaid each of Cedar's blows with another hidden weapon and soon Cedar's arms and hands were practically ribbons until the vampiric healing kicked in.

His healing wouldn't last forever.

Laurel jerked her bag open, digging through all the contents. *Where is it?!* Her thoughts moved too fast until she remembered the stunner was in her jacket. She snapped it out just as the Answer pinned Cedar again.

There was one way to stop an android.

His back was to Laurel and metal flashed out of his sleeve, forming a blade around his hand. Laurel threw herself to her feet and ran as fast as she could at him.

He must have heard her. It must have been why he didn't immediately eviscerate Cedar. His back straightened and he started to turn, but Laurel drove the prongs into the base of his skull, just under the helmet. There was a massive jolt, making the Answer's whole body jerk, and he screamed. The sound caught Laurel off guard.

Androids didn't scream. They simply shut down.

She didn't see him turn before his hand cracked across her face. Before she was skidding across the floor, her vision white from the pain. She'd hardly blinked it away, finding the room spinning around her, before Cedar shoved his fist skyward, catching it underneath the Answer's chin. The head went flying, crashing beside Laurel, and as she checked it, to make sure he was dead, she froze.

It wasn't his head that went flying. Just the helmet the faceplate was on.

The Answer stared at her, hardly breathing, and ash white hair fell across his very not android face. His eyes had the honey-yellow cybernetic glow. Except he was baring his teeth. Long fangs. Vampiric fangs.

He was a vampire.

He twisted away from Cedar, dodging the next strike, and snarled at him, all pretense gone. He dove on Cedar and sank his teeth into Cedar's throat. Cedar threw him off, pressing a hand to the puncture wounds, and the Answer steadied himself against the wall.

The place rocked again and this time, sirens blared. Then the power shuddered, sheathing the place in darkness. Laurel covered her head, ducking low, but nothing came down. All she heard was fists smashing against skin. Vampires didn't need lights, apparently.

As she uncurled, readying herself to stand, she felt the gun underneath her hand. She immediately snatched it up. Stunner was long gone, but this would do.

The emergency lights flicked on, showing Cedar and the Answer shredding into each other. They moved too quickly and frenzied to shoot and all Laurel could do was watch, praying Cedar won.

Cedar managed to grab the Answer solidly enough and chucked him through one of the research room windows nearby. The glass shattered on impact and as the Answer crashed inside, Cedar ran over to Laurel.

He was breathing heavy. Pupils were reduced to thin slits. There was blood running down his mouth. Before she could try to help somehow, he shoved her toward the way they'd come.

"Run!" he ordered and Laurel heard the Answer stirring. "Just fucking run!"

Because he wasn't winning and he knew it. If he went down, Laurel was defenseless even with the gun tight in her hand. A pinwheel shot between them, startling her, and Cedar charged the Answer stepping out of the ruined window.

She ran as fast as she could and hated doing it.

Cedar would live. She repeated it to herself like a mantra. He was Cedar fucking Woods! He *had* to. It gave her strength, especially as the Answer yelled after. The blows continued, each one more savage than the last as both vampires snarled at each other.

"Clary!" she shouted into her comms, dodging debris as another blast rumbled the facility. "Report!"

It wasn't Clary on the comms, but a fed recording. "Warning: the Galactic Federation of the Solar System will breach the Lowell Orbiting Research Facility of Pluto. Anyone inside is advised to surrender now—"

Useless. It must have gotten knocked when the Answer tackled her. Laurel tuned to a different channel, hoping to find Clary's voice.

"They're breaking the place apart!" Clary's shouting filled her ears after a few quick turns. "It's going to crack!"

Laurel rounded the corner, the room she'd left

Juniper inside was just in sight, and before she could answer Clary, she ran headlong into a trio of bodies. She screamed, fumbling with the gun, but steady hands pressed into her shoulders. She opened her eyes. Juniper was there, Aster and Morus behind them.

All her earlier apprehensions washed over her and she wrapped Juniper up as tight as she could. Until she remembered everything else.

She jerked back, eyes wide. "The feds are breaching!" she spat out at the same time as Juniper.

"Where's Cedar?" Aster asked, panicked.

"The Answer found us!" Laurel spit out. She jerked to look at Morus. "He came in through Clyde's dock. Why did it let him in?"

Morus' eyes grew wide. "Wilhelm."

"*Who*?" Juniper asked just as Laurel's heart sank.

"It has to be him. He-He could use Clyde's dock without the facility alerting us and the AI would treat his commands as Clyde's—I-I—"

Aster pushed between them and yanked open Laurel's bag. He took his anti-matter bomb out before Laurel could ask him what he was doing.

"Listen to me," he said. "I need you three to run. I'll drag Cedar out of here, okay?"

"Wait," Laurel breathed, eyes widening. Juniper was shaking their head, panicked.

"This will cover our tracks," Aster said slowly. "You three focus on escape. Do not come back for us, do you hear me?"

Juniper gripped his arm. "If you get caught up in that—"

Aster smiled sadly at them. "Then I've lived a good life. Worry about yourselves. I am not leaving without Cedar."

Laurel was shaking her head too, until she

remembered her last weapon. The ice needle. Before Aster ran off to the sound of Cedar and the Answer in the distance, she gripped his hand and yanked the necklace off.

"Cryo-ice is indestructible." She shoved it at him. "Just don't die on us!"

Aster pressed her close suddenly and kissed her forehead. "Cedar and I aren't done living, I promise." He pushed her toward Juniper and Morus.

"Go!" He took off in a jog, bomb under his arm, ice needle tight in his fist.

Laurel lingered beside Juniper, praying, and Morus tugged their hands. "We have to get to your ship. If the feds breach us all the way down, there is a high chance the heating will fail."

The whole place felt like it was coming down as they ran. Each time the facility rocked from bombs or whatever the feds were throwing down, the sounds of explosions echoed closer. Whole tiles were coming down from the ceiling now, plants littered entire walkways, even more wires were snapping and spewing sparks, and everything was a mess.

As they rounded the lounge overlook, Morus suddenly stopped them, eyes wide. They were bright. Almost white.

"Wait," he breathed. "Something's wrong."

Clary gasped over the comms. "GET OUT!" she screamed. "You need to move! Now!"

Bombs across the facility went off and blasted the three of them right to the floor. Laurel hit it hard, everything going black and silent if not for the ringing in her ears.

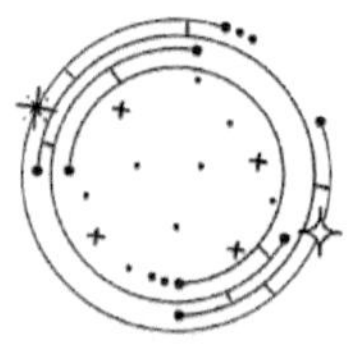

38
JUNIPER

THE WORLD BUZZED AROUND JUNIPER, but it felt so far away. Too far away. Drifting. Panic spiked through them and all they could think of was begging for help. Their augments ignited to the frantic plea. Too damningly familiar, but helped them remember to breathe. Good first start, even though it only let scorched air wash into their lungs. They coughed, and that allowed their aural augments to tune themself.

Beyond the ringing and the sirens was Clary crying over the comms.

"You better be fucking alive."

It *had* been her bombs, then. Juniper groaned and tested their limbs. Nothing broken according to their bio-monitor. "I'm alive," they said, voice weak, and Clary released a loud, relieved sigh. They glanced at their side, bio-scanner pinging signs of life. Laurel was tucked under their arm. Right, they'd thrust it out to cover her as they'd gone down.

"Alive too," Laurel choked out. All she had was a cut across her forehead and her glasses had a cracked lens. Everything else was intact. Miracle.

Juniper looked to their other side; Morus had moved the rubble back with one arm.

"All accounted for," he said.

"What *was* that?" Laurel asked as Morus unburied her and Juniper. Laurel winced as she put weight on her ankle to stand and needed Morus to keep her up.

Juniper's cortex computer immediately began estimating their chances of survival. The odds weren't good and they focused on quieting it again. The noise grew dormant, giving them peace, although Juniper immediately missed the strength it had been giving them.

"My bombs," Clary said and Juniper slid their gaze over the wreckage.

Fire. Smoke. Darkness. The feds were still pounding on the outside. Maybe they'd hoped the bombs within would have made the final layer open like a shell.

What made everything worse, however, was that Juniper didn't hear anything else. Their heart clenched.

There was clicking on Clary's side. "The feds must have scanned the place and detected the frequencies I was using. Half of them have gone off."

Juniper gasped. "Aster's bomb." Dread pooled in their stomach as they stared at Laurel and Morus. "You didn't prime it, did you?"

"No, but it might not matter," Clary said. "The feds probably don't even know what it is or even care if we told them. They want that place open, even if it ends up in pieces." She took in a deep breath. "Please. You need to get out."

That was Juniper's plan, but they had no idea where to go. With half the facility in ruin and shrouded in pitch-black darkness barely penetrated by sparking lights, they could hardly make out the path they'd been taking. How they were alive was a miracle.

Heavy booms thudded above, making the three of them flinch and look upward. More debris scattered free, but nothing breached. Given how loud it was, they must have already peeled back layers of the artificial moon. It was only a matter of time now.

Juniper pressed closer to Morus and noticed Laurel was still leaning on his other side. Her ankle must have been in worse shape than Juniper initially assumed.

"I know the way," Morus said. His eyes a light all their own. "Stay close."

Juniper matched Morus' pace and ducked under Laurel's other arm to keep her off her ankle. They consciously flipped their augments back on, just for the strength alone. It felt like a tingling warmth this time as it filled out their entire body, dulling the pain.

"I'm trying to disrupt their radars," Clary said. "Lily's sending out drones for distractions, but they are so hellbent to get in, they might ignore them."

If they were that hellbent, they'd also ignore the fact there were people alive inside the lab. They'd probably already done a thermal scan and saw their bio-signatures, but elected not to care. Juniper gritted their teeth, pushing themself faster. It'd be so easy to bury them with the lab at this point. No one would ever know.

Morus led them through a pair of shattered glass doors and into the stalled motorized walkway. He paused just inside, irises turning, and before Juniper could ask what was wrong, their aural augments picked up the footsteps above them. Morus flattened the three of them against the wall just as the ceiling caved in.

Their bio-scanner acknowledged the body that had come down with the ceiling and Juniper's jaw dropped. The Answer. Except he didn't have his helmet.

Juniper's confusion gave way to shock; he wasn't an android. The scan noted his vampiric fangs in full view, but Juniper was more distracted by his eyes. A shimmering honey-yellow.

He was a vampire with working cybernetics. Technological marvel the feds would tear apart if they even knew what he was.

If he was here, bloodied and bruised though he was, then where were Cedar and Aster? Juniper's stomach twisted and they glanced around him. A chill washed over them and anger clicked into place. They jerked a pinwheel into their hand.

"You fucker!" Juniper shouted and chucked it. The Answer deftly dodged it and the second one Juniper had also thrown. "You motherfucking—"

It took Morus stepping in front of Laurel for Juniper to notice the Answer hadn't been looking at them while he'd dodged. To realize their bio-scanner was detailing the blaster in his hand and how it pointed at Laurel. Juniper froze, holding back the third pinwheel. It was the gun Cedar had taken with him when they'd left the ship.

No shots went off. The Answer had hesitated, narrowed eyes fixed on Morus. Laurel for her part made herself small, hiding behind Morus, but her entire body was trembling. So was Morus' on second glance.

"Wilhelm," Morus whispered. "You will not shoot her. I won't let you."

The Answer stared intently at Morus, something human softening his expression, but he didn't lower the blaster. Juniper slowly dropped their last pinwheel, but the Answer kept his gaze on Morus.

"You were supposed to come back for me," Morus said, voice trembling, and he gripped Juniper's hand suddenly. They got the picture and slid behind Morus. A shield the Answer wouldn't shoot. "You-You didn't. For ten years I was here alone thinking you would."

The Answer lowered the gun. "I meant to," he said softly. Honey-tinted lies. If he'd meant to, he would have. "Move aside. I will not hurt you. Please."

Morus steeled himself, shoulders tense. "You move aside. There's nothing more to do here. It's done."

Neither of them would move, even Juniper saw the stalemate. Their bio-scanner pointed out the blaster in Laurel's coat. The plan their cortex computer was putting together was hardly formed before Juniper jerked the blaster free and put the barrel to Morus' head.

The Answer froze, eyes wide, and Morus let out a tiny gasp.

"Move," Juniper ordered, letting the blaster prime. "Or I'll shoot him."

The Answer scowled. "You won't," he said. "That's not you."

Sure, maybe not, but they didn't remove the blaster. It was evident he cared too much about Morus to chance it.

"Juniper," the Answer pressed on, "come with me. If they take you here and now, your friends will not get a chance to escape." He paused, as though giving Juniper time to rethink the hostage situation, but they refused. They were not leaving anyone in his hands.

Juniper had their cybernetics grow dormant again so all they had was their own body, just in case.

"I can promise that you will not die with me."

"Your job is to turn me in," Juniper snapped as their arms trembled. "I know what they want with me and so do you. Do *they* even know what the fuck you are? Do they even know you're *here*?"

The Answer didn't reply. Nope. Feds had no idea he was a vampire with cybernetic tech that worked. A prize they could dissect. Suddenly, Juniper had a bargaining chip.

They turned the gun on him and he didn't flinch. "You're a cyber like me, for fuck's sake. Why did you turn it all back on?"

The Answer sighed. "It has its advantages."

"And the feds don't know about your advantages. They really think you're a rogue android." Juniper drew the words out, relishing in the way the muscles in the Answer's face worked in discomfort. "Clyde set you up with all that, didn't he? And you killed him anyway."

Morus took in a sharp breath.

"Our history is irrelevant. He wanted to die. I let him."

"You let the feds starve him for ten years. Why didn't you do it sooner?"

That stopped the Answer. His jaw tightened. "They will breach if we keep talking."

Sore spot found. Juniper packed it away with the bargaining chip. "Is all this even worth it?" Juniper asked. "Worth one fucking job?"

The Answer glared at them so darkly, they should have felt fear. There was a distant click in their head, but nothing happened. His eyes widened and Juniper laughed. The scowl deepened, back to showing off his vampire teeth, and Juniper only laughed harder.

"You seriously tried to turn me off?" Juniper said between breaths. "You're a fucking asshole. Morus fixed me just like *you* were fixed! So go fucking eat shit and die already!"

If the feds had one thing going for them, it was timing. Bombs dropped against the facility exterior, violently shaking the hall, and a gust of cold air rushed into the passage. It blew past them, knocking debris and wires free, and the three of them looked back. Light shined inside. The feds had officially made a hole. Tiny, but there.

At least the heat hadn't failed. Not yet.

Juniper snapped their gaze back to the Answer, but he was gone. Juniper flipped their systems back online, searching for him, but no trace. Not even a sound in the distance of him hurrying away. Just gone. Juniper wasn't going to argue.

Their ship was within reach. Juniper shoved the blaster into their jacket and ducked under Laurel's arm on one side while Morus had the other. They had to get moving.

Clary gasped again over the comms as they entered the docking bay. "Shit! Shit!" she screamed. "They just primed Aster's bomb! They're going to ignite it! Guys—get the fuck out!"

Panic kicked in and strength flooded Juniper's limbs to help them run faster. "Can't you stop it?" they shouted into the comms. "Cedar and Aster are still in there!"

"I've been trying! They've locked me out!"

Morus practically threw Laurel into the waiting ship and she instantly situated herself into the pilot's side. Morus climbed in beside her and dragged Juniper in just as the systems engaged beneath Laurel's quick hands. The top shielded them in and all the systems revved, lights glowing gold along the console. Morus plugged himself into the ship's computer and threw in commands to start the lift.

The doors above opened quickly, letting snow spill inside, but their ascent was too slow with just the lift.

"Just start flying!" Juniper begged and Laurel ignited the thrusters. They took off at terrifying speeds, nearly nicking the first gate opening.

And right down through their entire body, Juniper *felt* Aster's bomb ignite. A tremor against the cosmos. Their cortex computer blared an immediate warning about imminent danger, but just as quickly went silent. Even their augments knew if they were caught in that, all the warnings didn't matter. It was a strange sort of acceptance.

Morus brought his arm around Juniper, dragging them close, and did the same to Laurel on his other side. Laurel had her eyes scrunched shut, but Juniper kept theirs open. The *Honeycomb* scraped the sides of the doors above, now jammed half-opened as the machinery began failing. But they'd make it. They'd make it. Juniper repeated it to themself so they'd believe it.

Darkness stretched around them, somehow faster than their ship, like it was trying to swallow them up alongside everything below. Too soon, it blanketed them and all Juniper could see was the haunting glow of the ship's controls.

It reminded them of stars. The ones they and Laurel promised they'd soar across together.

39
LAUREL

WHEN LAUREL OPENED HER EYES—BECAUSE she wasn't dead, somehow—all she saw was the sea of stars and nebulas above them. The darkness had spat them out. Hyperventilating, she fumbled with the controls, hardly believing they'd *escaped*, and her foot slipped off the thruster pedal. The *Honeycomb* careened to the side, threatening to send them right back into the darkness.

Until Morus secured a hand on the controls. His foot came over hers for the thrusters and between them both, they got the ship steady. Laurel's attention shot to the warnings pinging across the screens.

Thrusters slightly damaged. Running at lower than maximum efficiency, but still usable. Hull also damaged, but nothing was compromised. Grapplers still intact. Good enough.

Laurel swung the wheel to turn them but between her and Morus doing the same thing, they went too far and pointed themselves at the Federation ship looming in the distance. It was hazy in the blowing snow, but the sheer size of it almost eclipsed the moon.

Its large grappler arms held on with its fingers imbedded into the surface.

The surface that was very quickly being swallowed up by the receding darkness. The large ship lurched, straining against being pulled in, and the darkness raced across the arms, leaving dozens of smaller explosions in its wake as the circuitry blew. Pieces spewed across the slowing snow and the very same explosions raced across the body of the ship. The whole thing began to nosedive.

Laurel swung her gaze to the lab below them.

Odd. The darkness was still receding. Juniper let out a gasp.

"DON'T STARE AT IT!" they screamed. "GO!"

Because the bomb wasn't done.

Everything was being brought into a nexus point and only one thing was going to happen afterward. Laurel's pulse thundered in her ears as she pushed the damaged thrusters as hard as she could. Their ship shot higher and higher as everything below became smaller and smaller. The plates making up the fake moon's surface cracked, collapsing onto the outer layer of the lab.

Then came the next part: the explosion. Like a supernova, it blazed so bright, it hurt to stare at. The force was so strong, it sent them spinning. The Federation ship was thrown outward as well, and even more pieces flew off its husk. Laurel stabilized their ship before they were flung into the juggernaut and once she was sure all the systems still worked and nothing had fried, she let herself look out the window.

All was quiet. Still. The bomb had finished, leaving a destroyed lab in its wake.

The Federation ship had taken the brunt of the damage from the exploding landmasses. Half of it was a smoldering wreck, pieces of the moon imbedded within its decks, and even more dismembered ship parts were floating around it while the other half was barely holding on as it lay on a piece of the moon that hadn't outright exploded.

"LAUREL?!" Clary screamed. "Please, respond! You guys better not be fucking dead."

"Alive," Laurel said breathlessly. "Me and Junie are here." She choked the words and swallowed.

"Okay, okay," Clary whispered. "Lily has to clear our scans before she can grab you. Stay put, if you can for now."

Staying put let Laurel shake out her trembling hands. She couldn't see the *Gladiolus*, neither visually or through their own scans, but Clary must have had the sense to get the hell out of the way when the bombs were going off.

Debris was everywhere. What was left of the moon's plates drifted apart with pieces of the lab too destroyed to tell what it had been. The snow had turned into crystallized clumps glittering underneath the frozen searchlights from the juggernaut. At a glance, *nothing* was salvageable.

All of Clyde Lowell's research, all of his lingering memories, gone.

Tears filled Laurel's eyes, and she desperately hoped to hear Cedar on the comms. He couldn't be dead. Aster couldn't be dead. Not after everything they'd done.

She glanced at Juniper; they were working on something at Morus' other side, jacked into the console with their eyes bright. Morus was scanning the area on the ship's cameras, much better at parsing minute details than Laurel could with her cracked glasses. All she could do was keep the craft steady.

A distress call blared across the ship's speakers, making the three of them jump. It was soon muffled, and Clary sighed over the comms.

"I'm fuzzing that." Clary's voice was calm and detached. Laurel wished she was that calm. "Anyone that gets it would be too far out anyway, but better to be safe. Lily's almost done."

The part of the Federation ship still intact was attempting to peel away from the debris and its slow husk groaned as it moved. The grappler arms were toast, pieces of them orbiting the ship itself. Most of the thrusters had been taken care of as well. Good riddance to a ship that big. Smaller ships began to leave the hull, likely to see what they could scavenge while they waited for reinforcements.

There was a ping on the map and Laurel glanced over at Morus. The white circles in his eyes turned as he pinched the screen to zoom in. Not much more than a blurry speck. "Can you get closer?" he asked. "I think something's there."

Something. Laurel's heart fluttered and she eased them closer, switching her comms off to silence Clary as she began demanding they stay put. If there was a chance that something was Cedar and Aster, she was going to take it.

Pieces of the destroyed lab orbited around the nexus point of the blast, getting in their way, but Laurel eased them through. The farther in they went, the more Laurel was sure something shimmered at the very center. Where the bomb must have been when it went off. Her heart sped faster.

"Come back!" The comms switched back on— probably Lily's doing. Clary sounded desperate. "Those smaller ships *will* find you if you go digging."

"Not yet," Laurel stressed. "They have to be here.

We can't leave them."

Juniper sat up straight, eyes wide. "There!"

Morus stopped fiddling with the feed. Still pixelated and distorted, but it was clear enough. In the center of the shimmer, frozen despite everything else blown to bits, was an intact cryo-ice crystal. Tears ran down Laurel's cheeks as she shined their searchlight on it.

The crimson hair was what she noticed first. It was in a wisp around his head. In his arms was the man they'd practically brought back to life, his blond hair swirled around them. Both frozen in ice. Their lips locked in what they must have believed as the last thing they *could* do to find solace in what could very well have been their deaths.

But Cedar and Aster were whole.

"Ice is stable. The chance they are alive is high," Morus said. "We can extract them."

With renewed energy, Laurel glided them into range. She slotted her hands into the grappler arms and began extracting. Hints of colors from the Federation striders zipped around them past the debris, each time making Laurel flinch. Juniper had them handled. Her focus had to be on extracting Cedar and Aster.

The ice was an odd shape with spikes jutting off every side as though to grab anything else near them, making it resemble a star. Laurel twisted and turned the grappler hands until she found the divots the grappler fingers fit into. When the grappler console dinged a secure grip, she carefully eased the ice closer.

Only when she felt the thunk of the ice against the underside of the ship did she breathe out. She locked the grapplers in place to hold them there. "Secure," she said and retrieved her hands. "Clary, we're coming home."

"Roger," Clary said softly. "I'll get us ready to go. Lily's got her systems fully online again. Follow her ping until she's able to connect."

A blinking light lit up on her console. Not far off. As Laurel eased them back around, one of the Federation ships dropped in front of them, shining a too bright searchlight on them.

"Halt!" it came over the public channel. No hail needed. "Identify yourselves!"

Laurel and Juniper froze, but Morus looked absolutely nonplussed. He tilted his head.

"Oh, hi!" he said, his voice carrying over the comms. "I don't think that's such a good idea. You see, my father told me to never talk to strangers."

His voice distorted at the end into some deranged pitch of static, and the pilot on the other side screamed until the static took him over completely. The ship careened sideways, into a throng of debris, and Morus plucked his cord free from the ship.

"There," he said, proud. "Virus. Will keep them busy since they're all on the same network."

Juniper clapped him on the back, startling him. "Holy shit! You *can* be scary!"

"I'm joining pirates." Morus gave them a confused look. "I figure I have to be, right?" When Juniper laughed, throwing their head back, Morus chuckled. "They'll regroup. Let's get back to your ship before they regroup."

Didn't need telling twice. Laurel flew them out of the debris and once in open space, she pivoted the ship toward Lily's ping. Adrenaline was finally easing out of her, leaving her shaking. She was only glad when they came close enough to the *Gladiolus,* that Lily took control.

"I'll have to turn you," Lily spoke through their comms. "My apologies."

Laurel hardly had her seatbelt strapped across her chest before the ship turned on its side to land on the deck. Juniper yelped, falling against the side, but Morus managed to hold onto Laurel's seat, keeping himself from squishing Juniper. The ship made a horrible scraping noise as Lily dragged it into the hangar.

It was only when the doors locked, leaving them in darkness, did Laurel let herself truly breathe. They were home. Intact. Alive. Hopefully. Tears of relief threatened to spill, but she pressed her palms to her eyes. No more waterworks.

When Lily set the ship down inside their well-lit hangar, Laurel had the grapplers release Cedar and Aster. The ice fell with a thunk, making her wince, but nothing cracked. Once they were settled in, she popped the top. Juniper and Morus fell out, unceremoniously dropping to the hangar floor, and groaned.

"Sorry!" Laurel unhooked herself and climbed out to make sure they hadn't crushed one another. Thankfully, no, and she reached down to help them up.

Clary's footsteps echoed from above as she ran down the hangar stairway. She had another needle in her hand and quickly slammed it into the ice's surface.

The device hissed and then so did the ice. Clary stepped back, pulling the three of them away from it. The ice melted in waves, letting off clouds of steam with each layer that left a dusting of ice behind. It wasn't long before the two bodies within were free and clunked to the floor. Cedar gasped first, sucking in as much air as he possibly could, and pressed Aster in tighter. Aster did the same not a moment later, eyes flying open, and clawed at Cedar, trying to get him even closer.

Laurel's legs finally gave way and she sank to her knees, dragging Clary with her. Juniper somehow remained standing, but they'd covered their mouth and was leaning against Morus.

Aster blinked and glanced at everyone. "Good morning." He rested his head against Cedar's chest, closing his eyes. "Glad to see it has not been three years."

Cedar laughed, breathless, and winced in pain.

"You scared the shit out of us!" Juniper choked out.

Cedar huffed. "For the record, I was winning."

Liar. His arm was *not* in good shape. The skin hadn't healed completely, letting it bleed freely, and it was bent at an odd angle. The mark on his throat also hadn't closed, leaving evidence of the Answer's fangs. Not to mention the missing pieces of his bloodied shirt, hardly hiding the still festering wounds underneath.

"He was kicking your ass!" Laurel said.

Aster tucked his head into the crook of Cedar's neck and laughed. "He really *was*, love," Aster said and Cedar grumbled. "Would have kept at it if not for those bombs."

"Just give me my blood packs," Cedar said, resting his head against Aster's. "I'll live."

"You fucking better!" Clary snapped and Cedar shook his head. "Aster, you got any strength left? I think you're the only one capable of lifting him."

As Aster untangled his arms and legs from Cedar, giving him a soft kiss on the chin as he moved, the intercom turned on.

"Someone is hailing us," Lily announced.

Clary stood and waved her hand. "Tell them to go eat shit and die. I want us gone."

"Well, ordinarily, I would, but we seem to have... stalled." Lily's voice betrayed her annoyance, and everyone froze. "There is a lock on our systems from the recipient. My apologies: I grew careless with worry. I do not believe it's Federation, for what it's worth. The hailer is specifically asking for Cedar Woods."

Someone had been watching them. Laurel's body went cold. He couldn't have escaped, could he have? She looked at Juniper, but they were shaking their head. There was no way; he'd had no time. They'd barely made it and Clyde's dock had been clear across the lab.

Cedar grunted as Aster hauled him off the ground, Cedar's good arm across his shoulders.

"All right, all right," Cedar said. "I'll go tell 'em to go eat shit and die if they really want to hear me say it so fucking bad. What about the feds? God. Why's everything so blurry?"

Aster patted his back as they started moving and Clary quickly headed to Cedar's other side to help. Aster's legs were wobbling. "Loss of blood, love. We'll get you patched up soon."

"Feds have begun deeper scans of the area in light of Laurel's return," Lily replied. "We should not linger any longer than necessary."

Between Aster and Clary, they managed to get Cedar into the ship and then down the hall. Laurel needed her own help. With all the adrenaline and ship piloting, she'd forgotten how much her ankle was hurting. Juniper had their arm around her back almost immediately and she was glad to lean against them for support. Morus looked like he'd wanted to help, but when Juniper was already there, he lingered on her other side, as though ready if they both went down.

The bridge felt so much like home as they stepped inside. Laurel breathed in deep, glad to be back. Lily sat at the pilot's chair, eyes glimmering, and Cedar leaned against it.

"Here I am," Cedar said. "Patch it through."

The hail screen lit up with static as it established a connection. It took a moment before it cleared and revealed the Answer. Of course it was him. Laurel glared at the screen and Juniper tensed, their fingers digging into Laurel's back for something to hold onto. Morus was the only one who didn't outright react.

The Answer wasn't wearing his faceplate. Then again, it had probably been destroyed with the lab. His white hair was a mess, wisps falling across his face, and there were fresh bruises coloring his face. As soon as he was connected, he grinned smugly, and showed his fangs. With a low, contented sigh, he leaned back.

"There you are," he said, undaunted as Cedar bared his teeth at him. "It was a well-done extraction." His gaze fell to Laurel for a moment before he settled it fully on Cedar. "Cedar Woods. I tip my mask to you and yours. I saw the Juniper Austre of my job die this night." His eyes flitted toward Juniper until they eased behind Morus. The way the Answer's smile softened, however, said it all. He'd *seen* Juniper. He was lying.

"It's been such a long time since I last felt alive like that." He tilted his head as his gaze went right back to Cedar. "So exhilarated. And I have you to thank for that moment of radiance." He breathed out, like it really *had* satisfied him. "Though, I am dreadfully sorry about your arm there."

Cedar growled. "Like hell you are."

The Answer chuckled. Definitely not. "Next time we meet on opposite ends, you will not be so lucky to live." He peered at Morus and held his gaze for a silent moment. Morus didn't look away.

The Answer nodded at him. "Please, at least, take care of my seedling for me. He deserves better than what Clyde gave him and what I could give him."

That got a response out of Morus. He stammered on words already lost. Cedar just nodded, shrugging, and the Answer smiled again, showing his teeth.

"See you, space vampire."

The hail ended and there was a rumble beneath the ship. The cat hissed, her fur puffing out completely as she stood, and all of them watched as a ship shot out from beneath theirs.

It was sleek and as black as the cosmos itself, quickly becoming a distant glimmer in the stars.

"For fuck's sake!" Clary swore and shooed the hissing cat out of the seat. "He was riding along us to hide from the feds!"

"I will update my security measures," Lily said as the cat paced, annoyed. "I am taking us through to the backchannel gate now." The ship slowly eased around, facing away from the mess they'd made.

"He's letting us go?" Laurel whispered. "Why?"

Cedar rolled his good shoulder. "Near as I can figure, we saw his face. We know his secret. Isn't gonna do him any good to nab Juniper if we can easily make the feds target him next." He glanced at Morus. "And because he knows we could use Morus against him."

Morus tensed and Laurel moved beside him in seconds, glad to find Juniper doing the same.

"I'm not *going* to, mind you," Cedar said. "Give me some credit."

"Captain Cedar?" Lily interrupted them and they

all looked at the cat who had begun rubbing up against Cedar's legs.

"Yeah?" Cedar asked.

"Please get some rest. All of you. I will take us to the one station we haven't pissed off this month and let you know when we arrive."

Laurel wanted to curl up where she was. She didn't need her room. Just the comfort of the bridge. Juniper, unfortunately, had their arm around her back still, preventing any collapsing. She leaned against Juniper instead.

As Aster and Clary concentrated on getting Cedar out of the bridge, Laurel glanced at Morus. He lingered, eyes darting around the bridge as though searching for what to do.

It must have been overwhelming, never having set foot outside Clyde's lab in his life.

"You good?" she asked, gently rubbing his arm in lieu of anything else.

"I don't know if I'm good," Morus whispered. "Or if I will be." His voice was distant and he looked at her sadly. "But I'll try."

Trying was all anyone really could do in the end after the only home they'd ever known was blown to bits. Laurel pulled him closer, feeling Juniper reach around to squeeze his arm, and the three of them watched the wreckage of a life buried in the dark slowly become smaller and smaller.

"Laurel. Juniper," Lily spoke again and the cat was rubbing up against them too. "That goes for you both as well. You are about to collapse and my cat cannot drag you to your rooms if you do that. Please, see to your friend and then rest."

Laurel laughed and one bubbled out of Juniper as well. "We're going! We're going!"

40
JUNIPER

FOR ONCE IN THEIR LIFE, JUNIPER FELT refreshed when they opened their eyes. They'd slept. Really slept. No dreams, but maybe those would come back with time. Their cybernetics hadn't fought to keep them alert, pinging every single danger or how their body was faring. Sweet, sweet silence.

It was lonely, actually. Nothing else there by themself. Disconcerting. Still, in it was a peace of mind Juniper couldn't remember having before.

Unfortunately, sitting up made them realize just how many aches they had, but they smiled anyway. Evidence of having lived. Evidence they were still Juniper in spite of it all. Evidence that pain *sucked*.

They flopped back into their pillow. They hadn't realized how much their cybernetics suppressed the pain. Though it made sense; if cybers were meant to one day be unstoppable killing machines, pain was simply in the way.

It took longer to turn on their cybernetics this time. Adrenaline and panic had led the way before, and now calm and out of trouble, Juniper had trouble finding the so-called switch. They were sure they made many weird faces before something clicked, and the systems hummed to life. Immediately, their bio-monitor let Juniper know where their aches originated from. Some of the pain lessened considerably, too. A respite.

Until their systems began to notice everything else. How fast their heart raced using the cybernetics at all. Their bio-scanner fought for attention to tell them all the movement across the ship. Whispered words picked up by their aural augments only to be twisted by their cortex computer looking for danger. Juniper shut the whole thing back down.

They wanted the quiet today. No reason to run their cybernetics if they were safe inside the ship. Their home.

The word made them smile. *Home.*

Juniper sat back up, gentle with themself this time, and untangled themself from the blankets. Laurel had been curled up with them when they'd fallen asleep, but Juniper guessed it was simply their turn to wake up cocooned in warmth given how many times they'd done it to her. They threw their legs over the side of the bed and eased out a breath. Good first start. They stretched their arms, working out the kinks in their back, and stood.

As they folded the blanket, they distantly recalled Laurel jerking upright sometime in the night—or early morning; Juniper had no idea what time it was— and rushed off for the sad plants still in her bag.

Juniper must have drifted off shortly after she left. Maybe she was with Morus. Their new friend. Shy, sad friend, but Juniper had faith Laurel would make him feel welcome and they'd see a genuine smile out of him before long. Laurel was good at that.

Getting dressed was an ordeal. Juniper gave up after a pair of lounge pants and their undershirt. All they added to the ensemble was their cardigan wrap. Mostly complete. More importantly, cozy. They braved heading into the hallway and immediately almost ran into someone passing by.

Aster caught Juniper by the elbow and he was a lot more solid than he looked despite the willowy android frame he'd wanted. He smiled at them. No longer was his hair thrown in some slapdash style Cedar had braided it into and instead, he'd buzzed one side to a soft fuzz and left the other long and braided it across his shoulder. It was a little pinker than before too, like he'd washed a little dye through it. Much more like the Aster in the photos.

"Hey you," he said gently. He had a mug of bloffee in his other hand and Juniper regretted looking into it. "Yeah, yeah. Humans always find this a little gross, but Cedar needs a pick-me-up."

Juniper snickered. "Used to the body yet?"

Aster shrugged. "I'm still wired from the excitement, but my body feels more like me now. After I fixed my hair, I watched Cedar all night." He shook his head and glanced at the mug. "It still feels so dreamlike, like I'm afraid I'll wake up and I'll still be trapped in my head. Unheard. Undying. Oh! I'm rambling! How are you?"

"I hurt," Juniper said, laughing. "But it's nice? I can feel my body my way. Not through the veil of tech. I just really, really hurt."

Aster nodded. "That's how I felt when my cybernetics finally stopped, although I'd had a vampire bite to contend with." He gently reached forward and squeezed their shoulder. "It gets better."

"I know. How's the big guy doing?"

"Well..." Aster shrugged again. "Vampires bounce back, but he needs a lot of not getting his ass beat and some rest. And blood." He jiggled the mug and laughed. "We're going to have to find another stash at this rate." He leaned in, smiling. "Want to see him? I know he's wanted to check in on everyone, but I threatened to tie him to the bed if he got up."

Seeing Cedar would give Juniper a little more peace of mind. They nodded and followed Aster to his room, dodging Sprig as they went.

Cedar's room was lit in low tones, most of it lost in its dark shadows, and it still smelled the same. Maybe with more rosemary this time. Cedar lay propped up against the pillow and was covered in a blanket. The arm he'd broken was wrapped from the shoulder down and in a splint across his chest. Made sense. Vampires had to be careful with broken bones; set it quick or it could heal wrong. His neck was also bandaged up and his bare chest was riddled with black and blue bruises.

"You look like hell," Juniper said.

Cedar opened his eyes and laughed, wincing. "Nice to see you too." He tried to move, as though to make himself more presentable, but Aster set the mug down quickly and pressed him back against the pillow. "Okay, okay. I get it." He rolled his eyes at Aster and gazed at Juniper. "You finally sleep well?"

"I did. Best I've ever had." Juniper fidgeted with their sleeves, trying to piece their words together. "Thank you. For everything—you know."

"I should be thanking *you*," Cedar insisted. "If you guys hadn't come by that ship, accident that it was, I'd be gone."

"Don't be mushy about it." Heat rose to Juniper's cheeks. "We helped each other and it worked out."

Aster smiled still and sat at Cedar's side on the edge of the bed. "Without you finding us, we simply wouldn't be here. It means more to us than you know."

"I got mushy on Laurel when she checked in," Cedar said. "It's your turn. C'mere, let me hug you."

Juniper couldn't say no and moved in. Cedar immediately latched onto them with his good arm and pulled them in tight. Even with broken bones and bruises up and down his body, he was strong. Aster reached his arms around Juniper too, with a much softer touch.

It was strangely nice; this comforting warmth without their bio-scanner reading too much into it. Except it was also too mushy and sentimental; Juniper already felt tears in their eyes and forced them back.

Everyone let go before Juniper lost all composure and they quickly straightened their back, breathing in deep.

"Thank you," they said. "I don't think I'd be me without your help."

Cedar smiled softly at them and then flicked a sly glance at Aster. "Okay, go on now. I've three years of kisses to make up with this stranger here."

Aster laughed and it devolved into a giggling yelp as Cedar pulled him over his lap with his good arm. He planted a kiss on him without waiting for Juniper to turn and they laughed.

"Ugh! Gross! I get it! I'm going!" They turned sharply and heard both Cedar and Aster snicker as they slipped out. "I'll leave you guys to it!"

Back to the mission. Laurel. They felt like they were trapped in their head again and shuddered. At least the Answer wouldn't be showing up as everyone's face this time. They headed through the hall, passing their room, and found Clary coming down. She was halfway dressed and hadn't even tied up her hair yet.

"Hey." The word mixed into the yawn Clary failed to fight back. "You're chipper this morning."

Juniper grinned. "Slept great! How'd you sleep?"

Though Clary smiled, it was tinged with exhaustion. "Like hell, actually. When everything went up, I really thought you all died then and there." She breathed out and ran a hand through her hair. "I had nightmares 'til Lily sent the cat in to make me feel better." She held up a hand as Juniper's face fell. "I'm fine. Promise. Just make a nuisance of yourselves to remind me y'all ain't dead. I'm gonna head into the station for some grub soon. Food no one has to cook will make it better."

"That sounds great," Juniper said.

Clary came in so suddenly, Juniper yelped. Clary wrapped her arms around Juniper tightly.

"You're a good egg," she said. "I'm glad you guys reclaimed the ship."

Juniper squeezed her back. "I'm glad too."

Clary parted, sniffling, and nodded down the hall. "I think I heard Laurel and our new friend in the spare room messing with plants." She passed Juniper. "Hey, Lily, you finish maintenance yet?"

The spare room was at the end of the hall, the smallest one left, and the door was open, letting Laurel's and Morus' voices bleed into the hall. There was even a little music, inane coffin smashing cutting through the soft groan of the ship. Already trying to sway Morus into liking them, it seemed. Juniper chuckled. Smashing Coffins was growing on them.

Before, the room only had a single cot inside with shelves to the side. Now, it was filled. The cot looked more like a bed with proper sheets and pillows aplenty to make up for the lack of a good mattress. The shelves held the rescued plants and while some were in quite a shape, others had been split among multiple pots and bowls from the kitchen. At the other end, Laurel and Morus were hanging a row of sunlamps.

It was endearing how Laurel had thrown herself completely into making Morus feel at home. Both of them looked none the worse for wear, at least. Laurel's cracked lens had been fixed—likely Lily's doing—and she had bandages over all her cuts and bruises.

"I am so sorry again," Laurel said and from the way Morus' face pinched, she must have said it way more than she'd needed. "I didn't mean to forget them…"

"It's fine," Morus said, rubbing her back as she twisted a wire into an unlit sunlamp. "We survived two sets of bombs, a blackhole bomb I had no idea even existed, and then had a daring escape. They'll live. I'm sure they appreciated the excitement."

The sunlamp snapped on, a bright orange making everything warm, and Juniper's eyes watered.

"Junie!" Laurel called out past the brightness. "Good morning!"

"Hey," Juniper said, vision clearing. "I'm alive! How's your ankle?"

Laurel grinned and wiggled it. One of the bandages they'd lifted from the mall forever ago was wrapped around it. "Getting better!" she said. "How'd you sleep?"

"Like the dead." Juniper snickered and so did Laurel. "I feel like I reincarnated into a whole new me."

Morus came up beside Laurel, a little nervous still. He'd changed into pants and a tank like Juniper's. It showed off more of the tattoos he'd done and if he didn't look so shy, Juniper would have asked to see what was also on his chest and back. The design clearly continued, but Juniper decided they'd wait until he came out of his shell a bit.

"You look less tired," Morus said, smiling. "Are your cybernetics behaving? I must admit, we *did* rush the process. It's normally not that fast."

"Tested it under fire," Juniper said. "Besides, I knew exactly what I was looking for." They slid their gaze to Laurel. She tilted her head, curious. It was a little embarrassing to verbalize aloud and they held back. "It feels like it's my body again," they said instead.

Laurel squeezed her arm around Juniper and pulled them into a sideways hug. "You seem so much better now."

"I am." Juniper held her back. "Thank you so much for everything, Morus."

Morus lingered in front of them, unsure, and smiled awkwardly. Unfortunately, he resisted the call of the group hug Laurel clearly wanted to inflict on him. She pouted, but let it go. She was probably already planning another group hug opportunity.

"I am glad to have helped," Morus said and considered Juniper, like he had a question. Juniper raised their eyebrows, expectant, and he glanced away. "How long did you know Wilhelm? Er... The Answer?"

Juniper frowned; the one thing he and they had in common, but for far different reasons. Laurel watched them too, listening.

"Shortly after I ran away from the feds. So, for four years?" They remembered his voice oscillating through their satellite one day and the panic they'd felt. "He was the only one who knew which satellite I was hiding on. He left me alone when I threatened to blow it up." They chuckled. "Still found time to check in every so often."

Morus glanced away. "Was he always like that?"

"He was a bounty hunter and as far as I know, very good at it," Juniper said and hesitated before reaching out to touch Morus' arm. "Morus, you knew a whole different guy. People have many sides."

It felt weird not leaning into the fact that yes, the Answer was a monster, but from looking at Morus, Juniper knew that wasn't what he needed. Let him hold onto whatever nice memories he had of the man and let it be that. Maybe they'd never cross paths again.

Morus nodded slowly and peered up at Juniper. "Yes, I suppose you're right." He glanced at Laurel with a warm smile. "Thank you for helping me set up my plants, but I have processing I want to do on my own."

Laurel frowned. "What?"

"This is a lot." Morus drew his arms tight around himself. "I'm still not sure if this is real or a dream I made from loneliness." His smile turned sad and he cut his gaze away. "I just want some time. I'll come out when I'm ready."

"Yeah," Juniper cut in. "I get it. We won't be far."

Laurel still looked ready to argue, but she nodded in the end, smiling sadly. She peeled away from Juniper and spread her arms out toward Morus. He took the hint this time. One-on-one hugs was probably easier for him. Laurel squeezed him tight. She parted and Juniper gave him a wave in lieu of another hug. He seemed to appreciate the gesture and shyly waved back.

When the two of them stepped out, Laurel taking her palm tablet with her, the door whooshed shut, sealing him in with his plants.

"He'll come around," Juniper whispered.

"I know." Laurel pulled her palm tablet out and

went to turn off the music. Juniper stopped her.

"Keep it going. I might be starting to like it."

Laurel grinned at them, her eyes twinkling. "I knew I could sway you!" She slid her hand into Juniper's and held it. "Well? What do you want to do now?" she asked.

"We're docked, so we should have a view of the stars and the other ships taking off." Juniper steered Laurel toward the bridge. "Want to watch that until Clary feels sorry for us and lets us out so we can cause mayhem in the station?"

Laurel's grin widened. "I'd love that."

Clary never *did* feel sorry for them. She headed out alone to get everyone food, resisting Laurel's puppy-dog eyes. Juniper supposed it was just as well.

With nothing else to do, they sat on the couch in the bridge. Lily joined them soon enough, stretching across them both, and purred up a delightful storm. Laurel was curled on one side, leaning into Juniper, while Juniper had stretched out their legs and kept their arm wrapped around Laurel.

Together, they watched the distant stars sparkle, their view only disrupted when a ship left colors trailing in its wake. It was beautiful and peaceful. Juniper wanted to take the time to say words, have them mean something—like how much Laurel meant to them—but nothing sounded right in their head. Maybe they didn't have to say anything. Maybe this was enough.

Laurel broke the silence as she stroked Lily's head. "What's our next plan, do you think?"

"Exactly what we'd planned to do from the start." Juniper grinned at Laurel. "We'll go wherever the stars call us."

THE END

ACKNOWLEDGMENTS

The end of yet another book! I wrote this because I wanted a fun space adventure reminiscent of the space anime you'd find on Toonami or Adult Swim back when I was a teenager (just, you know, add vampires to the mix). Maybe it scratches that itch, maybe it doesn't, but I had a good time writing it and I hope you had a good time reading.

Major thanks always have to go to my mom who absolutely loved this book (and Cedar) and who always sat with us to watch weird space anime. Thanks also always goes to Miranda for being all over vampires in space as soon as I uttered the words.

Thank you also to M. Rhys Bail for helping me make all the tech sound techier and more believable. Juniper wouldn't be the same without you! Your amazing support got me through edits and I'm so glad you were there to help me.

To my beta readers, Aowna for always being down to read my stories even though they're not always your usual digs. To Julia for putting up with an early version (and somehow, it gained 5k words since you read it despite attempts otherwise). To Bri for all the lovely comments and for calling the crew a collection of lost puppies Cedar collected. And then to Jane for your sharp eye finding everything I missed.

And also! To you readers!! Thank you for taking the chance on my weird vampires in space idea. I hope you had as fun a ride as I had writing it.

ABOUT THE AUTHOR

S. Jean (she/they) is a queer sci-fi & fantasy author writing whatever strikes their fancy at any given moment. When not writing or dreaming of what to write, they can be found dabbling in game dev and drawing!

For more information, visit:
https://sjean.earlronove.com/